The Reef

Mark Charan Newton

To Sue

Best wishes,

Mark Charan Newton

First Published in 2008 by
Pendragon Press
Po Box 12, Maesteg, Mid Glamorgan
South Wales, CF34 0XG, UK

Copyright © 2008 by Mark Charan Newton
Cover Design & Illustration Copyright © 2008 by Darius Hinks
This Edition Copyright © 2008 by Pendragon Press

Mark Charan Newton asserts his moral right to be
identified as the author of this work.

No part of this publication shall be reproduced in *any* form without
the *express written consent* of the publisher.

Typeset by Christopher Teague

ISBN 978 0 9554452 6 2

Printed in the UK by
Biddles, King's Lynn

Acknowledgements

As with any book, more than one person has helped with its development. My agent, John Jarrold, for his faith, support, and ever-insightful commentary. I'd raise a glass of wine to him, but it wouldn't last long… George Mann, for his early assistance, kind book donations, and endless pub conversations. Graeme Harris, for his late night phone calls on the science of it all. Darius Hinks for his wonderful cover design. James Wilding, for listening to me ramble on about the book, and for the html. Jeffrey Thomas for his kind words. Finally, Chris Teague at Pendragon Press, for daring to take the gamble. If I've missed anyone out I'm sure they'll let me know soon enough…

For Kamal and Mick

Prologue

She cut down through the water in a precise, controlled movement. Further down this trench, pressure began to stretch her skin again, and it was at this level that she would usually forget the colour of the sun, the brightness, even the concept of warmth. Distances began to mean less, became more abstract. In the deep, life followed a different set of values. You could see filter feeders, bichir, gouramis, but you could also taste the salt more, sense the movements of the water in thick, unavoidable drifts. And you were required to perceive things on an entirely new level.

She fell for nearly a quarter of the day through differing shades of darkness.

A shark followed a school of tuna that circled with the currents, trailing one another, and within a second she could no longer sense them, only the drag they had left in the water. Bubbles of oxygen shot along her skin, through her hair, and she looked up for them to have long gone. She regarded a trickle of oil, spilt along the floor, black on black, could *sense* it. Organisms burrowed into the sediment, extracting minerals. With compassion, she hoped that they were waving their antennae in delight—she liked to think everything was satisfied, at one with their existence. For a moment she floated above them, feeling, then swam along the ocean floor.

Towards glimmering lights.

They appeared at first as a blur, but as she came closer they took the form of viscous diamonds. Soon they were all you could see, dazzling, an unnatural phenomena, but it was home. There were thousands of them, arranged in neat lanes, rows, built around a framework that hadn't yet presented itself clear enough—

At her side a vent spurted suddenly, forcing her to dive away as it vomited ultra-high temperature water, minerals. An explosion of heat, a change in currents. A moment too late and she would have been boiled, she knew that. However this needed fixing. It posed a danger to her, to the underwater community. Inside her head, she altered pressure. She generated a sound, called out through the water towards the lights. It was melodic, played along a certain scale, one that only her kind could hear.

Other sirens came.

She watched their shapes cut through the water until they were with her. With them they brought some encrusted piping. She couldn't sense if it had been extracted from a dense ore, salvaged from a wreck, or sculpted from coral. Dozens of the women hauled it to the vent and in unison they lowered it. The end covered the vent that had spurted out the heated water. The piping warmed up. Heat flowed along it, back towards the light. She had removed the danger for the moment, and with another group of harmonics she sent the sirens back home, back towards the lights. In their strange tones, they talked amongst one another.

But through the water, there was a disturbing groan—a deep bass that was felt in her stomach more than she could actually hear.

All of the sirens spiralled to a halt, turned to face her.

They could hear it again, and she saw the panic on their faces. Thin gills between her ribs flexed and exposed thin, translucent flaps as she breathed heavily. She knew what she needed to do. It was beginning to awaken, and her efforts were not enough to keep it for much longer. A decision was made: she called out, singing her request.

And ordered her women to become fecund.

Evening: the creature watched the waves fall onshore, focussed on the detail of the froth as each one covered the beach of the island of Arya. Behind him, palm branches swayed in the light wind, fizzing. He tried to calm himself. The sea was approaching, the sound of the waves not quite matching their movements. He noticed that tonight they possessed little pitch. They oozed back and forth, repeating as the wind swells were broken by the reef. Both motion and noise were hypnotising. The moon cast reflections offshore, and the water around Arya broke it up into a scattering of light. A shadow remained up ahead, where the shallow water was broken, and it looked as if a boat had sunk, spilt its cargo.

It was the darkness cast by the reef.

Despite his learning, which ought to have reassured him, his heart was beating fast. Whether or not there was something in the air, he couldn't grasp—but tonight it wasn't the reef that was making him frightened. The creature took steps back until he was in light of the beach fire, and glow illuminated one side of his body. Other such fires lined the beach, a thick, tailed shadow by each of them. Ashes sparked regularly off into the sky. Salt and decomposition filled his nose. To his other side he noted moonlit sand and the shadows of the palms that punctured it. Jasmine was pungent, offered somewhere in the distance, somewhere he wanted to be. Anywhere but here.

But he ignored that because he was afraid, and once again he regarded the sea.

The silhouettes of sharks drifted above his head. He swam down from the light, through air bubbles that stimulated his skin, past the photic zone in search of the ocean floor, the dark. A school of tuna swam in a circular column away from another shark in a never-ending chase. His tail heaved behind his stout legs, propelling him further down into the black. Each variant movement he made took him to within a grain of salt to where he wanted to be. His heart rate doubled, tripled.

He stopped, hovered in the gloom. Schools of luminescent fish dazzled him, and they flipped at high speed before soaring away. He shuddered, his long hair drifted around his head. He felt vulnerable suddenly, with a vague awareness of *something*, but he couldn't figure out what. Why didn't he listen to the others? They were right to think him foolish for wanting to find out for himself.

In a controlled thrust he swam to a piece of coral, did not touch it. Instead he simply stared at the strange substance. It was rock and animal and plant—that was what the doctor had told him, at least. It was precious. Life forms worked together, linking in vast and complex systems. And everything benefited.

The temperature fell further, not from his descent, and he shuddered. He regretted the decision to try and see what was down there, to find and penetrate the trenches the other side of the reef. The others warned him not to go so deep. He turned in a slow arc whilst looking around in an alert state, his eyes sealed shut by a translucent film. Bubbles rose from below, regular palpitations of air jetted along his skin, tickling him. He kicked his tail down, pushed up through the dark waters. Then he paused, as if in a trance.

He could hear the faintest of melodies. It was coming from deeper waters. The tune released him from his fear, he felt revived, the waters became warmer. Uncontrollably, he became aroused as the melody became more intense. His heart seemed to stop, suspending him in the waters, helplessly.

The fires burned lower, more driftwood was hauled on. The creature watched his own shadow grow with the flames. Determined to see the night through, his eyes were fixed on the tide, which came in further on each push. It fizzed on the rocks, the sand, the sea plants that lined the shore. He examined the surface of the water for discrete changes, or for any signs of the one whom swam in to investigate. Everyone knew he would not return.

The tide gradually approached the beach fires and the foam began to soak some of the driftwood before receding to ebb. His eyes were heavy, and spits of salt from the sea and the wind stung them. Halfway through the night, drizzle sparkled in the air. The mist of water was fresh, and his skin shivered. The night remained calm and the rhythm of the tide was soothing. The sound of the surf was monotonous. For how long would he have to stay here, to do this? Night after night? How long until his kind could rest easily?

A song rose above the sea.

He heard something tender, deep in his head. He focused on the water, tried to follow the waves, but couldn't. He walked forward, unable to feel the sea lettuces squelching beneath his feet, then touched the foam of the water, continued out into the sea. Still the melody played in his heads, more intense than before. He became aroused, could see that the rest of his kind were following him. They all waded out pushing the water around them as it reached their chest. The movement of the sea was sluggish, pushing him like driftwood. He was standing firm, tensing the muscles in their legs as they waited for the melody to climax, something it seemed to promise.

He glanced down into the water to see shining eyes staring back up at him, felt hands touch, caress, stimulate, crept up his thick legs. A primitive sensation flooded his body.

And, fatally, his kind was drawn further out to sea, underwater, suffocating him. In his final moments he was aware of his, of the pain, but he was disconnected, concerned with only the melody.

Morning: Doctor Macmillan bent down in the sunshine on the section of beach that was further up from the rocks. He looked at what he first thought was some strange, new piece of coral washed ashore, but stumbled back after had had brought it close. He recognised the segment of bowel, frowned, then noticed further organs, dry, open, next to the remains of the bonfires.

Even at this early hour his bald head perspired. Would he ever get used to this temperature, despite his years based here? A firm, onshore breeze aired his shirt. He turned towards the dense palm forest that was yards away from where he stood to see if there was anyone there. There was no one, nothing. The forest stood calm.

He couldn't work out why he felt frightened, as if his routine had been consciously watched. He walked further along the shore as the fine, warm sand squeezed between his toes, headed towards the sun. Holding his hand up to his eye, he saw one of the ichthyocentaurs.

Rather, it's remains.

He approached the washed-up carcass. Its chest had been cut open. He picked up a piece of driftwood to push the wound apart further, could see that the creature's heart had been taken. The doctor explored the tissue further. The creature's eyes were glazed open, a half smile on its bloodied face. Decaying flesh reeked, and he cringed as flies swarmed all over it like a fast-growing tumour. He stumbled back.

The bald man stood still, stared offshore. He closed his eyes so that he could hear only the wind racing along the beach, the wave motion yards away. The surf roared in. *Full of energy*, he thought. He opened his eyes to watch a small gull race over his head, arc out to sea, curving along the beach, looking down to the water's surface. It flew to the south, becoming a shadow in no time at all as it moved in front of the rising sun.

He lowered his head, shook it. *Not again. This can't go on. There'll be no more left if I don't do something. A fabulous race of exotics, wiped out. And I need them to survive.*

The movement of the afternoon waves tilted the small boat. The wind was noisy. The ichthyocentaur that were sitting inside the boat were visibly scared as the doctor lowered a sack of fruit on board the long craft. He thought it would be sufficient—they never ate that much, and they could always catch some fish should they need to. It was another hot day, but he noted that the two male ichthyocentaur shivered. The doctor looked at the anatomy of these creatures for a long time, as if, in this moment, it would be the last he ever saw of them. Of course, he wouldn't, there were more on the island. He handed over a bottle, sealed by a small piece of plant matter. Inside it was a note.

Foam brushed his toes and plants and detritus were scattered around. Sand was lifted, smoothed over as the saltwater trickled underground. It was these small details of the world that he appreciated, and was one of the reasons he adored the island.

This was doing the right thing. They would bring help, it will bring attention. I only hope they manage to do it safely.

He pushed the boat and it creaked. His muscles tensed, his feet slid in the sand, pressing down to create a deep scar on the beach. Water spat up at his shirt, and it became damp and heavy. Then an ichthyocentaur picked up an oar, began to row, then the other did, and they looked at the doctor, who nodded, trying not to display too much emotion.

It's all right, you will be fine, he signed to them.

They did not reply, their hands busy with steering the boat out. He sat on the sand, crossed his legs, watched the boat sail into the distance.

A bend round the reef and it was gone.

One

Manolin stared out of the window, as he often did, to watch the rain. To him, rain was a delicate, feminine violence. From his house you could see over the lines of ships that filled the docks of Portgodel South. Water was striking wood and metal with an alarming force. Behind intricate, rusted metalwork, people ran for shelter, newspapers or coats above their heads. One old man was regarding the sea with a primitive serenity, as if he wanted it to take him into a saline grave. A rumel dockworker jumped from one boat to another, his tail stretched out for balance as he dived into a metal shack. The sign on the wall said "cheap lunches". Half opened crates were left to become islands on the cobbled harbour, brackish ponds forming around them. Faces stared out from the yellow light of dry, top floor rooms. In these shades of grey, the horizon was imperceptible.

Manolin sipped from his glass. He didn't like to drink wine, but she would insist they drank it together. Still, he swirled the liquid around staring at it with some disdain, aware of the meaning within this action. This was how it always was: her decisions, her choices. Tasting the tannins, he grimaced, then set the glass down by the windowsill. A vague sensation came to mind that her eyes were beginning to burn with rage. He caught her reflection in the window as she tossed her red hair back, rearranged herself in her chair. Of course, he should have known that this was what she would be like. There had been enough signs.

The first night they were introduced: within minutes of meeting him she was already laughing at something that another man had said. From that moment, it created a need in him to keep her smiling, and when she did, there was comfort. Perhaps a man more aware of emotions would have stayed away from such a situation. Their love was intense at first, but he wasn't old enough to realise he should have left things merely at that. They'd spend evenings where they would drink wine and she would do most of the laughing, only for them to spend the following hours sweating in the bedroom, losing control of his urges. But he didn't like to drink wine.

She said, 'You never answered my question.'

'You know why,' he said.

'Why?' she said. 'Come on, you really *ought to* spend more time with me. You're never here. You're always working.'

He said, 'You know I can't get out of it. It's been arranged for weeks. I've told you about it every day more or less.' Then, 'So, you know, why don't you come along with me?'

'You know I can't stand them. They're always trying to outsmart each other. You *intellectuals.*'

He felt as if he was constantly on his own, that she never understood him.

Again, the elements distracted him. Manolin had always loved the sea. It was a reminder that there was something else, something *more* than the city. Something special that those who never left the shores would never experience, and they were poorer for it. He also loved storms. It stopped the city, for a while. It stopped the flow of people, forced a moment of peace. To him it was nature's way of reminding everyone that they couldn't control *everything* in their lives. Not that he ever wanted to control things. He was more than happy to sit back, let other people do that. Let decisions be made by those who feel the need to, he thought. Maybe it was the only reason that he stayed in this marriage.

He turned to look at his wife, still sitting in her chair, still reading a cheap newspaper. It was something he would have once dismissed as sweet, but now he hated it. *Why does that happen?* he thought. *Why is it that the things you love at first can be the things you resent, that cause bitterness. Or was I just blinded in the first place—that I always hated it?*

They had married only months ago. She was pretty, but that was not enough to go on. He was learning that the hard way. Red hair fell either side of her sweet face, which he'd seen turn into the nastiest of grimaces when required. And her slender figure was deceptive of the amount of strength it could generate. There were things he smiled at: he used to like the way that heels didn't suit her tall frame, had adored the fact that she wore flat shoes when out with him. At other times he had loved walking into a tavern with her. The feeling it brought. At first, he liked the fact that she made decisions. She was the one who convinced him to get married. She was the one who booked the honeymoon. She fucked him while he lay looking up in awe.

It hadn't been a bad start.

She'd been a waitress in an upmarket bar near Pennybrook Road, just outside the Ancient Quarter, but too near the side of the industrial areas so that it lost it's classiness. A new line of restaurants and inns had been slapped on top of six hundred year-old cobbles. She had worn a white shirt that was a size too small, cut to enhance everything she had. He was kind, considerate. Her ex had treated her badly.

It was inevitable.

An exchange of addresses, three weeks of courting and a quick marriage left them boxed up by the docks.

An oil lamp inside reflected off of the window, creating a warm haven for his eyes, and he gazed back now at his own reflection. Many considered him a handsome man, never short of admirers, but she was far more attractive. That was the way he had to have it. He wasn't much older, his black hair did not yet show any signs of age, his brown eyes were still bright.

'And why do we still have to live in this shit-hole?' she asked, flicking a page over. Then another. 'It's too near the docks. Can't we afford anything better than this?'

She hated the sea. He hated that fact. She told him that she felt lonely without people to talk with, because that was important. Her days had become uneventful, and she felt that that no one thought about her anymore. This conversation had been brewing for some time, was a point at which she would become angry from time to time. Today, she'd been drinking too.

The washed air that seeped under the windowsill calmed him. 'You know it's all *we* can afford. And, you know, I can't help the fact that working in science doesn't pay all that well.'

She made a disapproving noise, tilted her head. 'So why can't you get a proper job instead of buggering about with *him* all the time?'

He said, 'You never minded what I did when you met me. What's so different now? Anyway, what about your job?'

'You just can't expect me to sit here for weeks while you're on some expedition. You're probably shacked up with the first tribal girl who flashes a tit at you. And my job is very respectable, thank you very much.'

'Listen to me,' he said. He felt he lost more self-respect each time this conversation took place. 'If I'm with a girl as *beautiful* as you, why would I want anyone else?' He wished he hadn't said it to the window.

'For your information, I'm not a girl,' she said, 'I'm a *woman*.'

Since his marriage had run aground the silences were amplified to cause such an uncomfortable feeling. Each was left to their own thoughts. Unsurprisingly, to him, it was she who broke the peace.

She said, 'Will *she* be there tonight?'

'Will who be there?' he said, glancing back. There was a strange expression on her face, as if she fought with herself to maintain composure, but it looked as if she wanted to laugh.

'You know, his daughter—Becq. We all know she's fond of you. You've only got to look at the way she stares at you.' She was looking at the pages of the paper, but he could tell from the lack of movement in her eyes that she wasn't looking at any of the words or pictures. He turned back to look at the view. Then she said, 'Anyway, she's really ugly.'

'I hope you'd credit me with a little more than going for just looks.' He shook his head. 'Anyway, I don't know if she's going or not, but if Santiago is then it's more than likely.'

He could hear her kicking her shoes against the wooden chair.

'Have you ever... *slept* with her? Before I came along. I won't mind if you tell me, really. Do you see her much?'

'No,' he said, quite certain she would mind. 'No, I haven't. I haven't slept with anyone but you. And you know that.'

She said, 'You could've lied about it.'

'Look, I only see her whenever Santiago brings her to work.' Then, 'But now you come to mention it, I think she may be coming along on our next research trip. That's if Santiago deems it a part of her development.'

'You know, my friend Gathya said that she saw you with her two nights ago, leaving the research centre.' She paused for effect. The woman had clearly rehearsed this in her head. 'You were heading up Pennybrook Lane. You were together. She said you could've been holding arms but it was dark.'

He sighed, knew that this was a fragile situation. 'I walked her home. It was raining. You know how violent the streets are round there. Only last week that girl was raped. If she'd gone on her own and something happened... Well, I'd feel really guilty, wouldn't I? Besides, Santiago would've killed me.'

She stood up. Her paper dropped to the floor in a heap. His back was turned, but he could guess from her heavy breathing that something wasn't right, and for some reason he didn't yet want to look back to confirm it. She'd been getting like this all afternoon, working to some crescendo.

'I see that you're not even going to bother denying it,' she said. 'And she'll be with you then—on this trip? For how long, exactly, will you be *with* her?'

He said, 'It's likely, I'll be honest. But I don't know how long. Depends on the region we travel to. Anyway, I don't even know when our next trip will be, if at all.' Then, 'You'll have to cope with me being with her then.' He cringed, shouldn't have said that. He froze, his back still turned.

Glass struck his head with such force that he fell forward against the side of the window with a grunt. Splinters pierced the skin of his cheek as he slid down, fell to the floor.

'Fucking cheating bastard!' She started to kick him repeatedly.

'Hey, please, I haven't done anything wrong! I never have, fuckssake, please. Damn, you're drunk.' To stop her kicks he grabbed her shoes. His abdomen throbbed, but she bent over to pull his hair, to scratch his face, claw it. He cried out, closed his eyes, hunched into a foetal position. She reached for anything that was nearby to strike him with.

With his eyes closed he raised a hand above his head, caught her on the chin, grazing it.

She stumbled back before she regained her balance. The room became timeless with a pause. She examined herself, dabbed her chin delicately, as if applying make-up. She pulled her hand back, saw the blood. 'You hit me, you shit.' She sighed, smiled, as if she had been waiting for him to make such a mistake.

He stood up, brushed his shirt and breeches down, stumbled as he turned to look at her. 'Please, I... I only held my hand up, I didn't—'

'Never mind that, you hit me.' She glanced at the clock as it struck five. 'Get out now.' She looked at her watch. 'Leave, go on. Get out. I'll try and forget about this if you give me time.'

They held each other's gaze, but he knew better, stormed out towards the bathroom. He turned the cold tap, lifted the soothing liquid to his hot, scarred face. His hands were sweaty. It felt as if the chilled water burnt him. Gazing down into the basin, he watched the diluted blood spill down the plughole. Vaguely aware of his reflection in the mirror, he didn't possess enough pride to look himself in the eye. Instead, he viewed the two scratches down his left cheek, a token of her love. After he washed and changed his shirt, he grabbed a wax jacket before marching out of the room without a word to her. As he looked back one last time he saw her picking up pieces of the cup. He closed the door behind him.

She heard his footsteps as he departed and ran to the window. She watched him walk into the streets, with his collar turned up, and rainwater, stained yellow by the lamp, streaked down the window and smeared his figure as he disappeared into the docks.

She swallowed. A pang of guilt came to her—she hit him too hard. It was unnecessary. Why did he have to lie so much? It wasn't as if she meant any of that, it was as if something took over her body, anger forcing her hand. She glanced at the clock then her watch. Ten minutes had passed before the door was knocked three times. Smoothing her hair down and rearranging her dress, she shuffled to the door, sighed as she pulled it open.

A man with long, tied-back brown hair stood there, brushing down his thin moustache. He was tall, and she felt both safe and threatened under his immense shadow. He dusted down his damp clothes before speaking in a bass voice. 'I saw him leave early. Is it okay to see you now? I couldn't wait.'

'Yes,' she said. 'Yes it is.' She smiled, held out her hand to lead him inside. She kissed him on the cheek as he closed the door.

Manolin hunched up as the rainwater fell down his face, catching the line of his wound, running down his face and collecting, with tears, on his chin. He marched, head down, towards the tavern, knowing the others would be drinking in it by now. He flicked his collar to get rid of the rain, turned it up further, stared at his feet.

The water rattled on his coat and the cobbles, on the boats, the sea. The air smelled clean, forced a smile. For a moment, made him forget. He battled against the elements and he searched his pockets for memories. One side of his face was numbed by the weather, but he walked ignoring this discomfort. It was one thing he was good at.

He passed alleyways that were lit by lanterns. A legless man was crouched in the shadows against a wall playing a drum. The sign outside the shop to one side said "haircuts". The buildings here were old, towering over thin alleyways as if they would collapse into it.

It took him twenty minutes to reach the area of Portgodel that harboured the taverns and the whorehouses. Despite the weather, the prostitutes were out, holding down their skirts, loitering around the sides of buildings. On the streets it was said you saw the less pretty ones, where their looks or age had failed to get them a regular room. Out here, Rumel women were the most stubborn, with their thick, rubbery skins, their tails rigid beneath skirts. Some of them passed drug wrappers between each other. One of the coca-skinned rumel, with a low white top, approached Manolin as he shuffled past. His face darkened.

She said, 'After any business?'

Manolin shook his head, only glancing briefly at her broad face, not even wanting to connect with black eyes. He did not find rumel women all that attractive. It wasn't the fact that they were a different species, despite being a cousin to humans, despite cross-species sex having being legalised for nearly a hundred years so that it had become acceptable socially. It just didn't *feel* right, wasn't really his scene, although you got plenty of men that wanted nothing but the strangest of encounters.

He walked past her, stepped down off the pavement. From where he was you could see chimneys in the industrial quarter, chemical plumes standing out against the darker grey of the clouds. Next to it: the square housing towers. They were so bland, so ugly, represented everything about the city that he hated. There was so much decay, so much sleaze. With a snort of disgust, he turned away.

Manolin closed his eyes, sighed. Right now, wanted to die—then he changed his mind to wanting his wife to die in some freak yachting accident so that he could sell her jewellery and at least get some of the money he'd wasted. He thought it funny how the best lovers did not make the best wives. It said so in all the books he'd read. All the passion only went in to one thing. He could never work out her insecurities—wasn't him that she didn't trust, she had said, but other women. She was probably using *herself* as an example.

His held his eyes shut for a long time, the rain cleaning his face, letting his tension drip away, and with it his feelings for his wife. After some time he could think logically.

So he opened his eyes and the world seemed just that little bit brighter.

Two

Above her, a moon arced over the city of Rhoam. Jella glanced across at the hundreds of spires that punctured a starlit, black and purple sky. The city was vast, the centre of being something of a museum of preserved architectures. It was one of those places where life became predictable, routine. Irregular laughter spat out a few streets away, where cafés and inns were packed in mellow lighting, the tables spilling out onto the ancient streets. Hot drinks and spirits were being served somewhere in rooms with steamed up windows. You could hear a horse on the cobbles at an even further distance. *Probably drawing some lord or lady*, Jella thought bitterly. Couples were laughing, talking in hidden lanes, in their own private worlds. Cats ran in packs between people's legs, on their way to the canal.

From the balcony view of the cityscape, Jella turned back again to watch another scene with a strange sense of fascination. She was vaguely aware that she was internalising the irony. The room she had been spying on was illuminated by one thick candle near the far wall. On the bed, a young girl straddled an obese, old man. His fingers were covered with rings, his hands pawing the young girl in a primitive, distinctly animal manner. Every time his hands glided over her, they seemed to quiver with hesitation—perhaps fighting with his morals. Watching keenly, the rumel could tell that his nerves were overriding his body because of his clumsiness. The girl's smooth body rocked back and forth, and the man opened his mouth as if to groan as she ran her hands around the base of his neck. A constant expression of awe never left his face when he touched her small breasts. The girl flicked back her long, dark hair, and looked at him in a way to check if he was watching what she was doing.

So young and yet so aware of herself, Jella thought. *Of her performance.*

The man finished with a shudder. The girl seemed distinctly unimpressed, didn't seem as if she really cared, but she ran her small hands over the grey hairs with a distant look in her eyes. She didn't want to be there.

Whilst outside, in the shadows, Jella smiled. She thought about the money she would get from this operation. Blackmail was always worth it when done in such a calculating manner. She looked down off the balcony she had been crouched on for some time. The rumel waved to her comrades below knowing only her grey hand would be visible outside of her outfit. There were movements on the cobbles in front of the old house.

This ambient sound of civilisation was comforting. It was not so much a noise, but a sensation, one which calmed the rumel woman. Her tail became still, representative of her current state. But she knew that the wealthy lived out there, and that saddened her. Jella was conscious of the fact that she lived in that *other* place, one significantly removed from this painful glory.

A sound made her jerk her head. She looked into the window, back inside the bedroom. The door on the inside opened, and two men, one thin, one stocky, both dressed in the black outfits, formed shadows in the doorway. One of them held a box, the other a long, curved blade. Jella heard raised voices, but already knew the conversation off by heart. They were all the same. The shock, the self-disgust and panic. Blackmail using a young prostitute had worked. Again. The money was useful. It was all a contribution to her schemes.

It was so easy to do this way. A sign of the times. If a man had so much time and money, and he thought that he could get away with it, then he would certainly try anything. Sex was the driving force of the world, not money: this was something Jella was adamant about. That, and the fact that female morality was the *only* check on a natural male temperament.

She had discovered a radiograph unit, left out for rubbish near one of the lanes behind the opera house. It recorded sound onto a magnetic film. She did not know how it worked, or the technology behind it, but was aware of the potential. It was a relic, and it was all she needed. That was the thing about this world. Ever since the rebellion to science, an age that she would only know through rumours, stories, rare history texts, you could often find devices that no one knew of, or a technology of which they would simply be in awe.

With a few witnesses and a radiograph, Lord Barclay, the man in question, would lose his wealth, reputation, his house, his life. Finding the girl was the easy part. Jella thought that young girls were loose and curious in Rhoam. It made her angry. Some were spoiled, covered in make-up, putting it about, pretending they were much older, competing with each other for admiration. *Whatever happened to childhood?* She would have done absolutely anything for a childhood, a real one, with a safe family, security.

Her last city was called Lucher, but you would no longer find it on any map. It had been destroyed, and with it, so had *her* childhood. It was poisoned and left to rot by Escha, a dirty, oil-rich sprawl on the west coast of the continent. It was part of a war she'd known nothing about, never would. Settlements waged war with one another regularly. It was part of history. That, she could accept. But what she couldn't was the fact that it had ruined her life. The city of Escha and the west coast was responsible for that. It festered inside of her, a blossoming anger, and it was shared with others. Escha had acted with a military fist where possible. Her armies were vast, strong. However, Jella wouldn't be picking her fight with an army—it was with the entire settlement of the west coast.

She couldn't remember much about the time her life collapsed around her—vague thoughts of an endless walk out of the city, as if they were walking through some lower region of hell. A long dust march north. Her father had disappeared. Her sister abandoned her over a man. That was fifteen years ago. She was forced from a girl's into a woman's mind overnight.

She, like so many of the refugees, was promised sanctuary in Rhoam. Safety, comfort, love. In reality, she was delivered with thousands of homeless, to the outer regions of the city, where a large, dirty town was constructed from scraps.

Her childhood was ruined.

Back inside the bedroom, Lord Barclay was now crying into his hands. He had trailed the bed sheet over his gut, which had rolled over on itself. Then he stood, vanished out of sight, returned with a purse. He thrust it into the hands of one of the men, waved his hands for forgiveness. His voice was full of anger, desperation. He said, 'Take it! Just... please. You can have anything. My... I have a reputation...'

The young girl ran to another of the men, then one by one, they departed form the room leaving only Lord Barclay to sit and quiver. The candle flickered as the intruders closed the door. Jella watched the lord for a second more, her face expressionless, focussed. This was all part of a grander scheme.

She turned to the edge of the balcony, looked down as the group appeared on the cobbles. Both of them and the young girl ran in separate directions. Jella hooked her grey hands into the vine by her side, hauled herself up, leaf by leaf, swivelling her tail until she oozed up onto a sloped rooftop. Her boots gripped the tiles. She viewed the spires at a distance. A thin trail of cumulus clouds drifted like cigarette smoke, past the crescent moon. The night was calm, she could smell pine from the forests to the north. Her white hair was aired by the breeze.

She positioned herself at the edge of the rooftop before leaping on to the roof of the adjacent building. She ran south, up several steps to a second tier where there were shops that were now closed. She paused by a window. A doll caught her eye. She crouched down, focussing on the item. She smiled, vaguely, touched the glass. It was dressed in an expensive material.

Jella sighed, couldn't remember ever having a doll of her own that looked so good. She was certain she had one before she had to come to Rhoam—distant memories, picnics, bedtimes. Things that, as one gets older, become more crystallized in the mind, enhanced even, but for her they were not there. She frowned, concentrated on her memory, then slapped the window with her hand, stood up and burst into a sprint, which continued for several minutes.

Her movements hardened as if she ached. She dropped onto a limestone path, which stood a fraction lower than the roof tops on to the inner city walls and she looked beyond, to the mass, which lay in a heap, which had not progressed, but had remained stagnant and it was her home. A myriad of metal boxes formed symmetrical grids and squares, and this was the area that housed the former refugees of Lucher. They stretched out as far as her eye could see, lined with lanterns and barrel fires.

New Lucher expanded for miles. It was crude, muddy. She could smell the intense odour from the lack of good drainage, could see smoke as if the shanty city was visibly steaming. The rooftops were flat, sharing the same height and design. They were meant to be temporary, only for a month or two, but had remained for years. There was a flaw in that plan. It was obvious to her: Lucher had been a communal city. It did not use money. It was idyllic, some said naïve, but people were happy, sharing a wealth that others couldn't, would not understand. Those people had to make the transition to Rhoam, where money passed hands quickly, and with lasting damage.

Jella simply stared from the city wall. The limestone battlement made a wide arc around the main city, curving in a way so that from where she stood, and when she looked closer it seemed as if the city walls cowered at the edges from New Lucher. Pulling back, she thought, like a rich man would walk around a beggar, trying not to notice, struggling to avoid eye contact. Lines of clothes were hung out to dry, spanning across from one roof to another. Smoke blew into them. Dogs trotted in and out of people's way, wondered in to dark corners. People were gathering in streets, even at this time of night. They exchanged small pots and tools. Children ran excitedly with machetes.

Jella refused to acclimatise to this. It wasn't how it should be.

She had a plan to get out of all this. Blackmail was a necessary

cruelty, call it a redistribution of wealth.
   There would be justice.

Three

Manolin's arms ached as he pushed open the door, stepped inside the tavern. It wasn't as artificial as those found in the city. This was a proper tavern, one where women didn't like to go because it was too dark. Sometimes there was a smell like a creature had dragged itself out of the sea and died behind the bar, but he didn't mind. That smell, people said, was *character*.

A brown cat shot by his feet and outside, taking less than a second to come back in, damp. It looked up to Manolin, its eyes narrowed, before it trotted under a table. He looked across the large, wooden decked room to a group of humans and rumel that were sitting in their usual place in the far corner making much noise. They were hunched over a table with a lantern hanging above.

You either got sailors or fishermen littering this dim building—it was always the same, never attracted a new crowd, and there was something comforting about that. You got cats everywhere, mingling with the customers. Two old men were playing dice, as they always did. Others were engaged in passionate conversations or arguments, persuading the other that their opinion was revelation. Brass ornaments littered the walls, rare bottles, and antique books sat gathering mould in dark corners.

An old, black-skinned rumel looked up from the table in the corner as the door shut. He bellowed something incoherent across the tavern, gestured elaborately. His black eyes gradually focussed on Manolin, his thick black tail shook, his face creased into a smile.

'Hey, Manny. Whatever took you so long? Has that pretty creature of yours been beating you up again?'

Laughter filtered around the table as Manolin walked into the light. The beam drew across his face like a curtain revealing his scar.

Manolin became aware of awkwardness. 'No. I slipped over whilst having a bath. Damn soap.' He walked around the group, who seemed to pick up in spirit as he scraped a chair backwards. He slipped his coat off, sat down.

Opposite him was a middle-aged figure, wearing fine clothes: a grey silk waistcoat covered a white shirt, and he was crowned with a top hat. His name was Santiago DeBrelt, and his black moustache curved magnificently outwards.

Despite his age, Santiago was, by all accounts, a bounder, and a bit of a cad.

Manolin observed him for a moment. The older man maintained his usual cool, detached fascination with the world, as if he pulled all the strings for his own amusement.

Manolin nodded and smiled, and Santiago, tilted his head down slowly and surely, then brought a cigar to his mouth. He inhaled, presenting a glow at the tip. His violet eyes narrowed with sympathy at Manolin, rolled his lips inwards in a half smile. The two men had known each other for years. Manolin couldn't hide what happened to Santiago. You couldn't hide much from the man.

'Evening, Manolin. To fill you in, the party is just getting started and Tchad has not arrived yet as he's still signing the wedding contracts.' Santiago inhaled from his cigar again, his cheeks being sucked in, enhancing the angles on his face, making him look like a drug addict. He took a sip from his nearly empty glass, calm, methodically, as if it would be enough to pre-empt any complaints on him being a drunk.

'Ah, the secret wedding,' Manolin said. 'In that case I'll order a little something to get me started until he arrives.'

Manolin stood up and walked to the bar. He leaned forward as the barmaid wondered over. She was short, old and slender, and she looked at him and relaxed her shoulders.

'I've never seen anyone need a drink as much as you,' she said.

'True,' he said.

'You spend too much time here, you know.'

Manolin said, 'You know how to sell a drink, don't you?'

'Can't a woman care?' she said. 'You look troubled.'

'You could say that,' Manolin said.

'I've seen guys from all over Has-jahn with faces like yours. From that I've known of a lot of lonely women.'

'I have to work.'

'This isn't work, honey. This isn't work. Spend a little more time with her. Yeah?'

'You wouldn't understand. Life isn't that simple. Anyway, I'm not going to talk about it. Give me two malts, finest ones you've got.'

'All right, but this isn't the solution, honey.'

'No, but it'll help until I find one.'

After watching with cool interest as a waitress sprung up the stairs, pausing politely for people to pass, he returned to the table with two glasses, rested them on the table with reverence. He slid one across to

Santiago, who glanced down to the glass and back up.

'Malts, from the north,' Manolin said.

Santiago nodded, smiled, picked up the vessel. He held it to his nose, inhaled before taking a sip, his face showing that he was savouring the taste, again cool, calm, to say, *I'm not a drunk.*

'Many thanks.' Santiago placed the whiskey back onto the table, gazed at it like usually would a woman.

'It's the least I can do,' Manolin said. Then, 'I thought you'd given up smoking? I take it you still take the white stuff, too?'

'I've said no to drugs before,' Santiago said. 'They just won't listen.'

Their colleagues sat nearby. Jefry and Arth, two old, black rumel men who were both dressed in white shirts and black breeches. Arth was one of those jerky-motioned man, who walked as if his shirts were tied around his ankles. Jefry seemed as though he never took the care to think about what he said or did, but went in whole-heartedly anyway. As loyal as a dog, and just as clumsy.

To his left sat a middle aged woman with silver streaks, racing though dark hair. She was sitting alongside Santiago, a black cat on her lap, and she smoked a cigarette whilst gazing out of the window nervously, possibly imagining herself elsewhere. Yana was more handsome than pretty. Manolin always thought she looked like a starlet of the theatres. She was married to the rumel, Jefry, but it had occurred to him that they seemed to be more friends than lovers these days, and her husband did not seem to mind her spending so much time with Santiago. If indeed Santiago was fucking his wife, Jefry did not show such knowledge. Santiago seemed to know how make her smile. She possessed a straight nose and a firm jaw. Her eyes were silver, beacons against the dark outfits she always wore. Manolin gazed at her face, wanted a woman like that when he was older. She had laughter lines around her eyes and everything she did or said seemed almost secret, hidden, demanding more attention. Young girls looked up to her, wanting to be her. She rubbed one of the cat's ears.

Manolin suspected that only Santiago could possess her attention, like he did so many other women, but in Yana's case it was because he was her boss. He never acknowledged that fact. Santiago was a true ladies man: one with a good ear. He had set Manolin up with several women throughout their working career together, and had even introduced Manolin to the one he went on to marry.

Manolin felt frustrated at times. Santiago had been like a father to him, aiding him with his Doctorate and eventually providing him with a job for life. He felt that he owed Santiago a lot, much of what he was in fact. He still wanted more, but just what their relationship was anymore, was beginning to form complex shapes in his mind. He laughed at himself at the negativities that he found he had towards his mentor. Why should he have felt this particular way when he owed so much? Manolin shrugged off the notion as a peculiarity of the human animal. It was, he had declared, an inevitable predisposition to destroy relationships of any kind wherever they can. It contrasted with the natural world. It was where relationships formed and developed—never destroyed—but always transformed into new systems, and increased in stability along the way.

'Becq not coming out tonight?' Manolin said to Santiago.

'No, she's out at the theatre with her aunt,' Santiago said. 'She's leaning towards the Arts these days. I despair. You know, she's taken to making dolls in her spare time. Dolls. All that science I gave and she turns to crafts. I pour over journals and research notes, and she makes dolls.' He smiled at his drink. 'Still, I have to say, they're very realistic.'

Manolin was disappointed.

'You know, I can't remember what I was saying before you came in,' Jefry said. 'I'm sure I had a point to make.'

'What's that?'

Jefry said, 'I got lost in my thoughts—'

'Was that unfamiliar territory then?' Yana said.

Jefry saw the sarcasm in her eyes. 'No, my dear, your body is unfamiliar territory.'

Arth sniggered. Yana sat silently, fingering her cigarette. She rubbed its ears with her free hand, and the creature regarded her with narrow, satisfied eyes.

'So, any work this week?' Manolin asked.

'Not much to report,' Santiago said. He puffed on his cigar. 'Guano has gone to the Mayor's office though, and he'll be back soon with some possible news, but apart from that we're still going to have to burn that research grant for a month or two longer.'

Everyone nodded. A silence crept on them. Times were tough for DeBrelt's Freelance Exploratory Crew. They were mercenary naturalists. Together they travelled Has-jahn and lands further, for whatever they were asked for, animal, vegetable, mineral. Their knowledge was unrivalled. They came at a high price, but, as they told everyone, you got what you paid for: intellectuals who knew their subjects inherently. There wasn't much call for their specialist knowledge in recent times, and so they had become regulars at the tavern, drinking away research funds, eating into Santiago's personal pockets, which Manolin knew were luckily rather deep. Sometimes they even had mail delivered to the bar.

The door burst open. A couple strolled into the room to a standing roar from DeBrelt's table. The man was clad in a smart, black robe, with baggy white breeches underneath. His fingers were covered in dozens of silver rings, and at his side was a small woman with a large smile that Manolin thought was genuine. She wore the same styled outfit, but wore a white top and black bottom.

'Tchad, Dora, come over, many congratulations,' Jefry said, checking his stance as he scraped his chair back.

He was being careful not to stumble, and Manolin saw that Yana looked at him almost angrily at his loudness. Shame flashed across her eyes as if a candle had been blown out. Jefry sat back down, removing beer froth by raising his lower lip over his top. Manolin watched and felt pain as Tchad squeezed Dora's hand, their faces beaming. He could see they were happy. He breathed out, but smiled anyway, and he congratulated the pair.

Drinks were ordered. Food was brought. The table became full of rare curiosities: crab, oyster, certain cystoids, fish, eel, lizard were all crammed into the centre, sizzling and spiced. The main course, a large squid, was brought last, placed in the centre of the table and everyone gazed at such a delicacy. Each of them had a plate and filled it to the top. Manolin was not feeling particularly hungry. Santiago more than made up for it. He devoured the delights, being careful not to get any in his moustache. A crowd came and went, congratulating the couple, who were coy, gracious.

As the evening progressed Manolin drank more. He had bought the whole bottle of whisky so that he didn't have to move. For many minutes he stared at the cream label, the old style lettering. The noise of the crowd began to gather in his head, amplifying, aching. His eyes felt hot and his head heavy on his neck. His eyes focussed on the whiskey as he threw back another glass. The liquid fired his taste buds, sending a flash of alertness to his eyes. It took him away from the noise. Breathing became difficult. He tapped his chest with the ball of his palm.

Yana nudged Santiago, whispered in Santiago's ears, and he nodded. She felt sorry for Manolin. She had spoken aloud that his wife would ruin him, but even she would be surprised how rapidly this was happening. Yana cared for him. Probably in the absence of any attention from her husband, and in the avoidance of Santiago's lechery, she found comfort talking to Manolin. She'd told him that he was sensible, articulate, well mannered. He was, she would admit, cute, but that was hardly a word to feel guilty about. It helped to have someone like that around, especially given his situation.

Manolin felt eyes on his head, something typical of a heavy drinker. He looked up from his warm, liquid escape. He slid back his chair and slumped forward on the table. He stood up, pulling everyone's eyes with him. Santiago raised his head. Manolin walked to the door of the tavern, reaching out to hold on to chairs as he went. Cats leapt out of his path.

'Please, excuse me for a moment,' Santiago said, and followed Manolin.

Manolin burst out into the cold. The freshness hit him in the face. It was night and the sky had been washed by heavy rain. He inhaled deeply, walked towards a metal railing that separated the dock from the water. He found it difficult to walk on the cobbles and could hear his footsteps. Clutching the rail, he vomited over the side, spitting lumps and shapes into the black water. He coughed several times, rolled saliva around his mouth.

Street lamps lit the underside of the clouds, creating a dirty amber glow that illuminated the boats and the cobbled stones shone where they had been worn.

Manolin burst into tears.

'For Arrahd's sake, man. Pull yourself together.' Santiago gripped Manolin, pulled him close. Manolin put his head on his shoulder. He shook.

Santiago said, 'She did it again, didn't she?'

Manolin nodded into Santiago's jacket. Santiago hugged him so tight that it almost knocked off his hat. He nodded to himself, because he thought that it was difficult for a man to admit such a thing. Manolin had talked to Santiago about what his wife did. It was shameful for a man to strike a woman, but what happened when a woman struck a man? If the man was a gentleman, he would not strike back. He ought not to be a punch bag. Manolin did everything for her. He bought her presents, had never looked at another woman, when he was with her. He thought he was courteous, gentle, kind—qualities that did attract attention, but it was not his fault. He loved her dearly, dismissed her attacks as mere intimacy. It was accepted that beating a woman was wrong, but no Minister had felt it worthwhile protecting the male of the species from attack. Once, she had drawn a knife when he told her of a girl, a year younger than herself, who had a crush on him. He thought it an honest and open jest, but she had other ideas. Later that evening, he knew that she had gone out to show him that she, too, could possess attention.

A flock of white and black geese streamed by overhead heading south in a large V-formation. They were illuminated by the gas lamps. They cackled as they flew in low, swirling up over the three or four storey buildings. Manolin heard their voices fading and echoing down the bay.

Behind the two men, the tavern door opened and with the loudness of laughter and voices, Jefry ran out with someone else. The human and rumel seemed to Santiago to be eager, hastening across the cobbles. Manolin shook himself away. He didn't want a fuss made.

'Sorry to disturb, San.' He was almost out of breath. 'We've got some news.'

'News? What news, Guano?' Santiago said.

'Two species, unidentified, washed up last night, twenty miles south. Apparently, we're requested first thing in the morning, at the Temple, the Mayor's office. They wouldn't let me look, but they were under observation from the government's men.'

Santiago frowned and scratched his chin, propping that arm up at the elbow with his other hand. 'Alien species indeed? I wonder what they are?'

'They wouldn't show me. The officials will only allow you to see them. Apparently they don't trust anyone else as they want this kept away from the press—as if I'd fucking tell anyone. But, they seem really worried.' Guano shifted his weight from heel to heel.

Santiago smiled and paused to think before. He raised both his arms like a conductor, before patting his team on the back, steering them towards the tavern.

'Let's drink tonight and worry about these creatures tomorrow.'

Manolin watched them walking back towards the warmth and the light. He lingered, wondering what these new beings were. He turned to face the sea.

Santiago's voice could be heard just before he re-entered the tavern. 'Or, we could go and find out later tonight. The night, after all, is still young.'

Manolin looked down as a cat rubbed his leg then moved away. The creature stepped from cobble to cobble, avoiding puddles, looking up all the time to where the geese went.

Four

'**...of** the basic silicate tetrahedral structure, with varying degrees of feldspar and mica. These extrusive rock formations, as they stand, are composed of the typical minerals, but can be grouped into two major, separate compositions: Eschan Bed Sediments and the Pergamos Formation (*Tyaris et al*, 1603). The extinct volcanic island chain, that extends north from the non-volcanic island of Arya are Daleth, Gimel, and Samekh. Only Samekh retains this unique geological formation, possessing discrete boundaries to the surrounding country rock that contains large amounts of iron and magnesium, typical of any magma.

My other chief concern is the coral rock linked to these islands. The coral seems to move daily, with no reason as to a particular occurrence. The main frame in one particular region, expands outwards like a limb from the main coral system, which is nearest to Arya. This calcified rock gradually shifts as if the very world itself moves. I had not the ability to decipher its chemical composition. It must wait until another trip.'

Prof. Victyr Lewys (1694), *Geological Concerns of Tropical Islands*. Department of Geology, Al Terril Institute, Escha.

Five

Jella woke early as musky sunlight filled the room. Lula stirred, the girl's mouth open slightly revealing her tongue. Jella smiled, pushed Lula's jaw up to close her mouth. A few strands of long, black hair fell over her tanned face.

'You'll catch flies,' Jella whispered, still pushing the hairs back over Lula's ears.

'I'll shoot them from the sky first,' Lula said with her thick east coast accent.

'I believe you,' Jella said, smiling. She believed that Lula was one of the most proficient women with a musket she'd ever seen.

Lula's father had fought in wars, and settled in a small fishing village south of Rhoam, bringing Lula up on their own That was long before the couple had met.

The story always made her smile. Jella had stolen a horse from a rich-looking merchant who sold his wares through the shanty city outside of Rhoam. Jella had jumped on the steed, galloped into the desert scrubland south, in the direction the dead city of Lucher, her old home. She had ridden for miles through sparse surroundings, dazed in the streaming light from which there was no shelter. She dragged up dust, entered even more barren regions, until out of the corner of her eye she saw the sea. It was a bold blue that stood out from the land and sky. She rode towards it, having not seen if for years. Like greeting an old friend, she felt an awkwardness then rapid ease. She sat on the horse staring at it. She watched the waves, took pleasure from hearing the water hit the cliffs.

Eventually, those cliffs began to form a long shadow over the sea. Jella turned the horse along the coast, always remembering the pair of pterodettes that were flying together that evening. She was hypnotised, watching the green reptiles in unison and she jumped down off of the horse. She was still watching them glide in and out of circles, with their vein filled wings out wide, when she heard someone crying.

She turned on the spot, her feet drawing up red dust that blew inland. Walking towards the cliff edge and down several steps that had been carved into the rock, she came across a girl. She was hunched, shivering. Naked, so that her skin looked the same colour as the rock.

Jella walked down. 'Hello,' she said above the sound of the tide. 'You okay? Why're you crying?'

The girl looked up. Black hair fell back away from a pretty face. Delicate, with strong cheekbones. A handsomeness that came from within. Her eyes dazzled even at a distance. 'My father's run off with a new woman. He left me alone.'

Jella reached a hand down, offered it to the hunched girl, who looked straight up, full of confusion.

The rumel said, 'Where're your clothes?'

'What use are they right now?'

Jella nodded as if she knew what that meant.

The girl took Jella's hand and the rumel watched the slim figure rise. She was most definitely a woman, not a girl. The sea hit the cliff hard, they felt the vibrations. Jella took off her white shirt and placed it around the girl, who strained to get both arms within with the wind being so strong. They were both half naked. Jella's tough grey skin looked so different to the soft, brown of the human. They were uncertain of what to do or where to go. Both being lost in different ways, they stood together. It was only moments until they found each other's touch both desirable and comforting.

Jella held the girl. The exchanged names, then glances. The rumel drew her finger along the delicate jaw line, up to the forehead, pushing strands of hair from out of her eyes.

They rode back to Rhoam, where they would spend every moment together. When they made love, it seemed that there was no outside world.

'Will you love me?' Lula had said. She asked the question a lot.

Jella said, 'Of course I will.'

'Men and women have said this to me before. They all leave and forget what words mean. Sticking your tongue inside of me isn't enough.'

'I'll love you. I'll show you what it means.'

Jella did not care much for words, and although they felt awkward on her lips, those were ones she intended to stick by. And Jella needed Lula. The girl had softened her heart, made her feel something after such a long bitterness inside. One of the few things about her past that Jella wanted to remember was her father and the way he held her, looked at her, and Lula gave her exactly the same sensation. Lula was quiet, contemplative, and it was her gentle actions that soothed Jella, and the girl's presence was at times better than any drug. Lula thrived on taking Jella on walks, for meals when they had stolen enough money, brought her flowers. Lula was the romance that she needed.

***

'D'you get much money last night?' Lula asked.

'Yeah, Menz and Yayle have it. We've more than enough money now. We can stop tricking rich, gullible men,' Jella said.

'Good, now we can get on with it.'

'Yes, *now* we can. We should set off soon.'

Jella rose from the bed. There were few comforts within the metal hut, but Jella and Lula had tried to make it their own. Lula hung green drapes, burned incense day and night. They had managed to find wooden cupboards and a table. Jella thought the place much better than most were outside of the city. They could, with the blackmail money, afford better, but it was a matter of principal that they remained with their own kind.

She stood up, naked, and stretched, her grey skin taut over her muscles. Lula opened an eye to watch. The rumel's tail swung in order to wake up fully and Lula's eyes followed the tail left and right before it settled. Lula yawned.

'I've got to go to the City Library soon,' Jella said.

'More research?'

'More research.'

'What're you looking for now? I thought you'd planned every detail?' Lula asked. Her accent made her words sound lazy.

'I do, I do. But there's no harm in being certain, is there? It's fine to know what's there, but I need to make sure we're doing everything by the book.'

'You're like what you've told me of your father. You're such a control freak,' Lula said. Then, 'But sometimes I'm glad of your attention to detail.'

Both girls laughed. Jella walked to a cupboard, her muscles moved visibly. Her white hair swayed down her back, a contrast to her darker body. She opened the cupboard, thought of an outfit to wear, then put on a black gypsy skirt and a shirt.

'It suits you. I think I like what you're wearing,' Lula said. She turned, ruffled the sheets, pushed the side of her face further into the pillow.

'What? Don't you like this?'

'Of course I do. I think you look sophisticated,' she said to the wall.

Jella looked at the body of the girl in her bed. The sheet had fallen back and the curve of Lula's brown back could be seen.

She stopped the urges that were building within. She had work to do.

Jella walked through the wooden doors of the City Library, through the arched corridor, and into the book room. She always looked up to the ceiling that was covered in murals. From this end you could hardly see the other side of the room. She glanced over the area charts to find where the biology books were kept then she sauntered off to a far corner, humming a tune, her tail waving. The library was quiet. It was the way of things in modern Rhoam, she thought. People still loved the arts and books, but they liked to talk about them a lot in the street side coffee shops and dark music theatres.

She picked a title up: *Marine evolution surrounding the seas off Samekh Island.* She wondered around other sections, collecting books on mathematics and three ocean charts of the Sea of Wands, and the Island chain north of Arya. She settled on a desk in a quiet corner of the library.

For an hour or two, she made notes and calculations, until she was interrupted by the curator, an elderly man with a ghostly face. His eyes were enlarged behind his glasses.

'Good morning, Jella. How're we today?' He coughed, hunching into his jumper.

'Hello. I'm fine,' Jella said, looking past him. He was always helpful, always bringing her the books she needed. Never asked any questions, happy that someone wanted to read.

'Studying, eh? Good. Not like your friends then?'

'I'm sorry?'

'Menz and Yayle, those chaps in your little group that come here looking at maps. They were arrested early this morning'

'Arrested?' She looked him in the eye. 'What for?'

'Terrorism charges,' he said. 'They were caught in possession of some pretty lethal explosives and several dozen muskets.' One of his eyes squinted in a strange expression.

Jella waited for more detail, but there was none.

'Now, Jella, I don't want you getting caught up in anything to do with weapons and war. Does no good at all.' Even though Jella was looking at him, her mind was elsewhere. She could tell that another one of his stories was coming.

'I remember years and years ago, a library—not sure if it was this one, come to think. Anyway, it was under siege. The city's armed forces came in, knives and muskets everywhere. Said that there was information that could cause a revolution—political talk—within the walls. The government wanted all the books burning. Place was sealed off, with the staff inside.'

He burst into laughter and Jella forced a smile. 'Of course, that was back a long time ago when the government could do that sort of thing. Anyway, the soldiers picked up books and started to read. All sorts of philosophies went in their minds. All sorts of stories. One by one they stopped the burning. They ignored their orders. They read and enjoyed and read more. They put down their weapons and just read. Course, the government was ironically overthrown as a direct result, eventually, but just goes to show that weapons are no use, Jella. You're a good girl. I don't want you getting caught up in any such activities.'

She said, 'I won't, sir. When were they arrested, Menz and Yayle?'

'Dawn, approximately. But for some reason they weren't in bed like the rest of us. They're in the City gaol now.'

'Thanks.'

'No problem.' He turned, walked along one of the corridors of books, touched the shelves with his hand.

'Shit,' Jella said. She scraped her chair back, gathered her notes.

Six

'**F**ather?'

The boy prodded the doctor's bald head. He was sitting cross-legged on the beach, on the side of the island facing the reef. His eyes were closed.

The boy said, 'Father.'

Doctor Macmillan opened his eyes, gazed out at the water. His eyes focussed on the large, turquoise gem: the coral reef. He couldn't see any of the islands beyond. The glare off the water forced him to squint. The water was partially broken up about two-hundred feet from the shore, where green algae seemed to loaf like flotsam. It was, in fact, resting upon limestone pedestals in their thousands. Clouds stretched out thinly, in one or two small lines above the horizon. The heat was glaring.

Doctor Forb Macmillan turned to regard the boy. The child's skin was browned and he wore a white shirt and sand-coloured breeches—the same type that his father wore. He stood waiting for his father to speak, prompting him.

'Father, did they make it?'

Doctor Forb Macmillan shrugged, wiped a thin veil of perspiration from off of his bald head. 'I don't know.'

He stood up, pushing his weight down into the soft sand, leaving his imprint momentarily. He ruffled the boy's short, scruffy black hair before he walked towards the palm forest. He was limping as he walked off an ache. He felt a little dizzy. 'I hope no more've been killed.'

The boy shook his head. The tide followed them inland, water seeping through the indentations in the sand, which the doctor had made, and covered them up before removing them from the beach.

Seven

'I'm not sure if I like this route,' Manolin said, walking behind Santiago. The older man carried his hat under his arm, a lantern in the other. They shifted along a platform at the edge of the sewer. Rank fluids flowed past them and they dared not look at what was in there. Manolin swore he saw a decaying arm, clutching at the damp air, being swept away into the darkness. Snakes snapped by upstream. He could smell methane, sulphides. The only light came from the lantern, and the brickwork was black as was the water. Manolin's eyes were heavy with the weight of alcohol. Either that or the chemicals in the water.

'It means we get past any hired thugs used to guard the grounds,' Santiago said. He paused to look at the map in his pocket. 'Gets us right in there.' Then, 'This way.' He pointed to a right turn.

Presently, they surfaced outside of the rear entrance to The Temple—the offices of the mayor. Manolin looked up in and he felt awe at the perpendicular spires. Gargoyles loomed over. The building looked as if it didn't belong there. It was something so old that was immersed in hastily constructed buildings. The limestone was smooth. Santiago rubbed his hand over it, nodding. Birds clung to the top of the spires of the building. Birds or bats, it was so high up that they couldn't quite discern. Manolin could see the chimneys in the distance, the plumes. He wondered at how bad it would be to live under such conditions, breathing them in, allowing them to line the lung over time.

They heard stifled laughter and screams close by, almost so close that they could see the groups of people attached, but there seemed a strange otherworld quality to where they stood, as if the history of The Temple was enough to scare anyone off.

He was starting to shake a little as Santiago closed the lid of the sewer, being as careful as he could be. The old man dug in his pockets, pulled out a silver key and tried it in the large oak doors. He smiled, popped on his hat once again.

'Where d'you get a key from?' Manolin said.

Santiago waved a hand dismissively. 'Oh, I've many an old friend who can help me out with these things. I've got a stash of such keys at home somewhere. You never know when they'll come in handy.'

Manolin watched Santiago laugh to himself as he walked into the darkness of the building. He hoped that there was nobody inside. Manolin followed, taking one last look to make sure that they were not being followed. He wasn't cut out for all this stealth.

Santiago seemed to know his way around the government building surprisingly well, despite the fact that there were no lights, just corridor after corridor. Santiago took them up several levels of stairs before concluding that they were close to where he suspected the alien species would be being held.

'There's a room on the top floor that was used for scientific pursuits some years back,' he said. 'There was a botched up experiment by a rather hopeful mayor, but the room has been kept for research.'

Manolin said nothing. He thought that he should be at home, in bed with his wife. He missed her, despite everything that had happened.

'Righto, here we are.' Santiago pushed open the doors then walked into the black. Because he'd dropped the lantern in the sewer, after Manolin had screamed at what turned out to be nothing, he pulled out a matchbox from his pocket, struck a small flame. They walked to the next room.

Manolin stepped towards the window. From it, you could see the cityscape in its entirety. There were large, rectangular towers peppered with the little lights. Above he could see an airship turning in a slow circle. Down below were two men standing next to a barrel, which held a small fire. They rubbed their hands together, held them over the flames. People walked by, threw objects towards them. Glass shattered. A few paces away: a hooded figure was painting something on a wall, an explosion of colours and lines. Manolin followed the figure to a shadow, where a prostitute was leaning, her skirt hitched up to her thigh. Even from that height, he could hear a group of rumel were taunting a human female. Manolin thought that she could look after herself. She tossed a canister of liquid in their direction. The rumel scattered into the darkness.

He looked up towards the hills that the ancient train lines disappeared into, where he knew clansmen operated. No one travelled through those scrub hills.

Santiago's footsteps disrupted his thoughts. Manolin turned to face the room again. There was a glass panel separating that room from another. The match went out, so again, Santiago drew another. This time he noticed that the flame reflected off the glass panel. Santiago turned to look for lanterns on the wall, lit several of them to illuminate the scene fully. Manolin and Santiago walked up to the glass, placed their hands on the smooth surface. Their mouths fell open.

'Well, bugger me,' Santiago said.

Manolin nodded in reply before asking, 'What the hell are they?'

A voice broke in from behind. 'We were hoping you would be able to answer that, Santiago DeBrelt, but only when we invited you to.'

Santiago and Manolin turned. Several men pointed muskets and pistols at them. In the middle was a man in a black suit, hair slicked to one side, a wide, brown face, and eyes that were slanted, creased at the edges. He appeared utterly calm.

Manolin glanced between that man and Santiago, who held each other's gaze as if they knew each other, had done so for years, and were now ascertaining one another's thoughts. But what really bothered him were the weapons. To see these men who were so obviously used to intimidating people actually addressing him was more surreal than unnerving, but with the barrel of a gun pointed at you, you tended to take it seriously. His heart thumped in his chest.

'Good evening, Mayor Gio,' Santiago said, with an arrogant casualness that almost confirmed their history for Manolin.

'Step away from those Qe Falta creatures,' the Mayor said. 'We can very easily kill you.'

'Please, it's too late for such hard-talk, Mr Gio. I'm sure you've killed lots of people, but I'm tired and I haven't even had a cup of coffee tonight. Besides, you're incorrect on both counts.' Santiago turned to the glass panel, peered into the other room. 'They're not Qe Falta.'

'Santiago, I see muskets. This isn't the time for you to turn into a professor,' Manolin whispered. Santiago smiled, winked as if to say, *It's okay, it's all a game. Just tough guy talk.*

'Mr DeBrelt,' Mayor Gio said, 'you seem confident. Let me remind you that because of your political activities you're constantly being watched. Your little band of Collectivists may be underground now, but we still watch you.' Then, 'So, may I ask why I'm wrong on both counts?'

Manolin frowned. He knew Santiago was against the capitalist mechanisms of Escha—always said so in late night rants over a beer—but not that he was an *active* Collectivist. That political movement was forced underground years ago. The word was rarely heard these days. You more or less did what you were told in this city—for a quiet life—and being a Collectivist was far from that. Pure communism didn't sit well with a right wing government, such as the one Gio led.

'You may,' Santiago said. 'You see, you'll not fill me with shot, as

I'm the only one who has the faintest idea what these creatures actually are. And on the second count of your *wrongness*, sir, they are *not* Qe Falta.'

Mayor Gio turned to his entourage of several broad men. A couple of them shook their heads at him, shrugged.

'Not Qe Falta, you say?' the Mayor asked.

'No. Everything on these creatures is natural and has evolved for a reason. Nothing has been grafted on by weird science. You do of course know why they're called Qe Falta, Mr Gio?'

The Mayor was silent, his eyes perfectly still, regarding Santiago.

'They're called Qe Falta since the accurate translation is *the false people*. They live in the desert, with whatever poor features that have been bolted on by crack-pot genetics. Wings where there shouldn't be, four arms where there should be two—that sort of thing. Genetic freaks, and labelled so. What you see here is totally real, even though you've sliced them open to discover this. Trust you to think them outlaws. Not that there is anything wrong with the Qe Falta anyway. Unlike you they actually look after our lands, our environments.' His eyes turned to the window that faced the chimneys.

'Please, shut up. The Qe Falta are evil, everyone knows that.' Gio's face reddened. 'Plain and simple ghouls. So, what are these things then?'

'Ichthyocentaur, I think,' Santiago said, excitement clear on his face. 'Men and women who lie somewhere between a dolphin and a human, in the great tree of life. You can see that they possess a tail suitable for a marine habitat and a skin ideal for diving. The rest of their body is like you and I, Mr Gio, like you and I. And you have butchered them. I wouldn't imagine anything else from fascist fellows, such as yourself.' He smiled.

There was a pause while everyone took in this information. Manolin nodded. He remembered an old book or a lecture or something. He rested his elbow on his hand to prop up his chin. Santiago and Mayor Gio still held each other's gaze.

Santiago broke the silence. 'One thing puzzles me though. They're meant to be extinct. They should've died out during the Rebellion to Science, during the last age. Then, too, they were suspected of being Qe Falta. Where'd they come from?'

'We were hoping that you could tell us that,' the Mayor said.

Santiago turned around and nodded. 'Did they come with anything? Clothes or food? Anything of that nature?'

'All they came with is on the table on the side of the room. There were a couple of fruits and little else. The only thing to note was a bottle.'

'Fruits? A bottle? May I go in?' Santiago said.

'You got this far without my permission, why ask now?'

'Excellent!' Santiago said, rubbing his hands together. He walked around to the door and into the room. Manolin followed.

Two male ichthyocentaur lay on top of separate operating tables, their arms by their sides. Their chests had been sliced open from the base of their necks to their genitals, which had caused a musky odour. Metal clamps held tissue apart. Skin was pulled away from the incision, revealing a bloodied rib cage. Their organs were intact, and much of their blood had been removed, stored in large canisters that stood behind them. Their facial expressions were calm, their eyes closed.

Santiago studied their anatomy and made expressions of wonder. He moved in close to their open torsos and sniffed the flesh. 'They came from warmer seas,' he said, probably to himself. He walked to the table with the belongings, while Manolin stared at the cold dead forms.

Santiago found the bottle, which was dark, unopened, with a plant seal blocking the neck. There were medical instruments around the room, and so he picked up a pair of tweezers, poking the seal down into the bottle. After minutes of fiddling he pulled out a piece of paper. He glanced out of the glass panel to the Mayor, who stood with only two armed men, their muskets lowered to their sides now. Santiago looked again at the paper. It was coarse and grainy, made from basic sources, more like a plant. The kind that they used to make old notebooks out of, years ago. He unfolded it and called Manolin over, placing the bottle back down onto the table.

Manolin said, 'Come on, put us out of our misery. What's it say?'

Manolin unlocked the door to his home, walked in quietly, a million pre-prepared excuses for why he was late flashing in his mind. He closed the door, headed into the sitting room. He glanced up at the moonlight through the gap in the curtain. The light shone onto a small table in the centre of the room, where two glasses sparkled. He took a step closer and saw only one had lipstick on. There was an ashtray beside, the embers of two cigarettes were placed at opposite ends. Manolin blinked, turned to walk to his bedroom. His heart began to ache. He heard noises from behind the door and paused.

With some dread, he pushed down on the handle and opened the door.

He saw the back of a tall man. It was bigger, more muscular than his. He was standing behind Manolin's wife. She was bent over the bed, her legs apart, her arms resting on the mattress. Her hair had fallen over her face and was touching the sheets. They were both naked, wore only the light of one small candle that wavered in the corner. A cold gust filled the room. They both turned around, slowly. These details were captured as images in his mind.

Manolin's eyes were wide. His mouth fell open as if to say something, but nothing came out. The other man pulled the bed sheets up over himself. Manolin's wife stepped behind her lover for cover.

Manolin's heart seemed to stop. He felt his stomach turn, sink. Everything his marriage had been was brought to his eyes in the moment. His throat felt thick, preventing words from escaping, if they could have been much use to him.

'Manny, I didn't think you'd be back. It's not what it looks like, I swear,' she said, her voice faltering a little.

Manolin grunted a laugh. *It's not what it looks like, indeed*, he thought. He walked over to the wardrobe to his right. It was far enough away from the bed so he did not need to walk past this other man. He pulled down a large canvass bag, proceeded to fill it with clothes. He felt impressed that he had not broken down yet.

She said, 'Manny, aren't you going to say anything?'

No reply.

'I think you'd better leave now,' she said to her lover, who was stumbling whilst putting on his clothes. He glanced to her one last time before opening the door then walked out of the room, leaving the door open. She slipped into a night gown, walked behind Manolin, who buttoned up his bag, sealed it tight.

She said, 'Manolin, please, it wasn't what it looks like.' Her hand on his shoulder. 'I'd been drinking—'

'Fuck off. Spare me any of this—shit,' He shrugged off her hand. 'You accuse *me* of cheating all this time. It's you who's the jealous one. I guess you *were* judging me by your own standards then?'

'No. You didn't come home. I thought you were with her. You know, Becq DeBrelt, and I knew that you and her must be together.'

'Maybe I did,' he said. Then, 'Well I didn't. Never have, never will. Remember those vows? Wasn't that long ago. But you thought you'd get one in before you thought I'd have the chance anyway? Typical, the only way for you to feel accepted is to open your l—'

She slapped him hard across the face. It surprised and hurt him. They looked at one another in despair. Manolin could hear the clock chiming in the next room.

'It wasn't like that,' she said.

She said, 'You're never here for me, you're always out working, ignoring how I feel and ignoring my needs.'

'And that's where I'm going again, to work,' Manolin said. 'I'm going away and this time I don't want you here when I get back. Most of what's in the home is mine. All of this.' He indicated all four walls. 'I'm sure you can spread your legs to find other accommodation.' Inwardly, he cursed. He shouldn't have said that. It showed too much anger.

Her mouth fell open, obviously didn't believe him capable of saying such direct thing. 'Manolin, please, Manny. You can't do this to me.' She sat on the bed. Her eyes became filled with tears. He could hear her breathing become quick and heard the desperation in her voice. It was so frail that it made him want to stop, there and then. Hold her. Maybe forget it had happened.

Whatever he did would probably be wrong.

'Yes, I can. I'm leaving in a couple of days, but I'm not staying here any longer. I'll sell this place and have the money waiting for me when I return. I'll see an agent first thing. You, on the other hand, you'll have nothing.'

She looked at him through eyes that were full of tear. There was nothing she could say. She sat with her head in her hands, pushing her fingers through her hair.

'Where're you going? Please don't go. When will you return? Please, let me try again.' She looked up, her eyes red with sadness.

'You never even tried in the first place. I don't know when I'll be back.' He looked at her one last time and saw simply a woman that he had once loved and thought he had satisfied. He walked to the door, walked through, closed it behind. He waited to hear it click.

He could hear her crying from the other side, but it was no use because the door had been closed. No longer able to see her, he did not know if she was looking at the back of the door. Maybe she felt too much pride to plea now, but wanted him so much to come back. He fell to his knees and his chest felt tight.

Still, she did not open the door.

He lowered his head into his hands, he wept so hard, bearing his teeth and he found he was shaking. It was a minute before he could stand up again. His legs felt weak and he stumbled to the bathroom to retrieve a few final possessions before dragging his body outside. He walked down the steps carrying his large, canvas travel case. He set it down, breathed in the cool dawn air. Far off he could hear the sound of motors pulling large vessels out to sea. Gulls cried from a sky that was changing from black to purple. A rumel was brushing at the puddles of water that had accumulated from the previous day's rain, pushing the brackish pools over the side of the docks. Ahead, a small steamer was being loaded with barrels. Through the buoys and warning lanterns, which wobbled in the tide, there were two people on the top deck of an old yacht. They were holding hands, facing the expanse of waters promised as you sailed from this coast.

And he thought then, of how much she hated the sea.

Eight

The limestone bricks turned red, absorbing the colour of the new day. A man rode by on horseback, wrapped in black, and she could only see his eyes. The horse sauntered at the base of the wall, kicking up dust as it dragged its feet only yards away from where she was standing.

As soon as she felt the sun's heat on her back Jella fell into the shade of a hut to remain unseen. She was wearing sand coloured clothing, as was Lula, who fingered the barrel of a long musket beneath her cloak. Her long black hair contrasted Jella's white locks.

The rumel and her human lover were crouched behind the shanty huts that almost touched the large city wall. Jella had calculated that they were directly outside of the gaol section. She could see the barred windows that were spaced ten feet apart. But only she and Lula could see the small bore-holes and white wires that led from them down to the base of the wall. *What a waste of ammunition*, she thought.

All Menz and Yayle had to do was remember the plan. There was a pre-conceived idea, in the event of such a situation. The solution was simple: to tie material around the bars in the windows of their cells, all of which faced towards New Lucher. Jella looked at the tops of the city wall, forty feet up, and nudged Lula. gaol guards walked along the top, shifting black cloaks over their bodies. They paced back and forth. Lula nodded.

Jella and Lula kissed one last time, holding each other.

'Be careful,' Lula said, stroking Jella's arm.

'I will, I will.'

Every few minutes, Jella would check back that the two horses she had stolen were still fine in the heat. She stroked their noses. People began to stir in New Lucher. Market stalls were being set up. Dogs began to trot around in the dust. A woman began collecting drapes that she had hung over a washing line.

The morning bell sounded within the city walls. On that chime Jella picked out a box of matches from her pocket. On the second, Lula held her musket up, pointing it at the men on top of the wall. She waited, pulling the catch back on her weapon. On the third Jella took out a match and held it tightly. She nodded to Lula. On the fourth chime Jella lit the match, and on the fifth she stepped forward and lit the fuse at the end of the long wire at the base of the wall. By the sixth chime the fuse was sparkling halfway up the wall.

At the exact moment of a series of explosions set off, Lula fired a shot. There were seventeen snapping sounds followed by four deep explosions that couldn't be seen against the redness of the morning sun, and the wall coughed out large bricks and clouds of dust. Men fell from the top as Lula picked them off, one by one, before the dust cloud became too much. Men lurched off the top, seeming to hang in the air, before they plummeted. Their arms flayed beneath their cloaks, scraping the wall on the way down. Jella could see that one broke his neck on the bricks that were sticking out. Masonry fell in large knuckles on the huts below. People screamed, shouted. Jella watched a dog catch the full force of a square block. It crushed the animal's skull, smacking into the ground. Further explosions followed, sending vibrations along the ground. Huts were shattered behind them in the next boulder shower, the metal roofs collapsing easily as the masonry rained down.

Then the explosions came to a halt. All that could be seen was a silent dust cloud.

'I'm going up,' Jella said. She ran to the wall, Lula fired up behind her, covering.

Jella clutched a rope tied to a metal claw, looked across at her lover. Lula fired then reloaded. Her eyes squinted to block out the sun and the dust, but she picked the guards out. The men tumbled into the ground. One fell almost on top of her; he spread his body horizontally to slow his fall, but his head caught on the edge of a supporting pole of a hut. His neck snapped as it was impaled momentarily. His body slumped down and dragged his head that was still held by the cloak. Lula looked at the body without expression the resumed firing up through the dust.

Jella regarded the wall before her, tried not to be worried about Lula. She started to climb. Her tail was erect, poised, as she clawed her way up the broken brickwork. She could hear Lula firing and the sound of retaliation from above. She burst upwards, scrambling and grasping at stone, some of which crumbled in her hands. She tossed the claw end of the rope into an open gap in the wall.

A rumel waved at her through the dust cloud as if he were a friend on the other side of the street. He climbed down and she watched him all the way to the ground before she shifted along the wall to another gap from the explosions. She threw the claw end in. Another rumel made his way to the ground. He was stouter, older, and nodded as he passed. She leapt down after and rolled to absorb the impact and ran back to Lula, who was still firing shots. People had by now gathered to watch. Children stared at Lula, some cheering. There were ten bodies on the floor by her side, limbs broken from the fall.

Jella and Lula backed off with the two men, jumped up on the horses and rode through the middle of New Lucher, under canopies and the smoke from cooking fires. Lula through a large device towards the remains of the wall, turned, and listened to the noise of the explosion and screams, which faded as they moved away.

They rode to the limits of the shanty into a scrubland littered with spindly grasses, then in to the desert proper.

At midday the heat was painful. Jella could feel the sweat down her back, on her arms, even in her eyes. They rode on, every now and then looking back over their shoulders. They travelled until the horses couldn't cope.

They came across a small watering hole, marked by jagged trees that leaned over a stagnant pool. They jumped off, bathed and drank, allowing the horses to rest. Jella walked to the edge of the water and knelt down to wash her face.

She stood up, looked at her group, who were all laughing like children. Sometimes she felt the did not take it all seriously enough as her. Were they here for the fun, to feel that they had some direction in riding her anger based towards Lucher? She hoped not. She was annoyed at Menz and Yayle for costing her munitions, but they were part of a team. Together, they were working towards the mission.

A bizarre metal structure stood at one edge of the water, behind a tree. About fifteen feet high, was thin, skeletal, like a fossil, in the shape of a giant wing. It had oxidised ferric, red.

Lula walked behind, put her brown arms around the rumel. She said, 'What is it?'

'Don't know,' Jella said. 'I suspect it's something from an earlier age, some ancient technology of some description.' They held each other, stared at the structure. It cast a long shadow across the sand.

Menz and Yayle, the two other rumel, both with grey skins, were still dressed in the grey rags of the gaol and it had darkened where they had splashed in dirty water. Their tails stuck out of a hole in the back of the breeches and were swinging.

Menz took off his shirt and advanced to a deeper part of the pond.

'Can fat people go skinny-dipping?' Yayle asked, watching the heavy set Menz wallow in the cooling water.

Menz turned back sharply, glared. Yayle smiled. Menz returned to shallower water, put his shirt back on. The intense heat had already dried his back. Yayle stretched then rubbed his legs. He removed his breeches to wade into the water then came back out again, patted his legs dry. There was a scar that stretched from his knee, up along his thigh.

He saw Menz looking, and the older rumel looked away whilst Yayle pulled his breeches back up. 'You don't have to stare y'know.'

Menz said, 'I wasn't, lad. I wasn't. Still gets to you, doesn't it?'

'It would if it was your leg, too.'

'I know, I was just saying. We've all got wounds, some of which we can't see.'

'Yeah, well, this one you can see, as I have every damn day for the last ten years. You've got yours from the army, I made mine myself.'

'Weren't your fault, though, was it.'

Yayle turned to the flat stretches of sand in all directions. He didn't want to think about this. Not again. He was content being free again, was beginning to worry that their gaol plan would fail them. Although he'd only been locked up for a night, it was more than a relief.

They walked over to the women, coughed loudly.

'Come along you two,' Menz said. His white hair had been shaven off to stubble. He was almost fifty years old, his skin tough, creased. He was stout, solid, muscular and had a keen look about him that made him appear much younger than he was.

Yayle was younger, taller, with a liveliness in the way he stood, shifting weight from foot to foot. 'I take it you brought the money and the notes?'

'Of course she did,' Lula said.

'We brought everything that you'd kept under your hut and ours, everything. It's only the explosives that have gone, but that is, of course, your own fault,' Jella said.

Yayle did not say anything, but simply looked at her.

She said, 'What the fuck did you two do to get caught?'

'Guess our neighbours needed cash,' Yayle said. 'Grassed us up. Anyway, where to now?' He brushed his hand over his stubbly head. 'We haven't a guide this time.'

'Well, we've a couple of options,' Jella said. 'One, we go back and get hunted and shot down.'

'Hmm. What else you got?' Yayle smiled. He always smiled. Jella wasn't sure if it was something that annoyed her or not. Sometimes it helped, given the grimness of their work.

'Or,' Jella said, 'we've to get on with the mission, a week or two ahead of schedule. It shouldn't matter, this was the time of year we had hoped to leave anyway.'

Yayle made a cautionary noise, the inhalation of air through a small hole in his mouth.

'Look,' Lula said, 'we've more than enough money, and a lot of knowledge. All we need are the materials, which we can easily get from our *friends* in the desert.'

'Ain't no friends you're referring to,' Menz said.

'They can help us get the explosives. And last time they acted as a go-between for us and the guide. They're an organised operation. Look, just about everyone in Has-jahn hates Escha. It's a parasite. The Qe Falta possesses one or two effective fighters, and we need all the defence we can get, especially after the last time. We can't afford to lose any more of us can we? And we aren't taking any guides this time. It's just us lot, with our notes and charts.'

The group fell silent.

Lula said, 'If you two hadn't gotten arrested, we wouldn't be in this situation so soon, so I don't think you can complain.' She removed her arms from the rumel, put her hands on her hips. 'You're still in this, aren't you?'

'Hell, yes,' Yayle said. 'I want revenge like the rest of you.' Menz nodded.

'Good,' Jella said. It was reassuring, to hear it again. It always helped to hear the words spoken. A confirmation.

'What sort of protection we got though?' Menz asked.

'The best we can buy off of the Qe Falta,' Jella said. 'We've two sacks filled with coin, we can get rock borers, explosives of the most powerful quantity and a hired bodyguard that'll not allow anyone to be taken this time.' Lula nodded.

'I don't trust Qe Falta,' Menz said. 'I don't trust ghouls. They ain't gonna stop one of us being dragged into the sea again. It's bad enough with us disturbing things down there, without more weirdness.'

'No one was dragged into the sea, Menz, it was just your old eyes letting you down,' Yayle said, resting his hand on the stocky back of the rumel, smiling, always smiling.

'I saw it right. I fucking saw it with my eyes—two goodens—so just you shut the fuck up, 'cos no ghoul ain't gonna stop anyone from being dragged underwater.'

'I didn't see anything that time, nothing,' Yale said. It could've been the tides or anything that caused them to drown. And it was night time. When we took a submersible down, we didn't see anything that could've done what you say. There was nothing. Nothing but the reef.'

'No, you didn't fucking see anything,' Menz said. 'You didn't see his eyes when they went under, did you? You were on the other side, making your bloody notes. I was there, I watched all three of them go under—all good, strong, men they were—and you didn't see it. Didn't see the blood shootin' up nor the fright in those eyes. Ain't no ghoul gonna stop that.'

The wind picked up. A pterodette croaked from above. The reptile was gliding on a thermal with its vein-filled wings stretched out wide. It curved down over their heads before it arced to the north.

Jella broke the silence. 'We've no choice but to have some faith. Come on guys, all any of us have left is the plan. Think about all your relatives that died in Lucher, all those years ago. Think about them, choking, coughing up blood, vomiting, dying in their own excrement, withering away to nothingness, no dignity and with no justice. Think about losing everything, being shipped out of a city to live in a tin can surrounded by filth and shit and think about getting one back for them and then worry about trust.

'The Qe Falta can help us, sure they might be weird and sure, we might not know what creature we're actually dealing with, Arrahd may not have designed such a creature, but they can help us get one back for our families and loved ones.'

All of them nodded. Lula aired her shirt.

Jella said, 'We can head towards caves tonight. There're some about a two hours ride south then tomorrow we can head towards where the Qe Falta might be. They'll help us. They're known terrorists after all.'

She walked away from this, regarded the landscape to clear her mind. There was only ground and sky. Where the two met, the horizon wobbled. Beyond that there were only things that her imagination might make up so she shook her head and looked at the trees. The spindly branches and palms seemed to ache in desperation to suck water up. She felt her face gathering sweat and she wiped her brow, tied her hair back. She glanced again at the strange sculpture, the buried wing, and through its frame she could see a small plume on the horizon, where a yellow cloud extended upwards into the endlessly blue sky.

They were being followed.

Nine

They travelled through the centre of the desert for twelve days before Jella saw the boat.

Up until that point, everywhere that she looked she saw bright sand and blue sky at every point along the horizon. There was an intense loneliness about the desert that was welcoming to her. It meant no one was around to disrupt her thoughts, her focussed anger.

Sometimes she pointed out scrub plants to the others. Occasionally she pointed to things that disappeared, which were never really near anyway. The horses were tired and the group was almost out of provisions. Two days ago Jella had pointed out the Lo Gurate hills in the distance, which looked like low, blue rippled clouds.

They sat on horseback, wrapped in cloaks to stop the penetrating heat, were staring at a boat that was in the sand. Jella could guess how large it was because, as they approached it, it increased in size almost at the same rate as the hills in the background, which were some hours away. The group dismounted, stood by the horses.

'What is it, that thing?' Lula asked.

'The Aarc,' Jella said. 'It's where the Qe Falta live.'

'Ghouls,' Menz said. His face darkened.

'They live there?' Lula asked. 'How do you know all this?'

'The library had its benefits. Also, news and contacts are prolific, if you know where to look.'

'How d'you mean?'

'There're a few Qe Falta in Rhoam, although no one knew because their deformities are subtle, in certain cases. Like I keep saying, you know they've helped us on our previous scouting mission. They put us in contact with our guide that time, as a sort of in between. You meet many people in those cobbled streets, Menz, many people. People can hide by being right in front of you, because it's the last place you expect to look.'

A pterodette approached. Jella looked up at the small creature. At first a mere dot in the blue, became large, graceful as it flew above their heads in a circle, drifting on a thermal, hardly moving its wings, then turned sharply towards the home of the Qe Falta.

'They'll come for us,' Jella said, her eyes fixed on the creature.

Within the hour, shapes could be seen approaching from the boat, a plume of sand above them, unmoving with no wind to disturb its path. The shapes became larger, and soon Jella could see that it was in fact horses approaching. She counted ten in a wide line. On each of them was a figure wearing a dark cloak and she could see that because they rippled, obviously riding fast. Menz and Yayle opened a bag that was hanging on the side of their horse and each drew a musket.

'Put those back,' Jella said. She was facing away from the rumel, towards the riders. 'You won't need them.'

'Why? I ain't gonna trust no ghoul,' Menz said.

'Just put them away,' Jella said, turning to them.

Menz and Yayle placed the muskets back, closed the bag. It snagged against the rope that held it and fell off, smacking the sand. They held each other's gaze. Lula stepped in between the rumel, put the bag back on the horse, tying it secure.

The sun was directly overhead, the horses were almost upon them.

Lula stepped alongside Jella. 'I'm frightened of these things,' she said.

'Don't be, beautiful. Don't be.' Jella held Lula's hand, squeezed it. She could feel a pulse. Lula smiled, wiping further sweat off of her brow. The horses were almost there. Menz and Yayle stood closer. The group huddled alongside their horses. Menz's fingers tapped his side.

The horses arrived under a dust cloud. A figure in the centre raised his hand and the horses came to halt, which threw up even more sand and the wind had risen, sending it in an upward spiral. The cloud thinned, revealing the ten riders.

Yayle held up his hand to protect his eyes from dust.

Jella looked at the horses and her eyes widened. They ought to have been dead, they couldn't possibly be alive. They were grey, gaunt, each appearing to be no more than a walking skeleton. Jella's vision followed every bone that seemed to stick out like a fossil; their skin looked as thought it had been sucked inwards. Each rider wore similar black cloaks, and hoods were drawn over their faces. The central rider pushed off, jumped to the floor, airing his cloak. Muscular and tall, he stood still whilst it raised its right hand. Jella saw that it was not a hand at all, more of a claw that was like a crustacean's. She let go of Lula's hand and raised her own, then walked forward. It advanced towards her with its cloak flapping in the breeze. Menz, Yayle and Lula did not move, but stared with their mouths open slightly.

'Welcome to the seas around the Aarc,' the rider said. Its voice was frail, a hiss. 'You have not drowned in these sands then?'

'No, not at all,' Jella said. She looked straight at the creature and her gaze travelled around the body as if to see what it was, but there were no clues under such loose clothing. There was another long silence.

'Why're you here?' he said. 'We don't normally expect any visitors.'

Jella remembered all the stories about the Qe Falta, the false people. She remembered that they were used to scare children who misbehaved. Rumour being the main source of lore, in the absence of information. There were stories that they were a leftover from before the rebellion against science. The Qe Falta had all sorts of combinations of animal parts grafted onto them, in the previous age. Legs exchanged with those of a dog or a cat or worse, and stitched on by science. Monsters were grafted, the stories said, and the people of the age couldn't stand them or the science that accompanied them. They were forced underground, hidden, secret. They did not want the world to hunt them down, to kill them.

An Age passed, the Qe Falta rose again. Some took to the cause to fight for their recognition, for them not to be shunned as ghouls. Some began to focus on the cities, mainly Escha, since it was industrial, anti-nature. More recently, lives were taken by 'equality bombs'. A wave of terrorism emerged just so that they could be treated as normal, to live in peace. Small battles were fought. There was much blood, a failed attempt to rid the world of them once again, but they stayed. They remained undetected.

Now they were in front of her: the *ghouls*, the terrorists.

Jella said, 'We need your help.'

The creature turned his head without moving its torso, taking every one of the other riders in view, before it gazed at her again from within the darkness of his hood. 'Help you? Why should we help you? What do you want that would possibly be in our interest to help *you*?'

Jella turned to her companions, looked back. 'I've contacted others of your kind race. We've a plan that you may be interested in. We think you'd want to support our cause.'

The Qe Falta said, 'Oh, really? Please, tell more.'

Jella wasn't sure if the creature was humouring her, but she walked back to the horses to fetch her plans and charts. 'I'll show you,' she said out loud. She couldn't look at anyone, so she stared out to the desert.

That evening, Jella had watched what thought was possibly the greatest sunset she had ever seen. She was in awe as she sat on the sand with Lula in her arms, staring at the sun as it enlarged. The sky turned purple, and she could see desert mammals rising in the cooler climate. It had become cold now, so they had made a fire using a small pile of wood that the Qe Falta had brought for them. They cooked spiced meats, which satisfied even Menz, who sat with his legs crossed alongside Yayle, playing dice. The four of them remained seated under a dark sky, which seemed somehow larger than they had ever seen, now that they were so far from civilization. The stars came out in their billions.

Lula had said that it was quiet, calm, pretty—which was exactly what Jella thought of the woman in her arms. She did not tell Lula this, as she thought it would be patronising. Sometimes, Jella felt that she was controlling to the point of misogyny—a strange concept for a woman. She wanted a pretty, young girl, one who would not answer her back, and one who would pretty much just sit there, being attractive. It helped if she could shoot well, too. It wasn't shallow, just that Jella simply couldn't connect with people on a personal level. The problems she'd experienced in life forced her to focus internally. She was not capable of sharing experiences with someone.

Jella had worked through dozens of 'relationships', none of which she had told Lula about. She remembered her teen years where she wanted to have sex with as many women as she could, just to prove she could. She felt an absurd level of control and power when she had her tail inside a girl, rumel or human, though she always preferred the latter. She wondered if she was mistaking sensation for emotion, but in the end she didn't really care. It wasn't important. But what she had with Lula was special. Jella could lie in her arms sometimes, and let the girl's soft nature take over, or she could get a kick out of pleasuring the woman endlessly. There was always something so satisfying about that. Lula wanted simply to be loved, and that was not difficult—in the sense of showing love, tenderness.

Jella combed Lula's black hair with her fingers.

Yayle glanced towards them, pulling a hood over to conceal his face. He stared at them holding each other.

The group stood up as they heard hooves strike the ground. The low bass sound rode the sand across some distance. Lula could see that there were only three riders this time, silhouetted even against the night. They approached the fire, came to a halt. The claw-man dismounted and landed on the floor within a beat of her heart. He walked towards one of the other bone horses, which did not carry a rider but instead several large bags. Sounds seemed to travel across the horizon. The rider extended his claw, took down the bags, two at a time then placed them on the sand before her partner. She was discomforted by his presence, and feared for Jella a little. Lula wanted no harm to come to her. Sometimes she resented the fact that Jella was involved in such a dangerous lifestyle—but that was who she was, and she respected that. She'd not ever leave her, and that meant putting up with these shady operations.

'We have the rock boring equipment and explosives that you asked for. The devices are simple, and you should be able to use them. They'll detonate in deep water, so you needn't worry.' He turned, pointed his thick claw in the direction of the other rider then turned his hooded head back.

'Allocen knows how to use them. He is what we've promised to you.'

'Allocen?' Jella asked.

'Yes. He doesn't talk, but he understands what you'll say. He can sign to his kin, but you won't understand that. We have briefed him of his role—it's only protection that he'll offer. He won't do anything he deems too risky.'

'What good's that?' Menz said. 'What use is he if he ain't taking a risk?'

The claw-man was silent. He looked back at Allocen who was sitting still on top of the horse, beneath a cloak, hidden in darkness. The claw-man nodded towards Allocen who removed his cloak, dropping it to the desert floor. The group gasped.

Allocen had the head of an insect. Two hemispheres containing hundreds of tiny hexagons were bolted onto his shoulders. There was no discernable face, except for his proboscis and antennae. The abdomen was dark and glossy, resembling the musculature of a human, but it reflected the fire, as the claw-man's skin did. Lula could see a pair of thin, translucent wings protruding from his back and she wondered vaguely if they would be able carry such creature. She was hypnotised as muscles slid underneath the skin of his thin body, bulging, pushing ropy veins. Attached to his waist were two brown sheathes.

This fly-man twisted his head around his body as if looking far, far out into the desert night. It was as if he could hear and see and smell something that they couldn't.

The Qe Falta with the claws spoke, his tone lighter. 'Now, could someone throw something? You, human girl, do you have a musket?'

Lula nodded. 'Me? I do, why?'

'Shoot him,' he said.

'Sorry?'

'Shoot him.' Lula looked to Jella, who nodded back.

It didn't seem right somehow, but Lula walked to her horse, opened one of her bags, pulled out a long, polished musket. She prepared the weapon, returned to the others. As she did she feared what would happen. 'You want me to fire, then?'

The man said, 'I want you to fire. At him.'

She took aim, a little uncertain as to why she was being asked to kill this creature. She raised her weapon at it. He had not moved in the few moments she was away. She placed her finger on the trigger. He still did not move. Lula waited, thinking this some joke. She could feel her pulse in her hand.

'Shoot him,' the claw-man said.

Everyone else stared. She pulled the trigger. There was a snapping sound, followed by a high-pitched crack and a spark spat out into the darkness. Lula's musket smoked.

The fly-man was sitting calmly on his horse and there was a scimitar in one of his hands. The other Qe Falta walked a few steps away, bent down, picked something up off of the sand and carried it to Menz. The rumel couldn't help stare at the claw as it was extended. His jaw lowered as the claw-man dropped the distorted piece of metal that Lula had fired, and stepped away to rejoin Allocen. Menz showed it to Lula, and it took a second before she realised that this Allocen had sliced the projectile from the sky. They looked up at each other without sharing a word. The sound of the fire crackled in the background. The temperature was falling further.

'And so you see, he has his uses,' the claw-man said. He mounted his horse and reached for the reins of the horse without a mount. He slid the bags on to the sand. Then, he looked across at Allocen and nodded. The others said nothing. They looked up from Menz's hand towards the Qe Falta.

'If your plan works you'll be considered to be heroes by many, especially us. You'll be welcome here. We share your ideals, and so give you our most efficient fighter and some explosives. Not enough to destroy the whole urban sprawl of Escha. There will never be enough for that. I know, from an age ago, and from my travels, that what you seek will very much be able to destroy Escha, providing everything you say is performed accurately. If not destroyed, then damaged greatly. We support this move. Other Qe Falta have spoken of your plans of the contact that you had made to our kind previously, and they remembered both you and the plan. But, to cover our costs –' He held out his claw.

'Yes, right.' Jella walked to her horse, opened a bag. She drew out a purse, walked to the Qe Falta. 'More than enough.'

He nodded, reached out his claw, which snapped shut on the purse then it disappeared into his cloak.

'Good luck,' he said. 'Your plan's inventive. If it means anything to you, apparently someone received a message from our west coast contact. Your guide, if you recall. He remembered that you would travel at the end of this season, this year, but not so soon. For your plan to succeed for sure, you must not delay. There'll be a boat waiting for you in a town called Gaya on the west coast, on pier nineteen. Approach it by water, from any village that lies to the south, just to be safe. Make sure no one follows you. That boat's well equipped.' He turned his horse, drew the other with him. The animals kicked up sand before they ran off into the night. The thunder of feet could be heard for another minute or so, but after that, there was only the sound of the fire.

One by one they found themselves staring at Allocen. The fly-man did not move from the top of his horse. It left Lula with a strange feeling of protection and unease. Menz fingered the metal shot still. Lula couldn't tell if Allocen was staring back at any of them. Slowly they sat by the fire, but they all kept an eye in the stranger's direction.

Jella said, 'No one can know of our plan, surely? Only the guide knew, I hope it was him. Still, we'll find out in a few weeks when we get to that boat.'

Lula saw the worry on her face, so held her hand, as if the touch of another would be calming.

'Do you think someone's found it before us?' Yayle said. 'Officials in Escha or Rhoam maybe.'

'No, it's well hidden,' Jella said. 'We found it as our knowledge and assistance was advanced. Our guide was the best. Don't kid yourselves that a government know anything about the natural world.'

Yayle nodded. 'Well, let's just hope it's still there.'

'It is,' Jella said. 'It will be, right. So don't worry.'

Ten

There is a single beam of sunlight on the table that highlights a book. The little rumel girl runs into the room, looks at the book with a strange sense of awe—and the recognition of potential mischief to be had. The room is full of such books, diagrams, animal specimens. It smells musky. The child picks up the book, sits on a chair, commences reading. She reads for minutes, then what seems like hours. Outside she can hear the sea, a pleasant and soothing sound that only contributes to the moment's timelessness.

Her father is standing in the doorway, his arms folded, a wide smile on his face. His eyes are fixed on her with all the love a father could muster. Then he walks over to her, picks her up, sits down, places her on his lap, and all this time she is still holding the book as if nothing else exists.

This particular title, she discovers, is on marine ecology. There are wide diagrams of oceans, cross sections of animals that make far more interesting shapes, she thinks, than the animals themselves. Pencil notes decorated the vacant spaces to the sides, much of it incomprehensible.

'Enjoying it, Jella?' he asks.

'Dad, surely if there isn't much fish of one sort in the sea, won't it die if people keep fishing it to eat?' She looks up from the book and kicks her legs.

'Yes, yes it will.' He face is the picture of satisfaction.

'Why don't they stop?'

Her father shrugs. 'It's not for us to say. We can believe something on this inside, on our own, but unless everyone pulls together, things don't change.' Then, 'You know, you're a very bright young girl.'

'I thought my skin was dark though. How can I be bright if I'm dark skinned?'

He laughs. 'I don't mean literally.'

'Okay. I like this. The words are too long in places though. And it's like they don't want normal people to understand some of it.'

'Lots of books are like that,' he says. 'So, you going to be my pupil, then?'

'You bet,' she says. She puts the book down, squirms into her father's neck, puts her arms as far around him as they will go.

And just as the girl lifts her head to see his face—

—Jella woke up thirsty. Lula's head was rubbing against her shoulder. She sat up in her tent, the canvass door open and flapping. It was dark outside. Allocen was by the fire, and somewhere she could hear the men snoring. She lay down again and stared at the roof of the tent. She started to think about the mind, how memories played tricks, how time affected them. She wondered if what had happened in her dreams was true, if dreams recalled true events at all. Jella hadn't thought about her father in a long time, and this dream brought back some awkward feelings with in her, poking at something that she didn't want to wake.

She lay awake for some time, listening to the rhythm of her lover's breath.

Eleven

Lula looked up, saw the walls of a town. She turned to Allocen, could see that he was looking at it too in a calm way that suggested he had known about it's presence for days. She felt the wind on her neck, pulled a hood up, then nudged Jella who was resting her head on her back. 'Jella, look.'

Jella regarded the scene. 'Judra. We're here then,' Jella whispered. Aloud, she said, 'Guys, we're at Judra now, we can stay here tonight and get some sleep and real food.'

'Judra,' Yayle said.

'Aye,' Menz said, nodding. 'I remember a time years ago, before when Lucher went communal, and we had the army. I spent time here. I wonder if they still fight lizards. It was a beautiful city then.'

'Really?' Yayle asked.

'Yep, oh yeah. Was good, what I remember. But those lizard fights, you should really see 'em.'

Yayle said, 'Do you think they still do them?'

'We'll find out, but Arrahd it was a great place to be a young man.'

Jella nudged her horse towards the wall, the others followed, Allocen at the back. As they approached, Jella noticed just how tall the walls were, estimating them at forty feet, with battlements crowning them. She heard a sharp explosion from the other side of the wall.

'What the fuck was that?' Lula asked. She looked at the others, who said nothing. They glanced towards Menz.

'I think, and that's only if I remember, that it could be the fiestre,' he said, with some excitement on his face. This usually dour man had become something of a more younger self.

'And what the fuck is a fiestre?' Jella said. She could see a smile on his face, his eyes were bright.

'Fiestre? It's a celebration, and that explosion—'

Menz was interrupted by a sharp snapping sound. He jerked his head to see a bright light spark at the top of the wall. They looked up as more appeared and they watched until their necks hurt.

'Fireworks,' Menz said. 'I don't think we'll get much sleep tonight.'

'Great,' Yayle said. 'That's just what we need when we finally find decent beds.'

It was hot as they stepped out into the main square, despite it still being morning. The sun was making its way over the high stone walls, illuminating the stone centre of Judra. All the rumel and Lula were wearing similar styled long-sleeved shirts and baggy, sand-coloured breeches. They were sweating, squinted as the sun came into view. Gateposts were being put up to close the streets and to hold people back from a track that spiralled around the square, through a shaded, narrow corridor that led up a hill.

Empty firework canisters were being cleared from the street. Small boys walked with baskets full of dark bottles. People were beginning to gather. Everyone in Judra was human. Lula had said casually to Jella, Menz and Yayle that people stared at them and was it because they were rumel. Some of the elderly who walked by travelled in an arc around them, tilting their heads up and down to examine their tails. Lula put her arm on Jella's waist, as if to say it's okay, it's normal, they're normal, they're with me.

'Right,' Jella said. Let's just stick together. There're too many people around. I don't want us loosing our explosives or create any attention. Just in case we're still being followed.'

'We haven't seen anyone for days,' Yayle said.

'Doesn't mean they're not out to get us,' Jella said, regarding the street scene. There was so much activity, so many markets. Carcasses hung in the sun, drenched in flies. Giant paper dolls were being erected. This was a town waiting to enjoy itself.

The only room they could find during the fiestre took them the best part of the day to find. It was in a small tavern overlooking the town square, illuminated constantly with flashes of light. Fireworks coughed smoke and the smell of gunpowder into their room.

Their lodgings were about twelve feet square, with three beds of equal size, a chair and a table by the window. Menz looked outside while the others placed all their belongings in one corner. Jella had instructed them to bring everything in, all the explosives and tools.

'Be careful with those,' Jella said as Yayle was heaping the bags.

'I'm being careful,' he said. 'Although I'm not exactly happy sleeping with these things in the room.'

'None of us are, but we can't leave them outside with the horses can we? Just be careful with them. They're expensive.'

'I am being careful.'

'Good.'

Yayle placed the last of the bags on top before he stretched out on one of the beds. Jella and Lula sat together, on the bed that was next to the wall furthest from the window. Allocen had removed his hood, and although everyone else's heads were facing away, their vision was never that far from him.

Jella scanned down his face, once again, looking at all those eyes, his skin, which reflected light from the activity down in the square. She glanced over to the old rumel, Menz. He was still looking out of the window and on to the streets, leaning against the wall with one hand.

Around his frame you could see humans spilling out of every corner, wearing garish masks. Fire-crackers coughed, fizzed. Bonfires begun to burn large human-like dolls. Chants echoed around the square. The music invited you to dance and sing in drunken, happy voices.

Jella watched the lights flicker on Menz, as he stood at the window. She thought she could see a smile on his face. 'Memories, Menz?'

'Aye. Like I said, I served a season or two this way, many years ago.'

'Not all doom and gloom then.'

'No, not all. Saw too much of that, as you know. No, its times like this that I like. I think they'll bring out the lizards tomorrow. You all talk of bravery and no fear.'

'What do you mean, "bravery and no fear"?' Lula said.

'Exactly what I say. Men fight horned lizards, which they get from way down south. They breed 'em especially for this. Men will come and stand in front of those great beasts, facing death, staring into those eyes.'

'That's a little cruel isn't it?' Lula said.

'Cruel? Some might say that. Youngens, mainly. Horned lizards live a long life, better than most people ever manage to. Pampered, some might say. They make 'em tough and strong that way, before they bring 'em to fight. Then if the lizard gets killed, they give the meat to the poor. But it's killed in such a way, that they never feel a thing. You'll often see priests standing on the side to sense their pain, and if so then the killer is never allowed to fight again. So what's cruel about feeding the poor and giving the lizards a long and healthy life? Otherwise they'd rot in the sand. It's something you youngens don't always see. It's something you have to understand. Most types of people don't much talk about death. Killing is either for food or sport. Here it's different. We should think about it a little more.'

'Still,' Lula said quietly, 'it's not right.' Jella held her hand. Yayle nodded to himself. A firework exploded outside the window, spitting green sparks against the glass.

Menz smiled, walked to the bed closest to the window, turned then fell on top with a groan.

'I tell you what though,' Yayle said. 'I wouldn't fancy fighting one of those things by the sounds of it. They must weigh a ton.'

'Aye, they do, and the rest. They'd skewer you in a heartbeat, pushing you against the wall and turn you into pulp. They're beasts, but by Arrahd, they are graceful. I've heard of an undefeated lizard who would let its breeder rub its horns and nose like a pet, then in the fight it butchered three fighters.' Menz turned on his side, faced the room.

'I think it'll be fun to see it,' Yayle said. 'What do you think, Allocen?'

Allocen moved his head a fraction then turned back to facing the floor.

Yayle turned to Jella. 'Doesn't say much, does he?'

'Not surprised. He's probably seeking some intelligent conversation, and he's not getting much of that is he?' Jella said. 'Anyway, we won't have time to do this. This isn't a holiday, we're on a mission. We don't know if anyone's onto us so I want to get going. Come on, I need some sleep.'

'You can try,' Menz said.

Jella watched the old man turn to face the window again, draw the sheets over his body. You could still hear the singing and dancing, could smell the bonfires and the food that was cooking somewhere. There was a prominent melody where you swore you could hear a female voice. You thought of her dancing, maybe twirling in a long dress. You guessed she would have blonde hair, brown skin, bright, promising eyes.

Menz couldn't sleep. After he splashed his face with water, and changed shirts, he prepared to step outside. He was careful not to draw too much attention to his movements. Before he went, he whispered to Yayle, 'I'm popping out for an hour or two.'

Yayle waved a hand, said, 'Yeah, knock yourself out.' He turned over.

As he stepped out of his tavern, a tide of people flowed by. Within seconds he was gone, holding a bottle of wine in the wave. People were singing, dancing, smiling, he couldn't help but let the years fall away, and soon he, too, was singing with them. A young woman took his arm, led him away, smiling, not saying a word, and Menz did not complain as he ran with her past an alleyway in which a man was beating a drum. Menz looked up the side of the stone building where you could see people dancing on balconies, waving strips of coloured materials as they swirled. The woman next to him cheered. She was short, dark, her cheeks glistening with perspiration despite the cool evening. She dragged Menz into the main square where fires burned dolls that were twenty feet high.

In another alleyway he could see men crowded round something. As they approached, Menz and the girl could see two large pterodettes, with their wings clipped back, and they were fighting, scratching in the dust. Menz saw gold exchange hands as one pterodette stumbled before the girl dragged him away again.

'What's your name?' she asked, pulling him to a café.

'Menz,' he said, looking through a steamed up window. Inside was filled with smoke but quieter than the streets and the girl shuffled through and brought Menz and herself a cup of red liquid.

'Drink it,' she said. She tipped her head back whilst other men looked on and cheered. Menz, too, poured the liquid down. It seemed to both chill and burn his throat pleasantly. She danced him out of the musky café and out into the street again, back into the central square and Menz took a long look at the girl's beautifully plain red dress. It aired as she turned and he watched the curls of her black hair bounce on her shoulders. All of this reminded him of something hidden inside that he'd never looked at for years. Some incident in his youth, something of those military days. That was when he had a life ahead of him, full of promise, not like now, where all he had was Jella's mission. There was no one to coax him out of soldiering, to help him integrate with the world as it was without a musket and a sword. He'd seen so much evil in the world that it had effected him. He was glad to have met Jella, a youth with ambition, determination, and with their past being destroyed in Lucher, she presented him with something to focus on. It meant he didn't have to sit in silence waiting to realise that he had nothing really to live for.

Her chest heaved as she breathed in. Menz took another swig of the wine from the bottle he still carried. He looked around at the lanterns that hung on walls, tilted his head up as fireworks exploded and you could smell the gunpowder in the cool air. As he looked down, another tide of people passed him, spinning him and another girl, paler this time, looked him up and down, saw his tail and hugged him, kissing him on the cheek and ran off with the people.

No sooner had they come then left, Menz found that he was on his own. He never had the chance to find the name of the woman. He sighed, smiled, turned to face the celebration. From where he was standing you could see old men holding pipes, women, playing flutes. Whilst they waved the instruments in the air, there was a six-legged dog, which he took to be Qe Falta, hopping in circles. It was watched by a tall, handsome man, an ugly woman on each arm and they both kissed him on the cheek, touched his chest, their hands under his shirt.

It was over so quickly. Hours had passed, leaving Menz back up in the room, looking down on the square, except this time he was at least smiling. He knew the town would not sleep and it seemed that the air was filled with a charge, not unlike the night before a battle. It was something he was familiar with, something comforting. An old soldier at home with his feelings.

Twelve

The day after the fiestre, they were on the road again. Jella wondered why Menz was quieter than usual, but at least he occasionally smiled, although it was an inward smile, the type you don't share. They had been travelling for weeks, and more uneventful days passed. That was the nature of the desert: so little happened. Landscapes were identical, blurred, became one. Eventually it chanced again. The further west you went, the more farmland there was. Grasses appeared on the horizon, with cattle, sheep. There were old buildings here, ancient, half buried. You would see enormous rusted structures that cut so deep into the sand it was as if they had fallen from the sky. Skeletal frames leant this way and that, fallen, filled in by sand. Occasionally, you would see a human skull behind grasses, a remnant of some tribal conflict. All of these things suggested a time and a place Jella would never know. She wondered how many cities, how many civilizations had risen and fallen across Has-jahn. Today there were only remains that threw up more questions with no way of knowing. She wondered just how significant the rebellion against science was to all of this? Being the daughter of a marine scientist, she would never fully understand the desire of a continent's population to collapse the existing infrastructure of technology. In this age, there seemed a need to look back to the past, because it was a time that was infinitely richer than the one exited. Governments could only dream of what the elder civilizations were capable of, which made the constant cycle of existence in Has-jahn all that more frustrating.

One evening, they approached the coast.

Jella spotted it first. 'There, look.'

'Ah, the sea, the sea,' Yayle said. 'You swim, Allocen?'

Allocen did not move or say a thing. In fact, for the whole journey he had not said a word, or shown emotion of any kind. Yayle seem to find it amusing, although Jella began to wonder why they needed him. They had not been threatened in any way since they'd left Lucher, but it was a comfort—albeit a bizarre one—to have this creature on their side. He would just sit on his horse regarding the horizon, his hands never having once moved towards his scimitars.

'Who's got the map?' Jella asked. Lula, who was behind Jella, leant over to open a bag, pulled out a chart. She passed it forwards it.

'Can you read maps then, your lot, eh?' Yayle asked.

Jella turned, looked at Yayle. She did not say anything. The younger rumel raised his eyebrows. '*Not* a post-feminist, then?' He wiped sweat on to his sleeve.

She returned to look at the map as the horses sauntered towards the sea. Over this scrubland, beyond a few cacti, you could see the horizontal bar that contrasted sky from the sea on the horizon. The sea was dark and still, the sky a hazy pink, although clouds were fast approaching in long, dark streaks. The land became more uneven, and there were dips that suggested small, pleasant fishing villages, ones which possessed no concerns of the world, of its grief. For a moment, she imagined herself there, sitting on a dock, drinking wine. Out on the sea, you could see small, white triangles drifting in the winds.

'The village we need should only be a mile or two southeast. We should get there by night fall. Then, all that's left is to find a boat and buy it, or steal it, taking it up the coast,' Jella said. 'Of course, we have more money this time round, so we should be able to get a really good one. Hopefully, the craft we get up the coast should be perfect, if it came via the Qe Falta.'

The sand was firm, darker, becoming more like soil. Allocen halted his skeletal horse suddenly. Jella looked back at him, and he seemed to be twisting his head, viewing the panorama. She suspected he was examining every aspect of the desert. Allocen's head tilted then straightened.

'Allocen, everything okay?' she asked.

He nudged his bony horse forward, pushed back his hood, to reveal, again, his fly-head. The Qe Falta appeared agitated as he joined them. She could see his proboscis, black as it formed a silhouette in front of the sun.

For the first time on the expedition, Jella noticed that his hands were fingering the handles of the scimitars beneath his cloak.

They moved on. A trail formed in the ground, between the spindles of vegetation. The trail was only two feet across, but they took it to be the road they needed. After weeks of journeying, Jella was relieved to finally be following it. It lead down a steep slope, which curved to the left, revealing a settlement that looked as if it were hugging the land to escape the sea. Dozens of wooden huts veered away from the water, in the shade of cliff. In the middle of the main cluster of huts was a small harbour, in which several brown and white boats were kept. Their sails were unfurled, waving in the breeze.

As they approached down the slope, you could hear ropes tapping the masts, the gentle slush of the sea. Menz and Yayle's horse was in front, leading the way down to the harbour. Jella could hear the two men bickering again.

'Notice anything strange, lad?' Menz said.

Yayle said, 'Only the smell, but I put that down to you several days ago.'

'Comedian, eh? No, I don't mean the smell, idiot. Take a look around.'

Jella turned her head taking in the wooden town in its entirety. She looked up to the dark cliffs, which cast a bold shadow, and out to sea, where she could see boats in the distance, but they were moving parallel to the coast.

'Nope,' Yayle said. 'Nothing at all. There's nothing here but huts and boats.'

'Exactly,' Menz said.

The wind stiffened a little, bringing the smell of organic matter from along the coast, the taste of salt. The ropes tapped repetitively on the masts of boats and those same vessels banged against the wooden dockings. You could hear a door shutting and opening, or a window. Clouds were massing in large patches.

Menz pulled the reins on the horse, and the animal stopped before it approached the first of the town's dust-streets.

Jella and Lula's horse walked up to his as he watched an empty carton blowing across the street. Dust pirouetted in tiny whirlwinds.

'What's up, Menz?'

'Nobody here,' he said.

'What do you mean?'

'Look—' he indicated the town, his palm facing the sky. 'There's no one here. Not a soul.'

'Hmm,' Jella said. 'I see what you mean.'

'What's wrong?' Lula said.

Allocen brought his horse in front. The creature turned his head in a full circle, hardly moving his shoulders. His two half-globe eyes were scanning. The rest of his body did not move. Jella's tail was twitching on one side of the horse.

The street was lined with little huts, fishing stores, trade shops. Some of the doors were left open. Inside there was only darkness.

The town, still under the shadow from the cliffs, was cast in further gloom by the nimbus clouds. On top of that, night was coming. Jella felt the wind, shuddered. They inched their horses forward towards a well that marked the centre of the town. It was made from brick, with a thatched roof. They rode nearer. Jella thought she could see something sticking out from behind the well and jumped off her horse.

Menz and Yayle followed. Lula felt inside a bag, drawing out her musket, prepared a shot. Jella looked back up as Lula clicked the weapon, but Lula did not make eye contact; she was turning her head from side to side every time she heard the wind blow a door shut.

Jella walked around the well. A boot was sticking out from behind. It was connected to a man wearing black breeches and a white shirt. He was dead, his shirt stained red at the collar. What the hell could have done this? The town was eerie enough without the corpse in the centre of it.

'Stand back,' Menz said. He walked to the body. The man's eyes were wide open, staring up. His face was blue, withered, making the corpse look older than it ought to have been. Menz picked out a knife from his pocket and flicked it open, using the small blade to peel back the collar.

'What can you see, Menz?' Jella said.

'Puncture marks. He's been bitten by the looks of it. Although, there's something that ain't right. There's no tearing or scratching to indicate an animal attack.'

'What do you suppose did it?' Yayle asked.

'Some ghoul, I guess. I ain't seen anything like this,' Menz said, looking up at Allocen.

No one said anything. Jella kept glancing all around, paranoid at every creak of the boat or of a door, at every time the water splashed into the docks.

Menz stood up. 'We should find somewhere to sleep for the night.'

Yayle said, 'Damn right. I don't fancy sleeping around here, old thing. Not in the slightest.'

'I agree,' Lula said. 'It's too creepy.'

Jella nodded. She turned to see Allocen off of his horse. The Qe Falta was pacing in a strange, lurching circle around them. His antennae gleamed as the moon surfaced from above the cliff top. The wind picked up, but did not move any of the protrusions from Allocen's head. Jella marvelled at this man. Or fly, she couldn't be sure which was the dominant species in his body. With his cloak flapping now, she could see that his hands were clutching the handles of his blades. Every time she noticed a door shut, she could see that Allocen's head was facing it. She thought at first that she must have blinked to have missed his head turning so quickly, but she soon learned that it was a remarkable creature.

Lula fingered her musket, glancing around her. 'We should just take a boat and go now.'

A light rain began to fall.

'Aye, the lass is right,' Menz said.

'Okay,' Jella said. 'Let's see if there is anything left at the harbour side and take the first one we come to. We only need to travel a few hours up the coast anyway.'

They walked to their horses as the spots of rain became globules that slapped the ground spitting up small clumps of mud.

As they were about to jump on their horses, a shrill cry pierced the sky.

'What the fuck was that?' Yayle asked.

'I've no idea,' Jella said. Their eyes darted around between the columns of rain. It was pitch black. Allocen had drawn his scimitars and stood with his legs apart, facing up the street that linked the centre with the harbour side. They took out muskets from their bags and loaded, waiting to discover the cause of the scream.

'Just bring one horse with us now,' Jella said. 'Put all our belongings on it and let's just get to a boat as quick as possible.'

They led the horse between the wooden buildings, towards the harbour. The wind rattled; the rain drenched their hair and clothes. Allocen walked in front, his cloak waving around his body. He was spinning his scimitars, weighing up the blades as if they were an extension of his arm. Menz walked at the rear with Yayle, glancing from side to side, their muskets held ready.

Another high-pitched scream.

Wooden shutters on the buildings banged closed before opening again in the wind. Jella looked at one building to her left. She saw that the window had been smashed. The rain was relentless, but through the columns of water she could see there was definitely something inside.

'Lula, look. In there, I saw something. Two eyes, just... glowing.'

Lula stood next to her, looked. She couldn't deny that there was a pair of eyes inside. Allocen had already turned.

'Shoot at it,' Jella said.

Lula lifted up her musket and stared down the barrel of the weapon. She followed the tip, lining it up with the break in the widow. Pulled the trigger. A crack sounded, a scream erupted from the building. The eyes could no longer be seen. Lula lowered her weapon and reloaded.

A cacophony of screams filled the air.

Jella looked up as streams of water vibrated in the air, almost fizzing as if every drop had exploded. The group huddled around the horse, steering it towards the harbour. Allocen was walking faster, pacing, waiting. His head was nodding all the time in some strange primitive ritual. Jella couldn't discern where the screams were coming from, and she screwed her face with pain as the volume of them increased.

Then all sound stopped.

'Something's not right,' Menz said.

'Well done,' Yayle said. Despite the strong wind, the doors were no longer opening and closing.

'Look!' shouted Lula. 'The doorways. Look at the doorways.'

'What the fuck is this?' Jella said.

Figures were simply standing there, dozens of them, holding open the doors, becoming drenched in the rain.

'Look at their faces,' Jella said.

They walked out into the street, their eyes luminescent. There must have been at least twenty, clothes were ragged, torn. They groaned audibly as they came nearer. Their mouths were open, revealing canines.

'Vampir!' Menz shouted. 'I'd say now was a good time to shoot the fuckers.'

But, before they could raise their guns, a blur shot past them, circling them and all that they could see was a streak of metal in the air through the rain, and the displacement of water as Allocen sped through. A head fell at Menz's feet, blood spat up on his breeches. He stumbled back in disgust as the vampir's eyes faced him, cold, lifeless. The canine teeth must have been two inches long.

Again the blur raced by, blood arced through the air. Rain vibrated. They began to fire their muskets where they could whilst edging the horse forward to the end of the street. Allocen carved the vampir, hacking and slicing at a speed that dazzled, amazed. So impressive was his display that Jella couldn't tell what where the rain ended and the blood began. Vampir still lurched at them, clawing, but all that came close was a severed arm falling at their feet.

Allocen had formed a physical barrier. When he did pause, his held scimitars out wide, dripping with blood. He possessed a sheen that was neither sweat nor rain. His head flicked from left to right as the ragged figures clambered at them further, groaning. The vampir screamed as they fell, in ones, twos. The Qe Falta hacked and slashed, kicking, spinning, flexing into impossible forms and at improbable speeds whilst body parts were scattered and the floor became with blood. Lula aimed and picked at one or two of the vampir, but Allocen frequently beat her to it, leaving strips of the ghouls at her feet.

He appeared in a static image on all sides.

Jella thought that it was as if, in Allocen's eyes, the vampir moved at a painfully slow pace, walking like elderly with their hands out, ready to be severed. He hacked though bone, skin, slashed his blade through the vampirs' throats, picked lines in their veins for his own amusement.

Eventually, Allocen slowed. They could see him slicing the remaining vampir. A young female was spinning away, knowing she was defeated. The Qe Falta sliced a scimitar down her spine with the poise of an artist flicking paint at his easel. The vampir girl shrieked, she scratched the floor, then her eyes sparked out. Allocen stabbed both blades either side of her spine, brought them together, then twisted, generating a crack as he broke her back.

The last vampir stood a foot shorter than Allocen. He held his scimitars out either side from the creature's head. The vampir took one step forward, and Jella could see the glowing eyes become wide and bright as Allocen closed both blades around, through the neck, crossed his arms, and the body fell in fluxes, leaving the head in mid-scream to balance on his two blades. Blood spat on Allocen, who stood there letting the liquid drip down his face, indifferent. The vampir's eyes faded to black. Allocen let the head fall.

Soon all you could hear was the rain hitting the floor and the remains of bodies. The Qe Falta creature stood still, his chest heaving and falling. He turned to face the group.

Jella could just see bodies in the rain. Nothing moved amongst them. The wind echoed around the bay. Out on the sea, he foam on the top of the surf was intense. The rain fizzed on the ground by her feet.

'I think he's on our side, Menz,' Yayle said. 'No need to be so anxious about that anymore.'

Menz regarded Allocen, a look of wonder on his face. 'How does he move so fast?'

Yayle shrugged. 'Have you ever tried to swat a fly?'

'Look,' Jella said. 'Let's just get out of here and to a boat, before any more of those things get here.'

The wind strummed the masts and ropes and chains, tilting the vessel as it lurched out into the bay, and arced towards the north, the shore on their right. Menz stood at the wheel, and steered the boat through the ripples of foam that savaged the boat on all sides.

'Keep her steady man,' Yayle bellowed though the rain. 'I'm trying to take a piss off the side.'

'Arch your back,' Menz said, squinting through the rain.

While the others were above deck, Lula and Jella were below, their clothes hanging to dry, and they were standing, warming in candlelight, semi-naked. The rumel dabbed the soft, human skin with rags that she had found and all the time they talked of places that they had been to as a couple, reminding themselves of warm cafés, pleasant walks, sunsets—anything to take their minds off what they had been witness to moments earlier.

Lula told Jella that they would have dinner together one night, and that they would not talk of the mission. Jella held Lula close for several minutes, and for only a few of them could she feel the human shivering.

Allocen stood at the front of the boat, staring offshore. He wiped his scimitars clean with oil, let the rain wash his torso. Drops of water turned pink as they hit the deck. He appeared not to be concerned with this. He held himself upright, pushing out his torso to be cleansed by the elements.

Behind, Menz stared on as a sheet of lightening illuminated the distance, framing the creature's unnatural silhouette. *All this effort*, Menz thought, *not to be followed*

The boat weaved the surf, headed north along the coast.

Santiago Speaking

Voyage Diaries, Volume 8, The Trip to Arya. Day 2.

The first time that I heard about Arya, I was earning coppers on schooners during my holidays. That was when coppers meant something. My job was, amongst others, to maintain the rope, & I walked, every evening, to a fishing supplies store for various materials. There, amidst the bric-a-brac & the basket traps, fisherman came to talk. One man was talking to another about his expeditions to the far seas, past the Sea of Wands, & further southwest, to a chain of islands. There were two boats that went out & only his returned. The other vessel disappeared after some precarious deep-lagoon fishing, using explosives. No one ever heard of it, or even why the devil sank.

It will take some weeks' travelling to get there, so we have been quick to leave. I've once seen some islands just to the north of Arya, but they were a little far away from it, so I have never happened across the place. That was a few years back. When they told me what they found, I didn't believe them at first, but I went to see it for myself.

One must listen to the sea. That hypnotic noise that slaps the hull as the ship slices through each wave. The amount of nature below us is amazing. Only on these trips can I understand life. & I look forward to new lands—unseen places, to be the first!—because for me, seeing other things, the way other people live—*that* is life.

To stay in one place is to die.

It has been three days since we left, & three days since we left all our troubles behind. Well, almost. We still have those two bastards with us. Government agents. The mayor said that he didn't trust me. I can believe that. So, I must put up with them.

Arya is three months' travel southwest, providing we stand on with the wind astern. I don't know much more about the locale, except that legally it's still property of the Escha, & moreover, the mayor's responsibility. There has been some political wrangling over the island in the past, too long ago to make much of a difference. The mayor is keen to establish that there is no threat to Escha & her properties. However, I assume he wants to know what is there exactly, & this provides him with a most excellent opportunity to get me out of the city for a while.

My Freelance Exploratory crew are called for, & it's about time, too. I can't say that funds weren't running low. I nearly had to sell my third boat if it wasn't required for a private expedition—something which was fine by me, at least.

Hitherto, only three or four vessels are known to have returned from Arya. A small community was set up after a storm wrecked one ship, leaving it unable to leave, so history has us believe. But the island is not too small, according to the charts, &, I suspect there has been a fair amount of inbreeding with the natives. I don't know what we'll find there, with regards to its populace, but I do know they are being killed, & we're going to find out why.

A message from one Doctor Forb Macmillan reached us. The community of a species thought to be extinct, the ichthyocentaur, is alive—alive!—but threatened. An exciting day for science, but something from the sea claims them. Fifty have been taken this year, according to the note. There are humans on the island, too, & they are frightened (quite right). They are technically Escha's folk—some legal loophole—so, we must investigate. I am rather interested in the other things mentioned in that letter. Doctor Macmillan suggests that the ichthyocentaur possess botanical knowledge, & that the island harbours great cures that may be of benefit to mankind. This is also something that the mayor is interested in, for Escha is famous around Has-jahn for her drug culture. The rest of the continent believes her to be rather a rum place, & I can't say I disagree. I, myself have been an abstainer of the harder stuff, but there are others who cannot resist temptation. Perhaps the island holds the cure for damaging bodies in such a way. But, for now, we have left those problems aft. In all honesty, those deaths & that message provide a great excuse for us to map & sketch new territories, which can always fetch a shilling or two in the right circles. Information is, as they say, power.

We're one less in number. Tchad is on his honeymoon, we have decided to leave him to his new marriage.

We number as follows:

Myself, Manolin (whom I've a few concerns over. He is depressed), Becq, my daughter (whom has been suffering from terrible dreams of late—she keeps having nightmares about drowning. Not something to think of when at sea. She has brought her doll making kit with her—dolls, I despair!), Jefry, Yana (whom I can certainly say has blossomed since the last trip, although I've not succumbed to her womanly charms), & Arth.

Yana has spent the last couple of nights chatting to Manny, trying to cheer him up. I'm not sure if she has done any good. Maybe she can open him up a little—woman's touch. I'm not sure if it's what the lad really needs. What he wants, me thinks, is to plunge into his work like a real man. He needs to grow up & stop worrying about his wife (ex) & start thinking of these new shores. New horizons!

Oh yes, a matter of the addition of a Mr Calyban & a Mr Soul, as I noted. The two government agents are casting a critical eye over all that we say & do. They don't contribute at all. They keep themselves to themselves, when we're not up to anything interesting. I think they're here to follow up a story that one of the Eschan navy vessels went disappearing in the area years ago—it's a bit of secret, rumour perhaps, but more than a few ships have gone down in these sees. But, those agent fellows: I don't like them.

I can't help but think that because of their presence everyone is paranoid. Arth kept trying to persuade me that he saw me sending a pterodette off of the ship. He insisted on the fact, but became angry when I told him that it was the shadow of my hat on my arm. He stormed off, cursing those agents for making him suspicious. Much to my relief, of course, but that's a feeling that won't be expressed in these journals. That's what happens when you bring people like that on board. Interested only in gain, & on expeditions like this, one must be communal. In life, in fact, one must be. That's why I dabbled in politics.

One last thing: the wine supply that I've brought—all cracking vintages, of course—is excellent. There are some delightful specimens. My only concern is how long they will last. I've calculated I should still be drinking by arrival, & for a day or two more.

After that, I dread to think.

Voyage Diaries, Volume 8, The Trip to Arya. Day 20.

We were lucky to miss a storm last night—we're still alive! I could see it on the horizon, just before sunset. The anvil of the cloud, which must have reached hundreds of miles up, headed inland adjacent to our boat, *DeBrelt One*. The sky was a dark indeed, but we missed it. *DeBrelt One* is a typical schooner, just like one used for fishing. We have no need for luxuries. It's made from a rusting metal, painted grey. We have about four months' supply of fuel, but I've had large sails installed in order to carry us farther.

There were storms on the boat, too.

Jefry cannot seem to do anything but annoy Yana. I think, & I've seen this many times before, that she yearns for other lovers now. Not that there is anything wrong with Jefry, no. He is a good fellow, but, perhaps a little *too* nice. One can see when things are running aground. That's the problem with a rumel & a human. The differences are subtle, but as with differences in ethnic backgrounds, & I do only mean in one or two instances, it can be exciting at first—and why not?—something exotic that adds a fraction of spice to life, but when that goes one can only imagine the differences when comparing species. It soon evolves that that same fraction of spice becomes a friction. Love & hate are two sides of the same coin, after all.

No matter how many tens of thousands of years that we've been co-evolving, which is in itself an interesting aside (I have no time here), there are some things that just cannot click. Basic feelings just aren't there, no sir. Not being able to have any fertile children may be another issue. There are other issues, too. I've been at a theatre or show with Jefry & some others, & Jefry will always have the spare seat next to him. Old ladies even, they'd rather stand for a while than take that spare seat. Some of that sort still goes on & that can highlight an incompatibility between the species, even when she herself may have forgotten any differences. I can see the pain on her face clearer than these weather patterns, although in both cases, one has to know what to look for.

When women—and men like myself, I hasten (very much so) to add—reach a certain age, they get to think about what they have done in life—things to pass on, & all that. She's a beautiful lady, too, & Jefry has let himself slip in recent years. Men do not seem to make that extra effort with age, & it's no surprise when a woman jumps ship, if you ask me. They've been together for years, & maybe it's the plague of the human mind—that capability for illogical & self-destructive thought—which makes her want to go. But look at it from her view: she exercises regularly & eats well, & he drinks each night, getting quite a paunch on him I might say. He can see that she still makes that effort, but what greater sign of complacency is there than that? His rumel hide has expanded, & he has become vulgar. I know people love each other despite that, but good manners & good physique buy a lot. If no other woman wants him, why should she?

I've decided I'm not going to sleep with her though—even if she offers. I'm not the sort to do that to friends. I can see she wants me though, or at least, thinks it. But, if it isn't me, it will be someone else.

Manolin is still an enigma. I hear him crying some nights, through the cabin door. He has left her, I can see that, although it's not difficult to see. He has brought a bottle of whiskey with him & when he wakes up I can't tell what has made his eyes red. I think Becq is rather worried about him, although she has her sleeping problems. Last night she told me that she dreamt she nearly drowned again. The omens are not good. Manolin tends to ignore her, but I've told her not to take it personally, he's depressed, & depression is merely anger without enthusiasm. Yana has had a stab at mothering. Not entirely sure if that has had any effect whatsoever.

I despair.

Had a thought: they say that women are more irrational than men; but to be irrational is a major factor in separating humans & rumel from nature—we are irrational species after all—so does this mean that women are more human than men? Are we males more animal-like? That would explain a few things anyway. Just a thought.

What a sorry-looking bunch I've employed. Not to mention those two government agents. They have not joined us for supper, ever, & they spend most of their time in their cabin. If I didn't know better, I'd say they batted for the other team, but I fancy not.

I wonder how Tchad is getting on. Ah, to be married! I loved weddings. My own weren't much to talk about, but they lose their effect when you have too many. Well, we'll crack on without the fellow. I'm sure we'll do just fine. He wasn't one for sailing, anyway. Besides, he liked Escha too much.
    That, I struggle to understand.

I think it best if I read my zoology journals & see if there is anything that could explain what has been happening on Arya. I've recently discovered, from a very old article, that the island was discovered & claimed for Escha over two hundred years ago. There is a reef system in the local waters & fascinating palm forests. There was a small colony of humans, in addition to what were referenced as simply 'strange folk' who utilised plants in a previously unseen way. They must by the ichthyocentaur. Ethnobotany is Manolin's speciality, so that ought to take his mind off matters. Pigs were introduced once, & a boat set sail with rabbits as little as ten years ago, but never returned. I suspect both provide the staple diet, running wild around the island & its palm forest.
    Who this Doctor Macmillan is, however, remains a mystery. We will find out.

I drank a vintage red, from Rhoam, last night. It was delightful, full bodied, a great colour & packed a powerful punch. It rather reminded me of my second wife.
    And I shall not make that mistake again.

Voyage Diaries, Volume 8, The Trip to Arya. Day 55.

More thoughts, ramblings.
    One or two things I need to think over, for future reference. I'm just getting this straight, in my own mind, before setting to work. DeBrelt's is a cutting-edge operation. We do not need sophisticated equipment, but we do require sophisticated minds. We observe nature, her biological, chemical, geological, mathematical aspects as one whole science. We do not reduce, but adhere to the philosophy of 'systems', that is, nature is a

system & not a 'thing' to be broken down. She is a process, an interdependent mechanism. She changes through time. She is a web. The human & rumel species are not outside of her power. We study not each fraction of science on Arya, but conduct a wide, holistic survey, to understand nature accurately. This was Manolin's suggestion, initially, & I think it's a good one, although I must confess that the old ways do set in often. Only then, will we find clues as to whatever affects the ichthyocentaur &, more importantly, how it fits in to the bigger picture.

Always look at the bigger picture.

According to the charts we should be near the volcanic island chain, of which Arya is the largest. I hazard a guess at two days' sailing. The weather has been good; the health of all on board has been fine. Well, physical health that is.

Manolin, I think, has stopped crying himself to sleep. He talked things over with me two nights ago. As I suspected, his wife had an affair & he caught her—starkers & legs akimbo—with another fellow, a tall chap apparently (it makes a difference to a man, let me tell you). Manolin left immediately, distraught.

I, myself, love women too much to hate them. You could tell she was the sort: self aware & loved attention from all. Manolin was perhaps too weak a character for her. But alas he was bewitched by her looks. We've all been there. We've bled tears to satisfy their whims.

But, *by Arrahd*, we'd do it again in a heartbeat.

I think Manolin needs a girl with a good heart, who won't try to compete with him, & who will earn trust over time. Someone not so concerned with glamour, but what the stars mean at night. He would treat her well, I know it. He wants a girl to provide for, who won't become bored with his attention. He would like a girl who, after reading a good book, looks at their reflection in a mirror & frowns rather than brushes their hair. There used to be a saying that the nicer a woman is to a man, then the worse he treats her. I suspect it works just as well both ways, these days.

I slipped Manolin a touch of cocaine last night. Poor lad had never tried the stuff before. I thought he could do with a booster, even if it was only for an hour or so. I entered his cabin around about sunset. I found a book of Arrahd (what it was doing on my ship, I'll never know) & decided the best use for it was to use its leather cover to spread it out on. So, I lined it up for him & he was up for it. He's an experimenter, that one. I like that quality in a man. I even let him use my glass straw through which to sniff it. For his first time, he did pretty well. Straight in, no fuss. Within twenty minutes he could no longer feel the roof of his mouth, nor his front teeth, which meant it kicked in all right. However, did his spirits rise? Did he stand up with new-found happiness? Did he hell. He's so far in the doldrums that not even a little magic powder has any effect. I, myself, started babbling like a goose—as is usual—& think I managed to bore the lad to sleep. That lad's problem is that he can never decide things, never be a man. I reckon that's why she went. She went because he never directed her (possibly even in the bedroom—some of them like those shenanigans). He'd much rather escape then do things. When I knew him to be at university, I'd catch him the morning after some blind-drunk bender the evening before a deadline. Always avoiding decision, responsibility. Mind you, he'd always pass with distinction.

The two agents that Mayor Gio sent have done nothing but question me, & quite frankly, I'm becoming bored of it. They do not trust me one iota. They come storming into my cabin wanting to know all sorts about the island, any reports of sunken ships in the area, what the killings on the island could be. I tire of it. I had hoped for a great, intellectual debate, but one can be sure of one thing: you won't get it from government bodies. The thing is, I get the impression that there is something they know, & when I start to ask questions they have to leave. They're hinting at something, which I think lies not on the island, but, & this is the strange thing, something in the water. It's a good thing we have the submersible craft with us. It's old, yes, but there is no better craft for penetrating deep places. So to speak. Note to self: less innuendo on one's own. It is ineffective.

Yana was looking pleasant yesterday. She strutted about on deck, wearing a thin skirt, & I could see the shape of her legs through it as the sun was setting. Her hair is getting longer—I've always been a fan of long hair on a woman—and she's started dying it blacker. As the sun gets more intense, much more so than Escha, she is browning like a good roast chicken.

She's been sick a few times. Not sure she's made for the sea.

Her man, Jefry, has been getting drunk every night, although I must track his source for when the wine goes. She must be frustrated (perhaps sexually? One can only hope). Especially if Jefry's breath reeks of alcohol.

That reminds me. A crisis has besieged us: there are only three bottles of wine left, all of them cheap. I shall drink them alone, perhaps they will taste better that way.

Thirteen

A palm tree moved in the wind. The doctor looked up through its jagged leaves to see the sun, the light dappling his bald head. The trunk leaned inland by just a fraction of a degree. A section of scab-like bark fell naturally, tapped the sand. He picked it up, marvelled at its rough texture. Then he brought it near his mouth, took a bite, chewed. It tasted bitter.

Doctor Macmillan stepped out from the edge of the palm forest and onto the beach, warming in the morning sun. He was wearing a pair of brown, shortened breeches. Above his head a cluster of colourful birds circled the air then darted into the dense foliage behind. He smiled, waded out to the white sand, towards the sea. There, a woman was emerging.

He watched her walk out of the water. She took long, graceful strides as she pushed her browned body from the sea. Her damp black hair covered her breasts. The sun reflected off of her skin, but it wasn't the light that dazzled him.

He walked over to her, listening to the repetitions of the surf.

Her body was toned from years of swimming and he couldn't wait to touch her—never could. He embraced her, picked her up from the shallowest of waves, carried her up on to dry sand, where he lay her down. Kissed her. She opened her eyes, but the sky was obviously so vivid that she shut them again, holding him. She allowed him to run his hands over her prominent hips. In this paradise, she was what he cared for most.

After a short while, he lay to one side to take in the panorama. She stood up to brush the sand off of her damp body. Only a thin line separated the horizon from the sky, the water being a slightly darker blue. A shallow bank of sand meandered out for a hundred yards or so, carrying with it light turquoise waters, up to a point, where it stopped and the deeper sea began.

Further into the distance you could see the edges of one side of the reef. Plants were perched on top of the coral, bathing in the sun, as if some exclusive miniature islands. The surf lapped against them, foaming, then towards the island of Arya, where the foam oozed, with some pitch, onto the warm sand.

Tides surged through the coral heads, sparked the water with oxygen. Doctor Forb Macmillan wondered just how many eyes were staring back at him, peering out from under shells, from around gelatinous spines, in places where flat ribbons of tissue twisted, danced around in current induced spirals.

He stared out to sea, ran his hand over his scalp. He rubbed it, unconsciously, smelling the organic matter that had been washed up on the shore in the night: weeds and detritus that the sea had coughed up. His bright eyes focussed on a wave pattern further offshore. Instinctively, he knew where channels flowed. He knew of wind swells, of reef breaks. He turned to the woman. 'Myranda, I'm going to fetch my board. I'll be back in a minute.'

'Okay,' she said.

The doctor ran to the palm forest unbuttoning his shirt, and moments later he returned with a six-foot long shortboard tucked under his arm. A necklace of tiny shells rode up and down on his chest as he ran. Myranda was wondering along the beach, picking up small detritus, shells, driftwood, then arranging them idly in the sand. As the doctor passed she looked up, slung her long, black hair over one shoulder. They smiled at each other, before he trotted into the sea.

He strode in with his knees reaching up high then threw the board down flat and jumped on top, centring his weight, feet hanging off of one end. He paddled out, careful to keep the nose of his board a couple of inches above the water. For some time swam further, where he knew the greater waves travelled east across the face of the island and its reefs. The salt in the water stung his eyes, but it invigorated him. The sea was pleasantly warm. He could see the edge of the coral reef below him, columns of fish, and in this blue he noticed the shadows of rays drifting coolly.

The winds became stronger, his body felt the force of the water push his board up then allowed it to fall. He kept his mouth closed so as not to consume too much water and as another wave brought him up a couple of feet, he noticed, coming forth from the horizon, a large, grey boat.

His eyes widened with exasperated hope, but he concentrated on the waves, feeling a bolt of energy race through him. He paddled further still, the beach far behind. When a wave became high, he rode into it, diving like a duck under the oncoming water then out the other side. He placed each hand on the rail of the board, pushed himself up, felt his triceps quiver as he hauled his body out of the water then sat on the edge of the board, and allowed it to slide beneath him in a movement as fluid as the ocean.

He waited, rising then falling with each wave.

The boat travelled half a mile or so past him, was headed towards the eastern beaches of the island, before it came to a stop. A moment later, smaller, wooden boat made its way towards the shores.

He waited, watching the water, observing the swells. He was looking for a reefbreak. He felt the wind chill the water on his back.

Eventually, the wave came.

He used both feet and arms to manoeuvre the board so that it faced the beach. Then, holding the rails, he pushed his body up again. He slid the board beneath, freely, and placed his chest flat against the board.

The doctor committed himself, angled the board to the tide, began to paddle fast and caught a large wave, felt the wind, pushed himself up, positioning his feet at the rear of the board. The muscles in his legs tightened. He held his arms out for balance.

At some speed he surfed towards the beach, cut along the water, speeding still, and could feel the board vibrate as angrily a wounded shark, and he saw the island move towards him. The beach slid along his view, then he twisted the board into the wave, but turned the nose too far, caught the lip of the wave, and in a heartbeat, he plunged into the warm, salt currents.

He held his breath, clutched his board, and felt bubbles of air race over his body and he could see the light smear with water then disappear, before it revealed itself to him once again. The waters calmed. The tiny sparks of sunlight crammed into his eyes.

Then he surfaced.

He lay face down on the board, gasped for air, spluttered out water. Wipeout.

He wiped his eyes and he could see the palm forest close up, as he was at the far end of the east beach. Paddling, he rode the currents round to where he had set off from. The doctor smiled at the sensation of the warm waters on his arms. He glanced to the forest, liked to test himself on how many of the species of palm and fig trees he could identify. He could smell the perfumes of the pittosporum species lingering from the night.

Up along the beach, he could see an unknown figure standing next to Myranda. The stranger stared out towards him, shading his eyes with his hand, whilst Myranda was moving backwards. The doctor noted that the figure wore a top hat, was dressed unusually smartly. *Could this person have found the message? Could they come to offer help to us?*

He paddled towards the figures and into shallow tides, dismounted, landed knee-high in the water, hauled the board under one arm, and waded onshore. He thrust the board upright into the sand, headed to the stranger, his feet sliding back on the fragile sand.

* * *

Santiago turned to address him and, taking off his hat, extended one arm out to shake hands.

'Doctor Macmillan, I presume,' he said, and clasped the doctor's hand.

'Indeed,' Forb said. And whom do I have the pleasure of addressing?'

'Santiago DeBrelt, of DeBrelt's Freelance Exploratory Crew. And I believe, sir, that you left us a message.' He drew out the note that was sent, and held it up. It rippled in the wind.

The doctor nodded. 'Yeah. Well fancy that.' He stared at Santiago in a way that suggested he didn't expect it to have worked, that it was a final hope in an attempt to save the species.

'Fine island, you have yourself here,' Santiago said, turning to take in the dark, palm forest. He turned to face the green bush.

'She's not mine, or anyone's to own,' the doctor said.

Santiago turned to face him, nodded, took a good look at the doctor's face. Noting the fine lines around his eyes, he guessed him to be about forty, perhaps fifty years old, but young looking for it. His body was toned, browned, but not to the extent of a native. Two bright green eyes shone eagerly from an angular face. Santiago thought he was spoiled by a rather square jaw, then glanced at his own, expanding waistline. He looked back at the forest. 'Why, you've got figs and palms, orchids and acacia, heavenly birds and a… Oh my, I say, is that volcano an active beast?'

'No, it isn't,' the doctor said. He tilted his head to follow the newcomers gaze.

Above the thin strips of palm trees, was the blue-brown cone of a volcano, which from the boat he assumed to be a small mountain. Santiago followed the line of the volcano, which dominated the landscape. The sides of the rim had broken. Down the slopes, its edges were jagged, being claimed by the forests. Hugging the rim were two cumulus clouds. The shadow of the volcano cast one half of the forest in darkness. Santiago's gaze fell to the forest close up, and saw the blackness that the canopy sealed in. Vines hung down as thick as arms. Dense, exotic vegetation spiralled into any available gap, hogging what light there was. Santiago frowned as a hare dashed out onto the beach, generating a little yellow puff as it slid to a halt on the sand. Its head shifted from left to right.

'Your hares, I presume? They're not native I take it?' He placed his hat upon his head.

'That's perceptive of you,' the doctor said. When I came here for my second, and final time, I brought them, knowing they would flourish and feed the natives well enough.'

'No predators?'

'None.'

'There too many of them now?'

'We keep them in check where we can. Somehow the forest does its part.'

Santiago nodded, turning to assess the island's aspect toward the sea. Behind him, Arth and Jefry, the two black-skinned rumel approached.

'Ah, rumel,' the doctor exclaimed. 'I haven't seen them since I was on mainland Has-jahn nearly ten years ago.' He looked at the two foreigners with keen eyes, following the sweep of their tails as if he suppressed the urge to touch their black skins, to see if they were real.

'Allow me to introduce Arth and Jefry,' Santiago said. He stepped back with his arms wide. He took a sideways glance towards the woman who stood almost naked, with a small piece of cloth around her waist, her hands clasped together, waiting politely.

Arth and Jefry shook hands with the doctor.

'How do you do?'

'A pleasure to meet you. I'm Doctor Forb Macmillan. It's a relief to have visitors. So, you're here to solve our problems?'

'Well, hopefully,' Santiago said with a gentle chuckle. 'And to survey the place for our records. You have ichthyocentaur, so it seems.'

'We do indeed. They're some way up, through the forest.' Santiago felt excitement at a new species, another that was similar in race to the human and rumel.

'Well, Arrahd bless us,' Arth said.

'Arrahd,' the doctor said with a half smile, his eyes turning to the sky. 'Haven't heard that god's name for a while. No, not for a long time.' He regarded sea, squinting to block out the sun.

'Yes, we're quite keen on seeing them,' Santiago said.

'And you will see them, you will,' the doctor said. 'There any more of you? Three seems to be a damn small number to come out all this way.'

'Oh, yeah, they're still on the boat over there,' Jefry said pointing behind him. His shirt flapped in the breeze.

'We have another five to come, but I thought I'd let these two row me out first,' Santiago said.

The doctor frowned, analysing the comment. 'Is speciesism back in fashion on the mainland?'

'Not at all,' Santiago said. 'No, I just didn't want to break into sweat too early. One never knew who one is likely to bump into.' He glanced at Myranda. 'I'm sorry, I don't think we've been formally introduced.'

'Don't be coy,' the doctor said. He turned to the newcomers. 'This, gentlemen, is my wife, Myranda.'

'Charmed.'

'Pleased to meet you.'

'How do you do?'

Myranda smiled whilst Santiago ravaged her body with his eyes.

'Good,' Doctor Macmillan said. 'Well, now that we're all introduced, perhaps you'd like to have a tour and familiarise yourselves with the island. Will you take lodgings here, or do prefer to live on that tin can for your stay?' The doctor nodded towards the boat that was anchored offshore.

'What lodgings do you have?' Santiago asked.

'Bring everyone onshore and I'll show you,' the doctor said. He walked past them urging them to follow with his arms wide. Myranda ran up alongside to him. They exchanged a smile, strolled ahead, whilst Santiago, Jefry and Arth stared at her from behind, following every sway of her steps, scanning her tender, brown skin.

Santiago smoothed down his moustache with his forefinger and thumb.

Fourteen

Manolin watched Becq DeBrelt step off of the rowing boat and into the water. Her hair had become lighter since she'd left the mainland. She leant her thin frame to bring the boat onto the shore. Wearing a white vest and brown breeches that clung to her body, she turned, her hands in her pockets, to consider the island.

From their vantage point you could see her father, Santiago, talking to Doctor Macmillan in the shade of a hut, and he was lounging in a hammock as a woman cooled him down with a large palm leaf. She took out a piece of cord from her pocket, tied her hair back. Her face perspired and the skin on her shoulders had already started to peel.

Manolin jumped off the boat and stepped next to her on the sand, scrunching his face in the sun and he dropped a large bag at her feet.
'Here you go.'
'Thanks.'
Manolin was wearing a white shirt. His breeches clung to his skin he could see sweat trickling down his leg. He thought the weather pleasant until the wind dropped. The air had become oppressive, humid. He looked towards Santiago, rolled his eyes. Hauling his own bag on his shoulder he walked forward, glancing around eagerly. Becq followed.

Yana stepped out in her thin skirt and vest top. She breathed, drawing in the fresh island's air. She smiled. She had begun to die her greying hair to its full black, and waves of it fell down her shoulder. Stepping on to the sand, Yana walked towards the others, spiralling whilst turning to scan the horizon. Her arms were held out wide as if she had been liberated. Manolin suspected she probably had, in some way.

The last two men stepped off of the boat, wearing smart trousers, identical blue shirts, with a black tie. They fanned themselves with straw hats, stepped off of the boat hesitantly, looking out to sea more than towards the island.

Manolin overheard their annoyingly formal conversation.
'So this is it, then, Mr Soul.'
'Indeed, Mr Calyban, indeed. No sign of any of our ships then, wrecked or otherwise.'

'No, not yet. That Santiago fellow has a submersible. I think that should reveal some more.'

'Shall we?'

'After you, Mr Soul.'

DeBrelt's crew assembled themselves by the hut that Santiago reclined in. Greetings were exchanged with Doctor Forb Macmillan, his wife Myranda, and their eight year-old son, Lewys. He was small, tanned.

Manolin began to open a small file of papers and notes that he had prepared, began to sift through them.

It was at that moment when Manolin saw Myranda for the first time.

He drew in the moist air and his chest felt heavy. He pushed it out, sucked his stomach in. His vision followed the gentle ridges of muscle and her. He placed the folder under his arm.

She looked at him, shaking his hand when he offered it. She held it, and his gaze, for longer than he thought necessary. She dazzled him with the whiteness of her teeth. He wanted to speak to her more, to say anything in fact, but his throat had swelled.

Manolin dropped the folder then a breeze tore the notes from him, scattered them across the sand and sea. He cursed, looked on helplessly. He ran after them, across the beach. Pages unfurled on the wind, darting away whenever he tried to grasp them. They were his notes he made in the city, many of his essays an observations. There were maps, charts, even some leaflets back from Escha, should he begin to feel homesick. It was all he had to remind himself of home, of the city, and it was being lost on the island winds.

The doctor called out, 'Don't worry, young man. Leave your paperwork. There will be much more than can be put on paper here, anyway.'

Manolin didn't acknowledge the words. He sighed, looked at Santiago, who simply shrugged. Reluctantly, trotted back to the group.

'Let them be,' Myranda said.

She offered him a piece of fruit. Manolin took it, examined the new specimen, then devoured it delicately, savouring every morsel. Sugary fruits burst in his mouth. His spirits soon picked up with the charm of this native woman. She paced away in a way that made sure his gaze remained on her.

The doctor turned to Myranda. 'I say, what've you got lined up for this afternoon's class?'

'Well, I'm finishing off the painting lessons,' she said. 'Mhuela is proving to be quiet talented. I wanted you to take over next week, as they need to study plants a little more. Little Juhhn had a bad reaction to something in the forest, and his hand has swollen.'

'Okay.' The doctor smiled. 'Poor fella. Yes, tell them to bring some specimens they know of, and I'll take it from there.'

Drinks of freshly squeezed juice were brought out. The foreigners didn't feel as if they were exploring new shores, so much as going on a holiday. The doctor made his guests feel welcome, then took them to the human settlement, a few hundred yards south.

'Luckily we have three cabins, which the ichthyocentaurs used to stay in, but they won't come this close to the shore any more.' Doctor Macmillan led the group, his son by his side, to the main village.

The sand was so bright that they could hardly look down and the soles of their feet felt hot. They were presented before a lagoon, by which forty or so huts clustered. This formed the village, and wooden shacks varied in shades of brown. The water of the lagoon was almost green and, to the right, Manolin could see dozens humans, working, playing. Some carved wood. Others wove fishing nets. He could see baskets in various stages of production and, from the forest, browned men carried nets of fruit. Children jumped into the green, hot water. Shrubs grew to the limits of the settlement and Manolin noticed three shacks that were on stilts, standing over the lagoon itself.

He said, 'Doctor Macmillan, what are those houses for?'

'Ah, glad you asked. Those were where the ichthyocentaurs stayed. That'll be where you'll be sleeping.'

'Must we stay there?' Mr Calyban said.

'Indeed, I'd rather stay on firm land, if it's all the same,' Mr Soul said. 'And I very much doubt there are any facilities?'

The doctor looked long and hard at the men in straw hats. He nodded. 'Suit yourself. I'll find other places for you. And yes, we do have *facilities*. There's a pit just inside the forest. We collect all our faeces there so that it can be used as a fertilizer to grow specific things by the ichthyocentaurs.'

'Charming,' Mr Calyban said.

The doctor continued towards the lagoon. 'Oh, I forgot to ask, what weaponry did you bring?'

'Well, we've muskets and knives,' Santiago said. 'Why?'

'Precautionary, that's all. It may be worthwhile installing someone to lookout at night, keeping an eye on the sea.' He paused for a second, running the palm of his hand back over his head. 'I suggest you give this role to a woman, because it seems that only males are affected.'

Santiago said, 'The ichthyocentaurs—where are they now?'

'They've fled to the hills,' the doctor said, indicating the dormant volcano that loomed above the forest. 'It's safer this way.'

Manolin looked up, saw birds with bright, colourful plumages scattering from the forests. In the village, the locals had stopped what they were doing, were massed in a long line of brown bodies, were standing still, staring.

'By Arrahd's loins, there're hundreds of them,' Jefry said.

'I'd no idea that there were humans away from the mainland, on an island,' Arth said. 'Let alone this many.'

'Oh yes,' the doctor said. 'We've about a hundred and fifty or so. Not forgetting the ichthyocentaurs. There're about, what, another hundred of them. It should be two hundred, but as you know, they're threatened.'

'I see,' Santiago said.

Manolin turned towards the lagoon and sea. Waves struck the sandbars that marked the rim of the lagoon, which was, he estimated, about fifty-yards wide and as long as he could see. The motion of the sea was distractingly repetitive.

Santiago said, 'If you don't mind me saying, you're awfully calm considering creatures are dying. And you don't seem overwhelmed at us being here.'

'Oh, I'm sorry, have I not made you feel welcomed?' the doctor said in earnest.

'Well, yes, but—'

'Mr DeBrelt—'

'I'd prefer Santiago. We're all friends here.'

The doctor said, 'All right, Santiago, I've spent ten years here now. These killings have occurred before, but this time they're rampant. I've asked for help only for their sakes, and to save my own curiosity before it's too late. Neither me nor these islanders are particularly keen on outsiders.'

Santiago said, 'You were one yourself, at one point, weren't you?'

'Yes, but I had to earn my right to be an islander. And I brought with me an inexhaustible supply of meat. I brought a pair of hares. They respected me for that and I hope that we can learn to respect you.'

Manolin looked at the doctor and recognised the concerns and scepticisms that flickered in his eyes. 'We'll earn your respect, Doctor Macmillan.'

'Please, call me Forb.' He smiled, nodding slightly. 'Come on, I'll show you to your lodgings. There're three empty huts here. You don't mind sharing, do you?'

Their habitations were minimal, smelled of damp wood. To access it, you had to row a small raft, securing it to the stilts. Palm leaves were woven intricately for roofing, leaving strips of sunlight to filter through. If you sat on the doorsteps of the huts, you would be able to dangle feet in the sea at high tide. To the right was the beach, in front the lagoon. To the left, the ocean. The stilts on which the huts stood were capable of withstanding a storm. Santiago shared a hut with Manolin. Arth with Jefry. Yana with Becq.

Sunset: and a vast orange horizon proved warm, pleasant. This was the time when most of the islanders socialised, out of the extreme heat of midday, during which they appeared to do little. Men, women and children scampered on the shore with long shadows in the sand. Manolin had seen some sights in his life, but this was one of the most impressive he'd witnessed. Not only for the natural beauty, the almost inherent quality of the island, but for the feeling it presented him with. There was a peace, a sense that you could be yourself here, find yourself. There were few people, none of the square and oppressive buildings in which he'd grow up with. None of the thick plumes of smoke trailing across the sky, the constant industry, the competition, the need to improve, get the next best thing, do this and that socially. No, there was peace here.

Myranda began to swim in the lagoon.

Manolin sat on the doorstep, his toes cooling in the water, watched her ooze out into the middle of the lagoon, about twenty feet in front of the huts. His breeches were rolled up, his shirt was out loose.

'Why don't you come in?' she said, treading water. 'It'll make your body feel good.' Her accent was clean, her voice almost hanging in the air above the lagoon. Manolin thought that the doctor must've educated her well.

He said, 'Oh, no, thank you. It feels pretty good already.'

She laughed before spinning underwater then back up. Her skin shimmered in the low sun. He smiled. Water sparkled.

She said, 'It's your loss, stranger.'

'Oh, I know,' he said and was convinced she made sure she held his gaze before swimming further out into the lagoon. There were small rafts out at sea, the inhabitants arcing nets over schools of fish, pulling in traps.

Manolin turned to face Santiago in the cabin. Out of the corner of his eye, he could see Becq's legs dangling out of her hut.

'Fine lady,' Santiago said, standing over Manolin. 'Very convenient to have an island beauty.'

'Yeah, she's pretty pleasant. Nice-looking sort.'

Santiago said, 'Be careful. Remember what happens when you

don't follow the head and let that—' he indicated Manolin's groin '—think for you.'

'Hey, I'm not thinking with that. I'm not thinking with anything.'

Manolin rested his head on the doorframe, allowing the breeze to blow a few strands of black hair over his forehead. He reflected for a moment, was in no hurry to make a comment. 'I tell you what, San, I could get used to this.' He watched the silhouette of a gull glide in low over the beach.

'I know what you mean. It's easy to forget that we're here to investigate and to survey the place.' Santiago rested his hand on the doorway above Manolin's head. The trees generated a sweet perfume, as they could open up in the cool evening climate.

Manolin said, 'Don't you feel a bit uneasy about staying in these huts, what with those creatures being killed? There's talk about ghouls and ghosts from the islanders.'

'Not really. There is always a rational explanation for these occurrences. I spoke to Forb earlier, and he suggested we look at some of the carcasses that were washed up a couple of days ago.'

'I wonder what *Mister* Calyban and *Mister* Soul are up to?'

'I've no idea, Manolin. I really don't know why they're here at all apart from making sure I get up to no harm.' Santiago smiled.

'I forgot to ask you about that,' Manolin said. 'Why *doesn't* he trust you?'

'Oh, you mean the Mayor? Gio and I go way back. You see, I used to be a member of the Collectivist Party, and Gio, as the rest of Escha tends to be, is a devout capitalist. Our political history is… *colourful*. Too many arguments and rivalries. He even tried to hit me once, in a debate.'

'You've never mentioned this before?'

'No. No need to. Anyway, Escha is no place for a Collectivist. Not these days.'

Manolin nodded, looking down into the water, at the strange shapes that the light made. On the sides of the doorway symbols were carved. He'd seen them on the other huts too. 'San, what d'you think of these? Some sort of tribal designs?'

Santiago looked closer. 'They're old mathematical and scientific symbols. Bizarre. They're not used in this age. Some've changed, but we don't use these ones. You seem them in the odd book, here and there. Old books, mind. They remind me of some that we saw way up north—that place a few weeks' travel past Rhoam. Small village and that archaeological dig. '

Manolin nodded and could see that fires were being lit on the beach. 'We going to this shindig then?'

'You know me,' Santiago said. 'Not one to miss a party.'

Becq sat in the doorway of her hut. She hung one leg over the side and reached for the rope, which secured the raft, with her toes. She kicked it, played with it. Then she glanced over at the fires that were burning on the beach, at the people gathering around. You could smell meat or fish being cooked on the fires. She felt the peace and beauty of the location, but her personal troubles brought her mind some imbalance that challenged her ability to appreciate it fully.

It was getting darker, the sky purpling. The temperature became much more bearable for her. Despite Escha being located on the edge of the desert of mainland Has-jahn, on the edge of permanent high temperatures, the island had proved stifling on arrival. Some part of her suspected it wasn't an environmental factor. Perhaps the heat came from somewhere else more internal.

She turned towards Yana, who was changing into a white shirt and long black skirt. 'Do you think he'll ever actually notice me?' Becq said, resting her head on the frame. She placed her hand palm down on the wooden floor and touched the panels almost affectionately.

'Who?' Yana said. She sat down on a small mat next to her luggage.

'Manolin.'

'Oh, him.' Her face darkened. 'I can't say, I'm afraid. I think I've given up on men. I obviously never know what I'm doing with them.'

Becq stared in disbelief at this woman who she respected so much, almost aspired to be like. 'You? But you could have any man you want. Look at you, every year you get better looking.'

Yana rolled her eyes and smiled. 'My *husband* doesn't seem to notice.'

Becq said, 'Jefry does, I'm sure of it.'

'Whether he does or not, I can barely look at him.'

'Why?' Becq sat up.

'You wouldn't understand.'

'I would. I know he loves you—'

'But I can't stand him,' Yana said. 'I can't bear to listen to every crude thing he says anymore. I can't stand the way he eats. I detest his smell. He doesn't care about himself, let alone me.'

'Are you sure it's not because he's a rumel or something?'

Yana said, 'I wouldn't have married him if that were the case. Anyway, hardly anyone's bothered by that these days, much the same as if he were human and black. No, my prejudices against him are different. They were planted years ago. You know, I can't even remember the last time we had sex. Not that I can't get turned on you see. I do, I love sex, and more so as I get older. I have desires, but I can't if he is *there*, touching me.' She screwed up her face and Becq could see her tendons lifting in her neck as she turned away. 'He does try but, well, I'd rather not go to all the effort. Not with him anyway.'

There was a lingering silence.

'So, you don't know if Manolin likes me?' Becq said. 'You know, I'd do anything for him. I just want to hold him because he looks so sad sometimes. What his wife did…'

'It's not always enough, Becq, not always enough. He's had a tough time. Just hang on in there if you really feel that way. I'm not sure you can fix his problems. He was seriously scarred by her. He puts a brave face on it, but deep down something fundamental has shifted. These things always do, if you dig deep enough.'

'I think he's interested in that Myranda girl.' Becq turned her gaze to the floor. 'She's so damn pretty and her body is so much more bloody attractive than mine. Just like yours. That's what he wants, not me.'

Yana smiled inwardly. 'Men always look for something better, Becq. They're never satisfied. They'll give you explanations like "men aren't meant to settle down with just one woman". They're just weak and will use any philosophy to justify what happens in their pants.' Then, 'It's amazing how, these days, any immoral act can appear to be justified.'

'I think Manolin's different. He's really shy usually. He's an absolute gentleman, too. Unlike dad. No, Manolin is a different guy.'

'Is he a man?' Yana asked.

'Yes, of course.'

'Then he'll do anything in his powers to possess a girl like Myranda. It may be a subtle effort, but he'll try. Half the time he won't even realise he's doing it. But I think it'll do him some good to have a flirt with someone different and new. It'll make him feel mildly alive again. Don't hate him for it. He's one of those guys that will ride waves for years, being taken in many directions, and he'll cling on to whatever he can to survive.'

'He can cling on to me.'

'I think he needs someone to order him about. Tell him what to do. And a stereotypical island girl maybe the thing to help mend his shattered ego.'

'It's so unfair. She's gorgeous.'

'And she knows that these new foreign men that have arrived think that too.'

Becq nodded in agreement, turned her head. She leaned out of the hut, above the water and looked up at the sky. 'Yana, look. I've never seen so many stars.'

Yana stood up, leant over Becq to see the sky. It wasn't yet fully night. The stars littered the sky in powder trails or thin white smears. The light pollution in Escha had always prevented such a sight. Becq sat up as Yana lingered in the doorway. She sat back down near her bags and after she had rummaged for a moment, drew out a stuffed doll and some thread.

She closed her bag, drew the doll over her lap. It was about a foot and a half long, had a thick crop of black wool for hair. She had made two brown eyes from small gemstones, had dressed the doll in a white shirt and black breeches.

Yana turned from stargazing and glanced towards her. 'Oh, that's nice. Did you make that yourself?'

'Yeah, d'you like it?'

Yana leaned down over. 'Can I have a look?'

Becq passed the doll carefully across.

'Yes, that's really good. The stitching's very tidy. How long did it take you to make?'

'Oh, I've been making it for a couple of months before we came over. I've made a few before, but none as good as this one.'

'Yes, it's good.' Yana paused. 'You know, it kind of reminds me of Manolin.' She examined the doll further. 'Yeah, now I mention it, it looks quite a lot like him.'

Becq said, 'Can I have it back, please, it's not finished yet.'

'Sorry, of course.' Yana handed the doll to Becq who placed it on her lap. She could see that Yana frowned stared at her as she placed the doll with care into the bag.

You could hear the sea fizzing against the fringes of the lagoon, the gentle rhythm of the water against the stilts underneath the hut. Birds called out from the forest. She walked to the doorway, leaving Becq sitting on the floor. The volcano was fading into the darkness of the night and the fires that were on the beach. Through the sounds of the forest she could hear children laughing, saw their tiny brown bodies lit up as they danced around a fire.

'Come on, Becq. We should be on the beach having fun.' Yana sighed, rubbing her abdomen.

'Are you okay?' Becq said.

'Yeah, I think I'm not used to the food or something.'

* * *

Santiago's team huddled around the fire, watching a native turning a hog on a spit. The local man wore only a loin cloth, but it was the foreigners who felt embarrassed. A crowd of natives stood yards away, watching them. Children looked out from behind their mothers' bare legs, the firelight warming their faces.

The doctor sat within the newcomers' circle, chewing meat. He briefed Santiago. 'The people that watch you have been here as long as they can remember. They descended from a naval vessel, which was wrecked upon the reef. There were about five women on board that came from a place that I never really understood when they talked about it. Needless to say, five women amongst fifty or so men meant that they were in demand. That was several generations ago, round about the rebellion against science. The sailors weren't ruffians though, no. They were scholars and academics—scientists fleeing persecution. Deemed as immoral, they decided not to try and leave for the mainland, but set up their own little bit of paradise.'

Manolin nodded, gnawing a hunk of hog, which had been roasted in herbs.

Santiago sat on a palm mat, with his hands clasped over his knees. 'Makes sense. There's plenty to keep them going here. And that would explain why they speak the same language.'

'Indeed. It's been easy to get along since I came here.'

'Yes, I've been meaning to ask. Why did you come here?'

'For the ichthyocentaurs, originally. Plus I was caught up in some trouble about ten years ago.'

'What trouble was that then?'

The doctor placed the meat he was chewing onto a bamboo plate. 'Ten years ago was the time when a mayor resurrected one of the ancient technologies, the ones that were outlawed in their time. Well, I got caught up in helping her, and, needless to say, when the shit hit the fan, I left, because the trouble went right down to the street level— gangs and whatnot. When the mob decide to take things into hand, it's advisable not to be there. There was nothing left in Escha, so I decided to follow up a line of research with the ichthyocentaurs. Sure there was some risk, but it was easier than sticking around.'

'Ah, yes, I've heard that these little beasties know a secret or two,' Santiago said. His eye followed a native girl as she walked past the fire and towards the sea.

'I'll say they do,' the doctor said. 'Know much ethnobotany?'

'That's Manny's department,' Santiago said. He slapped Manolin on the back. The younger man coughed out a strip of pork.

'Splendid!' The doctor turned to Manolin as he looked to where the piece of meat had landed. 'You'll love these things then.'

'Why's that?' Manolin asked.

'The ichthyocentaurs know how to use every plant on this island, so they never get ill. It's why they've survived for so long here. If you get a headache, then there are three things in that forest that will stop it. If one of them has a stomach ulcer, then there is a bark of a palm tree that needs to be chewed. They're in superb health, which probably explains why this lot—' he indicated the natives '—don't suffer much illness either. They've lived alongside the creatures for so long, but none of them know what plants do what. It's the ichthyocentaurs who know all the secrets.'

Manolin said, 'I'd love to see some of this tomorrow.'

'Oh, you will,' the doctor said. 'You'll want to spend as long as you can on this island.' He smirked. The fire crackled and the waves encroached. The smell of pork lingered.

Santiago's gaze travelled to the lagoon, where two women were shifting a small boat onto the land. He could see their muscled bodies rub together as they struggled with the weight. Once on the sand, they brushed each other down. They were some way away, and there was only the moon to illuminate the scene, but he swore that they lingered long on each touch. They seemed sensual as they brushed sand off of one another's arm. Maybe it was his mind playing tricks. Maybe it was the weather and good food. Maybe it was because he was, simply, a dirty old man—he would freely admit it—but he watched them, following them running, hand in hand, towards the forest then disappearing into the darkness behind the huts.

'I can see you wouldn't want to leave a place like this,' Jefry said.

'You like the island then?' the doctor asked.

'Oh yeah, I'd say. Everyone seems so peaceful here. It must be relaxing. Yana, maybe it would make you feel a little better?'

'What d'you mean by that?' Yana said.

'Well, you were feeling unwell on the boat. Now that you're on dry land you might, you know, be a little happier.'

She grunted. 'Nice for you to show an interest.' She stood up, brushed sand from her skirt, stomped to the village. She stepped over Manolin's legs, which were spread out, and she glanced at him, but Santiago noticed he looked away. He watched her walk to the huts, she pass a group of natives. She held her hand out in greeting.

Mr Calyban and Mr Soul stepped out of the trees behind. They were staying in huts in the forest and dined alone. They stood behind

DeBrelt's crew.

'Everything in check?' Mr Calyban said.

'Why don't you do something useful and fuck off?' Santiago said.

'I'm sorry, what was that, Mr DeBrelt?'

'I said why don't you help yourselves to some pork?'

'Thank you, but we've already eaten.' They walked towards the lagoon, along the beach, their straw hats in their hands, the surf spitting at their feet.

'So, Forb,' Santiago said. 'You said we need to protect ourselves tonight?'

'Yes. Yes that's true.'

'What from, might I ask?'

'Well, from the things that have murdered around sixty or so ichthyocentaur.'

'Well, I think if we're to help you, we need to know what we're dealing with.'

'True, true. Every week or so, up until I relocated the ichthyocentaurs to the side of the volcano, we lost about five of them. We don't know what has killed them, just that the remains are found the next day with the hearts removed and their testes severed too.'

'Testes? So it's just males that are taken?'

'Yes, only the males. I sent the message to you early on in the killings, because I knew, from what the natives told me, that it had happened before, a generation ago. I suspected they would go on and I wanted to preserve the race. So, knowing that only a scholar would know what they were, I asked for help.'

Santiago said, 'You say you don't know what is killing them?'

'No. But they come from somewhere on the other side of the reef.'

Santiago's eyes narrowed. 'Deep sea?'

'Possibly. You'd be surprised how close the nearest abyss is from here, Santiago. I've never known of such a formation, but the reef stretches for miles and marks the edge of what I think is the abyssal plain. I've never had the technology to know further. You don't get many remnants from the past out here. To be honest, since the killings began, I've never had the nerve.'

Santiago nodded. 'Luckily we've brought a decent submersible craft. Maybe it's something we could investigate at a later stage.'

'That'd be excellent if we could. Like I say, we don't go past the reef. If you like I'll give you a full tour of the island tomorrow. I'll show you where the ichthyocentaurs now live.'

'That'd be fantastic,' Manolin said.

'You'll love them. You'll never have seen a race use plants the way they do.'

Manolin said, 'I'm looking forward to it.'

Santiago suspected that, for the first time since he had left Escha, Manolin had something to be excited about. Studying how tribes used plant matter was a major aspect of his life. His Doctorate was awarded, with Santiago's assistance, of course, on the same subject. The young man stood up. 'I think I'll need to sleep then, if we'll see these chaps tomorrow. 'Night all.' Manolin turned, sauntered to a raft, then pushed it out into the lagoon as the others watched on.

Santiago's turned his attention to the two rumel.

'That's the first time I've seen him smile all year,' Arth said, sprawling back and staring at the stars. 'I think the little chap'll come out of his shell on this island. He hasn't got that terror of his causing him grief anymore. And this is the sort of territory he loves to study.'

'Aye,' Jefry said. 'It's good to love your work, even if nothing else loves you.'

'Oh come now, Jefry. Shall I fetch my violin?' Arth said.

'I know, I know. But I can't help think that I've done something to upset Yana. She's never been like this with me before.'

'Well, you can't go blaming yourself,' Arth said. 'It's natural to think so, but coming away to a foreign place can make people a little upset. Sort of homesick. People just get uncomfortable, and don't forget, she's been stuck on a boat for a good while.'

Jefry nodded.

'Just stay cool, Jef, stay cool.'

Santiago stood up, said goodnight to the doctor, and meandered along the beach then to the lagoon. He picked up a pearl-white shell and skimmed it along the sheltered water that the lagoon was. The shell bounced four times off of the water before shooting over the edge and into the sea. A young native girl came tugged on his breeches.

'Oh, hello,' he said. 'Aren't you a pretty little thing? You're going to break some hearts, I can tell.' She looked up, frowned so he ruffled her hair. 'So young, so young. To be so innocent. Arrahd, I wish I could be so innocent again.'

He spent the next half an hour teaching her to skim shells across the lagoon. Pretty soon she had spun a twelver, leaving Santiago wide-eyed. After she had gone to sleep it was two hours before he had bettered her and felt he could retire to his hut with a fourteener.

After he pulled his raft up to the hut and had climbed in, he checked his belongings for a musket and kicked Manolin awake. 'Here, you take first watch. Wake me in an hour.'

Fifteen

'Well, this is pier nineteen,' Menz said. 'That must be it then.'

'She's a big one. Let's take a look on board,' Yayle said.

The rumel were standing on the docks, staring up at a large, grey boat. Behind them, other worker rumel in overalls were sitting eating their lunch, whilst seagulls screamed down from above, circling them, eyeing the bread in their hands. These docks had a sense that nothing really happened, and that was the way of things. Nothing in terms of progress, at least. You could smell it in the organic matter that only ever accumulated. It was one of those places where people did what they did, what they had to, earned some coin for some food, and that was about it. Days would probably drift into years and nothing would happen. People would stay, marry, take their parents' jobs, have children of their own, quite happy to keep doing this. The mere concept of development or migration would unnerve them totally. Menz had seen a thousand places like it in his lifetime—but perhaps he missed all this because his home city had gone. Maybe that was where his bitterness came from.

As Menz and Yayle climbed a step ladder, they could see over the tops of red-brick buildings, four or five floors high with steep-pitched roofs that reminded him of Rhoam, squeezed together overlooking the harbour. Hundreds of white masts punctured the sky. The sound of engines echoed around the bay.

'This'll do nicely.' Menz leaned over the side of the boat, rested his arms on the rail.

Yayle joined him. 'I'd say. Hey, have a look at this submersible.'

Over the side hung a brass rimmed cylinder, with circular glass panels. It was about ten foot long with yards of piping coiled at one end. Walking over, Menz noted what they took to be generators that would supply air to the craft.

'That should definitely do the job,' Yayle said. He tapped the roof of the craft with his knuckle.

Menz said, 'Right, all we need is a couple of people to man this thing and we can go.'

'Is Jella right in saying we need a skipper? Can't we just do this ourselves?' Yayle asked, gripping the rails.

'No, lad. There's no way I can navigate this thing for four months. Remember last time we had a guide, one with experience at sea.'

'Why do we have to find one? I bet those two are at each other right now.'

Menz said, 'Don't be so crude.' Then, 'Anyway, you're only jealous.'

'Of who?'

'Both of 'em.'

'Probably true.' Yayle sighed.

'Anyway,' Menz said, 'I doubt they are, lad. Not with that ghoul hanging around.' He didn't trust Allocen, despite what the creature had done. Mildly annoyed at his prejudice, Menz thought it a peculiar feeling that people have towards anything that looks strange, unnatural. There's an inherent lack of trust to the more freakish—and why? It's purely a physical thing. Perhaps it was some biological consideration, an evolutionary learning—to dislike anything other than what is accepted.

'Hmm,' Yayle said. 'He's a strange one. Endearing, I suppose. If you like that sort of thing.'

'Aye. I guess he's proved his worth, what with that little carve-up the other evening.' Menz walked along the deck, glancing at the gulls, which seemed to float in the air, waiting for food. 'Still, he makes the mind boggle.'

'How do you think he got like that? You know, half fly and half man?'

'Well, they say that scientists did it to them, the Qe Falta, in the last age. Some book of sorts, held the recipe for altering their... what's the word?'

'Hairstyle?' Yayle said.

'No, fool.'

'Sex drive?'

'Idiot.'

'Genes?'

'Genes, that's it. Altering their Genetic make up. But the secret for that has long been forgotten. Allocen's one of the leftovers, I suspect.'

Menz stared out to sea. The weather was still, a bank of grey cloud hung low over the horizon. The local waters were filled with trawlers.

Yayle said, 'I suppose we'd better find someone to drive this bugger then? If we sure as hell can't.'

'Yep.'

The tavern was quiet, the lunchtime period having finished. The sign on the bar said 'No Beggars'. Yayle walked up to the bar, where a well-built man was polishing tankards. His face was red, as if he had just swum to work. His shirt was stained with oil.

'My good man, we're looking for a sailor,' Yayle announced, placing a hand on the bar.

The barman looked Yayle up and down, his eyes narrowed as he put down the tankard, he draped the cloth over his. 'Aye, you look the sort,' he said. 'If you want those sorts of shenanigans, you'd better walk up Juiliper Street after six. They cater for your lot.'

Yayle raised his chin then turned to Menz, who shook his head.

'What he means is,' Menz said, 'that we need to hire someone to skipper our boat. We need a good sailing type, someone who knows the western seas. Sea of Wands, and beyond.'

'Ah, I see. Right, well, anyone in here after lunch probably doesn't have a job to get back to. Take your pick.'

They looked around the tavern. In one corner, a window cast a grey light on an old woman, who sat with her head tilted back, her mouth open as if she had died only that morning. There were two young rumel, who sat playing cards. They looked too young to know the sea. By the other window, next to a staircase, a young woman touched the edges of her wine glass, before dabbing the crumbs on her plate then licking her fingers, smiling.

In another corner was a man with a black beard that covered most of his face. Ah, Menz thought. Now he looks the type. He tipped a naval hat back as Yayle and Menz approached.

'Good afternoon,' Yayle said.

The man looked at them and nodded, then scratched his beard. Yayle glanced to Menz.

'Do you sail?' Menz asked.

'Aye, I do.'

'Can you read charts?' Yayle asked.

'Better than any book.'

Yayle said, 'Can you read a book?'

Menz kicked Yayle. 'Do you know, sir, the way to Arya?'

'I do. And what're you wanting to go there for?'

'That's our business,' Menz said. 'We need a skipper to take us there. You'll be away from land for months, at least.'

'You got a vessel?'

'Yep. She's a gooden. Parked over there, number nineteen.' Menz indicated out the window that overlooked the harbour.

The bearded man did not follow Menz's gaze. Instead he sat back, the seat creaking. 'They say you have to be mad to set sail round there.

Not many have returned.'

'Sailors' stories, mostly. Besides, we have money.' Menz produced a heavy purse, tossed it onto the table.

The man looked at it. Then he glanced between the two rumel, sipped from his glass. He sighed whilst he set his glass down again. 'There's a lot of money around these days.'

'When was the last time you had a job?' Menz asked.

'It's not all about work now, is it?'

Yayle said, 'True, true. Okay, tell me this. You anything against Escha?'

'Ain't we all. Why?' He looked up, suddenly interested.

Menz said, 'How old are you?'

'Seen fifty-four years and can remember most of them.'

'You know a lot about the sea then?'

'More than anyone you'd know, aye. Most people talk too much these days though.'

'Look, we want you on board, okay. You seem a good sort, and if you got jip with Escha, we're your people too. I'm Menz. This is Yayle.'

Yayle leaned forward to shake the man's hand. 'There's three others coming along too. Two women and someone else. You'd better come back and have a chat with us. We're staying at another tavern a few streets back. You got digs here?'

'Yep, been staying here a few weeks now. The name's Gabryl.'

'Pleased to meet you,' Menz said. 'What exactly was your line of work?'

Gabryl flicked his hat. 'Navy. Was thrown out six years back.'

'What for?'

Gabryl said, 'Killing another officer.'

Menz and Yayle looked at each other, still standing at the side of the table. Menz said, 'Why?'

''Cos he didn't follow my orders. We were months away up the north coasts. Some of the tribes' people up there didn't like us being there, so they got nasty, started being all difficult with us, not cooperating. Got messy. One night, my second-in-command decided he'd take one of the local women into the forests. I caught him raping her, saw it all. Saw her face full of tears and teeth marks. So, I dragged him off and gave him the beating of his life. Beat him for ten minutes solid, which is a long time when you're hitting a man. Ten long minutes and the tribeswoman watched, then she thanked me, so did the rest of the tribe when they found out. They even paraded his body afterwards. Didn't mean to kill him, but I got furious. You just don't do that. Gives us all a bad name. But we had to pull up after that, and we came back shortly after, and I turned myself in. My crew tried to persuade me otherwise, but I'm an honest man, Menz. Apparently, our government seems to think that the natives are a lesser people than our forces.'

Menz looked at Gabryl, who glanced down. Menz turned to the barman. 'Can we get three beers here?'

Gabryl stared vacantly across the room. Menz thought he smiled, but couldn't quite see under the beard. 'So before you know it, I'm out of work and away from what's been my whole damn life. Been messing around on schooners here and there. Hired knowledge and so forth. Ain't the same, though.'

'Listen, can I trust you to keep something to yourself?'

'Do I look like a gossip? Does it look like I know many people at all?'

'Right, well, have you ever heard of...' Menz leaned in closer, and whispered, 'Ever heard of Quidlo?

The bearded man's face darkened. 'Yeah. You don't wanna be sayin' that too loud, you hear? Not round the coasts anyway. What in Has-jahn are you talking about that for?'

Menz sat back. 'We're going to get it.'

'You don't *get* a thing like that?' The bearded man took a long sip from his glass then gasped after swallowing. 'So, you actually know of it then?'

Menz smiled, 'Seen it. So's the lad.' He indicated Yayle.

The bearded man looked at the purse, to Yayle, back to Menz. 'What you want me for? What the hell d'you want *Quidlo* for?'

'We're taking it to Escha, or at least trying to. Sounds crazy but we got it all worked out. You don't have to come that far necessarily. We just need you to get us there. We got everything planned in detail you'd never imagine. We got plans, notes, sketches, maps. Got the lot.'

There was a pause while the bearded man looked out of the window then back to the table, pouted his lips, narrowed his eyes. 'Well, it looks like you have yourselves a captain.' He extended a blistered hand that was as thick as a blacksmith's.

'What's your full name then, captain?' Menz asked, shaking it.

'Captain Gabryl Miller Fontain.' He nodded to the two seats next to him, and took the purse. He opened it briefly, tied it shut, buried it inside his coat.

Lula lay on the bed, a newspaper resting on her chest. Her eyes were closed, but Jella could tell that she wasn't asleep. Jella sat at a small table in the corner, by the window, which overlooked an alleyway. You could smell the rubbish piled up outside the tavern, two floors below. On the edge of her chair, Jella could just about see the harbour front, the litter that blew around. Earlier she had seen men cutting nets of fish, allowing the cargo to spill into crates.

Allocen sat at the table, too. He leaned over and his fingers formed intricate shapes. Using hand movements, he was trying to communicate with her, starting with simple things such as his name, his weaponry, objects around the room. Jella made notes, in an attempt to bond with the Qe Falta creature. His hood was, as always, hauled over his head, but she could clearly see the light from the window shine off of the numerous shapes that formed his eyes. She felt a strange bond forming between herself and Allocen. Perhaps it was because of the fact that they were both isolated individuals, that they both felt unable to connect to the world in a normal way—albeit for different reasons. They had been brought together, with a common aim of destroying Escha.

There was a knock at the door. Jella looked up, but was reassured by Allocen's lack of action. Lula reached for her musket that was on the bed next to her. Jella pushed the chair back along the floorboards and walked to the door. She pulled it open. Menz shuffled in, Yayle behind.

Menz said, 'Afternoon.'

'Hey, Menz.' Jella turned, sat back down at the table. 'So. Did you find anyone?'

'Certainly did.' Menz and Yayle stepped aside. 'Presenting ex-naval Captain Gabryl Miller Fontain, thirty years service in the Eschan forces.'

Gabryl stepped in, hunching as he stepped through the door. His boots were loud on the wood and he stretched out his hand to Jella, looking at the back of the cloaked figure sitting opposite. 'Please to make your acquaintance.'

'Likewise,' she said. At the instant she heard the fact that he was in the Eschan navy, she felt defensive. Why would these two idiots have brought someone from Escha?

With a gesture, Menz said, 'This is Jella and over there is Lula.' Lula gave a slight wave.

'And this is the other chap we were telling you about. Allocen.' Menz leaned across to Gabryl, whispered, 'He's Qe Falta.'

'By the balls of Arrahd...' Gabryl took a step back as Allocen stood up, inches higher than the bulk of the new captain, stared right at him. Jella could see that this man he could feel the immense and complicated eye structures analysing him.

'He's a quiet one,' Yayle said, 'but he grows on you. And he's saved us all once, so we've decided we like him.'

Gabryl nodded. Allocen sat back down and Gabryl watched him all the way. Even after Allocen had settled, Gabryl's eyes were still wide. Jella regarded this man, his large frame, his bearded face. She never trusted beards: you couldn't see people's full facial expressions.

Yayle broke the silence. 'Well, now we're all friends then, when shall we set sail?'

'Tomorrow, I guess.' Jella looked around and everyone nodded. 'But let's just check this guy out first. I take it we can trust him.'

'The sooner the better,' Gabryl said. 'I can't wait. And of course you can trust me.'

Jella said, 'So you've worked for Eschan forces. You still got any links with the city?'

Menz answered on Gabryl's behalf. 'He don't like 'em, he don't care. We've all ready briefed him.'

'I'm a simple man of the sea. And I can't wait to see Quidlo.'

'You've heard of it then?' Jella said, suspicious.

'What man of the sea hasn't? I didn't think it was alive though. I didn't think it was *real*.'

'Oh yeah, we've seen it.' Jella nodded to him.

'So Menz said. But listen, you're going to need a lot of whale. One thing I don't understand is how you're going to get that. We ain't got the skills.'

'We've got to intercept a whaling ship on the way,' Jella said.

'Menz never mentioned that.'

'Didn't he?' Jella looked up at Menz who had retreated to his bed.

He fell on it, sighed, flailing an arm, his tail twitching by his side. 'Small print. Won't be a problem, will it?'

Gabryl smiled. 'No, I guess not. I tell you what though, you guys sure are bad hosts.'

'What do you mean?' Jella asked.

'Haven't been offered a drink, and I've been here five minutes now.'

'Think he'll fit in nicely,' Yayle said, reaching in a bag. He drew out a bottle, grabbed a metal cup from a shelf. He opened the bottle and filled the cup, then offered it to Gabryl. 'Here you go, captain. Rhoam wine, vintage. Took it whilst at a rich man's house.'

Gabryl frowned, rubbed his beard, took the cup with his other hand. He swigged from the bottle, gasped, raised his lower lip to remove liquid from his facial hair. He felt the drink fall down nicely. 'You know, think I will fit in nicely. I think this calls for a celebration. Yayle, do we have more wine?'

Jella opened the window to let some of the cool night air rid the musky smell that a group of people tended to produce. Gabryl sat at the table, Lula on the bed. Behind were Menz and Yayle, leaning against another bed. Allocen was sitting on a stool in the far corner, oiling his blades. Jella could smell the fresh air and it felt pleasant on her face. She sat back opposite Gabryl and topped his glass up, being careful not to knock the candles over.

They shone on Gabryl's face, and his eyes seemed full of life, despite his age. It suggested an eagerness about his character. 'Thank you, young lady. More for yourself, too?'

'Sure, why not.' She poured her cup full.

Gabryl leant back, said, 'So that, Menz, was my last battle. The navy was under funded and decreasing in size each year.'

'Always the way with the military, ain't it?' Menz said from behind, between from his cup. He crossed his legs.

A thought-filled silence descended.

Gabryl rolled the wine around his mouth. 'Look. I've been meaning to ask. Why's it you plan to use Quidlo on Escha? What do you hate so much about that place?'

Jella glanced over the candles and Gabryl's shoulder to Menz and Yayle. The men nodded approval.

'You might as well tell the man,' Menz said.

Gabryl saw her wide eyes. 'Look, I've seen a lot of shit in Hasjahn. I know that people have agendas of their own. This continent's seen its fair share of deception, of slaughter.'

'Over ten years ago, we lived in Lucher,' Jella said.

'Oh yeah, east coast.' Gabryl nodded.

'Yes,' Jella continued. 'For whatever reason, ten years ago, our homes were destroyed.'

'Poisoned,' Menz called out.

'Poisoned,' she said. 'Our homes were *poisoned*. Escha dumped a load of toxic substances, amongst other things, into our waters. The concentrations were phenomenally high. It accumulated in our food chain, which means it got more toxic through the fish we ate. It destroyed our mangroves, every single tree. That meant that there was nowhere for marine life to breed and we were susceptible to the elements. We were a communal city; we used no money. Thousands were poisoned. I was only a little girl at the time. My father went missing.

'I remember seeing a cousin of mine—she must've been ten years old.' Jella shook her head. 'When our families prepared to leave, I watched that girl. I watched her on her bed and you could see the blood come out of her mouth when she coughed and you could see it all on the walls. I remember her white hair going pink at the ends, where my aunt tried to wash it. She cried to have her doll but she vomited on that, too, but she wouldn't let go of it. When you see that happen to a girl you remember it. A ten year old girl holding on to a blood-drenched doll, she wouldn't let go. Then, two days later, they had to burn her body to stop the contamination from spreading.'

Gabryl looked down at his glass.

Jella went on. 'We had to leave the city and go to Rhoam. Lucher was uninhabitable, and soon desert clans came to take what they could. Took advantage of the refugees that left. I've got aint memories of my sister leaving me on the way, but we were luckily not affected by the clans. Unlike Yayle.'

'Yeah,' Yayle said.

He took a gulp of wine, as if to help. Jella had heard his story a dozen times, but it still caused her anguish. Her own narrative she could tell with some boredom. She'd internalised her rage, focused her anger.

Yayle's tail flickered. 'I was sixteen when the clans came. Came from a family that lived on the edges of the city, so weren't hit by the greatest contamination. Our water supplies were stocked and kept in tanks. For a while we were fine. Anyway, when the refugees left in the first wave, the clans came to take what they could. My family had some decent things—nice pictures on the walls, lovely jewellery—all hand made of course. Nice stuff.

'My mother and father were preparing a basic dinner, since food was rare and we were about to set off for Rhoam, when our windows were smashed and our doors were kicked in. I was upstairs and looked out of my window to see four men climbing over our whitewalls with the roses on. They were wearing rags and carried machetes, and so I ran into my parents' room and grabbed two pistols then ran to hide in a cupboard. I heard my mother scream, which is something no one should hear. From the cupboard I heard people run upstairs, and I remember hearing things sliding off of tables and strange voices I had never heard. I heard the clansmen go away and I ran to the window to see three of them throwing a bag over the walls and then jumping over after.

'I walked to the top of the stairs and heard my father call out something but he was cut off. Then I walked downstairs, carefully, and loaded the pistols. At the foot of the stairs, I heard my mother crying. Through the kitchen door, which was half open, I could see her lying on the kitchen table, and a dirty clansman pushing up her skirt. Without thinking, and I still don't know how I had the know-how, I fired one of the pistols. The clansman gasped, grabbing his shoulder. He turned and came towards me, and I could see blood on his blade, and he started to swing so I lifted the other pistol and fired, but as I did the machete struck me on the thigh. It was my fault—I should've shot him right away. I shouldn't have hidden in the damn cupboards.' Yayle moved his leg, perhaps self-consciously. 'I stumbled back and he fell forward, holding his stomach and when he was on the floor I could see his eyes were wide, really wide, and he opened his mouth to say something but nothing came out. I ran to the kitchen and saw my father on the floor, not moving, and my mother crying on the table, and I remember seeing the dinner was still on it and it looked nicely laid-out as my mother had wanted to make a good meal. She had wounds to her head and she was crying, but almost not, it was strange. She died minutes later from the bleeding.

'I buried both of my parents by the rose bush in the back garden, and after some time I went back in the house and saw that the clansman had moved. I thought he was dead, but he had inched towards the kitchen. I saw his machete on the floor so I picked it up and looked at the long, curved blade. Then at the strange rags of the man, and saw the tiny animal trophies—teeth and feathers—he'd used to make a necklace. Then I hit the clansmen in the arm with machete. It was a strange feeling. It was like chopping wood and I had to put my foot on his body to pull out the blade. Hell, I was young. I kept hitting until my arms ached then went outside. It was evening, and cool, and only then noticed the wound in my thigh. It was about that same moment I saw Menz.' Yayle turned to smile sensitively at the older rumel, who was nodding in the dark. 'He had been fighting off a group of tribesmen in front of my house.'

'Aye. I remember it well,' Menz said. He pushed himself up off of the floor, walked to the table. Jella smiled at him, her eyes raw with sadness. He poured his cup full, patted Gabryl on his shoulder. Gabryl looked past Jella, out of the window, where there was only the night.

Menz said, 'We hadn't had much of an army for several years. We'd no need to. So I took to making weapons, mostly ornamental. Kept a little place about a five minute walk towards the centre and coast. An old lady had spotted some of the clansmen coming up the hill, and she walked, quickly, to my house to find me. Took what weapons I could and headed up the hill. Took down about three of them, but there must've been ten more that got away. Saw young Yayle there, pistol in his hand, clutching his front gate. Couldn't let the lad be, so took him under my wing. Two days later, we joined the refugees heading north to Rhoam. That was one hell of a walk. Then, over the years, we all met up, didn't we lass?'

'Yeah.' Jella nodded. 'Yes, there were more of us, too, but that's another story. I think we've bored Gabryl enough for tonight.'

Gabryl looked up. 'Why don't you hate me, then? I mean, I'm from Escha, aren't I?'

'Good question,' Jella said. 'You're helping us, so I guess that counts. Anyway, it's not the individuals we hate, it's the whole city, the whole government or whatever, the whole damn thing. They say it's people that make up a society, but that's just crap. People do what a handful at the top will say. People just get on, do their thing. They don't give a fuck about ethics and values. They just want to live. Anyway, you were chucked out. You're not an Eschan anymore. As you know, we hope to just damage the place. If people die then so be it. We have our reasons.'

Gabryl stared into his cup. 'I think I should head back to my room for the night. Drunk a lot tonight so should try and recover for the morning. Shall I meet you here around midday, and you can show me this vessel of yours?'

Jella nodded.

'Right-o. 'Night everyone.' Gabryl stood up, swayed a little. He paused as if to say something. He rested his hands on the table as he straightened up to walked to the door. Everyone wished him good night.

Jella watched him leave the room, and after he'd gone she stared at the door, and the room was painfully silent.

Sixteen

Manolin woke with the sun. He rubbed his eyes, sat up, saw that Santiago was in the doorway, leaning on a folded up pair of breeches. He was snoring, his musket on the floor, about a foot away from his reach.

Manolin stood and stretched. His body ached from lying on the wooden floor of the hut. He could hear the sound of the waves. He walked up to Santiago, nudged him with his foot. 'Hey. Wake up.'

Santiago opened his eyes.

'I thought you were on watch? That normally means keeping your eyes open.'

Santiago said, 'I was merely resting them, as they say. Anyway, I was only gone for a moment, but you chose to wake up at a very opportune time.'

'Sure. Or perhaps it's just your age getting to you?'

Santiago said, 'I'll have you know that I'm as agile as you are, and my years just bring me more experience and advantages than the rest of you.'

'Okay, okay.' Manolin patted the air. 'You're a bit sensitive at this hour. You see anything last night after me, then?'

Santiago grunted and sat up. 'Nothing. Not even sure what it is we're looking for.'

Manolin stood over him, looked outside, breathing in deeply. He could see the long shadows of the huts as the sun rose behind. The waters of the lagoon were green. Two native men pushed a boat on to the sand. 'Fine morning.'

'I rather suspect they all are here.'

'Feels like a holiday still.' Manolin stepped back to allow Santiago to stand up.

'Well, after the tour this morning, we'll get straight to work.'

'Can't wait to see the ichthyocentaurs,' Manolin said.

'Me neither. It's pretty exciting stuff. I mean, a genuine extinct species—found again. Not just any species, one that's semi-human.'

Manolin said, 'I reckon we'll be famous in Escha once we get back.'

'Can't take this excitement on an empty stomach. Wonder what they eat for breakfast round here?' Santiago brushed his hair back.

Manolin and Santiago walked along the beach towards the rest of the group, where breakfast was being served. Arth and Jefry sat with Forb on three logs facing out to sea. Yana and Becq were standing alongside a muscular native woman, who was wrapping some sort of fish between leaves.

'Morning all,' Manolin said.

'Hi, Manny,' Becq said, her eyes bright.

'This fish is good,' Yana said.

'Yes. Where doest thy go today?' the native woman said. She was wearing a rag around her waist, and her long brown hair hung to her stomach. Her jaw was square, her skin dark brown.

'I think we're going to see the ichthyocentaurs tribe,' Yana said.

'Ah, thou seemest happy. When thou sees them, thy will be.'

Manolin frowned at the native girl's strange and old speech.

Forb stood up. 'Ah, good morning, Manolin, Santiago. And what do you think of your first dawn on Arya's shores?'

'Beautiful,' Manolin said. 'Absolutely stunning.'

'It's a shame that you didn't watch the sun rise from the beach,' Forb said. 'Amazing colours, especially for this time of year.'

'Say, Forb, why does she talk like that?' He indicated the native woman.

'Yes, quaint, isn't it? Well, they were the remnants of the last age, so I've always suspected their language didn't change like ours did. There's not much to modify it. Very few things happened here to require their words to alter. Like nature, language must adapt and change, too.'

'What's on the menu?' Santiago asked.

The doctor put his arm on Manolin's shoulder and steered him back to the others. 'Depends on what you want,' he called out to Santiago. 'We've some hog left, or hare, or fish, or any number of plants from the forest.'

'Excellent,' Santiago said. 'I think hog is in order. A few strips of that'll be most welcome.'

'Hog it is.'

After breakfast, DeBrelt's crew formed a circle around Forb. Santiago stood alongside the doctor and looked at the faces of his colleagues. Only the black-skinned rumel, Arth and Jefry didn't have cheeks that were red from the sun and salt.

'Right,' the doctor said. 'The moment you've all been waiting for... the tour.'

Everyone smiled, mumbled approval.

''Bout time, too,' Jefry said. He smiled, thinking it a joke, then caught Yana's gaze just in time to see her turn away in disgust. Arth patted him on the back.

The doctor said, 'Firstly, I'd get some stout boots on. Also, you could fetch any note books you need. There's a lot to say. There's plenty of food in the forest proper. Fruit and whatnot, but we can bring some meat along, too. Wear light clothing because it's pretty humid up there—' He indicated the sprawling forest that clawed at the top of the dormant volcano. 'Now, you'll all be able to see the ichthyocentaurs, but we'll have to take you in twos. They're rather nervous these days.'

Manolin frowned.

'There was no action in the night. No deaths, so we were lucky... Are those two agents coming at all?' The doctor turned to Santiago.

Santiago shrugged. 'No idea. I'll go and see what the little buggers are up to.' He walked off into the forest.

As soon as he set foot under the canopy Santiago could feel the humidity. It took a minute for his eyes to get used to the surprising darkness after being in the sunlight on the beach. He focussed ahead, at a small hut at the end of a trail through the vegetation, walked to it. Santiago loathed these agents, resented the fact that they were here, following him. On the ship they'd acted with the usual tough guy mannerisms, the set jaws, sideways glances, the precision silences. In the right bars you'd see men like that in Escha all the time, huddled away from doors, talking only with themselves in steep lighting, shaded hats, as if the rest of the population was an inconvenience to their image. They'd look at you sideways, with an expression somewhere between suspicion and disdain. You knew better than to interfere with looks like that. He understood their serious talk, the posturing. Gio seemed to have a hundred of them keeping him in power, but that was because he had the money to. Santiago knew that was why he'd always fail—his principles, all that he stood for would ensure he never had such a power. So he'd spent a slice of his life dealing with these agent types. To be on an island with them bothered him so much more, because they had no right nor use to be here.

Insects sprang across his face. The sound of the sea became muffled, the nearer he got to the hut, as if he were in the middle of a rainforest, not at all on an island. Above the hut, he could see sparks of colour and calling sounds that he did not recognise, as birds fled his footsteps. He approached the hut, knocked on the door. There was no answer. He put his ear to the wood, could hear a strange sound, muffled voices—a constant fizz, not unlike the sea. Listening for some time, he deduced the sound was constant. He knocked again, wafting his shirt to escape the humidity. Dappled sunlight burst through the canopy. A small bird sat on the roof of the hut. It was bright red, with yellow streaks on its face that made it look like it wore a mask. It had a curved beak and an elegant tail, which unfurled over the edge of the hut.

There was a noise from within the hut and Santiago thumped on the door again, calling out this time. 'I say, are you two coming out of there, or not? We're about to tour the island, and thought you ought to come along.' Then he said, 'Not, of course, that any of us want you.' He pushed the door back, noticing that it didn't have a catch, peered in.

Inside, was dark, but he saw Mr Calyban and Mr Soul hunched in the corner. There was a clear sound of static.

Santiago said, 'What are you two doing?'

Calyban and Soul looked up, startled.

Santiago could see that they were leaning over a small box, with brass dials on top. 'What's that?'

'It's none of your business, DeBrelt.' They stood up to usher him out.

'What is it?'

'It's not your concern.'

'That's a relic, isn't it? What's it for?'

'It's not a relic.'

'Yes it is, you've brought that with you. What's it do?' Santiago stepped in the doorway, pushed the door fully open.

Calyban and Soul stood shoulder to shoulder, arms folded, in front of Santiago. 'Mr DeBrelt, kindly leave now. We'll follow you in a moment on this tour thing. Get out.'

Santiago looked from Calyban to Soul and back, several times. The moment stretched in time. Before he left he glanced at the device one last time, slammed the door behind him as he stepped out and he saw the red of the bird flash as it flew from the roof into the forest.

'They have a relic,' Santiago whispered to Manolin as they pushed forward into the forest. Forb was up ahead, leading them on a gradual ascent.

'A what?' Manolin said.

'A relic.'

'Do they know how to use it?'

'I guess so. They must've worked something out back in the city.' Santiago wiped his brow.

'What's it do?'

'No idea.'

'How d'you know it is one?'

'I can tell. It isn't any technology I've seen.' Santiago pouted thoughtfully, nodded.

'A relic, indeed...' Manolin said.

'Yes. Heavens, man. Your mind must be on that woman still.'

'Shush, keep your voice down. I don't want him hearing, do I?' Manolin indicated the doctor, who was leading the group.

Santiago said, 'Anyway, yes, they're up to something.'

'Come on, you must have an idea what it does? Did you get a good look?' Manolin said.

'I'm not sure,' Santiago said. 'I reckon it may be something for communication, which means that there must be at least another such unit, probably back with Gio or somewhere out at sea.'

Manolin grunted, stepping over a tree root. He and Santiago followed Forb, who seemed to skip up the slope and over the foliage with the agility of a deer. Becq and Yana followed, and Arth and Jefry were behind them. The two agents brought up the rear end of the group.

The heat crept up like a predator, catching the foreigners unprepared by mid-morning. They plodded through the forest, their shirts becoming damp with sweat. Manolin could see the perspiration on the doctor's head.

Forb explained that they were at the foot of the volcano. Their ascent to the ichthyocentaurs would take about a two hours' hike, but it became cooler as the forest was less dense and a fresh onshore breeze was received with open arms, open shirts. In shaded paths were butterflies, the bright colours a sharp contrast to the forest. More birds added to the variety—species they'd never seen. Sounds became intense the higher you climbed.

Forb pointed out some of the flora and fauna. When they were deeper in the forest, Manolin followed the doctor's extended arm and finger to a hog.

'Do you catch them often?' Manolin asked, leaning back with his hands on his hips, drawing in deep breaths.

'Yes. Every couple of weeks we have a hunt. The next one is tomorrow, which you're more than welcome to join. Hog is a good source of meat. Tasty, compared to fish. Only once every now and again. All things in moderation.'

After an hour, at a point where the volcano was exposed, they came across a bright clearing, and the horizon could be seen from a significant height. Manolin gasped as he approached the edge and you could see all they way down to the lagoon. The wind ruffled his hair pleasantly, cooling the sweat. The sun was overhead, and you he looked right up, you could see the edge of the volcano towering.

He turned to face the sea once again and noticed, as Forb joined him, a large patch of bright green in the sea.

'Ah, you've spotted the reef, Manolin. Excellent.' Forb turned to the others. 'Come and have a look at this view. It offers a perfect aspect of the reef.'

The travellers gathered, caught their breath. In one long line, they stood in the clearing, looking down the slope to the reef. Manolin saw Santiago smile

The reef extended for a good half a mile, then faded beneath the deeper waters. There were patches of sand, here and there, where the reef was more stable, and in the distance, you could see the edges of another island. Even Mr Calyban and Mr Soul seemed impressed, nodding approval to one another.

'Are those the other islands then, Forb?' Santiago asked.

'Yes. That's Samekh, about ten miles away,' the doctor said. 'It's much smaller than Arya. There are two others that extend the chain beyond. We don't ever go there.'

'Why not?' Santiago asked.

Forb turned and looked at Santiago, smoothing the sweat off of his bald head. 'There's nothing of interest there. We don't go there.' The doctor walked away from the group, into the forest.

Yana turned, stepping back behind a bush. The others looked on as she hunched double, with her hands on her knees, her pack almost tipping over her head, and she vomited behind the bush.

She coughed twice, emptying her stomach, as Jefry ran over to her.

'Yana, dear, is everything okay?' the rumel said. 'You all right?'

She waved him off and stood up, wiping her mouth on a leaf. 'I'm fine, I'm fine. It's probably something I ate.' She reached for her pack, pulled out a water bottle. She took a sip and wiped her mouth, placed the bottle back, then walked into the forest. Jefry simply watched her enter the shade of the trees again, and turned to the others, a look of helplessness on his face.

Santiago wore a frown and turned to Becq. 'She had the same fish as you earlier. Are you feeling okay?' He placed a hand on the girl's damp shoulder.

'Yes, absolutely fine. A little out of breath, but fine.' She smiled at her father, then glanced over to Manolin, who turned away to walk after Yana and the doctor.

Becq looked on as the others continued. She dragged her heels a little. Maybe it was the heat, maybe not entirely.

She wasn't having a particularly good expedition so far. This was the worst to date.

Was it too much to ask for him to even acknowledge her presence? She would admit that she wasn't the prettiest of girls. Her mother was pretty, but had died when she was three years old. She thought that might have made her close with her father, but work was always his first love.

One day he had brought home a promising young student for supper: Manolin. He had ignored her from that first day, where she spent the evening watching him talk to her father. Then she waited by as he married a waitress from the place where her father had taken them all for a night out, a time to celebrate.

Manolin was the type of man that looked as though he needed looking after. Needed a good meal and a wash, and for some reason— and Arrahd knew from her prayers she wanted to be an independent woman—she felt she wanted to care for him, to pamper him, to provide for him. He had the kind of hair that she wanted to ruffle. Deep down she knew she had only the doll. The only way to get closer to him was to follow in her father's footsteps, to study nature.

Don't start thinking like that, Becq DeBrelt, she thought. *You're here because you want to be, not because of a man who barely looks at you. At least he's single now, I can work on him. I just need to be patient. On this island, we've all the time in the world. Just wait it out.*

An hour later, DeBrelt's crew were three-quarters of the way up the volcano. There were some pleasant moments where they walked in parts of the forest that stood under the shade of the volcano. Vines hung down. The vegetation crowded them. Clear shafts of light burst through the canopy, casting illumination on clouds of insects, on bright flowers. Manolin's alert vision noted many species of spiders, which, as Forb explained, were probably the first species to pioneer the volcanic islands, being able to weave gossamer balloons to carry them to each of the islands along the fringes of the reef. Manolin dreamt scenes of squadrons of spiders all flying to invade the archipelago, to have a crack at setting up home again, somewhere far off.

Everyone was tired, dehydrated, drenched in sweat. It took them several seconds to come to a halt by Forb's extended arm. The bald man was peering into the forest, his neck stretched.

Manolin stood alongside the doctor. 'What is it? What's wrong?'

Forb was silent. His eyes flickered from tree to tree as a bead of sweat ran over one of them. He rubbed it clear and turned to Manolin. 'Hear that?'

Manolin turned to the forest and back. 'Hear what?'

'That drone.'

'No. I can't hear a thing over those birds.'

Santiago approached, taking long steps. 'What's the matter?'

'Drone bee,' Forb said.

'Oh, well, a bee isn't going to be much harm is it?' Santiago said. He brushed down his moustache.

Forb took his pack off of his shoulder, opened it and pulled out a folded-up blanket. 'Here—quick.'

'What's this for?' Manolin asked.

'Just unroll it and take the other end.' Forb flicked the blanket to unravel. 'Everyone, get under this.'

'What the hell for?' Mr Calyban shouted from behind.

'This is most uncalled for,' Mr Soul said.

'Just get under, now.' The doctor and Manolin held the blanket up for everyone to crawl under. The agents went under first, sighing, then the others followed. Manolin lowered his end and the blanket touched the ground, the travellers underneath. Manolin joined the doctor and sat crossed-legged, with Santiago at his shoulder. Everyone seemed too tired to speak, or disagree.

Manolin nudged Forb. 'Is this necess—?'

As soon as he spoke he heard the deep drone that seemed to come from everywhere at once. Then, Forb pulled the blanket over their heads.

'What's that noise?' Soul said.

'Quiet,' Forb said.

Manolin stared through the gaps in the fabric. The drone became louder and the vegetation rattled ahead, could feel his heart beat high in his chest as the large black shapes moved into vision, then could see them break the light, shift leaves and vines. The shapes hovered a few feet off of the ground and Manolin guessed them to be about a foot long. The large shadows glided, loudly, and he stifled a squeal as the shapes passed overhead. They flew in twos, achingly slow, passing like airships over their heads, casting thick shadows over the blanket.

After a couple of minutes, when the sound had gone, Forb lifted the blanket. Everyone spilled out, gasping at the fresher air.

'Now, sir,' Santiago said. 'What where those exactly?'. He wiped his brow, stared into the forest after the sound.

'Drone bees,' Forb said.

'Bees?' Santiago asked.

'Bees,' Forb said.

'But they were huge,' Manolin said. 'A foot long, at least, and I lost count of how many there were. They can't be bees—they're too big to be able to fly. I mean, their wings wouldn't be able to lift them.'

'Ah, but according to theory, the ordinary bee shouldn't be able to fly anyway,' Forb said. He wrapped up the blanket, placed it in his pack.

Manolin and Santiago looked at each other before staring back at the group. Everyone regarded the darker forest.

'Don't worry,' Forb said. 'They'll not be back. They're not normally out this late in the year.'

'Where's the nest, and the queen?' Santiago asked. 'Surely they should have a nest and a queen. Where is it?'

The doctor stood under a shaft of light and waved the others over. Then he pointed upwards, through the trees, at the volcano that stood silent and large over the island. With the gentlest of smiles, he said, 'Seen the queen once, only once. Not sure I'll try again.'

'By Arrahd's balls,' Jefry said.

'I'll second that,' Arth said.

'I'll third it,' Santiago said. 'What flowers do they use?'

'Some of the other islands have larger flowers. A foot long petals in places. The bees live here though. It must be safer for them.'

Manolin took a notebook out of his pocket, began writing scribbling notes. The doctor patted Manolin on the shoulder. 'You remind me of me when I was younger,' he said. Then he walked further into the forest.

The doctor stopped the group, who were now walking in a single line along the shaded path. Manolin had noticed that the trail had become well-trodden and wide. Vegetation had been cut away, and in the distance there was a wide patch of light. He could hear clicks, too, and looked around the canopy to find what he assumed to be a bird. He waved Arth forward. 'Hey, Arth. What bird do you make that to be?'

Arth bounded keenly towards Manolin, stood beside him, glancing, wide-eyed, from tree to tree. 'That's no bird, Manny. At least, not one that I've heard.'

Manolin said, 'You sure?'

'Pretty positive. It's too guttural for a bird.' Arth's black tail moved from side to side.

'Arth's right,' Forb said, with a smile. 'That isn't a bird. It's what you've all been waiting for. From here on, I'll have to take you two at a time. Manolin, Santiago, shall we?'

The men nodded. Mr Calyban and Soul grunted disproval.

'Good,' Forb said with a glance towards the government agents. 'I suggest the rest of you sit down for a few minutes, relax, enjoy the forest. There's fruit from those trees—' He indicated a cluster of dark-leaved trees behind them, with small, yellow globes hanging in bunches. 'We have to go in twos so the tribe will accept you. Don't move from here, I'll come and find you.'

He ushered Manolin and Santiago forward along the path.

The rest sat down, one by one, grunting as they hit the dry forest floor. The wind was stronger, some way up the volcano, and the refreshing breeze filtered though the forest sounding like the tide.

'I don't see why we can't go first,' Mr Soul said to his colleague.

'Hey, we'll all get to go at some point,' Arth said. 'Let's just calm it down and stay cool.'

'Yeah, so just relax,' Jefry said.

'I really don't think you should talk to us like that,' Mr Calyban said. His eyes rested on Jefry, casually, as if he was a tree.

'There's not enough room on this island for your attitude,' Jefry said. He brushed his mop of white hair away from his forehead. 'We're all here for a job, so let's do it.'

'We're here to watch you people, not any ridiculous tribe,' Mr Soul said.

That maybe so,' Jefry said. 'But I wouldn't be so rude all—'

'Jef, they're not going to shut up so let's just keep it quiet, okay. I'm not feeling too good,' Yana said. She slid back against a tree. Then she reclined, reached in her pack for some water, poured a few cool drops over her scalp.

Jefry said, 'Sorry, Yana.'

'That's okay I just want to relax a bit, that's all.' She smiled before closing her eyes as she poured more water on her face.

Jefry was relieved when he saw her smile. He watched Becq move in a little closer, place her hand on Yana's shoulder.

'Are you sure you're okay,' Becq asked, crouching. 'It's not the food is it? I had the same thing and I'm fine.'

'Sure, just a little sick that's all. I'll be fine. Probably not used to all this walking.'

'Me neither,' Becq said. 'Just so long as you're all right.'

'Hey, I said I'm fine,' Yana said. Then, 'But thanks for worrying.'

Jefry stared his wife as if he were at school, watching a girl, one he had a crush on but could never talk to. That was no way to look at his wife. He couldn't put his finger on the point when he'd begun to view her from such a distance. Two years, maybe three. He knew of several couples his own age, and some of the husbands had even confided in him that they, themselves, had not made love to their wives for months. That made him feel better. He knew the problems of a human-rumel marriage, too. He knew the only children he would have would be infertile, just like a mule. Maybe that was what was wrong, that she wanted a long family tradition. Then he remembered her dedication to work.

She was a geologist at heart, and it was something she would complete her life. She had said it herself—and that was a reason he fell in love with her. It didn't help her being more intellectual than him. She was the bright one, and she certainly made sure he knew it. He was a chemist, and helped the others when they needed his skills. The others did all the glorious work, bringing new species back, finding new gemstones and other precious finds. He played with test-tubes, measuring liquids, telling them combinations of this and that. It wasn't glamorous. It certainly wasn't alluring. He was useful, but not exciting in both his marriage and his work.

He sighed, again, looking at her hair blow in the breeze. Her face tilted back, the moisture from the water she had poured glistened. He still thought her beautiful.

Manolin shaded his eyes from the sun, as they stepped near the clearing, so he could take in the scene. Arranged in a layered circle were numerous huts, about fifty, he guessed, and the soil was light, dry, almost a sand. Charred leaves indicated the vegetation had been burned back. Then he shook his head in disbelief, he saw what they had been looking for: ichthyocentaur, and dozens off them. His mouth fell open to say something, then decided against it. Forb stepped aside, allowing Manolin and Santiago the full view. The ichthyocentaurs were as tall as a man, and as grey as some rumel were, but they possessed stubby tails, such as on dolphins. Their faces were strange, broad, although eerily human.

A large group of them turned simultaneously to face the newcomers.

Manolin looked towards Santiago as each man sought to find any words to describe what they were seeing. They could hear staccato clicking. Forb stepped forward, moving his arms and hands through the air. To Manolin and Santiago's surprise, the ichthyocentaur began doing the same, and just as they did, the clicking ceased.

Forb turned and waved an arm to beckon the strangers forward. 'Come on, Santiago, Manolin. Come over.'

They walked towards the doctor, out of the shaded forest, out into the intense sun that beat the clearing as if someone had opened a furnace. Manolin looked around, counted dozens of these creatures, naked, staring, clicking. He could see the doctor signalling with his hands as they approached and two tall ichthyocentaur came towards him.

'Well I'll be,' Santiago whispered to Manolin. 'Look, he's signing to them.'

'Really? Thanks for that,' Manolin said.

Santiago looked at Manolin for a moment, then nodded.

Forb broke the silence. 'I've introduced you to them. I've told them you're from other shores and that they have no need to fear you. That you're hear to help.'

'Splendid,' Santiago said. 'They're interesting creatures, aren't they?'

'Forb, how do I sign "hello" to them?' Manolin said.

'I'm glad you asked. Look—' Forb indicated a circular motion with his right hand, whilst keeping his left palm facing upwards.

Manolin repeated the gesture, making eye contact with one of the two ichthyocentaur, and smiled. He thought if all else failed, the smile should break down barriers. He noticed that they possessed small, gill-like flaps on their sides. His vision drifted down, and noticed the penis that gave away their sex, and that their legs he would have normally expected to find on a horse, or a lion.

The two creatures repeated the sign back, his smile widened. He turned in a circle, repeating the gesture to all the tribe collectively. Some of them replied. Forb laughed, patting Manolin on the shoulder. Then, he signed to the two creatures standing next to him and they turned, allowing Manolin and Santiago to see the full torso from behind. There was a tiny fin on each of their backs. They did not walk at all awkwardly, which Manolin thought they would.

The clearing was on a slope that he suspected was the gentlest section up to the volcano, which he could see large and clear to his left. There was forest surrounding the settlement, and the huts were made of bamboo, of woven palm leaves. It was achingly hot. Ferns littered the floor near his feet. Butterflies flipped behind huts whilst bright birds examined him from above. Everyone was silent for sometime, although it was not uncomfortable, as if each of the men knew that they were simply taking in details.

Manolin watched the tribe at work. They were still building their new settlement, after being relocated from the shore. They moved with precise, graceful motions. They were communal, too, gathering in large groups, generating those audible clicks, which he had discovered were their own form of communication. On one side of the settlement, women were hauling large quantities of plant matter. 'Forb, what's over there?'

'Keen eye, I see,' the doctor said. 'Well, that's where they store plants.'

'Can I have a look?'

'Yes,' Santiago said. 'That'd be good to see what they're storing.'

'Okay,' Forb said. 'But be careful there. They're extremely protective about plants here.'

They approached a large building that was made from the same bamboo and palm leaves as nearly everything else. It was twenty feet long and dwarfed the other buildings in the settlement. The three men approached a female ichthyocentaur, who signed a greeting to Forb. Manolin signed *hello* to her and she returned the greeting, with a look of puzzlement on her face.

Forb signed something which he translated to the others as, *They have come to help with the deaths. They have come to try and stop the deaths. I am touring them here. Okay to enter?*

Yes, she signed back.

Manolin looked at her legs, which were horse-like too. She had small breasts, long black hair that was tied back. Her skin was grey.

'We're all right to go in now,' Forb said.

They stepped into the darkness of the hut and Manolin noticed the immediate musky smell. Once their eyes became accustomed to the change in light, they could see the hundreds of bundles of plants, shelves on one side, with short, sealed bamboo tubes, and on them were etchings that he did not recognise. In another corner were large bundles of leaves in netting, and everything was organised in neat rows. The female ichthyocentaur cast a shadow in the doorway as she looked in. Manolin turned to her and smiled. She stepped inside. Santiago walked around the room, cautiously, being careful not to tread on any of the bundles. He knelt quickly by a sack of bulbs and one of bark chippings.

'Everything here is categorised by usage,' Forb said, wiping his head of sweat. 'Each of the bamboo samples on the shelves contains relief from all sorts of medical problems, from headache to depression, anaesthetic to hallucinogenic powders. Very potent of an evening, I assure you. They even have plant extracts to test for pregnancy.'

'By Arrahd,' Manolin said. The female ichthyocentaur came up close to him and stared intensely at him. He grinned at her again and she stepped back. He noticed that there were several ichthyocentaurs gathered outside of the hut, and he could hear their clicking noises as they chatted amongst themselves.

'Pregnancy?' Santiago asked. 'Well I never. How does it work?'

'Simple,' Forb said. 'Take the powder in the tube, and a sprinkle to the urine sample, shake it around. Then, heat it and add a little more of another extract, and do the same. There's some light-coloured bark chippings in a jar next to it and dip it in. When the back soaks it up, if it contains red streaks, there you have it—she'll be dropping children.'

'Amazing,' Santiago said. 'I'd like to see it in action.'

'Unless you know of a likely lady, there's not much point'

'Still, I'd like to see the processes. Could we borrow some? I'd like to see some of the other things in action, too. Something with a bit of a kick in it.'

Manolin said, 'We can't take their stuff without permission. It's pretty rude.'

Santiago glanced at Manolin, then the doctor. 'I'm sure it will be all right, won't it, Forb?'

Forb said, 'Well, I'll ask them.'

'Splendid,' Santiago said.

'Anyway, we should be bringing some of the others in now. We've already been here ten minutes.' Forb turned away and left the hut, the female ichthyocentaur trotting after him.

Manolin saw another of the creatures run up to the doctor, and it was carrying a cluster of some herb. It was too far away to see properly. Then they went out of sight.

Evening came suddenly, as it always did. Most of the travellers sat on the rim of the lagoon, allowing their feet to be refreshed by the cool waters. Manolin was sitting with Forb and Myranda on the edge of the lagoon, which was calm and still, and a breeze came from left to right, rippling the palm leaves behind. Myranda was wearing only a ragged brown skirt, and when she sat cross legged Manolin had to force his eyes away for politeness. She had finished giving another brief art lesson to the children. She seemed in a happy mood.

Manolin talked with Forb about the island, about the ichthyocentaurs. He was keen to learn about their histories, or as much as Forb knew. Forb did not know their origins, only that they had been there for as long as anyone knew. They had catalogued every plant on the island, even some of the other islands in the chain, but they dared not swim anywhere except a lagoon on the south coast of Arya in recent years. They had no political structure to speak of, much like the natives. Just a council of the older ichthyocentaur, and it was they who decided, after discussing some options with Forb, that they should stay away from the coast at night. That was when the deaths occurred. They were allowed to swim at selected times, and some native humans stood guard with blow-darts, bows and arrows, sharpened bamboo spears. They had survived for so long on the island, Forb assumed, because of the way they harvested and utilised plants. This was something Manolin was especially interested in. He told Forb about his keen interest ethnobotany—how tribal communities used plants in culture. That, too, was one of Forb's reasons for coming to Arya to study. 'I will show you my notebooks,' he said. 'I've an immense collection of data.'

Myranda was quiet whilst her partner and Manolin talked. At one point she had walked off, returned with some shells. She handed one to Manolin, who accepted it with overwhelming gratuity. Forb glanced between the two and seemed content, then he told Manolin about her background, steering the subject to what Manolin was concerned he was being too obvious about. Although Forb found her alluring, to say the least, Myranda was considered ugly by Arya's standards. True beauty on Arya consisted of two things: large thighs and sharp teeth. A large thigh was rare, and showed that the woman was healthy and virile. Sharp teeth were handy for cutting vine and making rope. If a man had the two in a woman, he had much to be proud of. So Myranda, much to Forb's delight, was not sought after. She was as sleek as a ray, just as graceful. On the mainland she could have found work as a high-class model or escort, and made her fortune in either. Forb knew it, and so did Manolin. Her mother had died during childbirth, her father only two years ago. She had no siblings. Forb found her charming, kind and beautiful. It was a matter of weeks before he had wed her in the local tradition. Forb had also taught her the dialect of the mainland, so her voice was satisfying no matter what she said.

Myranda and Forb's son, Lewys, approached once again. The young lad wore just a pair of breeches that came to just below his knee, and a shell necklace. His black hair was scruffy, quivered in the wind.

'Hello, Lewys,' Forb said.

The boy said, 'Hello.'

'You've met Manolin, haven't you?'

'I haven't, father. Hello, Manolin.' Lewys walked up to Manolin. The boy offered his hand in such a gentlemanly manner that Manolin chuckled.

'Hello, Lewys. Pleased to meet you.' He shook the boy's hand.

'Manolin's a nice name.'

'Thanks,' Manolin said. 'It's a lovely home you've got here. You've the beach and the forests to play with. It's so calm and peaceful, too.'

Lewys said, 'It's okay, I guess. Not many other kids that I like playing with though.'

'Lewys is quite an independent boy. He likes keeping himself to himself. He reads a lot of my books that I brought with me. I had nearly two hundred, and he's half way through them.' Forb ruffled the boy's hair.

'A boy after my own heart,' Manolin said. 'You remind me of when I was your age. Still, we can play a game of something tomorrow if you want, before the hunt.'

The boy looked at Manolin with keen eyes, nodded, curling up one side of his mouth in a smile that was like his fathers. He also had his mother's feminine looks.

Manolin said, 'And maybe you could show me some of your favourite books, too.'

'Yes, I'd like that,' Lewys said. 'I could teach you to surf if you want.'

Manolin frowned. 'Surf?'

'Yes, like father. He could teach you with me.'

Forb glanced at Manolin, raising one eyebrow. 'He's good,' he said.

'Why not,' Manolin said. He gave a shrug and a laugh. A bright bird came out of the forest and sailed above the beach.

'Good,' Lewys said. 'I'm going to find some books to show you tomorrow morning.' And with that, the boy ran along the beach, weaving in zigzags before disappearing into the settlement.

'I see that both Myranda and Lewys speak like you, like on the mainland,' Manolin said, watching the boy go.

'Yes, yes. I think I'd go mad if these two didn't speak like me.' Forb touched Myranda's arm as she looked out to sea. 'It was inevitable that the boy would, and Myranda is pretty smart. That's why she's the teacher here. She occasionally slips back to the traditional form every now and again, but I just ignore her.' Myranda turned in a mock-offended manner, pouting her thick lips, before smiling at both of the men.

Manolin thought her profile irresistible. *Stop it! This is ridiculous. She's not yours.*

The three of them watched the sun pass over, and the thin trails of clouds that tried to cover it, but failing. It was a pleasant temperature, with the wind cool, steady. The air was filled with pungency as certain species of trees opened up to breathe. Soon the natives would be cooking fish.

Manolin looked over to the rest of his group, feeling that they were further away than he remembered. For some reason he couldn't identify, he was uninterested in how they were, or what they felt of the island. Santiago pulled Yana up off of the sand, and the two of them walked further up the shore, past the lagoon and the native settlements. They did not seem intimate in any way, nor did they seem to be arguing. Manolin wondered what they were up to. Minutes later they came back, walking several feet apart in the sand, each apparently in their own thoughts. Santiago walked to the raft, paddled out to the hut.

Then, as Manolin looked back out to sea, after supper, and after Forb and Myranda had bid him good night, his mind fluttered across a thousand ideas, as he imagined it would, given such an expanse in front of him. He sighed, tipped his head back as the usual concerns spilled into his mind like a giant wave. Maybe Myranda provoked the thoughts. Maybe it was the isolation, which forced him to think about it. It was probably both. He knew, from other journeys, that there was something about isolation that at first made you panic as you were forced to face your thoughts of life.

Santiago managed to corner the doctor before he had retired into his hut. DeBrelt had been drinking a couple of glasses of rum, which he had brought from the boat in his luggage.

'Doc, won't you have a drink?' Santiago held up a beaker.

Forb was with Myranda, on the foot of his hut. He nodded to Myranda who walked inside. Forb looked to Santiago, whose eyes followed her in.

'Santiago,' Forb said. 'Looks like you've drunk most of it.'

'Chance'd be a fine thing. So, take a pew, let's chat.'

They both sat down on the sand together. 'What's on your mind?'

'Nothing and everything. The usual,' Santiago said. 'Lovely evenings, you have here.'

'Yes, and mornings and afternoons. Very pleasing.'

'Indeed. Lovely wife, too.'

'Yes. I love her, dearly.'

'Quite a perfect little set up, you have here,' Santiago said.

'Yes.' Forb looked at Santiago carefully. The man was staring out to sea. 'Many a man could be jealous of this.'

'Me for one,' Santiago said.

Forb assumed he would be. 'Why so?'

Santiago said, 'Well, you've everything. You've nothing to worry about.'

'True. I've had too much to worry about in my life. Done too much on the mainland. Wanted to get away, and this is what I've got. Can't argue with this place.'

'Indeed.'

'So, why would you be jealous, Santiago? You don't seem to be a man who would be.' It was at this point that Forb wondered if Santiago would actually offer him any rum, but it wasn't important.

'Ha. I'm not really. Well, yes I am actually.'

'Why?' Forb said. 'You've a good team, although I noticed a bit of tension between you and Manolin.'

'Yes, yes. Well, boy's got a good future ahead of him. He just gets excited when on trips.'

'Futures. Forgot what those were,' Forb said, smiling. 'Done all I need to, you see.'

Santiago grunted something.

'Tell me,' Forb said. 'I never came across any of your research when I was on the mainland. I would've thought at some point our paths would've crossed sooner.'

'Well, you see I never had the chance that young Manny has these days. When I did my research, I couldn't publish it.'

'Really?' Forb said. He crossed his legs, sat up straight. He was always keen to discuss matters of science, and found Santiago intriguing, highly intelligent. A man that held secrets, knowledge, respect.

Santiago stared out to sea. 'When I was studying for my Doctorate, I discovered some very unpleasant things about the government. They were polluting in such a strange way that the public never knew about. Their industry was affecting waters and air in *very* odd ways, and my research would've made this public knowledge. Of course, the government would only allow my Doctorate if I gave way and researched down a different line. Basically, I couldn't win. I'm a man of principle. You know, if I'd been allowed to publish my work, I'd have been a legend.'

'What did you do?'

'The only thing I could—I refused my Doctorate.'

'So, you're not a Doctor of Science?'

'In all but name,' Santiago said.

The doctor slapped Santiago on the shoulder. 'That's not important.

You did a very admirable thing. We must talk more about this research. I'd like to know more.' He stood up. 'I really must get some rest though. It's been a busy day. I'm not used to giving tours.'

Santiago stared out to sea. Forb patted him on the shoulder once again, and walked back to his hut. As he walked in he thought he heard Santiago say, 'I could've been a legend.'

Santiago was still sitting on the sand, the breeze on his face as he stared towards nothing in particular. Forb never realised just how much the foreigners looked out to sea since they had arrived. They weren't reading it, like he did, for signs. They seemed to stare longingly, as if the sea itself affected their thoughts, as if it could change them. But he realised that the sea did indeed do that, if you weren't used to it. Even if you were, it seemed a motivation for change. It had the raw power to penetrate the mind. It felt strange, having these people here, on Arya. He was glad of their company, but he had not been amongst his own people for so long that they no longer felt real to him. Except Manolin. There was something about the young man that Forb admired deeply—a quality that suggested he wanted to know about the natural world so badly that he could almost stand in the forest perfectly still and allow lichen and moss to cover him. An interesting young man.

Yana sat down next to him on the sand and regarded the dark lagoon. 'Hey.'

'Hi.'

She said, 'Stuff on your mind?'

The moon had arced noticeably in the sky. She felt sad for him, but not surprised. She had comforted him on the journey to Arya, but knew that scars like those never really left a man, that men didn't forget things like that. A woman might have to, of course, but this wasn't a night for her concerns.

'You know, this could be quite romantic, given the right couple,' Yana said.

Manolin turned, laughed. 'What a waste.' Then, 'So things not good between you and Jef?'

Yana said, 'Course not. They haven't been good for a long time. It's been over for months as far as I'm concerned.'

'What made you realise it was over?'

She paused to think, searched her mind for the moment that lingered in her memory. 'One day, we were just sitting there in one of the harbour inns. It was raining, so we went in and had a bite to eat and a woman walked by. She wasn't much. Petite, a little younger, but

I saw Jefry's eyes follow her across the room and out the door. I could cope with that. Then, two rumel friends of his—not close ones—passed by and he stood up and talked to them for several minutes, whilst I just sat and ate, and he didn't introduce them to me.

'In the evening, I felt I needed to be wanted, so I dressed up in some nice, silk underwear, and when I went in the room he was fast asleep. He didn't even say he was going. I put some clothes on and went out. I went to some new city bars on my own. Don't know what for. I was dressed up and needed to go, I guess. Guys came up to me—me, a woman of my age. They bought me drinks, made me laugh. I felt desired. You have no idea how long it'd been, Manolin. I didn't do anything that night. I went home, and in bed I just hoped he'd but his arm around me, or even his tail, but nothing. One day, and that was it. I don't expect flowers or perfume or anything like that. Just a genuine smile and a look to know you're wanted, that would've done.'

Manolin nodded, by didn't look her in the eye. He was still entranced by the surf. Yana wondered if he felt her pain, having been in a similarly situation. Was this young man capable of focussing on her, not his own thoughts? But out here, away from Escha, it didn't seem to matter so much. Her problems weren't trivialised, more put into a wider perspective.

She stood up and the wind threw back her hair, and she could hear the palms behind her shaking. She brushed sand from her clothes.

Manolin stood up to join her. 'We should be getting back. Who's on lookout tonight?'

'Santiago and Arth are. I don't know what they're exactly looking out for though.'

'Me neither. There haven't been any ichthyocentaurs killed for a while now, from what Forb says.'

Yana said, 'You're getting on well with him, aren't you?'

'Yeah. We think alike, you know?'

'Yes. You both like the same things in a woman.' Yana smiled.

'That's not what I meant,' Manolin said, smirking. 'Is it that obvious? She's pretty, but I'm not up for any of that. No, Forb's a good man. He seems a bit odd though.'

'How do you mean?'

Manolin said, 'He doesn't open up much. I just assumed being back to nature like this, it'd make someone quite, well, philosophical. Sensual. I don't know, he doesn't say too much about himself. He's pretty mysterious.' He could feel the spray from the water, high in the wind, and along the beach to the settlement, he could see shadows of humans entering huts.

Yana did not reply. She held her hair back from the wind, gazing out into the black. 'Okay, let's get back. We've got the hunt tomorrow. Another busy one.'

'Should be interesting at least.'

Santiago gave Manolin a hand up out of the small raft and into the hut. It was totally dark, and Santiago clutched a musket in his other hand as Manolin stepped by him inside.

'Thanks,' Manolin said, then sat on his bedding. He could smell the intense fragrances from the forest, the salt in the air. 'See anything, San?' Then, 'You been drinking again? Arrahd, I can smell it on your breath.'

'Hmm,' Santiago said, staring out into the darkness over the sea. 'I think so, well, not really *seeing* as such, just *hearing*. And only a small glass of rum, nothing much.'

Manolin shrugged. 'What d'you hear?'

'If I didn't know better, I'd say I heard a song.'

'A song?'

'A song. Rather, a gentle melody. Like a woman singing, then harmonies. It was almost soothing, if it wasn't so damn eerie.'

Manolin sat up, the blankets around his legs to keep of any chill. 'It's probably the wind. Or your imagination, it's eerie out there.' Manolin stood up and walked to the door. He looked to where the volcano was now a shadow, and he could see tiny flames near the ichthyocentaurs' settlement. They moved around like sparks from a fire, but slowly. Then, he too heard the sound, that soothing song. 'I think I can hear it too, you know. Do you think it's coming from the settlement?'

Then the sound stopped.

'No,' Santiago said. 'The wind would've taken it away. This is coming from out at sea. I've been watching the ichthyocentaurs and whenever I can hear the sound, I can see their flames. It's been happening on and off for the last three hours.'

Manolin said, 'Do you think the disappearances are related to the sound? Suicide?'

'Not suicide, no. Forb had said that the bodies were torn open.'

'Oh yeah, I remember,' Manolin said. 'But the sound?'

'Possibly. It's too hard to tell. They've been moved up there to stop them being killed, and it seems to have worked for now, but they seem busy with those flames.'

Manolin watched the tiny fires spark in and out of darkness when concealed by the forest. 'What do you propose then? We've got the hunt tomorrow, and a fairly big island profile to start work on.'

'Well, I guess if whatever happens occurs at night, we should bring an ichthyocentaur down and watch the fellow.'

'You mean bait?' Manolin said.

'If you put it like that, yes,' Santiago said.

Manolin said, 'You can't do that.'

'We'll keep an eye out. Plus we'll have muskets and pistols. He'll be quite all right, I can assure you.'

'Well, I don't think it's ethical.'

'Ethical, indeed. We're here to investigate, Manolin, not ponce around on holiday. And I don't want anyone mixing with the natives too much, all right? I'd prefer it if we kept ourselves to ourselves. I don't want anyone getting too attached, nor do I want anyone catching some disease.'

Manolin was silent, walked to his bedding again.

'What did Yana have to say?' Santiago said.

'I'm sorry?'

'Yana. What were you two chatting about on the beach?'

Manolin said, 'Oh. Nothing.'

Seventeen

Santiago lit his freshly rolled cigarette, and the wind took one of the loose leaves from the pack in his front pocket. The paper skimmed along the bright sand, raced along the edge of the sea, missing the foam, then up towards the native village, where Manolin and the doctor's son were playing catch. Then, it hung in the air, gliding between the two. The boy seemed happy, and despite the strong breeze, Santiago could hear him laugh. Out at sea fishermen were rowing back with nets that were full from the evening. Along the green water of the lagoon, you could see the shadows of quick-flying birds.

It was early and he had just had a swim in the lagoon before preparing for the hunt, which was an hour away. Despite being early, it was hot, but not uncomfortable, and the wind, he hoped, would be a benefit later in the day. The others were making their way to the native village for breakfast. He walked up the beach, could see Becq standing a few feet behind Manolin, her eyes fixed on him.

She was smiling as Manolin threw the wooden disc to Lewys, who dived at any given opportunity. Manolin, too, was ambitious to please the lad, or himself. His daughter had caught the sun from the tour, and her cheeks were red.

Santiago put his hand on her shoulder. 'Morning, Becq. Are you coming from breakfast?'

'Hi. Sure.'

They walked along behind Manolin, who turned to see them walking towards the village.

'Hey, Lewys,' Manolin said to the boy. 'Fancy some food?'

'Okay.' The boy trotted up next to him and they followed Santiago and Becq.

Forb bent down to pick up a leaf of cigarette paper, brought it close to his face to examine it. He frowned, folded the paper up, placed it in his shirt pocket. 'Okay, everyone,' he said to the group. Two native men women walked behind him, further into the village. They were carrying long, wooden spears. 'It's the morning of the hunt. I hope you're all looking forward to it?'

'Certainly am,' Manolin said.

'Will it involve much running?' Yana asked.

'Quite a bit. Look, those of you who don't want to can just stay here in the village. Nothing's compulsory. If you like to experience life on Arya, then this is the way to do it. That's all the hunt is really—experiencing island life in its most natural state.'

'Okay,' Yana said. 'Look, I've been ill, so I'm not going to go.'

'I'll stay with you then,' Becq said.

'That's all right,' Forb said. 'Who's up for the hunt then?'

Manolin, Santiago, Jefry and Arth nodded their inclusion.

'Great. I take it Mr Calyban and Mr Soul won't participate?'

'Best if they don't,' Santiago said. 'They're liable to get a shot in the head. Accidents will happen.'

Forb smiled. 'We won't of course be using muskets, Santiago. If you miss once with a musket, everything will clear right off at the sound, and you won't get a second shot.'

'What will we use?' Manolin said.

'Poisoned darts. We, or rather the ichthyocentaurs, help us coat the tip in spider venom. Very silent way to kill them. Hogs don't last long. The levels on the tips of the dart are rather a high concentration, and therefore anything that gets in the way dies, but dies peacefully, in a drug-endued state. We like to think that the hogs suffer less this way.'

'I see,' Manolin said.

'Now, we only hunt for three months of the year. That allows the hogs to breed sufficiently. And this is one of the last of the season.'

The natives began to gather around the group. They were wearing black paint on their dark faces and bodies. One man carried a large conch. Two others carried a drum. There were surprisingly more women then men, and they each carried long, thin tubes through which they blew darts. Three more women had spears.

'I say, Forb,' Santiago said. 'We're not properly dressed for this.'

'Well, you can take your shirt off and we'll put some mud and paint on you so that you blend in.'

'Sounds fun,' Manolin said. He unbuttoned his shirt with little hesitation, wanting to involve himself fully in the workings of the island. He folded it up, placed it in his bag. He had lost some weight since leaving Escha. He had not eaten much at sea, and he had browned in the sun, which made him look lean. *Give it a year and I'll be like a native*, he thought. He was half conscious of Becq staring at him as he turned to face Forb.

Forb gestured towards Myranda, who entered a small, thatched hut, then returned with a wooden pot. She and Forb then began to apply the mud evenly to his skin, blending the paste in. They applied it softly, yet firmly and Manolin felt a little embarrassed of their hands, yet at the same time was glad that Myranda was touching him. He glanced towards Becq, who's eyes were narrow, and she turned away to say something to Yana.

Santiago took his shirt off to reveal his paunch, and pasty skin, which he had not allowed to brown, because of the smart manner in which he dressed. Myranda handed the pot to a native man, who began to apply the paste to Santiago, who looked not a little disappointed at the change. 'Go easy, man,' Santiago said.

'Thou worries greatly,' the native man said. He had a wide face, a broad nose.

Santiago said, 'Just not use to tribal ways.'

'It will be so.'

Jefry and Arth looked at each other and shrugged, taking off their shirts to reveal their tough, black, rumel hide.

'See, being black just gets better,' Arth said.

Forb laughed, looking at the rumel as he finished painting Manolin. 'Will you want any, anyway?'

'No, you're all right. I'll stick with what I've got,' Arth said. He shook his arms loosely as if to prepare for a fight.

Jefry laughed, flexing his arms like a bodybuilder. 'Still got it, eh?'

Yana grunted a laugh that Jefry didn't hear, and she and Becq began to walk away from the village and to the seafront.

Arth jumped around on the spot like a child waiting for a trip. Despite his age, he was full of energy. He always took on new tasks with the excitement of a puppy. Manolin had always assumed that because Arth had no family to speak of, he became excited at any activity at all, and he could afford to apply his whole being into whatever project it was. He was always happy, always willing to throw himself into any job. You'd find him spending his free time with his head in a scientific journal, keen to further his knowledge in a way Manolin could identify with.

Forb disappeared around the back of a line of huts further in the village, then returned carrying several long poles and a bundle over his back. He placed them on the sand, handed a pole to each of the men.

'These are your weapons, gentlemen. You may want to practice on a piece of fruit or something. Get some good practice in, as we don't have too long until the hunting begins.'

The hunt, as Forb explained over an hour or so, was to start when the conch was sounded. From then on, no one was allowed to talk loudly. Only certain hand signals were to instruct what to do or where the hogs were. Forb led the group to the edges of the forest. A troop of natives ran into the darkness carrying blow pipes and darts. Manolin thought that they looked savage, with the body paint and weapons. He, too, seemed to take on a different persona—felt feral and he liked it. He liked the feeling that he was closer to nature, not necessarily in harmony with the rhythms of the island, but some way to understanding it. For him, something such as the hunt was essential on any voyage or travels. That was truly experiencing a culture. It was part of discovering the true essence of a people.

Years ago, when DeBrelt's was a larger company, there were some scientists who never participated in cultural phenomena. They wanted food cooked to Eschan recipes. Their bedding was made of Eschan material. Their idea of surveying a territory did not include talking to the people, despite, as Manolin knew, that people were the best barometer of any land. Escha would always be there, so why bring it abroad?

'Be careful,' Forb said. He held the group back with the tip of his blow pipe. 'These are poisonous.' He held a bundle of blow darts. 'Shoot them carefully when you see the hogs. We take as many as we can and we do it quietly. The hogs are large, and the males can be deadly. We had a child go missing one day, and his necklace was found near a colony of them. All that remained were bones—they'll eat anything, so if you're knocked unconscious that may well be the last we see of you. Any questions?'

Manolin shook his head.

'Good, now let's go, and remember: silence, else we'll catch nothing. And we must be very quick. Those little blighters can run like you wouldn't believe.'

They entered the forest. The native people ran into the trees. Arth, Jefry and Santiago stood in a line behind Forb and Manolin. Forb turned his head as he crouched and, bent double, trotted into the trees. Manolin turned, shrugged, then followed, crouching also. The others did the same.

The conch sounded and they ran through the trees. Manolin felt the humidity as sweat formed on his forehead and he ran despite this, being careful to make his footsteps light, and he watched Forb's feet, stepping where he stepped, being careful not to show himself up. Santiago, Jefry and Arth were all trotting behind in single file, their blow pipes held high, their heads tilting from side to side. The natives were spreading out wide, their painted bodies hard to discern against the ferns that crowded him. Forb signalled for everyone to slow, then he indicated for the group to split. Jefry and Arth darted along a path to the right, and Santiago and Manolin to the left, along a small trail, following Forb and some of the other natives.

Small groups reflected the dappled sunlight in flashes as they skipped through the aromatic undergrowth, and his heart began beat alongside the drum that he could hear, low and powerful, and he jogged, eyes wide, behind the doctor into darker areas. Arth and Jefry vanished along an adjacent path, and Santiago was following, the sweat leaving streaks in the paint on his body as the older man struggled already in the humidity.

Whether it was the hunt or something else, everything around him felt wild.

Manolin had only seen a hog cooked and he did not know what he was looking for, but he turned left and right looking for movement that he thought would be his prey. He had only an inkling, from what the doctor had told him, that they were a reddish-brown colour, that they were about four feet long, wide at the shoulders, with powerful legs that, should the need occur, could cause a man some serious injury.

As he ran, Manolin glanced at the blow pipe, marvelled at the instrument, smiling as a primitive thrill raced through his body. He remembered his brief practice against the fruit on the beach, where he found his shot was accurate and deadly, whereas Santiago, who always assumed himself to be superior couldn't strike the fruit in several goes.

Manolin and Santiago caught up with Forb, who was crouched behind a tree, his bald head seeming to glow with sweat, and the doctor was making a flurry of hand signals to a native was standing so close to a tree in the distance that Manolin could almost not see him.

Now that he had paused, he could hear a hummingbird. He turned to see its body hovering alongside what he thought were beautiful flowering plants. He did not recognise the species, nor could he see the bird's wings. Next to the hummingbird he saw two trogons with their black and white tails a sharp contrast to the lianas that grew in a bright spot. He took two steps closer to Forb.

Forb leaned back, whispered, 'Gnundo thinks that there are a cluster of hogs further up, about a five minute run.' With that he ran again. Manolin and Santiago followed him, breathing heavily, struggling to draw the dense, hot air in, and there was colour in the canopy as birds stood on branches, looking down with curiosity as men sprinted under their homes.

The three of them ran, following the natives, their blow pipes in hand, through a clearing, the intense and burning sun. Manolin halted, turned to see Santiago resting his arm against a tree, hunched over, and his chest was rising and falling, his mouth wide open and his eyes slanting at the ends in despair.

Whether or not it was a primitive, competitive sensation, Manolin found this mildly amusing.

He cut his thoughts, scorned himself for laughing at the old man, who was clearly struggling. He thought that it was probably the feral nature of the hunt that made him wilder. But he realised it wasn't. If he was feral then he wouldn't think in such a way at all. A wilder side of him would make him support Santiago, support his own species, especially in a situation such as a hunt. It was the fact that he was a human that made him think this way, and he couldn't blame the hunt nor the natives.

It was at that point that he realised the drumming had stopped. He couldn't remember when it had.

He walked back to Santiago, helped him upright. 'Come on, it's about my turn to start paying you back in some way I suppose.' He smiled.

Santiago nodded, his mouth wide open, and Manolin could hear the older man wheezing.

They walked to where he had seen Forb go, along a small trail that lead though a cluster of acacia trees, where branches had fallen, making the path difficult. It was a matter of minutes before they caught up with Forb again, who stood alongside some of the natives, peering over a large, branch, that Manolin could tell had only recently fallen because the colour of the wood inside was light.

Forb turned to see the foreigners catch up, nodded at their arrival. He stepped back towards them, and leaned into Manolin's face. 'They're over there, back behind the trees. About twenty feet away. The other group should be around the other side, so it'll be difficult for the hogs to escape.'

'How many are there?' Manolin whispered, wiping sweat from his forehead.

'Seven. That could feed everyone for a while. If you want to have a go at shooting one, come alongside Mbuht and Gnundo. They wanted to wait for you two to fire first.'

'Ah,' Manolin said. 'That's good of them.'

Santiago nodded, still breathless

They approached Mbuht and Gnundo, who nodded a greeting as the foreigners arrived. They reached out to tap Manolin's blow pipe, indicating the clearing where the hogs were. Manolin nodded and regarded Santiago, who had regained some composure. Manolin raised his long pipe, rested it on a fallen branch, long leaves providing ample camouflage. Santiago rested his alongside They looked down the weapons to the clearing, where, against the grass, seven hogs were standing. Their heads were down, their ears fallen forward over their faces. Manolin could see their tanned skin, marvelled at their size. He thought he couldn't miss. Forb handed a dart to each of the men, careful to keep the poisoned end up. The men placed the slender darts, which were as thin as matchsticks, into the pipe, and, watching four natives along to their right do the same, placed their mouths to the pipe.

Manolin held the bamboo pipe with both hands underneath, like he had been shown, one hand further down the shaft than the other so that it was easy to control. He steered the pipe towards a hog, noting that Santiago was still doing the same. He looked to Forb who nodded. Manolin inhaled then gave a short, sharp blow then heard the natives follow suit.

Two of the hogs, the one he had been aiming at too, began to grunt deeply, and four other hogs lifted their heads, and turned to gallop through the forest and the natives reloaded and fired trying to get them and Manolin could hear the hooves thundering along the forest floor.

He and Santiago fired a second dart off into the forest, but they did not strike any hogs. Satisfied that he had struck one, at least, he and Forb walked into the clearing. The other natives had run off into the forest after the other hogs, bounding through the clearing and over the fallen branches with great ease.

Manolin noticed a silence around the clearing.

Forb, Manolin and Santiago approached the hogs before he heard a shout about thirty feet away. The three of them ran towards the direction of the sound. They stepped over the branches, through large-leaf shrubs, and back into the forest the other side, and the shout came again. Manolin noticed the voice was Jefry's.

When they arrived they found the rumel crouching over Arth, who lay on his back and was shaking in short spasms. Standing four inches up from his throat was a dart, the poisoned tip deep inside. The rumel's blow pipe was on the floor next to him, the dart hanging out of the end.

Forb called through the forest. The sound of his voice was muffled by the density of plants. Seconds later one of the native women arrived, striding over ferns, and Forb reached for the conch in her hand. He put the shell to his lips and blew through one end, and the loud, horn-like sound echoed despite the dense foliage. He blew three times, each noise breaking through the roof of the forest. Then, he walked over Arth, dropping the conch to the floor. Manolin and Santiago fell to their knees, watching helplessly as Arth shook as if lightening was travelling through his body.

Jefry simply repeated the words, 'Fuck, fuck, fuck.' His eyes were slanted at the ends and he was gasping as if crying, but was too shocked to cry.

'What happened, Jefry?' Forb said, staring down at the dart. He reached his hand over the four inch spike. Using his forefinger and thumb, he plucked the dart from Arth, who jutted continuously. 'I asked you what happened?' He turned to face the rumel, who was sitting crossed legged next to Arth, his hands out in front, shaking.

'I don't know. We were with some of the natives one minute. Then they turned to run after some hogs and when I looked back Arth was on the floor.'

'Hmm,' Forb said, turning his attention back to Arth, who was groaning. Forb leaned in and saw traces of foam around the tiny wound. 'Damn,' he said.

'What's wrong?' Manolin asked.

'Yes, will he be okay?' Santiago asked, shaking his head.

Forb said, 'He's dying.'

'Fuck, no, please, no,' Jefry said.

'Look, I'll see what I can do, but it isn't looking good. You two stay here. Wash this wound with water—Thyumba has some in her bag.'

'Where're you going?' Manolin asked.

'To the ichthyocentaurs' village. Maybe they've something. There're only a couple of poisons on Arya, but I'm not entirely sure we have anything to cure them. I'll be back as soon as I can.'

Manolin watched the doctor bound up the gentle wooded slope, run into the darkness of the forest. Santiago stood. A dark-skinned woman handed him a skin of water. He thanked her, leaned over Arth's body, pouring the water over the wound. Manolin could hear fizzing as the water passed over the hole in Arth's neck. Jefry ran his hands through his hair. No one said anything. Manolin's eyes were fixed on the wound. He watched blood come to the surface then recede like a wave. Manolin was determined to help Arth as much as he could. He wanted to ease the suffering that was apparent on the rumel's face. Manolin's eyes were red with desperation. *Come on you old bugger,* Manolin thought. *Come on. We'll have you out of this. Just hang in there.*

Arth had died some time before the doctor returned. As Forb took long strides downhill, he could see the group standing, facing away from each other, with the exception of Jefry, who was standing with one hand on his hip and the other clutching his hair at the front of his head. His tail was still. Forb walked the last few yards, knowing what had happened. He thought it unlikely that anything could be done, but he was ever the optimist.

He wanted to believe everything had a cure.

An ichthyocentaur followed him, trotting awkwardly down the slope and through the vegetation, to the clearing in which everyone was standing. The ichthyocentaur made a clicking noise, deep within its throat. Manolin walked over to the doctor and the creature, who was clutching a handful of dried herb.

'He died about ten minutes ago,' Manolin said. His voice was weak.

The doctor nodded, turned to the ichthyocentaur. *We're too late*, he signed.

Forb drew a deep breath. The ichthyocentaur inched towards the body. Jefry was standing next to it. His black eyes gave away little emotion. The creature crouched over the rumel, jutting its neck to analyse the body. Forb knew that had only seen a rumel when Jefry and Arth were introduced to the village. The ichthyocentaur prodded the wound, which had foamed considerably. Tiny flies began to crawl around the viscous substance, moving with purpose.

Forb and Manolin rejoined the body, and it seemed a relief of sorts, as the rumel was in great pain before he died. His black rumel eyes had glazed, seeming to stare at the canopy and the specks of sunlight that filtered through. The scene was strangely calm and you could hear the sea now, clear and sharp. Two more ichthyocentaurs came down the slope carrying a stretcher made from bamboo and woven leaves.

Arth's body was loaded onto the stretcher.

Everyone made their way back to the beach. Manolin led with Jefry, his arm around the rumel.

'I feel rather guilty,' Forb said.

'Why should you feel guilty, man?' Santiago said. He felt ridiculous in his body paint. He wanted more than ever to be wearing respectful clothes again, to put all the savagery behind him.

Forb said, 'Well, if I hadn't invited you to the hunt, none of this would've ever happened.'

'Nonsense,' Santiago said. 'We came of our own accord. It was an accident, plain and simple. There were quite a few of us firing those darts, and I guess Arth was just in the wrong place at the wrong time.'

Forb reflected on the thought for a moment. 'You don't seem too bothered.'

'I am, doctor, I am. I just expect some sort of danger or threat on these expeditions. I've not had a trip yet where someone hasn't been injured. DeBrelt's has lost more than a few people. There used to be more of us, but some don't want to take the risk. That's why I'm surprised those government agents are here. Anything could happen on a place like this.'

Forb said, 'How are those two, anyway?'

'Oh, I'm sure they're fine. I'm not entirely sure what they're up to. I know that if anything happened to them, it wouldn't be long until the Eschan Navy is sent out here.'

Forb stopped, turning to face Santiago. 'We can't have that, Santiago, we can't.'

Santiago said, 'I know—'

'This is paradise,' Forb said. 'We can't have any navy here. They'll come and tear up this place, destroying every plant and animal, and I simply can't have that.'

'Okay, okay,' Santiago said. 'That won't happen.'

Forb was silent after that. When they arrived at the beach, the sun was weaker, the wind refreshing. They walked out in a line to the village, their painted bodies dirty and smeared with sweat.

Yana and Becq were swimming in the lagoon when they saw the line of men and women returning from the hunt. Yana pointed out the stretcher. She and Becq hauled themselves out of the gentle green waters, on to the beach. Yana was wearing a white bikini, Becq a black swimsuit. White sand clung to their feet as they marched up to the village and the two women halted when they saw the body.

'Oh no,' Yana said. 'What... what happened?'

Manolin approached the girls, his arms wide. He managed to steer them back, and they looked over his arms, their eyes still red from the salt water.

Manolin said, 'There was an accident, during the hunt.'

'What... Is he all right? Becq asked.

Manolin looked her right in the eye, and shook his head. 'No. He passed away. I'm sorry.'

'Oh, no,' Yana shouted. Then, more quietly, 'Oh, fuck no.'

'I'm afraid so,' Manolin said. 'He took a dart in the neck. We tried to help, but it was too late.'

He let go of the two women, and they didn't move. Their bodies were stained by the paint from Manolin's torso. They stared at the corpse that was yards away.

Manolin waited for a reaction but none came.

'He's with Arrahd now,' Manolin said. He didn't know whether saying something like that would have any effect, particularly because they were people of science, not spirituality, but it felt right. When it came down to it, Manolin thought, to the stresses of life, science went out the window. People clung to their basest beliefs, no matter how rational a person was. It made everything easier. Or perhaps, science went only so far to explain things. What it couldn't yet explain, people dismissed as spiritual. But he was more open to suggestion than that.

'What happened, Manolin,' Yana asked. 'I mean, what *actually* happened?'

Manolin glanced back to watch the body being carried towards the village, the line of natives that followed. Santiago, Forb and Jefry were walking with them. 'He was struck in the neck by one of the darts that was meant for a hog. The darts are deadly. Somehow he got in the way.'

'Who fired the dart?' Becq said.

'I don't know. There were a lot of us firing. It could've been any one of us, I suppose.'

'So, one of you killed him?' Yana said.

'I haven't looked at it like that,' he said. 'It's an accident. Nothing more. I think it would be helpful if we didn't look at things in that way.'

The three of them walked towards the village. The two women picked up their clothes. The sun had dried their bodies. He watched Yana, focussing on her skin, which had browned since they had left the shore. Becq was a little too slender for his own liking, not that he'd even consider doing anything with her. He looked at the two of them, side by side. They were so different from each other. Yana had curves, her hair had grown long. The sun had made her look younger. Becq seemed to burn in the sun. Her face was red from the wind and heat. He thought her nose was a little too wide for her to be pretty. Yana had a more pointed nose. Sure she was older, but he found her much more attractive than Becq. Aware of what exactly he was thinking, he shook his head. It seemed as though he wanted to be distracted by the day's events.

As the women got dressed, Manolin caught sight of a group of villagers that were strolling from the forest. They carried hogs on spears that were placed on the shoulders of two individuals per animal. He counted five hogs in total. They were large animals, their weight tilting them upside down on the spears so that their stocky legs pointed to the sky. Blood had congealed in streaks across their bodies, the wounds from the darts had turned black like a tumour.

He felt a little guilty as, in his mind, he compared the hogs to Arth—he couldn't help it. They'd both shared the same fate, yet he looked at these animals with barely any emotion at all. The hunt was part of an island cycle, a natural cycle, of which death was an essential feature. That was no way to think about a friend though. He watched the group pass, then he and the women followed.

They approached the others that were gathered around Arth's body. The silence may have come from respect, or sheer shock at the fact that someone, a foreigner, a visitor had died. The natives seemed peaceful and comfortable with the corpse. Jefry was crying, crouched next to the body. Yana walked up to him. For the first time in as long as he could remember, she put her arm around her husband. She crouched down next to him, and he turned into her and nestled on her neck. His black tail lay still. Yana looked up at Manolin, who then regarded the sea.

He sighed, strolled thoughtfully over to the lower shore, near the ebbing tide, where the water was clearest. From where he was stood you could see the shadow of the reef, the waves that were being broken upon it, some way in the distance. At this hour you had to squint to protect your eyes from the sun. From there, the reef was a darkness on the surface of the water, as if a ship had sunk. He could tell it was there, longed to be able to sit on one of the tiny coral islands, where only one or two species of seaweed existed, lying in the sun.

Suddenly, he couldn't be sure if he heard a song.

It was like the previous night. He could hear it, but quieter. A shiver descended his spine. The sand was bright. He felt isolated. No sooner had he heard it then it had gone and all he could hear was the sound of the waves.

To one side, an ichthyocentaur was standing ten yards away, also staring out to sea. It was the one from the forest that came with Forb. Manolin coughed, held his hands up ready to sign the greeting he had learned the day before. The ichthyocentaur didn't move. The sand was so bright behind the creature that it appeared at first in silhouette.

It was just staring towards the reef.

Forb joined Manolin and placed his hand on his shoulder. Manolin shuddered as he was brought out of a trance.

'Weird at first, aren't they?' Forb said.

Manolin said, 'They'll seem weird for a long time yet.'

'Amazing place, isn't it.'

'I have to say I've never seen anywhere quite like this. I can't believe how clear the waters are, especially down by the lagoon. And

I've never seen so much life as in that lagoon.'

'Yes,' Forb said. 'It's quite something. You know, your huts form little artificial reefs?'

'Really? I hadn't looked too close at them. I expect if I were a creature I'd set up camp there. Nutrient run-off from the land. Stability and protection from the sea by that bank of sand. I'd be one happy fish in there.'

Forb laughed. 'I'm glad someone like you is here. I suppose we could've had anyone come, but it's good to know you *understand* the place. Sure, that Santiago chap is bright, but you've really got a *feel* for things here.'

Manolin said, 'Oh, there's still a lot for me to learn.'

'Exactly. It's always that way. So then. What do you think will happen now?'

'Not sure,' Manolin said. 'It's up to Santiago really, but I can't see him wanting to leave without surveying the island and finding out what was killing those chaps.' He indicated the ichthyocentaur.

Forb nodded.

Manolin said, 'I really don't think we'll be going anywhere for a while.'

'Good.'

'Don't know what we're going to do about Arth's body though.'

'No, tough one,' Forb said, rubbing his chin. He ran his hand over his bald head, as was his habit. 'You know, we can perform some sort of funeral if you'd like.'

'It'll have to be talked over with the others,' Manolin said. 'I think it's going to be a bit of a shock for a while. We've been here, what, only a couple of days and one of our team has died. Not in a pretty way either.'

Forb said, 'No, it wasn't nice. As long as I've been here, no one has died in the hunt. I'm surprised no one has blamed me for it yet.'

'Oh it's no one's fault. It's just a shock that someone's died, and so early, too.'

'We're used to death here,' Forb said. 'We've lost so many ichthyocentaurs now. I guess that's why none of the villagers seem all that bothered by another body. I guess they're only curious as they've never seen a rumel.'

'No, I guess they haven't. I guess they're just as interested in us as we are in them.'

Forb said, 'I doubt it.'

'Really?' Manolin said.

'I had the same problem of you,' Forb said. 'I called it "newcomer ego". They're not all that bothered about you. Sure, they wonder what you're doing here, and yes the rumel are interesting to them, but they get on with life in a different way. They'll welcome you, but don't think that they have a boring existence without you.' Forb spoke in a gentle, kind manner.

'I know,' Manolin said. 'I guess we're curious in them and this island because life on the mainland isn't all it's cracked up to be. We've been waiting a long time for something like this to come up. A real chance to explore the world. And within two days someone dies.'

Forb nodded.

Manolin turned with the doctor to face the village. He could see the dark forest, the palms being aired by the easterly breeze. They began to walk back.

'Tell me, how much do you know about the ichthyocentaur deaths?' Manolin asked.

'Not a great amount, I'm afraid. I usually find them first thing in the morning, at some stretch of the beach. Mostly on the other side of the island, when I'm out for my morning surf. Like I said to Santiago, their innards are removed. Sometimes you get just stab wounds.'

Manolin said, 'Ever seen one of them get killed?'

'No. No, the island isn't huge, but there's still a lot of beach to keep an eye on.'

'Hmm. I don't suppose, and I know this sounds stupid, but I don't suppose you *hear* anything when they're being killed?'

'How do you mean?'

Manolin said, 'Like a melody? I know that sounds ridiculous.'

'You've heard that too, then?' Forb said.

'I was hoping it was my imagination.'

'No, I've heard something. A slight sound. It's the only common link, since you mention it. I don't always hear it though. Often, it's out of my hearing.'

'How long have the deaths been happening now?' Manolin said.

Forb said, 'Oh, about a year, on and off. Apparently, years before I came, there was a similar spate of deaths, but it stopped after a month or two. This had been happening for four months on and off when I sent those ichthyocentaur to the mainland. You see, no one knew these creatures were still alive. They needed to be saved, purely in the name of science and ethics. It was just right that more people see knew about them. Didn't want them all to die, you see? I knew sending them to the mainland would provoke interest from knowledgeable quarters.'

'Well, we're here. We'll certainly try and find out what's going on,

Forb, but it looks as though we can't even save ourselves.'

Forb was silent.

Manolin said, 'So how come you're here then?'

'Sorry?'

He was intrigued as to why the doctor would not return home, to Escha. Certainly, it was a beautiful place, but was that really enough to leave life behind? 'Why've you chosen to stay here, on Arya, rather than go back to the mainland?'

'Oh, well you only have to look at the place.'

'It certainly is beautiful.' He looked at the forest, and the elegant cone of the volcano leaning up behind.

Forb said, 'Not just that, of course. I got sick of the city and all the politics in Has-jahn. I came here for research, my own research after following up rumours of the ichthyocentaurs. That's another reason I'm here: I wanted to study how they used plants. People say they can cure nearly anything with their botanical knowledge. People say that they never get ill. Most medicine comes from plants or nature, and here, somehow, that tribe are leagues ahead of anything we human or rumel have managed. I've got a *need* to learn from them.'

Manolin said. 'That's why I'm pretty excited to be here, too.'

After a moment of listening to the tide, Forb spoke again. 'So what else are all going to be doing here?'

'A thorough survey. Mapping, geological mapping, biological survey. The usual sort of stuff. We've submersibles to check out the coast. They can go pretty deep, too. We're in the employ of a mayor, funnily enough. But we can also sell a lot of this knowledge to academics. That's how we'll make most of our money. The maps of the seas fetch a lot, but scientific theory has a price, too. There's a first for knowledge. Tends to be the way this age, after the rebellion to science, and all that. Plus we enjoy doing it.'

'Sound's good. Just the sort of thing I'd used to be involved in, once.' Forb glanced down. 'Well if you need a hand with anything, just come and find me, or Myranda. Local knowledge is useful. Any of the villagers can help. Take little Lewys along, I'm sure he'll find it exciting.'

'Myranda is certainly beautiful. I guess that makes staying easier.'

Forb laughed. 'It certainly does, you know. Yes, she is beautiful, in my eyes and yours. But the other islanders, as I said before, don't find her all that much. Strange, isn't it?'

Manolin said nothing.

Forb said, 'She thinks you're attractive, too.'

Manolin stopped, frowned. 'I'm sorry?'

'Oh come on, you must've seen the way she looks at you.'

Manolin gave an uncomfortable laugh. 'Forb, that's your wife you're talking about—' Forb gave what Manolin thought was a genuine smile, which made what he said seem even stranger.

'You should join us for supper. I know little Lewys lights up when you're around. He's quite a bright boy. He doesn't much like playing with the other children, and you're the first person I've known to talk to him like he's normal. As if he's a grown man. Kids like that.'

'Well I, uh, that is, um, yes, sure, okay. I'll have to see what we're going to do with Arth's body first. But sure, that'd be great. I take it there'll be no feast from the hunt though, now that Arth's dead?'

'To the villagers, that's even more of a reason to celebrate.'

'I'm sorry?' Manolin smirked, thinking he had a lot to come to terms with.

'Well when someone dies here, they celebrate their life, not mourn their death. You see, to them, death is around every corner. We just never look at things like that. They're prepared for death, and so celebrate the life of whoever's died. I really think you ought to mention it to Jefry. I think he'd like it. Perhaps he could tell stories about Arth. There'd be dancing and food. I tell you what, Manolin. When I go, I sure as hell want a celebration. Couldn't stand seeing all the people I know crying.'

Manolin nodded, deep in thought.

They approached the group, who were standing around Arth's body. It had been covered over with a blanket. Only Jefry was looking at it.

Santiago said, 'Right, well someone had better tell Calyban and Soul what's gone on. Are they in their little shack?'

'Don't know,' Yana said. 'Probably.'

'Probably sucking each other off,' Santiago said as he stalked into the forest, fists clenched.

Manolin walked along the edge of the lagoon after retrieving a bottle of whiskey he'd stashed on the ship. At a particular point during the trip to Arya, he had realised that drinking wasn't the best solution for getting over his wife. The moon was not quite full, but he could see thousands of tiny reflections of it out at sea. The village was cast under an amber light from the funeral pyre, the flames noticeable above the ring of thatched huts. Another mild night, pleasant in the breeze. The aroma of roasting hog wafted nearby. Manolin clutched the neck of the bottle tight in his right hand, advanced along the firmer sand. The sounds of drum beats and chanting echoed along the shore, rhythmic, enchanting, and it filled him with anticipation as he approached. Santiago, who had donned his top hat for the evening, was silhouetted by the fire. Next to him was Yana and Becq, and they were all watching a group of natives dancing around the flames. The movements of the locals were strange, spasmodic, and it made him smile because it reminded him of some of the bars back in Escha. People liked to dance no matter where you were.

Jefry was standing the other side of the fire, still talking to a group of native children, who were sitting crossed legged on the sand, their faces bright and warm in the firelight. Jefry made exaggerated movements, his voice occasionally audible over the drubs. He was still telling the children about Arth and the antics that they used to get up to. Manolin felt warm inside, relieved that Jefry was happy in this moment. Manolin couldn't exactly hear what the rumel was saying, but he heard the children laughing and giggling throughout the performance. His mind raced across many stories that Jefry had told him before. They were always getting up to no good in the labs, playing pranks. Sometimes they'd even fake remains of a bizarre creature to pass it off as Qe Falta to frighten people. Always, there was drink involved, a laugh, a shared love of gambling.

Manolin joined Yana, Becq and Santiago.

'Ah, Manny, you've got the strong stuff then?' Santiago said, his gaze flipping to the bottle in Manolin's hand.

'Oh, yes. But it's for later. The doctor asked me to have supper with him and Myranda, so I thought I'd bring something special along. You know, make it nice.'

Santiago said, 'Did he now?'

Manolin couldn't read his face clearly. 'Yes. I find I get on quite well with him. We've a lot in common.'

'Did you say Myranda was going to be there?' Becq asked. She was playing with a strand of her blonde hair, watching him idly.

'Um, yeah. I think we'll talk science—Forb and me. And I think little Lewys will be there, too. I think Forb thinks we have a laugh.'

'Quite the happy family, eh?' Santiago said.

Manolin said, 'Sorry, San?'

'I said quiet a happy family, the four of you.'

'Well, I don't know about that. It's just a bit of food anyway.' Manolin turned to Yana. 'Is Jefry doing well?'

'Yes.' Yana smiled. 'Yes, I think he'll be all right. It's a bit of a shock to all of us I suppose. They've been friends for years, haven't they.'

Manolin nodded. 'So, what's our plan then, San?'

'How do you mean?' Santiago scratched his moustache.

Manolin said, 'I mean, are we staying or leaving, now that Arth has gone.'

'We're not going anywhere, Manny. We've a job to do and we'll damn well do it. Besides, we need the money and it's just a thoroughly splendid island. We'll be here for a few weeks yet. There's plenty of food. Much to explore. Besides, Arth had no family did he?'

Manolin said, 'Not that I can think of. Yana?'

'Nope. And I think Jefry was his only close friend.'

'Well that's that then,' Santiago said. 'We're here for a long time yet. We've got to produce a thorough assessment of this island. And some of the others, I'd like to see them, too. Most of all we have to find out what it was out there,' he indicated the sea, 'that's been killing those ichthyocentaurs.'

'Right you are.' Manolin felt relieved. He had a lot to learn on Arya, needed to stay to explore the shores. Hell, he needed to explore himself a little. That's what the island was making him do. 'Well, if it's all the same to you, I'm off to join the doctor for some food. See y'later.'

'Bye, Manny,' Becq said.

He walked towards one of the large huts at the far end of the village.

Santiago was staring at the fire for some time. He could no longer see Arth's body in the centre of it, although he thought he could see the skull, glowing amidst the charred remains. After a few minutes, he wondered away from the others, sat down on a large palm leaf on the edge of the forest, facing the stilted huts that was their temporary residence.

Despite the strong easterly that brought the fragrance from the opened pores of leaves from the forest further up, and despite the calm rhythms of the tide, Santiago was fuming.

Why the devil should he be having supper with the doctor? I should be the one. I am, after all, the leader here. He thinks he knows everything. That's the damn problem with those youngsters. You give them the best fucking start they could hope for; you help them with work and hobbies. Then they think they're so much damn better than you. Damn fucking boy owes me so much. Well, I'm not put out that easily...

He pushed himself off of the leaf, slipped without being seen to one of the rafts. He pushed out, looking around all the time. There was only darkness here. He secured the raft to a stilt, climbed up into his hut.

Within minutes he was back on land again. Now, without his top hat, he loitered within the edges of the forest, carrying a dark cloak around him. He could hear the drumming still, even the crackle of the fire. Through the shadows that the plants formed, he focussed on Yana, crouched. Behind, in the forest, were strange and uncomfortable sounds, but he put them out of his mind, waited. He watched Yana for some time. Eventually, as he knew she'd have to, she stood up, headed into the forest.

By the time she had passed the palm trees on the fringes, Santiago was at the place he knew that she would be walking to. A minutes' walk into the forest was a tiny pit, which was what his group had been using as a toilet to collect fertilizer. The pit was small, a raised plank placed across the top. Santiago was laying face down close to the pit, the cloak covering his entire body, under a cluster of thick ferns that concealed the toilet from all sides. He could feel his heart beating on the floor of the forest. The wind was moving the tops of the trees, which was good because it provided noise cover. His nose, despite being hidden by the ferns, was near enough to the pit for the intense and vile smell to make him feel sick. He breathed through his mouth.

Yana approached.

He drew the cloak over him fully making it impossible for him to be seen. He leaned on one side, shifted his right arm in to a freer position. In his hand was a small glass container that was typically used by him to collect water samples. Yana sauntered closer. He could see her moving slowly with precision, her arms raised slightly, which meant her eyes were adjusting to the slight change in darkness. The elements were on his side. He watched as she stepped through the ferns on the other side of the pit area, watched her lift up her skirt then slide her lace underwear down to her ankles.

Very impractical undergarments for an expedition, he thought. *Typical of a woman.*

He could see the curve of her body as she lowered herself onto the raised plank that was cast across the small pit. The wind was strong and the palm trees rattled loudly. With discreet focus, and scientific rigour, he extended his arm and the glass container directly underneath her rear, which hung fractionally over the edge of the plank. She leaned forward, let out a small groan as she began urinating. Santiago inched the glass to the left to capture the liquid, careful to hold the container at an angle so her urine would not make any sound striking the bottom of the glass. She stopped, wiped herself with a palm leaf. Santiago brought the container back through the ferns and under his cloak and placed a small cork in the top.

Yana pulled up her underwear, dropped her skirt, bounded back down towards the beach.

After a few moments he crawled out from the ferns, gasped as he drew in cool, clean air. Proudly, he held the container high. The liquid captured some of the firelight through the gaps in tress, and he swirled the urine around inside.

This ought to wipe the smile off Manolin's face, he thought.

He walked along the beach to the raft. After washing his hand in the water, he rowed across the lagoon back to the hut. Once inside, he set to work. He reached for the plant extracts he had pocked from his visit to the ichthyocentaurs' village the previous day and arranged, meticulously, a combination of glass beakers. Every movement of his hand was calm, methodical. Occasionally he glanced outside to see if anyone was rowing across the lagoon. Santiago recalled what Forb had said previously. He had pestered the doctor for more information, wanting to know every detail. He started a small, contained fire using a box of matches, and began the process of mixing the extracts. Minutes later he added the bark chippings, which were to be used as indicators, and there were indeed red streaks through some of the fibres.

A grin appeared on his face.

Santiago jumped off of the raft, on to the sand, gazing casually at the fire that had now burned low. He marched along the beach basking in the cool wind. Ahead, Yana was walking on her own, further down the beach away from the village. He headed towards her. She was staring out to sea, her chin raised high and he could see the firelight on her profile. He thought her handsome indeed and wasn't surprised with Manolin.

She glanced across as he approached.

'Good evening,' he said, stepping towards her. It amused him to see her now, after what he had done, after what he knew.

'Hey.'

He said, 'Everything okay?'

'Yeah,' she said. 'Just enjoying the view. Tough day, wasn't it?'

'Indeed... Yana, can I ask you something?'

She turned her body to face him directly. 'Sure. Something wrong?'

'With me? Not at all.' Santiago paused, then said, 'Yana, is Manolin the father?'

Her eyes widened, her mouth opened as if to say something, then closed. Then she said, 'I don't know what you're talking about.'

'Come now, Yana. I'm not a scientist for nothing.' He held out the bark strips. 'These are indicators of pregnancy that the islanders use to test for it. Forb says that the method is one hundred percent accurate.'

'What—where the hell did you get that? What the hell did you test?'

'You can test anything. Besides, that's not important. I have to ensure the health of my crew is fine. It's my responsibility.'

'Look, it's island hocus-pocus.' She began to play with the strands of her black hair, then prodded the sand with nervous precision.

'Yana, the morning sickness? You *are* pregnant aren't you? Come on, it's my job to help you all. How long have we known each other? Look, when you start having a baby on this island, I think we're going to know about it.'

She was silent and sat on the sand, cross legged. The word 'baby' seemed to have struck a blow with her. Santiago sat down next to her, placed his hand on her arm tenderly.

He said, 'Everything will be fine.'

'No, it won't.'

'It's Manny's, too, isn't it?'

She sighed, nodded. She glanced out to see, to the reef, her eyes welling up.

'Why?' Santiago said. 'Why him?' If there was jealousy in his voice he didn't want it shown. He watched this beautiful vulnerable women intently, almost like a scientific subject. Somewhere in all of this was a study of his emotions, although that was forced some way back. He did not like to get emotional, did not like to draw on something that could be a weakness.

'Oh, I don't know,' she said. 'We just spent two nights together, on the way here. Two nights.'

'Hmm.' Santiago flattened his moustache. 'I don't suppose you could call it Jefry's?'

She said, 'No, you wouldn't understand.'

'Try me.'

She said, 'I haven't had sex with Jefry in two years.'

'Ah. Indeed.' Santiago nodded. 'So, why *Manolin*?'

'Oh I don't know. We got talking. He'd split up with his wife and wanted to talk. So we talked. Look, you wouldn't understand. He gave me a drink and I could see him looking at my figure. He's young, what—mid twenties? I'm over forty.'

'You could still have anyone,' Santiago said, as if to say *you could have had me if you'd have only asked*. He raised his chin. 'You're quite delightful, and you know it.'

She appeared to ignore his compliment, which was something that wouldn't normally have hurt. 'When someone that young looks at you in that way—you know. Come on, if a young girl looked at you in that way you'd snap her up.'

'It has been known,' he said. 'I'll not deny such an accusation.'

'Well there you are then. Manolin looked at me in a *dirty* way. He'd had a little to drink and I had a little sip or two. He made me feel *dirty*, then he acted all gentlemanly. He wanted to be polite and suppress it. He looked really vulnerable and I when I walked around the room I could feel his eyes on me. There was just a candle on. Then he said I had a nice ass. You know, no one has said that to me. He said, "Seriously, Yana. You have a tremendous bum." He was slurring a little, and I said he'd been drinking too much, but as soon as I said that he tried to reassure me that he had always felt that way. You know, the way young guys do. Sometimes they'll do anything for a piece of you, and this time, when I saw his bright eyes on my body, it did something to me. I hadn't felt that way for a long time. And he's handsome. So, one thing happens, then another. Before you know it, I'm on top of him.'

'There are,' Santiago said, 'other ways to cheer a man up.'

'I know,' Yana said. 'Look, I never planned any of this all right? I never wanted to get pregnant. We had sex twice, and after that I felt too guilty. I'd never done anything like that before. Never. I'd never hurt Jefry intentionally. I'd never do it again.'

Santiago nodded. He drew out a pre-rolled cigarette and a box of matches from his jacket pocket. He lit the cigarette, pocketed the matches again. As he inhaled, the tip of the roll-up glowed, attracting insects until they were caught up in the smoke and were repelled. *There's some vague metaphor in that*, he thought dryly. 'So when are you going to tell everyone?'

She said, 'I don't know.'

'You ought to do it as soon as possible. The longer you leave it, the worse it'll be for all of us.'

'I know,' she said.

'Do you want me to tell Jefry?' Santiago said.

'No. No, I'll tell him, in the morning. I'll tell him first thing. I don't think he could cope with two upsets in a day. I know he's a stable guy, but this'll be enough to really break him.'

'And Manolin?'

'I'll tell him at some point,' Yana said.

'I think you ought to tell him before he gets too involved with the doctor. And his wife.'

Yana glared at him. 'Look, I'll tell him when I'm ready, okay?'

'Okay.' Santiago inhaled, stood up, then brushed the sand from his breeches. 'I'll leave you to it then.'

She didn't reply.

He turned and walked up the shore back to the village.

Jefry was still talking to the children and he could hear their laughter. Seconds later he saw Manolin stroll out of the doctor's hut, the boy, Lewys, running along behind. Manolin ruffled the boy's hair. Lewys ran up to the other children. Manolin walked past Jefry, patting the rumel on the shoulder. They both smiled.

And just to think their lives are about to be shattered, Santiago thought. *I'll sleep well tonight. Manolin needs to realise that I'm in control. Damn boy, after all I've done for him. Still, I'll be there to pick up the pieces when he does find out no doubt. He'll come running back needing my guidance. It's amazing what one can achieve be being rational about it all. Poor Jefry though. I'm sure he'll cope. He's a stubborn and dedicated chap. I'm sure he'll not blame Yana. Probably Manolin, but that's his own fault. Damn him, the way he struts out of the Forb's hut as if the doctor's bitch was the main course.*

Manolin looked at Santiago, gave a wave. Santiago nodded back, turned to regard the palm forest. The foliage possessed a sense of eeriness at night, when the paths couldn't be seen. A small crab that was inching towards a palm shrub. Santiago reached down to pick it up, and looked closely at its tough, white belly and its black claws. He smiled, placed the crab down again, watching it enter the darkness. *Go on, little fella. If you dare.*

She was clinging to the top of the reef, staring towards the shore. There was fire. She lowered herself so it was only her eyes that looked over the tiny coral island. It was dark. The water sloshed against the coral, gurgling as it passed through the tiny pores. Still she watched, feeling the water move her body and hair.

She waited and the fire became low. A marlin passed somewhere behind her, but she remained fixed on the shore, waiting for the fire to stop, for a total darkness that never came. More wood burned, the flames reached skywards. She was aware now that there were *others* on the island.

The moment would come soon enough though.

Eighteen

'Well,' Santiago said, looking down at the mutilated corpse of an ichthyocentaur, 'I most certainly didn't see that one coming.'

'Now, are you sure you didn't see anything in the night,' Forb said. 'Any of you?' He prodded open the wound with a piece of driftwood. The wound extended from the neck of the creature to its groin. The ichthyocentaur's intestines hung out its side in a bag of blue flesh, and you could see the trail of veins. He stood up, familiar with the type of killing, but it never worsened the despair he felt. These creatures were so precious. Their knowledge was essential.

'Not a thing,' Santiago said.

'Me neither,' Manolin said. 'Any of you guys?'

Yana, Becq and Jefry shook their heads.

The villagers had left the scientists to stand around the body, as if totally at one with the casualties. Forb looked up. It was a grey morning, with low cloud. It would probably blow away by lunch.

Manolin walked around the body, then crouched next to the wound. 'No heart, you say?'

Forb nodded. 'Taken. Same as the others.'

'Nice touch,' Santiago muttered. 'The wound is clinical, considering the environment we're in. It forms a near perfect line, bisecting his torso, and there are no obvious signs of struggle. A most impressive cut. Very fascinating.'

'Yeah. Bet it hurt like hell, too,' Manolin said.

Santiago glanced at Manolin and back down at the body. 'When do you reckon he was killed, Doctor?'

'In the night, same as the others. Couldn't give an exact time.' Forb looked offshore as if to find something out there now that would explain this. The movement of the water suggested nothing. *Why does this keep happening? When will it end?* It was of course more than personal for him, but he couldn't tell the others that just yet.

Manolin said, 'There's traces of dark red seaweeds on the body. I take it he was killed further out?'

Forb said, 'Yep.'

'How can you tell?' Santiago asked, with both hands on his hips, his waistcoat hanging slightly undone.

'Colour of the species.' Manolin scooped up a fragment of seaweed and held it up. 'Light doesn't penetrate deeper waters, so any plants won't be able to absorb the light and so chlorophyll is pretty useless, and because red light travels farther underwater—'

'Yes, yes,' Santiago said, 'I know that. Spare us the botany lesson. So it got tangled up further out to sea.'

'No, Santiago. *He* was tangled up out at sea,' Manolin corrected him. Santiago was unimpressed.

Forb sensed a tension between the two. The men appeared to have brought with them some personal issues. They would inevitably surface on such a small space of land. It was always the way on islands. Small groups of people in such an enclosed space could only lead to confrontation.

'There's only one thing we can do to find what's killing these chaps,' Santiago said.

'What's that then?' Forb asked.

'Well, it's really quite simple,' Santiago said. 'We haven't seen what's killing them, right?'

Forb rejoined the circle, nodded in unison with the others.

'Well, we know that since they've been up there,' Santiago indicated the camp near the volcano, 'very few have died, until now.'

'What are you suggesting, Santiago?' Forb asked.

'Bait.'

'I see,' Forb said, suspicious of the man's idea.

Manolin shook his head.

'Yes,' Santiago said. 'It's quite clear that we need to have one of the fellows down here, on the beach, so we can see what it is that's getting them.'

'I'm not sure about that,' Manolin said.

Santiago looked at him in a way that said, *Yeah, I'm well aware of what you think.*

'What do you think?' Santiago said to Yana. She turned away to walk behind Jefry.

'I don't know,' Becq said. 'I don't like seeing all these deaths. We've seen enough.' She rolled her lips together, making her face look peaceful and innocent. Forb liked the girl. She was shy, quiet, always seemed to retain her thoughts inside as if she knew speaking them would do no good.

'Too true,' Jefry said. 'Too many deaths already.' He sighed. Yana held his hand. He looked at her and she smiled uncertainly at him.

Santiago brushed down his moustache, which was becoming

ruffled in the sea breeze. 'Doc?' Santiago asked.

Forb reflected on Santiago's statements. There was a strange logic to what he said. This man was obviously good at convincing people, at persuading them to his way of thinking. *A powerful leader, this one.*

Santiago said, 'The chap would be well protected. We'd have our muskets and pistols and whatnots. He'd be quite all right.'

Forb nodded. 'We don't have many other options.' He looked at Manolin who gave an cautious nod.

'Excellent,' Santiago said. He paced around, his hands behind his back. 'We can plan this later. We're going to be here for a while, and we've a lot of work to crack on with. Now with your approval, Doctor, I'd like to begin surveying your island.'

'As I've said before, Santiago, she's not mine, but feel free to catalogue her. It'd be a shame to let all the villagers' and ichthyocentaur' knowledge go to waste. And I'd be glad to help with anything you want to ask.'

'Okay, you and Manny can crack on with some of that,' Santiago said. Then he turned to his daughter. 'Fancy giving them a hand, dear?'

Her face lit up. She turned to Manolin. 'Please, if you wouldn't mind?'

Manolin said, 'Sure, many hands make light work, n'all that.'

'Good,' Santiago said. 'Well, Yana, Jefry, if you wanted we could plan a geological survey of sorts?'

'May as well,' Yana said.

Jefry nodded.

'Great,' Santiago said. 'Well, I'll get some equipment off of the ship. Shall we crack on before midday?'

Everyone approved.

'Fantastic. Well, onwards.' Santiago marched off along the beach. Yana and Jefry followed.

Manolin looked down at the corpse. Its face was strangely serene, as if to suggest it's death was relaxed. He walked around it in a circle. Becq stepped away holding her nose.

'What're we going to do with him?' Manolin asked.

Forb said, 'We'll send someone up to the ichthyocentaur settlement. They'll collect him and take him up to the village. Probably burn him tonight.'

'Why do *you* think they're being killed, Forb. I mean, it's not as though the killings are random are they?'

'Nope. I can only guess it's something to do with reproduction.'

'Why so?' Manolin asked, and noticed that Becq had turned around to listen.

'Each death I've found—and we're well over the fifty mark now—each death has seen the genitals removed. It certainly isn't empirical science.'

'No, but it's all we've got,' Manolin said. 'So, what, you reckon their sperm is being used?'

Forb said, 'If the genitals are gone, that has to be the most likely thing. I can't think of anything else.'

'You think females did this?' Becq asked.

Manolin and Forb turned to face her.

'Possibly,' Forb said. 'You see a lot of violent females in nature. Stronger and more devastating than males in many circumstances.'

'True,' Manolin said.

'Presuming they're using the sperm, they're after breeding, but I can't see how. I mean, you can't just take sperm from one species and put it in another. It doesn't work like that. There're all sorts of barriers to reproduction that keeps a species separate, distinct.'

'How about mules?' Manolin said. 'And even rumel and humans. You still get a kid, be it a human or a little rumel, but it just won't have any of its own—infertile offspring and whatnot.'

'Hmm,' Forb said. 'Food for thought. Bit of an extreme way of going about it though.' He nodded towards the body.

'Lot of lonely hearts out there then,' Manolin said.

Forb grunted a laugh.

Manolin walked to the sea with his hands in his pockets and his head held high as he inhaled the fresher air away from the open corpse.

They came to Arya to work, and that morning was the beginning of real business. Manolin and Becq, with Forb's assistance, would study the ichthyocentaurs. It was something Manolin couldn't wait to do. Santiago, Yana and Jefry brought geological tools from the ship, which was still anchored away from the lagoon. Their plan was to hike up to the volcano, sampling the rock types on the way so that they could build a geological map of the island. Santiago had wanted to walk around the rim of the volcano in order to get a good view.

He also wanted Yana to tell Jefry that she was pregnant. He had told her that delaying the matter would only make things worse. She had agreed, would tell him that evening, but she didn't like to think about it too much.

They were beginning to acclimatise to Arya's conditions, so the hike didn't prove as tiring as the previous trip. Santiago appeared to be still a little exhausted from the hunt, but threw himself onwards. Jefry's spirits were, Yana thought, unusually high, considering.

The rumel seemed to smile at everything around in the forest. Colourful birds and insects. Tiny fossils he found in sedimentary rocks. He laughed at the one giant bee that droned by, whilst Santiago and Yana hid under a blanket behind a small acacia shrub.

Yana said, 'Hey, Jef. How come you're in a good mood?'

He turned to face her. 'Well, love, you've got to take every day as it comes. Live every day as if it were your last. We're not here for long, are we?' He turned back and continued marching up the slope with vigour, and Santiago stomped by ignoring the comments.

Yana sighed. *Does that make my decision any more easy?* she thought. *Maybe he won't hate me or want to kill me or Manolin. Hell, I wish I'd never straddled that guy. No, actually, I'm glad. I mean, it's a baby, isn't it? A child. And how long have I been waiting for one? Jef never did me any favours in that department. Not that the poor kid would've had much of a life, being unable to have a kid of its own. No, I want this baby. I don't expect Manolin to have any role if he doesn't want to. I must have what, four of five months to go anyway, so that's plenty of time for everyone to get used to the idea. If we leave in a month, I may even give birth on the mainland. Should I tell Manny? Would it ruin his life? I hope not. At least no one else is affected. Apart from Becq, fuck. She'll hate me because she's besotted by Manny. So, everyone hates me, hurrah.*

Of course, what's really annoying is the fact that I feel so damn turned on since I left Escha. I'm usually so good at controlling my hormones. I'm not one of those drama bitches. I think Manolin's opened something inside of me. Hell, I've had no fun at any point in my life. I married that dull man when I was too young to know any better and I've wasted my life on him. I think this could be good. I think it could be really good—a chance for me to break free from everything. If Jef won't support me then I'll divorce him. It's about time I get some respect. I'm not getting any younger—

Who am I kidding? No one's going to want me with a baby. Any 'man' would run a mile at the sight of my lump. Maybe I'd better stick with Jef. At least he'll look after me. I won't be really happy, but that's all a bit late now. So, happiness or security?

Halfway up the volcano, a half a mile past the ichthyocentaurs' village where Manolin and Becq were working, Santiago sat down with Yana.

He could see over the forest canopy that extended down to the beach and thought the view was spectacular. Terns flew along the beach, hovered above the shallow waters then jutted out to sea. The sun was strong, having filtered through, and there were only a few cirrus clouds in the air. You could see the shadows of the birds over the lagoon, and an unobstructed view of the reef. In the distance, you could see the vivid brightness of the sand banks against the pure blue waters. The reef began about two hundred feet away from the beach proper, there was a change in the darkness of the water as it extended farther from the shore. The small coral islands, dark on the water, seemed tiny from that distance and you could see the white tips of the waves around them.

In the haze in the far distance, he noted ridges that Santiago thought couldn't be the sea, although cumulus clouds appeared to hug them.

'D'you think that's land over there?' he asked Yana.

She followed his gaze and squinted to ascertain what the horizon revealed. 'Possibly. I reckon those clouds give it away.'

'Indeed,' Santiago said. His face felt hot in the uncomfortable heat. He had taken his waistcoat off before the hike, and wore a long-sleeved white shirt to protect his arms from the sun. They were almost at the top of the small volcano. Another half an hour and they'd be at the rim. Yana had taken rock samples along the way, as had Jefry, who carried most of them in the bag on his back. They were beginning to build a profile of the island. It was standard procedure.

Santiago shifted onto a stable rock, brought out a pad and pencil from his bag. Starting with the lagoon, one of three, he began to sketch. Yana looked over his shoulder at his work every few seconds. Jefry was crouching by a tiny bush further on, then smiled as he stood up. He waved to her, and she waved back.

'So then,' Santiago said, looking at his sketch pad. 'When're you going to tell him?'

Birds flocked over their heads. 'Soon enough.'

Santiago said, 'As I say—it will, of course, be easier to do this sooner.'

'I know, I know.'

'We're all here to support you, no matter what happens. And I care about you, I do,' Santiago said, still sketching.

'Thanks. That's kind. He seems in a good mood at least.'

'Indeed. Funny thing, death. Makes some try and put it all in perspective. New lease of life. Utter balderdash, of course. Month's time and he'll be his usual self again. I'd tell him now, if I were you.'

'I'm not sure, Santiago.'

'Go on. Do it now. You'll feel better. I'll still be here, sketching and getting sunburned. I think he'll be fine. It's not like you've been the closest of couples the last year or two.'

'No,' she said, with a half smile. 'No, that's true.' She sighed. 'I'm not sure though…'

'Go on. He's in a positive state of mind. It's a good time.'

She said, 'But his best friend died yesterday. It's too soon.'

'Ah, but you didn't listen to what I said, did you? State of mind. Does funny things to a man, death. He's found some vague religion at the minute. Take advantage of his new, kind god.'

'Maybe you're right.'

'Seen this sort of stuff many times before,' he said. 'Seen the effect it's had. Know when it's best. Now is a good time, Yana, a very good time.'

'Right.' She turned to stroll after Jefry.

Santiago did not turn to watch her. His sketch was coming along nicely. He thought it one of his better pieces of work.

A man of science should not be able to make art this good.

'There're dozens of note books here, Forb,' Manolin said.

Forb said, 'Yes, I've made a pretty good catalogue.'

Manolin picked up one of the brown books from the shelf. The hut was humid, being in the sun, and he could hear the clicking that the ichthyocentaur made in the doorway. He opened the book, looked at the sketches and notes that Forb had made. 'How long've you being detailing this?'

'Oh, a decade or thereabouts.' Forb stood, arms folded, watching Manolin pour over the catalogue.

'Wow, I mean, this is no easy job. Did you say you were an ethnobotanist too?'

Forb said, 'Not at first. A botanist at times, an archaeologist at heart.'

'I don't understand,' Manolin said. 'There must be a reason that you've done this. I mean, this is incredible. There are hundreds and hundreds of species in here.'

'Thousands and thousands.'

'I can see.' Manolin turned the pages with a sense of awe. There were detailed sketches of the anatomy of certain species, all arranged into similar looking families. Each book appeared to have a group in, with extensive notes alongside. 'I take it that these notes are the medicinal values?'

'Forb leaned over to where Manolin's finger pointed. 'Yes that's right. Everything the ichthyocentaurs have used them for in the past.'

'This is an phenomenally detailed piece of research, Forb, very detailed. I can't say I've ever seen anything quite like it.'

'I'll admit it took me a while.' He rubbed the palm of his hand over his bald head.

Manolin said, 'Do you have any idea of the potential here?'

'Oh yes, quite some idea.'

'You could save thousands of lives with these notes. Seriously, Forb.' Manolin looked up at him as he walked around the hut, smelling plant specimens that were arranged in bundles by the window. Outside the window were two ichthyocentaur looking in. Behind them was Becq, who was busy making detailed sketches of the village.

'What were you looking for in particular?' Manolin asked.

Forb did not respond.

'Forb?'

The doctor turned around. 'Sorry, was in a world of my own.'

'What was it that you were looking for?' Manolin closed the notebook. He placed it on the shelf again before taking another one down. He glanced up at the doctor.

Forb's face darkened. 'I'll tell you, soon. Not now. Later.'

Manolin nodded. He read through the notebooks for an hour, scrutinising the drawings, the research. The ichthyocentaurs knew how to utilise every plant on the island. It was remarkable. They could genuinely make—and Forb had detailed—cures for any ailment, from headache and stomach ache, to anaesthetics and even hallucinogenic drugs. There were appetite suppressants and stimuli, erection enhancers, fertility drugs, antidepressants. Manolin's mind was struggling to come to terms with the potential. If this knowledge reached the mainland, he could only imagine the number of cures it would bring.

The ichthyocentaurs' village was calm. Many of them were in the forests, gathering plants.

Manolin saw the ichthyocentaur woman who looked heavily pregnant.

'How far gone is she?' he asked Forb.

'Ten months. She should be due in the next couple of weeks, providing there're no complications.'

'Ten months. Interesting.' Manolin walked with Forb up to the female. He signed *Hello* to her, and she returned the greeting. He got a small thrill every time he could communicate with them.

Forb began a conversation with her for a few moments before turning to Manolin. 'All is well. She's looking forward to becoming a mother. Should be any day now.'

Manolin said, 'Who's the father?'

Forb smiled and shrugged. 'Could be any of them.'

'I'm sorry?' Manolin frowned.

'Any of the males could be the father.'

'Not sure I follow.'

Forb signed something to the ichthyocentaur woman. Manolin thought the clicks she made formed a laugh.

'The females can take as many partners as they want, as many times as they want, even if all at the same time.'

Manolin was silent for a while. 'Blimey.' He looked at the female and around at the others. He'd never noticed it before, but there were no 'couples' around. 'Not shy ladies, then. And I take it there's not a great deal of courting going on either?'

'Quite so.' Forb laughed. 'If indeed anyone *courts* these days. But seriously, it works well. How many times've you been to one of those clubs or inns, or bars, where you see a guy standing on his own in the shadows, and you knew he was thinking unsavoury thoughts, because you were thinking them yourself. All guys look at the women and want them, but can't have them. A dominant male wins and the weaker ones go home depressed and drunk and alone.'

Manolin nodded. 'Been there, my friend.'

'Well, here, there're no *dominant* males as such. They're all winners this way. And, the females are seldom satisfied with just the one male. They require multiple partners to be stimulated fully. It's really rare, because it's outside of nature, outside of evolution. You see, they're choosing not to compete. In that way, you could say that they're superior to us humans and rumel. If only we could get our heads around it.' He smiled.

Manolin scratched his head, looking at the female ichthyocentaur.

'So,' Forb said, 'the males are happy as they're always releasing their seed, and the females are happy as they're getting maximum pleasure. No one ever fights over a woman, too. There is no sexual violence at all. Never had a rape here. What's even stranger is that they do occasionally take a partner as companion, but they never get jealous of one another. It's as if feelings never come into it. I would add, before one goes running around fertilizing everything, that humans and rumel are *vastly* more sophisticated. We let feelings and morals get in the way. And that's a whole different thing all together. It complicates things.'

'Can't argue with that logic.' Manolin thought about the notion. It unsettled him a little, made him silent. He remembered the last scene in his house, with his wife, her lover. It seemed so far away. In his head, he was beginning to justify her actions. Perhaps she needed more partners. Maybe it wasn't because he was a bad lover to her, or unattractive. Perhaps her actions were a little more base, more natural. He settled on the word 'primitive'.

Perhaps all people are *primitive, deep down*, he thought.

Yana joined Jefry as he held a pink flower. He was spinning it, at the stem, between his forefinger and thumb.

'Look at these colours, Yana. Aren't they amazing?'

'Utterly.' She watched him spinning the flower. 'Jefry, are you okay after what happened, uh, to Arth?'

She could never read his feelings.

'You know, the strange thing is, I've never been better. Now, don't get me wrong, I'm sad that his gone, but that ceremony was different—you know, celebrating his life. That's a really good thing to do. And it's made me look at the world differently.'

'How so?' she said.

'Well, I guess I don't take everything so seriously. I'm not getting any older, and I know for a fact that death is around the corner for all of us, all the time. And when you're on this island it's like…' He searched for the word. 'Well, let me put it another way. This morning I ate an orange.'

'Okay.' Yana smiled, frowned.

'I eat oranges all the time in Escha. But this morning I knew it came from a tree. I peeled it back and smelled it. I felt the juice spitting on my fingers. I ate it slowly. I was mindful of the fact that I was eating it, and that it came from a tree.'

'And?' she said.

'I had never tasted anything as good. It was the most delicious thing I've eaten. It's the pace of things here, you know? Away from the city, you begin to live again, to remember those things that really satisfy.'

'Yeah, I think I know what you mean,' Yana said. 'Kind of sensual.'

'That's the word. Sensual.' He dropped the flower, turned to address her face to face. 'I know I've been a crap husband the last few years. But I will change, I will be whatever you need, I promise. We've had troubles, but let's start afresh.'

Her throat felt thick as she forced a smile. A moment passed as he leaned towards her as if using telepathy. She thought it ridiculous. 'Look, Jefry. I know we've had our problems. I... I want to be open with you.'

'Of course, dear, of course.'

His kindness made it all the more difficult for her. 'I've done something. Something I'm not proud of. Something I am really ashamed of. I wondered if you... had the kindness to listen and not judge me.'

'Of course. Look, I'm a different man now. I'm a sensitive man.' He held her hands in his.

'Okay. Look, Jef, I do love you. I love you a lot.' She looked down, to the right.

He said, 'And I love you.'

She looked at the bright plants that lined the path up to the volcano's edge. 'Right. Well, it happened months ago. I was confused and lonely. But remember I love you, and I... Damn, this is *really* hard to say.'

He said, 'Go on.'

'Well...' Her eyes settled on the reef, down in the distance. 'There's no easy way to say this. I'm pregnant.'

His head moved back fractionally. 'Oh.'

Yana's eyes reddened. She could see his face change.

'Really?'

She nodded.

Jefry said, 'I'm not the father, am I?'

She shook her head, a tear running down her cheek.

He nodded, sighed then was silent. He let go of her hands and they fell limp.

She said, 'Tell me what you're thinking, Jef.'

Jefry turned away towards the sea. A flock of birds caught his eye, graceful as they dove down the side of the volcano.

'Jef—please. Tell me what you're thinking.'

He sighed, still looking away. 'What d'you want me to say?'

'Something, anything. Just tell me what you think. Of me.'

'What I think of you?' He laughed coarsely.

'Yes,' she said. 'Please.'

'You mean, you tell me all of this, and you want to know how *you* are to me.'

'No, no,' she said. 'Not like that. I just want to know what you're feeling.'

'Oh, for fucking Arrahd's sake...' He looked her in the eyes. She turned away. 'If you gave a fuck about what I was feeling we wouldn't be having this conversation, would we?'

She glanced down and noticed vaguely how bold her shadow was in the intense sunshine.

'Who's the father then?'

She stared right into his eyes. 'Manolin.'

He nodded. 'Why? Was I just not good enough?'

She shook her head in tiny jerks. 'It wasn't that.'

'Well what was it exactly? Come on, you might as well tell me. Get it all out in the open. Had you been having an affair?'

'No, not at all, no. It was a one-off.'

'Right.'

She said, 'No, it *was*. Just the once.'

'Why *him*?'

'I don't know,' she said. 'He was sad because he'd just split with his wife, y'know.'

'That's no reason.'

'I know,' she said, fully ashamed of herself. He was cutting her with precise, thought out words. She felt ridiculously young. 'Look, it wasn't that. We chatted and had drunk quite a bit.'

'You were drunk, was that it?'

'More or less,' she said.

'Was he good?' he said.

'What d'you mean?' Yana said.

'Was he good? Did *he* fuck *you* better than *I* could?'

She began to cry. 'No, of course not, that's not the point at all. It just felt good talking—'

'You could talk to me!' he said.

'Please, don't raise your voice. I'm truly sorry, Jef. I've never done anything like that before. You ignored me before. That night he made me feel good about myself. He complimented me. Made me feel special.'

The rumel turned and sat on the ground. He placed his hands either side on the lichens.

Out at sea were two fishing boats, their sails unfurling as they watched.

Yana sat down next to him. 'You'd shown no interest in me for months. What was I supposed to think? That you found me attractive? I need to feel attractive to someone, Jef. Everyone does, don't they?'

He said, 'Are you asking me or telling?'

'I'm telling you.' Her voice was stronger. 'Manolin doesn't know yet. We both regret the act. It was a one-off, and now look at me. I'm pregnant.'

'Yes, yes you are.' He looked up and down her body. 'What're you going to do about it?'

'What d'you mean? I'm going to have it, that's what.'

'You've always wanted one, haven't you?' Jefry said.

'Yeah.'

'You want it, don't you?'

'Yeah.' With her eyes wide she rolled her lips inwards in a smile.

'Guess I should've seen it coming,' he said. 'A rumel and a human is never a good mix.'

'It's not that at all, Jef. I love you for who you are, not what you are. Anyway, we're not all that different. There're loads of rumel and human families.'

'Couldn't give you a kid though, could I?'

Yana remained silent, rubbed her hands along the grass-like surface of the lichens that lined the path to the volcano. 'Look, you've been so nice about this. Really nice. Please don't hate me.'

'I don't hate you,' he said.

'You do, you hate me, I can tell.'

'I don't hate you.'

She said, 'What about Manolin?'

'I don't know how I feel about him yet.'

'You've been so nice about all of this. You're such a kind person, I've always thought that.'

'Yeah, I'm a real great guy, aren't I?' Jefry grunted a laugh.

Yana was silent for a moment. 'Do you want some time alone?'

Jefry nodded.

Yana pushed herself onto one knee. She leaned in to kiss him, but stopped seeing his expression, pulled back, stood up. She turned back down the path.

'Looks like rain tonight,' Forb said

He gestured vaguely at the bulk of cumulous that were massing to bring a storm. Repeatedly, smoke from a cooking fire in the village rose a short way before being beaten down. 'Yep, I'd say we should wrap up tight tonight.'

Santiago, Manolin, Yana and Becq all stood around the doctor's hut. Myranda was preparing some fruit inside, and Santiago, out of the corner of his eye, saw that she was bending over to pick up something. He wasn't concerned with what it was.

'How long's Jefry going to be?' Forb asked.

Yana shrugged. 'I don't know. He wanted some time to himself so I left him there.' She indicated the volcano. 'That was a good few hours, though.'

'Is everything all right?' Becq asked.

'Yes, yes. Nothing to worry about. You know us.' Yana looked towards Becq. 'I'll tell you later.'

'Another hour and I'll have to go look for him,' Forb said. 'It's pretty dangerous up there, especially if there's a storm coming.'

'Storm? I thought you said it was rain?' Santiago said, still glancing behind the doctor.

'It's going to be bad whatever it is. It's a bit early. The storm season isn't for a month or two yet. Guess you lot have brought bad weather with you.' Forb smiled. Everyone else remained silent.

'Will it be a bad one, then?' Santiago asked.

'I should hope not, but you can sleep further inland if you want. We've huts here and there all the way to the other side of the island.'

Santiago said, 'When do you think we can use one of the ichthyocentaurs, Forb?'

'Not tonight, Santiago, not tonight. It's going to be far too rough without any extra troubles.' Forb turned to where the upper beach bordered the forest. 'Ah, Mr Calyban and Mr Soul. How honoured we are to have you join us. And what the devil have you been up to these past couple of days?'

Calyban and Soul stepped out of the darkness of the forest. They were carrying fedoras, and put them on whilst approaching. Their blue shirts rippled in the escalating breeze and the palm trees were fizzing behind them.

'We've been here and there,' Soul said. 'Watching what's being going on.'

Forb said, 'I trust you've been making use of our fine facilities?'

Calyban laughed. 'Chance would be a fine thing.'

'So, what *have* you two been doing?' Santiago asked. 'Two men spending all that time in a hut together. Alone. Must be... intimate, no?'

'Mr DeBrelt. Kindly refrain from such accusations. I would've assumed someone such as you would've been above that. Someone who postures as a gentleman.'

'Indeed,' Santiago said.

'Well,' Soul said, turning to Calyban, 'he's a Collectivist, after all. A rather rum lot.'

Santiago tried not to fall for their bait, but felt such disdain at their presence, at their language. He strolled up to them, said, 'You two'd better watch your backs. You're a long way from home. Anything could happen.'

'Tut tut, Mr DeBrelt. Should anything happen to us, the navy would be here within weeks. They'd scour the seas for you. They'd hunt you down.'

Santiago looked between them. 'Just what *are* you doing here?'

'Keeping an eye on things,' Calyban said. 'Someone needs to by the looks of it.'

Santiago said, 'We're doing pretty well without government shits interfering.'

'Yes, one dead already,' Calyban said. 'Impressive.'

Santiago reflected on this for a moment, considered their words carefully. They were a secretive lot, as were all agents for Mayor Gio, so you had to examine each hint, each expression. 'How *exactly* are the navy going to know you're gone?'

'That's for us to know, Mr DeBrelt,' Soul said.

Forb walked up behind Santiago, placed a hand on his arm. 'The navy must never come here, Santiago. Never. Let them be.'

'Our host is right, DeBrelt, let us be,' Calyban said.

'There's plenty of fish in the village, if you're hungry,' Forb said. 'Go help yourselves. You'll need feeding before the weather turns sour.' He tilted his head up at the grey sky as the government agents walked behind the doctor's hut, to the village as Myranda stepped out with a basket of fruit.

'Ah, splendid,' Manolin said.

Myranda smiled at him. Santiago noted that they held each other in their eyes for a moment.

'Very sweet of you, Myranda,' Manolin said.

'Thanks, Manolin,' she said. She turned to offer the fruit to the others. She was wearing a bikini top and a pair of baggy trousers, which he assumed were Forb's, as they were tied tightly with vine, bunching over at the top. Manolin glanced to Forb, who had a strange smile. Santiago suspected that the young man was being obvious about his attraction, but somehow the doctor did not mind. Perversely, he seemed to encourage it.

He turned to the sea. Nearing dusk and under a grey sky, had lost some of its colour. It was rough. White tips of waves gathered in large numbers. The wind was strong and you could see the huts in the lagoon swaying. Birds were returning to the island in great numbers. It was cooler than before.

'It's not going to be a quiet one,' Forb said. 'Still no sign of Jefry?'

No one said anything.

'Right, I'll go look for him. I'll leave you in Myranda's capable hands.' Buttoning his white shirt, Forb marched barefoot along the beach, hopped up onto the grassy bank that bordered the forest, then into the darkness.

Forb jogged through vines, ferns, over boulders, fallen branches. He wanted to get to the volcano before it was dark. Although he knew the paths well, he was well aware how dangerous they could be. You had to respect nature. You had to play by its rules.

He headed up the slope. The forest was pungent as plants opened to breath in the cooler evening air. This far in you could hear the sea, so sounds were travelling further noticeably. He knew the storm was on its way.

After a while scrambling through the undergrowth, he came across the path that he thought Jefry, Yana and Santiago would have taken earlier. It took large strides to pull himself out into the clearing, but he wasn't out of breath. To his right he could see the sea through an area where the forest was cut away. It was grey, and cumulus had massed, false cirrus were forming below, tiny wisps of white under a dark thunderhead. It was some way away yet, but the winds had risen since he had been running. To his left the slope lead up to the rim of the volcano, about a short run away. The ground, littered with lichens, would be slippery later, but at least it was soft underfoot. There was no sign of Jefry. Forb thought that he would have intercepted him on the way back, but it was possible he was back at the village already.

He jogged up the slope to the volcano at an angle. When he was higher than the forest canopy, the wind rattled him, but he had a perfect panorama of Arya. He stopped for a moment to watch the tide foam with energy. At that point, he wondered if there would be any end to the ichthyocentaur killings. Their survival was essential. Forb looked up to the volcano but there was still no sign of anyone.

It was some time until he reached the summit of the dormant volcano. As scrambled up the last few feet, his hands clawing the moss, he could see a figure crouched over the rim some way away, silhouetted against the clouds behind. Forb walked along the crest, which was a couple hundred feet across, glancing down into the darkness below, treading carefully one side of the plants and shrubs that lined the edge. A stumble to his left and he would be dead.

The figure was Jefry, and his face was over the edge of the volcano. Forb paused, watched, wondered what the rumel was doing. Jefry's tail was curved around a rock behind, and he was swaying to and fro, as if to suggest suicide yet uncertainty.

Forb walked forwards, next to the chasm. 'Jefry,' he called out above the noise of the wind. 'Jefry, are you all right?'

The rumel turned to face the doctor. The distress in his face was too apparent.

'I suppose y'all know now, don't you?' Jefry said. 'Eh? About my slut of a wife?'

'I'm sorry,' Forb said. 'I've no idea what you're talking about.'

'Don't fuck with me, *Doctor*—if you are a doctor at all.'

'Well, as a matter of fact I am, of archaeology and zoology. Botany, too, but that's besides the point. Look, Jefry, are you quite all right? I'm not sure I follow what's going on.'

'It's clear when I'm not wanted. It's clear I'm no fucking good for anyone. My closest friend has been killed. All within a day.'

Forb could see his body shake as he sobbed. Jefry stood up, and placed his feet at the edge. His muscles in his legs were quivering with nervousness. That made Forb think he was likely to jump. You could feel the wind channelling across the edge of the volcano, a sudden and saddening groan, and it came at you from different directions. 'Jefry, please. Will talking about it help?'

'Not going to do any good,' he said. 'Might as well go.'

'No you won't. Not now, not ever.' Forb was angry. 'Don't be so damn stupid.' Why should someone give up something so precious as *life*.

Jefry turned to face him. 'Why should you care about me? I've only known you a couple days.'

'No one should kill themselves,' Forb said. 'A man should never kill himself.'

'I'm not a man anymore. Slut's just proved that.'

'This is one afternoon's thoughts, Jefry. You'll think differently in the morning, believe me.'

The rumel shrugged, looked down at the fall. 'Couldn't give a fuck.'

'Yes you bloody well could. Look, I do give a fuck about this, Jefry. Please, don't do anything stupid—'

'And why should I listen to a jumped-up shit who's got everything? A gorgeous and loyal wife, a beautiful home. Not a care in the fucking world. Just why would you bother about me?'

'Because I'm dying.' Forb said the words with precision, exasperation. There was silence before he continued. 'Because I'm dying. I have cancer, and I'm dying quicker each day.' He ran his palm over his head.

Jefry turned his body to face him. He looked shocked, curious, his grin had changed to a sneer. Tears were streaming down his face, although you wouldn't have guessed that by his calm voice.

'That's right,' Forb said. 'That's why I'm here on Arya. That's why I'm so interested in the ichthyocentaurs.'

Jefry did not show any emotion now except discomfort. 'I don't follow.'

'I have cancer, Jefry. In my head is a tumour, and it's killing me.'

'You're only saying this to stop me.'

Forb said, 'D'you think I'm that fucking stupid? Go kill yourself then, rid me of your damn ignorance.'

Jefry stared at the doctor.

'Think about it. I have cancer. I've tried everything. Why d'you think I've no hair? D'you think this is to enhance my cheekbones? I don't think so. Had all sorts of chemical treatments back in Escha. All sorts of therapy. Everything failed. Myth had it that the ichthyocentaurs on this island had cures for everything. They can use plants to stop you dying. That's why they live so long and never have diseases. I've catalogued all the plants they know of. Thousands. And only one of them's any good for me. Extract from an orchid root. It's kept me alive for longer than I should be here, but I've no idea how long I've got left and that's why I sent for help: to investigate and stop them being wiped out. To preserve the race and preserve a cure for my... illness.'

Jefry stepped away from the rim of the volcano. The wind was strong, ruffled his white hair. 'I'd no idea. Really...'

'Yes, well now you know,' Forb said, his anger fading. What he was angry with he didn't know. 'It's all right. I'm pretty used to it by now. I've survived for this long. Who knows, there may be another plant that'll reverse the tumour and my weakness, should I be lucky enough to find it.'

Jefry said, 'Who else knows this?'

'Just Myranda.'

Jefry nodded as Forb walked up to him. Jefry put his hand on the doctor's shoulder.

Forb smiled, sighed. 'Hang on to life, Jefry. Don't throw it away so easily. We all have moments of weakness. Just think about it for more than an afternoon. You'd be surprised.'

Jefry nodded again. 'Look, I don't know what I'm thinking. I've had to try and come to terms with some real heavy shit.'

'It's easy to give up,' Forb said. 'Harder to face things.'

'Tell me about it.'

'You want to get back? There's going to be a major storm tonight. It does help talking Jefry. No matter what it is. I should know.'

Jefry looked as thought couldn't argue with a dying man.

They walked back along the rim of the volcano, down the slope. The breeze was strong on their faces so they had to walk with their heads down. Forb could feel the first drops of rain on his head shortly before they entered the forest. He turned every minute or so to check that Jefry was following.

It was quieter in the shelter of the palm forest.

'So, what happened earlier then?' Forb asked as they followed a well-worn path through fig re-growth.

'Told you. Wife's a slut.'

'Jef, you can tell me. I've seen a lot of things and I hardly know you enough to be judgemental. If anything I can give good advice.'

'She's pregnant.'

'Pregnant?' Forb asked.

'Yes.'

'And it's not yours?'

'No.'

'I see.'

'Exactly.' Jefry shook his head.

'Do you know whose it is?'

'Yes.'

'Who?' Forb said.

'Manolin.'

'Manolin?'

'Yep, Manolin,' Jefry said. 'Who'd've thought it, eh?' He looked up at Forb, then down to the path.

Forb said, 'Seems very unlike him.' Forb had a lot of respect for the young man who'd come to his shores to help him. There was a bond between the two, one that formed over an interest that was common only between them.

'Apparently not,' Jefry said.

'How do you feel?'

'How d'you think?' Jefry stifled a laugh.

'Not good, I know. Sorry. I'll rephrase that: what do you think you'll do?'

'Can't say,' Jefry said. 'You can never tell until you're confronted with it. When I see them again I'll guess I'll know.'

Forb said, 'Do you want some more time alone?'

'How can I? I'm stuck here with 'em.'

'I can take you to another hut in the forest,' Forb said. 'There're loads of empty ones here and there. Part of the island's history, and whatnot.'

'If you could, that'd help.'

'Sure,' Forb said. 'If it's any consolation, I don't think anyone else knows.'

'Wouldn't matter if they did.'

'Will you stick by Yana?'

'Oh I don't know, do I? I'll need to think about it for a while.' Jefry paused for a moment as they climbed over a trunk that had fallen across the path. 'She's always wanted a kid, you know?'

'Yana?' Forb said.

'Yeah. Always. I couldn't give her that.'

'Sorry to hear that.'

'Oh, it's all right,' Jefry said. 'You get used to those sorts of things as you get older. She wouldn't care even if it was an infertile runt, like a mule.'

'It's tricky, rumel-human relationships,' Forb said. 'From what I remember, anyway.'

'You can say that again. It's the mingling, really. Whenever you're out and about, you tend, normally, to stick to your own species. No one talks about it, and rumels and humans have lived side by side for so many generations, but still, there's always *something*. A disapproving look, or something.'

'That's one thing I like about being here,' Forb said. 'You stay away from all that politicking. Well, it's not completely free. I had a row with Ghula a few weeks back because he cut down the wrong trees for boat wood. Wouldn't talk to me for days.'

'You're lucky, very lucky. Being close to nature, those sorts of things are much less important, I guess.'

'True. Working with the land and the sea, you lose all that. Doesn't matter what you are, you think of the island as one entity. And I suppose she is really.'

The forest became progressively darker as Forb turned onto another path, one that the hogs used often. It led to the aromatic pittosporum grove that ran parallel to the beach, on the north side of the island. The constant bombardment of different scents seemed to drag the mind off in different directions.

'Was it too difficult for us?' Jefry said. 'Or did she just crave a human?'

'You can never know, really,' Forb said. 'There're all sorts of things in a person's mind that can press the self-destruct button. It's not so much the difference between rumel and humans, but men and women. If it's any consolation, you're not alone, Jefry. Thousands fail. It's nothing personal, although you can't help but think it is.'

'I don't understand why? I'm so good to her. I've never cheated.

I'm always there. I know I'm not the most exciting person in Has-jahn, but why? And why him? Why Manolin?'

'You shouldn't ask yourself those questions, Jef. They'll only destroy you.'

'But I want to know why Manolin? Was it the human thing? What do you think it could be?'

Forb said, 'It's really not my place, Jef.'

'You *must* have a theory, at least. You seem to for everything else.'

Forb overlooked the bitterness in Jefry's tone. He led the rumel to a small, solid hut, about ten feet by ten with a sloping bamboo roof. Forb pushed the door open, allowed Jefry to walk in first. Then he stood in the doorway. 'There's flint and kindling in the corner to make a fire by the hatch on the side.' He indicated a tiny fireplace. 'I used to spend some nights here, to think. It's rather pleasant at times. It's going to be a rough one tonight. There's fruit on the trees nearby, should you get hungry. I'll come and find you in the morning.'

Jefry nodded, sitting on the floor by the fireplace.

'Now you'll be all right, won't you?'

The rumel looked up, nodded again.

'Good. I'll see you tomorrow,' Forb said. He closed the door.

'Oh, doc…' Jefry said.

Forb leaned in again.

'Thanks.'

Forb rolled his lips in a smile, exchanging a warm look with the rumel. He stepped out, closed the door, stomped into the rain.

Jefry was sitting on a mat in the corner of the hut. His neck hurt. He watched the fire through half closed eyes. The flames were a bright blur through tears that had now settled. The hut convulsed as the wind rocked it. With a careless gesture, he placed some kindling on the fire. The wood took the flames, burned, filled the room with a strange green smoke, filtered through what acted as the chimney, but was more of a wooden pit. Jefry frowned. He hadn't smelled that type of smoke before. It was more of a sweet scent, heady, penetrating.

Somewhere outside you could hear trees moving, but there were no windows through which to see them. As he leant back he felt water on his right hand. He looked down, noted saw that it was beginning to rain as there was a small hole by his hand. He slid along the floor to keep dry, brought his knees up to his chin. Outside, the wind screamed.

His head felt heavy, and he wanted to go to sleep, but it was too noisy. The rain had rattled against the bamboo. Then, something caught his eye. To his left, through the small hole, something was moving. He could see a glistening, which was not water. The thing appeared to hover, then crawled around the hole. long. He could tell from the markings that it was an adder. It hurled itself into the dry.

Jefry pitied it. There was a storm outside. He would leave the snake alone, let it have some warmth inside. He watched the creature coil then almost roll forwards, spilling opposite him. About three feet long, he watched it with detached fascination. Crawling, it moved nearer the fire, then remained still. Jefry ignored it. Minutes passed and he listened, still, to the rain outside.

'Terrible weather,' a voice said.

Jefry looked up, his head hazy from the smoke. He looked around and saw nothing. The snake lay in the corner, still. Jefry shook his head and rested it on his knees again.

'I said it's terrible weather.'

Jefry looked up again. Nothing. Curious, he felt at ease. He stood up then opened the door, which, once it was unlocked, was pushed open by the force of the wind. It was dark, but could see the greens and blacks of the leaves shimmering with rain. The trees groaned under the strain of the wind. There were no animals that he could see. No people. There was only darkness.

He turned, closed the door, returned to his position on the floor.

'Told you so,' the voice said. It was a baritone sound.

'Who said that?' Jefry asked, placing his hands on the floor either side, as if feeling the wood would help his search. His eyes widened.

'Well, let's narrow it down, eh?'

Jefry looked at the snake. Its head was pointed towards him, its body uncoiling with precision. 'You?' He laughed.

'Well, who else?'

Jefry leaned back against the side of the hut, his heart beating a little faster. 'It couldn't... Am I talking with myself, or something?'

'Well, then you were. I'm talking to you now.' The adder moved in front of the rumel, and Jefry shuffled to a cross-legged position. Was he going mad? Had he been stung by an insect that had brought on some momentary insanity?

'Yes, well here I am,' the snake said. 'You can close your mouth, too.'

Jefry said, 'What, um... what do you want?'

'Charming. A bit of shelter wouldn't be too much to ask.'

Jefry felt a sudden guilt, but then he chuckled at the absurdity of feeling such a thing towards a snake.

'What's so funny? I amuse you? Yes?'

'I didn't realise there were talking snakes on the island, that's all.'

'There aren't. Singular, if you will: *snake*. And yes, my

conversation adds a little something, I must say.'

The snake didn't appear to move its jaw much. Jefry leaned forwards to study the creature in depth, but there was nothing to suggest it was capable of speech. It looked like a regular snake. 'So, um, what's your name?'

'Oh, please. Shut up, Jef. Right, so what are you going to do?'

Jefry convinced himself that its jaw was moving. 'How do you know my name?'

'Don't insult my intelligence, Jef. We serpents have a bad rep, admittedly, but give me some credit. What *are* you going to do?'

''Bout what?'

'Oh, for pity's sake,' the snake said. 'I *despair*. About your wife, and Manolin.'

'Oh.' Jefry looked down, feeling embarrassed that someone—something—had penetrated his emotions. More than anything he wanted not to think about his wife or Manolin, content simply to listen to the rain drumming against leaves and wood. 'I'm not sure.'

'Well, it's quite simple, isn't it?'

'Is it?' Jefry asked.

'Yes.'

Jefry said, 'Well what then?'

'You must kill Manolin.'

The rumel raised an eyebrow.

'Don't look at me like that,' the adder said. 'Kill him. He's humiliated you. He's screwed your missus. He's hurting a lot of people. You're angry, aren't you?'

'Well, yes,' Jefry said, inwardly surprised at the intelligence of the creature.

'Good. Good. We ought to act more with our emotions, Jef. Emotions get things done with *vigour*, don't they just?'

'Well, I'm not sure.'

'It does. Believe me.' The snake oozed nearer the fire. 'You might want to put more kindling on. Getting damn cold.'

Jefry shuffled across, placed more of the scraps of bark on the fire. The room filled with the strange smoke again.

'Much better,' the snake said. It turned its head towards Jefry, who had sat back in the corner again. 'Upsetting, isn't it?'

Jefry nodded.

'You'll stay angry forever, you do realise this?'

Jefry said nothing.

'You'll take it out on any female you're with. Can't shed your skin like me. You'll wear the scars. So, you might as well try and do something to feel good about it.'

Jefry tilted his head to the snake. 'Are you for real?'

'Are you? Give me evidence of that, if you are…'

Jefry was silent. He couldn't be dealing with questions of a philosophical nature, not in his state.

'Thought not. No one ever does. Had a whole host of things to say to enforce the point, too.'

'Thought you might've,' Jefry said.

'You give in too easily.' The snake moved across the floor to the hole on the other side. It stopped, looking out. 'It's going to stay like this all night. By morning it'll be still again.'

Jefry could only manage a sigh.

'You don't say much, do you?'

Jefry said, 'Oh, I *am* sorry. What d'you want me to say? Sing a song, perhaps?'

'Damn, no. Can't stand songs. Get enough of that from the islanders. Talk, Jef. Talk. What's on your mind?'

'You know damn well what is,' Jefry said.

'So, tell me the plan then. What you going to do?'

'I don't know,' Jefry said. 'I'm still hurting, all right.'

'Could always poison him,' the adder said. 'And her.'

'No.'

'Do you still want her? Could you still have her?'

'It's not as simple as that,' Jefry said. 'You can't just have it black and white. You can't simplify what people do like that. Who knows what I'm going to do? I still love her, if that's what you mean.'

'You're a tough one, Jef, I'll say. Course, if she's done it this time, she's probably done it before…'

'You're not helping here.'

'Just pointing out the facts, Jef, just pointing out the facts.' It coiled up by the hole, tilting its head outside. Then, it turned back again, as if unable to decide what to do. 'What's to say she hasn't?'

The room was still filled with the smoke from the unfamiliar wood, drifting in hypnotic drifts.

'Plan B—kill the man, keep the woman. Pretend the baby's yours.'

'And when the baby has a child of its own one day? It'll be plain it's not a hybrid, so it can't be mine.'

'Kill them both?'

'How about I kill no one,' Jefry said.

'Your call. You know, up forest, I've some friends who pack one hell of a bite…'

'Thanks, but I can handle this.'

'Suit yourself. Think about it though. He's younger than you are, smarter, more handsome; he's a human, too. She'll keep the child; you know she wants one badly. Fact is, Jef, you haven't slept with her in ages, and he walked straight in. He's more man than you, Jef. More man.'

Jefry could feel his heart pumping against the wall of the hut. His tail twitched. What this reptile said certainly held some truth—ones he didn't wish to acknowledge. A bitterness blossomed inside of him, focussed, strong.

'You're angry, I know it. It's not a bad thing. But play it cool, Jef. If you're going to kill him, there's a whole host of ways in which a man can die whilst on an island.'

'Go away,' Jefry said.

'I'm sorry?' the adder said.

'Go away.'

When Jefry looked at the snake he saw only the tail flickering through the hole. There was a puddle inside. He glanced at the fire, blinked, rubbed his eyes. It had died down a little. He had no idea what time it was, but he felt tired—a sense that hours had passed and he wasn't aware of where to. Inside him there were still hot ashes of anger. Whatever it was that the snake was saying had generated some much needed clarity and direction in his mind. For a moment he considered if the snake was even there, whether it was a figment of his imagination. The issues the reptile had raised were ones that only Jefry could have figured out himself, eventually, but it was as if his thoughts had sped up. For a good while afterwards, the rumel simply gazed at the final wafts of smoke that drifted from the fire in a single, steady stream.

Yana Speaking

On these pages I feel the need to write everything down in some fancy prose, but I think the bare facts say more than a false style ever can in this instance. Besides, I know that if I exaggerate, I'll lose the essence of this island. I'll loose the sense of place.

So, in simple, clear words then:

I am lying on my front, my cheek touching the white sand. Before me, the sea stretches. I am at Mnebu Bay, and everything is bright. Each drop of water sparkles. It's simply too hot to move. Maybe it's my current health, or maybe it's the island, but everything is so sensual.

I think it's the island.

It's mid morning and the wind is enough to stop me from sweating. My skin still tingles from the heat. I can see little fishing boats coming in. The men are silhouettes, and there are at least four shades of blue that merge with one another. And there is every wave spilling up the beach, receding then being overtaken again.

Repeat and fade, I could stay here forever.

We've been here a few days and everything has gone wrong. I did not anticipate returning to Escha with a child. I did not anticipate returning to Escha a single woman, either, but both ideas appeal now I come to think about it. I like the idea of having a child. I can't pretend that I've never wanted one. Santiago thinks I've been lucky to escape so far. He's not overly fond of children, poor Becq. All my friends and family have had them. I remember my sister, Yvena, telling me, when she first had Estella, the little thing cried all through the night. She cried so loud that Yvena couldn't sleep. When Estella stopped crying, Yvena had said, the silence was so blissfully intense. I want that, I want that very much. I'm putting on weight and I love it. I look down at my stomach and know that I'm creating something, and that I love him or her very much.

Of course, telling Manolin will be something altogether more difficult. I still can't tell him and I'm not sure what he's going to say. I'll also have to let Becq know, too. She's not going to like the fact that the 'untouchable' Manolin succumbed to this old woman's charms. She'll be clinging on to her doll for a little while longer. Santiago insists I tell him and everyone as soon as I can. He's cornered me several times. I can't see why he'd want me to ruin Manolin's life though. It seems strange that someone who has helped another so much would want to cause them such a problem like this.

Manolin has been freed from the city since we've arrived. Quite right, too, as he's had a lot to deal with. The island has turned him into something of a free spirit, unlikely to be claimed by anyone, let alone Becq. She'd be no good to him anyway, and he'll never want her. He's one of those men will only stay in a masochistic relationship, like his last one. He's the sort that does not like the responsibility of making a decision. I remember days like that.

I've learned more about people, but look at the idiot I ended up with: Jefry. Of course, I'll get the negative spin from it. He's so kind and so gentle. 'How could you do that to him?' Thing was, he never got me *excited*. At least Manolin, for the brief moment it was (not his fault, he claimed), made me feel like a *woman*. Jefry has always been so predictable. I wanted to feel a surge of something, of simply anything, race through me. Is it a crime to be bored by things? Should a marriage just turn to being distant acquaintances; saying good mornings at the breakfast table does not constitute love and affection.

He stayed the night in a hut on the north of the island. The doctor thought he needed time to think. Perhaps I am being too harsh, but sometimes you have to be. He joined us again in the morning and acted as if little has happened. He even spoke to Manolin, although I could see the look in Jef's eyes. I could see it clearly, because I've never seen it before.

I hate to say it, but I think him being a rumel affects me greatly, the older I get. I can't quite put my finger on what it is. It's not the sort of thing to be said these days. Initially there was this excitement of him being non human. And I know my mother never approved, which gave our nights a certain zest. He was never a great lover, not that these things matter in the long run, but it was certainly different: feeling his tough skin upon mine; feeling that tail wrap me up. But I guess no one likes to hear the same song endlessly.

I'm confident it's over. I feel, quite simply, nothing but sympathy for Jefry. This baby provides me with the ultimate escape. I don't want a relationship with Manolin, either. Wouldn't want to lumber him with an old thing like me anyway! I can do this on my own. He'd run a mile anyway. No, this child is simply mine.

It's a gift.

I'm bored with geology. I don't care what constitutes the sedimentary layers here. I don't care where there are geological faults. I should've given this up a long time ago. Santiago bores me. Jefry bores me. Everything is so frightfully dull. If it weren't for my beloved lump I'd probably run off with one of these native men. They're so awfully generous and so sensual.

Sensual: I think that is most definitely the word to describe the island. This is all getting more like one of those ghastly diary entries now. And how self-aware can one get? I'll continue sensibly.

One forgets about the city and remembers what it is to touch and feel and smell and taste and hear. I was talking to Mghuno, one of the village men this morning. He was hauling his boat on to the beach and took a bundle of fish to his family. He was manly and brown, too. He did everything so slowly, as if he had forever to do it in, and I watched him for some time. He is so gentle and strong. He speaks to me as if I'm a deity. Perhaps these sun-kissed men think that of a pale woman such as myself—I'm the exotic to them, after all.

There are so many things I could write about: the colours, the smells, the weather, the people, the forest, the reef. The ichthyocentaur: now they *are* an interesting lot. So peaceful. I can't understand why anyone wants them dead. They are killed so brutally, too. Such a ghastly vision. I know Santiago is planning something. He is an observant man. I think he's been frightfully nice about everything—the baby and my situation. He wants to use one as bait, to flush out the beastly things that are doing the killing. I'm not sure what I make of it. In essence it is does the job, but think of the poor creature being dangled out, waiting to be killed with just our weapons to protect it. It is so risky. I don't want any of them to come to harm. They're quite loveable, and just simply remarkable. It's insane to think that these creatures were thought extinct, and that we're here, with them, touching them.

And Santiago wants to play with their life? I'm really not so sure. That's just my opinion. I don't want to get into politics.

Anyway, I shouldn't write of frightening things like that, I should stay here, with my book and my pencil, and concentrate about what really matters because it's all here for me to see. Or, failing that, I'll turn over and let my back get a little browner.

I can do both.

I woke up sunburnt. There is a crab that has just crawled out of a shallow pool; I am redder than the damn thing. Sometimes I think I might be too harsh on Jefry. I guess over the years I've just become bitter, progressively. It happens. Some people are shocked when suddenly they wake up one morning, look across at their partner and suffer a stab of regret. The partner has given up; lost their charm. They no longer make any effort. Is it intentional, or do they simply forget? That's when people have long affairs; flings with someone who can provide comfort, a welcoming touch.

I remember when I met Jefry I felt a surge of excitement, and I knew it would of course one day go away, but I had hoped it would develop into something else. That was back in the days when it really was frowned upon for a human and a rumel. Legal, yes, but there was an unspoken essence in the city, the kind of talk that happens only behind backs. It's not wrong, in my opinion, for that to provide excitement. We are all attracted to things that are different. When a man with another accent walks into a foreign community, he is viewed with suspicion, but he is surrounded by an allure. It happens everywhere. But for that man to be of a different physiology, well, that certainly had people talking.

He used to be so nice to me. I'm not someone who accepts grand gestures because, quite frankly, that is too predictable. It's the most warming feeling to have someone ask how my day went, or to have him run a bath for me. It made me feel secure. And that is important, despite what anyone says. For me, I need security. Or I once did, at least.

Sometimes I think that being on this island is not all good. It is alarmingly dislocating. Home equals comfort; and it is amazing how that makes me feel. Being here where I'm not in my own bed, where I'm not eating the comfort foods I'm used to, where I can't chat to my friends or family; it makes me crave someone's attention so badly. I feel like a small girl again, who is restless when she is not back at home.

I'm not sure if Jefry can make me feel happy anymore. I know that in reality one should not rely upon anyone else for happiness, but it's easily forgotten. It's a basic human desire. I suppose being rational won't help anything. I suspect making lists of good and bad points will do little to help. I should see if that unspoken *thing* is there, whatever it's meant to be. None of this makes sense. Looking back over these words, all I can see is that I'm really confused. Nothing makes sense, nothing seems structured. I'd rather hoped that writing everything down would be beneficial, but all I've done is worked myself into paranoia.

Nineteen

Three days passed and no more ichthyocentaurs were killed. The doctor had agreed to Santiago's plan. That night they would use one of the creatures as bait. Forb spent the morning talking to some of the elder ichthyocentaurs. They had agreed, and were cautious, but Forb had described the extent of the weapons at their disposal.

The team continued their studies. Manolin and Becq focussed on the ichthyocentaurs. Yana and Santiago, with Jefry's help, had built up a geological and physiological profile. Jefry had sampled soils from various points of the island. Scientifically, they were coming to the conclusion that they were on paradise.

Yana was continually silent. For hours at a time she did not speak at all to Jefry. Manolin could tell something was wrong, but he was enjoying the island too much. He dined with Forb, Myranda and Lewys as often as he could. Manolin had great trouble hiding his feelings for the doctor's wife. He felt it odd that the doctor and Myranda must have both known about it, too. He sat with Myranda whilst Forb went for his morning surf. They talked about nothing that mattered. Manolin had his suspicions that the doctor, on seeing this, had extended his surfing each morning. Manolin and Myranda talked for longer each day. They would sit, on some remote part of the beach. She would perch on a rock, her hands in her lap and she would look down and smile when he asked about her past. She said there was nothing to tell. To Manolin that was beautiful.

She would walk slowly. Everything she did was mindful. She had no desire to understand Manolin's scientific rigour, but she always listened. She did not ask about his past, and it seemed to him that there was no need to discuss the past in their culture. It didn't matter. All that mattered was the present moment. Manolin appreciated this fact: his ex-wife had extracted, with precision and strain, every detail of his life. When he came to think of it, all his girlfriends had. They wanted to know who he had had dinner with, whom he had kissed. They would bleed out the details, hurting themselves and, he despaired, they would make him feel bad for it.

On Arya, none of that seemed to matter. Life was a totally different creature here.

Santiago, after a few days' exploration, became well acquainted with Arya. With the help of some of the villagers, he began to collect specimens. There were a few good butterflies, and countless beetles of which he had no record. Nets were held under trees in the middle of the forest while he threw up a little gas bomb, which exploded, then the plume knocked out hundreds of insects. They fell stunted to the nets. Santiago marvelled as he recognised none of them, clasping his hands together in an exclamation. The villagers would carry his samples back to the ship every evening.

He kept a close eye on Calyban and Soul. He did not trust them, wondered why they were even on the island. He would follow them on their daily constitutional to the north of the island, where for a brief section, the beach encroached a rocky shore. There, water gurgled in crevices, and the island had a different tone. He watched them as they sat on the rocks scanning the horizon with their telescope. Occasionally they would stop and converse with a few of the islanders, then, when the conversation had finished, they would take notes. The two of them always walked together.

The doctor found Santiago slouched in a hammock on the edge of the village, nestled between to palm trees, his right hand hanging down to a bamboo cup of water. His top hat was pushed over his eyes.

'Ah, Santiago,' Forb said. 'There you are. I've had my chat with the ichthyocentaurs.'

Santiago pushed his hat back and struggled to sit up. 'Splendid. And?'

'They've agreed to it.'

'Splendid, my good man. Splendid. This is the only way.'

'I suspect you're right, but I don't want to see any more die.'

'Not going to happen, doctor. Not going to happen. Mark my words.'

'You've several muskets and pistols?'

'Indeed,' Santiago said. 'I think we'll need a couple of small boats. If these things come from the water, as you say.'

'Yes, that's not a problem.'

Santiago met the doctor's gaze. 'They'll be quite all right, y'know.'

'I hope so. I've seen so many of them die. If the death rate continues as it has, they'll be wiped out within a year. I don't want to see that happening.'

'Of course, it would be a great shame,' Santiago said. 'You care for them a lot, don't you?'

'Yes, very much,' Forb said. 'They know so much about plant use it's amazing. I often thought of returning to the mainland and showing my findings. Think of the lives I could save. But then, I can't ever leave here. I couldn't take my wife and son to Escha.'

'No, they'd hate it. I know I do, especially after seeing this place.'

'Really?' Forb said.

'Yes. Well, I never quite liked that place truly. Well, not Escha. You get some nicer spots out further across Has-jahn, but of course all the work is on the west coast. One always hopes that government and society change, but people are too greedy. Anyway, people never care about politics unless they themselves are effected. It makes being a scientist a difficult job, at least. Especially studying the natural world.'

'I overheard that you were engaged in politics, once?'

Santiago smiled, reclining further. 'I did. Once. That was a long time ago now. Before I got into this business. But I got forced out of it. Don't much like to go into it.'

Forb nodded. 'Manolin tells me that you've been to one or two of the other islands in the chain before?'

'Indeed. I don't know why I never came here in all honesty. This is one of the smallest in the chain, isn't it?'

Forb found something disagreeable in Santiago's tone. Whether or not the old man told a precise truth was debatable. 'I think it's in the middle actually. But I don't go to the others.'

'No,' Santiago said. Well I went there not all that long ago as a matter of fact. Acted as a guide—you know, the usual malarkey to try and make ends meet. I had three vessels to pay for. They were rather pleasant places, although a little on the barren side. There's not much there. The group didn't want to see this far south.'

Santiago tilted his head to the sea then back towards Forb. They were silent for a moment. Neither of them felt it worth saying anything, which surprised Forb, being men of a shared interest. Forb didn't dislike Santiago at all, but the old man wasn't as engaging as Manolin on a personal level. Santiago didn't want to connect with the island in the same way Manolin did.

'Well,' Forb said, 'I guess I'll leave you to it. I'll get everything ready for sunset, if that's okay?

'Splendid. That's a good time to start.' Santiago sat up. 'In fact, I'll row to my ship and collect our weaponry now.'

'Good.' Forb turned, walked away. He looked over his shoulder to see Santiago edging his way cautiously off of the hammock.

The air was pungent, especially further out in the shallow water. Manolin breathed it in deeply, his hands on his hips, his white shirt rippling in the gentle winds that were more refreshing than being on land. He turned to see the ichthyocentaur that was sitting back on the beach. Jefry was standing behind him, a musket in his arms, a long shadow across the sand. Manolin waved, but he did not reply.

The water was gentle, hardly making a noise against the reef behind them. Santiago, who was sitting hunched over in the boat next to Manolin, studied his pistols. He drew one up, rubbed the smooth barrel, glancing up from time to time as gulls arced to the north. Manolin turned to the other boat, where Becq and Yana were sitting, with the doctor beside them. They were fifty or so feet away, sitting in a line facing him. He gave a wave. Only Forb waved back.

'San?' Manolin said.

'Yep,' Santiago said, looking up from his pistol.

'Are you sure Yana's all right? She hasn't really spoken to me properly for days.'

'She's a lot on her mind.' He looked back down.

'Such as?'

'She'll tell you when she's ready. Complex beast, a woman.' There was a smirk on the old man's face.

Manolin shrugged. The forest had darkened in the poorer light. In a purple sky, the moon was a third full, low and large against the volcano. Fires were being lit on the beach. He said, 'You think this'll work then?'

'Indeed,' Santiago said. 'Not a lot else we can do.'

'True. Where are Calyban and Soul?'

'Should be on the beach,' Santiago said. 'I think they're getting a small boat too, but I haven't seen it yet.'

'Found out why they're here?'

Flicking the mechanism on a pistol, the barrel aimed to the water, Santiago said, 'Hmm. Not really. I *think* it has something to do with disappearing ships.'

'Disappearing ships?'

'Yes. Rather a lot of trading ships have gone down near this island in the past. I've heard tales all my life about it. Great exploratory ships being sunk. Fishing schooners never being seen again. I was, in all honesty, surprised we made it here without any event.'

'You think that Gio sent them to hitch a ride with us then, not just to keep an eye on us?'

'Not entirely. I'm certain he wants an eye kept on us, for sure. People don't like not knowing things.'

Manolin nodded, his hands still firm on his hips.

Santiago glanced up. 'Sit down—you're making the place look untidy. And it's going to be a long night, I reckon. We may not even see anything.'

Manolin sat with a sigh, rocking the small fishing boat. Santiago raised an eyebrow.

The sound of the tide became monotonous. Manolin lay on his. The night was peaceful, the sky still fresh from the storm a few days ago. The stars were clear, numerous. His wonder had still not ebbed since he had been on the island. It wasn't long until he wished it was Myranda on the boat, and not Santiago. She would have made the wait more bearable.

Myranda. The only woman to have taken his mind off of his ex-wife. He smiled at the thought that she was not considered a beauty of the island, and he did not want her to be either. She was perfect as she was: her eyes, bright against her browned skin. Those slow and precise walks along the beach.

But Manolin could not, would not. He had an unparalleled respect for the doctor. There was something almost mystical about the bald man, a quality that someone so knowledgeable seems to possess. Between the two was a bond, a sharing of values. Manolin was conscious that his fantasies would not ruin that.

He let his thoughts flow.

Manolin and Santiago were both silent, both watching the horizon, the beach, the reef. Three hours drifted by. Nothing happened. The ichthyocentaur was still sitting on the beach, Jefry still behind. On the other boat, the doctor was standing up, scanning the horizon, but his body was in a relaxed pose, one hand rubbing his bald head. *Why does he always do that?*

The moon was higher. The fires of the village were bright. Manolin could smell something being cooked. Villagers went about their business. Their silhouettes and shadows moved discretely between the huts, the fire and the forest. Another half an hour and the fires were nearly out, thin trails of smoke rising in a line.

Manolin glanced back to the ichthyocentaur and it was now standing. Perfectly still, it was staring out past the reef.

Manolin nudged Santiago who turned to see it.

'It's standing,' Manolin said.

Santiago was silent. He craned his neck to follow where he guessed the ichthyocentaur was staring, but the sea was calm, nothing unnatural moving on the surface.

The ichthyocentaur stood there for some time. Then, it began to shuffle towards the sea. Jefry followed it to the water's edge before the creature moved into the shallow water.

'What's it doing?' Manolin asked.

Santiago didn't reply.

The wind was picking up. The ichthyocentaur waded further out to sea, but was only up to its knees. Its arms were motionless. Jefry had his musket in his hands. Manolin could see him walking back and forth, his eyes fixed on the ichthyocentaur, which was nearing the two fishing boats.

There was a distinct sound. It was like a breeze racing along the beachhead, but silent, almost out of range for them.

'It's definitely related to the sound,' Manolin said.

Santiago nodded, pointing at the ichthyocentaurs' village, some distance away by the volcano. Fires were moving. He glanced towards the reef, the direction in which the creature was headed. Manolin followed his gaze, picked up a pistol. He could see nothing except the flat coral platforms some way off.

'Row nearer,' Santiago said, indicating the ichthyocentaur.

Manolin placed the pistol on his lap, picked up two oars from the middle of the boat. He pulled them onto the side, began to row across to the ichthyocentaur. The creature was waist high in the water.

'This'll do,' Santiago said. They were about twenty feet in away from the creature. Santiago had his musket in his hands and rested it on the side of the boat. Manolin pulled the oars in, picked up his pistol.

Manolin never realised how dark it had become now that the fires had gone and the moon had fallen behind a cloud. It forced Manolin to rely on his hearing and the sound became noticeably clearer. 'You hear that?'

Santiago 'Yes, indeed. It's clearly the sound bringing it out. Keep your eyes fixed.'

Manolin, watching only the ichthyocentaur, could hear the clinking of metal as Santiago loaded his musket. His heart began to beat a little faster, and his hands were clammy against the pistol. The creature seemed to be in a trance, not aware of its surroundings. It was struggling against the tide.

Santiago stood up, lifted his musket, placing the butt against his shoulder.

'What've you seen?' Manolin asked, standing up and rocking the boat.

'Movement,' he said. 'Keep your eye on the creature.'

Manolin turned to see that the ichthyocentaur was standing still, the water lapping at its chest. Forb's boat was coming along the other side, the women with pistols in their hands.

The moon came from the behind the clouds, and illuminated the scene. Barrels of the pistols and muskets shone. On the water where Santiago was aiming, there were distinct shadows. Something was breaking the surface of the water.

The current carried their boat further out, nearing the reef. Three distinct lumps had surfaced, which Manolin took to be seaweed, drifting forwards. His heart raced and he held the pistol at arms length. Santiago was calm and methodical, the weapon natural in his grip, and with the tip of it he followed the movements.

'When should we shoot?' Manolin asked.

'Not until it's right there, on him, and we can see clearly what the hell it is. I want to see what it is and I want to know where it comes from.'

Manolin's throat felt dry as he passed the pistol from hand to hand in anticipation. Almost immediately he heard a melody, faint and almost untraceable.

'Get ready to row, Manolin.'

'Why?'

'Because if we shoot, it's going to swim very far, very fast, so I want to know where it goes.'

Manolin picked the oars up again, set them ready to row. Three heads appeared clearer, near the ichthyocentaur. Still there was the soft melody. The heads surrounded the creature. He couldn't believe his eyes. The heads had long hair and delicate faces: they were women. Three women. The females circled the creature, which was standing motionless, either waiting or showing no control of its own. The women closed in, and Manolin could see their breasts, full and round, rise above the water. In their hands were blades.

A shot punctured the sky.

The sound echoed around the bay and there was a piercing scream as one of the women fell down. The other two stopped, turned. Santiago fired, a tiny explosion of water appearing to the right of the remaining two.

'Row to the reef,' Santiago said. 'Quick.'

Manolin began hauling the boat through the water, not knowing where he was going, and he could see the two women's heads cutting cleanly towards the reef. He started off ahead, but they were parallel then edging ahead. He lurched forwards, pulled the oars backwards, propelling the tiny boat. He was level with the reef, careful to steer the boat away from the coral platforms. Santiago fired, and a spark shot off the rock. He loaded again and fired across, following the heads all the time.

Manolin had passed the first ridge of the reef, continued, falling behind, sweat pouring off his head. Then the heads sank. Santiago fired once again into the water where he last saw them.

'Fuck,' Santiago said. 'Fuck it, we've missed them.'

Manolin put the oars down, collapsed backwards, his chest heaving.

Santiago looked at him. 'You're unfit. We've lost them.'

Manolin lurched back up with a sharp gasp of air and stared, cold and hard at Santiago. 'They went underwater. You want me to row underwater?'

Santiago stared at the sea, his foot up on the side of the boat. His head moved from side to side as he tried to see where they could possibly have gone.

A minute later, and Forb pulled his boat up alongside. Becq and Yana held their pistols uneasily.

'I got one,' the doctor said. 'The ichthyocentaur's still back there, a little dazed. I'll head back and see what it was I hit. You see what they were?'

Santiago nodded. 'Heard of creatures like this, but never thought I'd see one.'

'What was it?' Forb asked.

Santiago said, 'A siren.'

'A siren?' Becq said. She looked at Manolin, leaned over the side of her boat. 'You okay?'

He nodded, smiling with his mouth open, still catching breath.

'Yes,' Santiago said. 'Thought they were myths. Still, absence of evidence is not evidence of absence, as my old lecturer used to say. I'd be very intrigued to see one close up, not that I've ever seen one before.'

'A siren,' Forb said, shaking his head.

'I've never heard of them,' Yana said.

'Fishermen's tales, usually,' Santiago said. 'Never known anyone to have actually seen one.'

He looked over the side of the boat, down into the water as the boats tapped each other with the water's movement. 'The water changes depths here, doesn't it?'

'Yes, by quite some incline. The reef follows the floor down a very steep fall.'

'How far?'

Forb shrugged. 'Can't swim down particularly far. None of the villagers has ever gone deep. The ichthyocentaurs used to be able to go down for dozens of minutes at a time. Even an hour. They're great underwater, but ever since they started being killed off, none of them went down that far.'

Santiago raised an eyebrow as he sat back down in the boat. 'Really?'

'Yes. But they'll hardly swim at all these days.'

Santiago said, 'Well, that's where our ladies went, so... Let's take a look at one then.'

Manolin looked back to see the ichthyocentaur had turned as was running up the beach then into the forest.

Forb hauled the body of the siren on to the beach. Manolin helped him by pulling on the siren's other arm, and her body carved a trail through the sand. They couldn't help but stare at her. She had a shot wound through one eye, and where the it had punctured, a thick, black liquid had leaked. Half her face couldn't be seen. A group of villagers had gathered to see the spectacle. Yana and Jefry stood further back. Yana looked across at Jefry for some time. He never once looked her way.

Pain gripped Yana's face. Becq walked up to her, took her hand. 'Are you all right? Please tell me if something is wrong. I can help you.'

'Oh, I'm not sure you can,' Yana said. 'I'll tell you when we go to bed.'

Becq rolled her lips thinly in a smile.

A gasp went up from the huddle of villagers as Forb and Manolin lay the body down in front of them. The villagers muttered amongst one another. Santiago flicked open a small knife then walked up to the body. Forb, Manolin and Santiago crouched down next to it.

The siren was disturbingly beautiful.

Five feet long, she looked like a woman, up to her waist, where a thick, oddly-textured tail extended. It looked like half a giant snake, with two fins strapped on the end. Ribs contained thick flaps, like gills. Her breasts were firm, round. Her hair was long, black and slick, face was almost translucent.

'You know, she's quite an attractive creature, all things considered,' Santiago said. He pulled back her remaining eyelid. A ghostly orb stared at him. The old man shuddered and he laughed awkwardly as he kneeled back, then dropped the knife as the lid closed.

'You really think so?' Yana asked. 'I can't see it myself.'

Jefry grunted. 'Well, you've never had any taste, have you?'

'I know what you mean,' Forb said to Santiago. He looked up. 'Mhuli, what say you?'

A tall villager stepped forwards, his slender limbs oozing forward. He had cropped hair and a wide, elegant face, and wore shortened breeches. 'Thy speaks truths, Forb. A man could wonder greatly at her beauty. For why did thou ask of my opinion?'

'You have different tastes than us,' Forb said. 'What you find attractive isn't the same as me, usually.'

Mhuli stepped back into the group.

'Gilli, and you?' Forb said.

A plump, stout woman, who was considered beautiful by the islanders, bounded forwards. She was almost naked and her hair was tied back, revealing large, low-hanging breasts.

'What say you, Gilli?'

'She possesses no beauty. I pray you could do much better than this, doctor.'

'Where's this going, Forb?' Santiago asked.

'I find it peculiar that every man finds her attractive, but none of the women. Moreover, we're men with differing tastes, yet we all find her pleasing to the eye. I think that'd very odd, that's all.'

Manolin nodded thoughtfully, his vision bound to the siren. He picked up a strand of her hair and it felt gelatinous, almost like kelp. His eyes settled on her face with ease. She was indeed pleasant to look at and he felt sad that she was dead. It disturbed him to look at her wound. An inexplicable urge took him. He wanted to hold her. He wanted to take her with him. He didn't know where.

Forb leaned over her, pressed her body to feel the texture. Santiago, too, touched her. All three of them were touching her, hunching over her, a primitive and suggestive display. They seemed lost and their eyes glazed over as they focussed on the siren.

Yana stepped forwards, shook each of them in turn. They looked up, confused at what she was doing.

'You're under some sort of trance, you idiots,' she said. 'Stop looking at her.'

Manolin couldn't explain the deep sensation that had just filled him. Stunned at what was happening, he rubbed his face vigorously. Not only was there mystery here, but danger.

Forb stood up, followed by Manolin and Santiago. They glanced down at the body as they stepped away.

Yana said, 'You men are useless at the best of times. There's obviously something in her make up that affects males.'

Forb nodded, rubbing his chin. He blinked rapidly. 'I think you're right. Incredible stuff. I've never seen anything quite like this. What about you, Santiago?'

'Nope. Only heard of these things and seen drawings. This is something quite special indeed.'

Yana, with her arms out wide, steered them back. 'I'm sure you think that, all right. But how about we focus on facts? This thing has some strange effect and tried to kill.' She stepped aside as some of the villagers moved in around the body.

Manolin looked up as if he had been reminded of something he'd done whilst drunk. 'Of course, yes, she did. Right, well what I want to know is how come the ichthyocentaur was stuck dead in his tracks. What was it this thing did?'

'It had to be the sound,' Santiago said. 'We all heard that sound. It was gentle, like a song. I've noticed it before. The ichthyocentaur up there,' he indicated the volcano, 'were stirring, too. It didn't really have an affect on us though, so I suggest it was outside of our hearing range. Too high, or something.'

'I think you're right,' Forb said. 'Question is, where did they come from?'

'They're obviously local, else these killings wouldn't be frequent,' Manolin said.

Santiago turned and looked out to sea. It was night, and he couldn't see where the horizon was. He could hear the water lapping against the shore. 'What's the other side of the reef, Forb?'

'Depends how far you go. Islands further up, as you know.'

Santiago said, 'What about down?'

'Come again?' Forb said.

'The other side of the reef, and down,' Santiago said. 'What's there? The sea floor drops steeply, you say.'

Forb shrugged. 'As I said, don't really know. Can't dive particularly deep. Don't have the equipment to go down that far anyway. And don't know of the technology to do so. All the diving equipment I've known only takes you down so far. After a while, the air from the surface becomes toxic, doesn't it?'

Santiago nodded, smiling. 'We have the technology.'

Forb raised an eyebrow. 'Really? How?'

Santiago leaned closer to the doctor. 'Relics.'

Forb smirked, then laughed. 'Where the hell did you get one from, and what is it?'

'You know 'bout relics?' Manolin said.

'Course. I was involved with government when I was in the city. I know about stuff the public doesn't.' Forb turned to Santiago, respect suddenly in his eyes. 'So, what've you got?'

'Submersible. Seats up to six. You can get gas mixtures in Escha, just had to get them in the right containers. We can follow the reef as far down as it goes. And more. Just have to be careful we do it slowly, else it isn't pretty.'

'Where did you find it?' Forb asked.

'Money can get you anything in that city,' Santiago said. 'Too much. So it wasn't difficult, if you know where to go. And I do.'

'We'll go tomorrow, if you want.'

Calyban and Soul barged through the group, and the villagers muttered annoyance as the two approached Forb. The two agents paused to look at the siren.

'So, that's our killer then, eh?' Calyban said.

'Indeed,' Santiago said.

Manolin couldn't read their faces in the dark, so he trusted them less.

Calyban said, 'Why didn't you tell us you were after one tonight? We should've seen this. It all needs to be recorded.'

Santiago shrugged, turning his back. 'Really? I could've sworn I did.'

'Where did it come from?' Soul asked.

'Not sure, but possibly the other side of the reef, in the deep,' Forb said.

Calyban nodded. 'You're going to see what's down there then?'

Forb nodded.

'We're coming with you. Whatever you find, we want to know. Okay?'

Santiago said, 'Why? Why must you?'

'Keep telling you, Mr DeBrelt. Whatever you see, we also need to see.'

Santiago smoothed down his moustache, then rubbed his face. 'Fine.'

'Good,' Calyban said. The two of them turned and joined the group of villagers that were huddled around the siren.

Santiago walked away with Manolin and Forb. Yana, Becq and Jefry followed.

'We'll have to bury the siren, you know,' Manolin said.

'Sure,' Forb said. 'It'd be a shame to let the beauty decompose out here. We'll do it when all the fuss has died down. I did think that Santiago expressed an interest in keeping one. For use as a specimen. Either that or one of the ichthyocentaurs. I can't keep up with him at times.'

'You and me both,' Manolin said.

Yana and Becq took a stroll along the edge of the forest. It was late, but neither felt tired. The tide was ebbing. Yana was silent for most of the walk, although the quietness wasn't awkward. She seemed content merely to listen to eh sounds of the island. Occasionally, she would laugh to herself.

'Amazing thing, the siren,' Becq said.

'Yes, very,' Yana said.

'You wouldn't think something like that could kill, would you?'

'I guess not.' Yana looked at the patterns in the sand, and at the thin strips of detritus that marked the changes of the tide. She walked with one foot either side of a line.

'What's on your mind, Yana? Come on, we're close aren't we?'

Yana sighed, stopped walking to sit on the sand. Becq crouched down beside her. To their right, the island curved out slightly, a knuckle of rocks protruding, slowing down the water.

'A lot's going on, Becq. My life is changing.'

Becq was silent, fiddled with a strand of her dark, blonde hair.

'Jefry and I are having some major problems.' Yana's eyes focussed somewhere in the distance. 'I had an affair, Becq. I slept with someone else.'

Becq looked across at Yana. 'You had an affair?'

'Jefry and I are very much over. Have been for ages. Oh come on, it's not like I felt anything for him. It's been over for months and months and the very sight of him makes me sick. D'you hear me? Sick.'

Becq said, 'When did all this happen?'

Yana held her head at an angle whilst she drew her knees to her chest.

'When?' Becq said again. 'Since we left Escha?'

'Yes.'

'Who? Who did you sleep with? It wasn't my father was it?'

Yana laughed. 'Hell, no. Not him.'

'Manny?'

Yana's face creased slightly. It was a mixture of pain and relief, as if she were about to throw up the admission. 'Yes.'

Becq choked a gasp, wanted to be sick. She felt desire to strike out at her. She wanted to scream in the woman's face. Instead, her head quivered and she looked down. A sense of betrayal filled her. Yana knew how she felt about Manolin.

'I'm sorry, Becq. It's not how it seems. It was nothing, just one night. I regret it was with him.' She rested her hand on Becq's arm.

Becq said, 'Please let go.'

Yana released her grip. 'I know you like him. I'm sorry.'

'Did you enjoy it?'

Yana looked across. 'What do you mean?'

'Did you enjoy it?' Becq said. 'Was it good? No. Don't tell me. I don't want to know.'

'I'm really sorry. We were drunk. He would've slept with anyone the way his mind was.'

'Stop talking,' Becq said.

Yana slumped back with a sigh, tilted her head up at the stars. Her hands were clasped over her stomach.

Becq stood up, stepped over Yana, marched back to the village. Tears streamed down her face, her eyes became hot. She walked towards Manolin, who was standing with the doctor outside his hut.

Manolin looked up from his conversation with Forb as Becq strode with some purpose across the beach towards him, her arms moving with jerkiness by her sides. Manolin said, 'Hey—'

'Don't you give me that, you bastard.'

'Hey, what's this about?' Manolin looked at Forb sheepishly.

'You know perfectly well what this is about?'

'I'll leave you two alone,' Forb said. He stepped sideways and up into his hut, took one last glance before walking in.

Becq focussed on Manolin. 'You... you slept with her, didn't you?'

'What?' Manolin said.

'You slept with her didn't you?'

'Look, Becq, I don't know what you're talking about.'

'You slept with Yana.'

'Please, keep your voice down.' Despite the darkness, he could see her red eyes and the wetness around her cheeks.

'Why?'

'Look, Becq... Did she tell you that?'

'Yes, of course she did. What d'you think I'd make it up?'

'No, I... Look, I think that's between me and her.'

'No, not when you go ruining other people's lives. Not when you hurt other people?'

'Does Jefry know then?' Manolin said. He glanced around in case the rumel was somehow nearby, the sense of paranoia all too sudden.

'I don't know,' Becq said. 'I hate you, Manolin. I hate you. I want you to know that no matter how much you think of yourself, you are the vilest man I've ever met.'

Manolin watched her turn and stomp down the beach to the rafts, and her feet slipped on the sand. She pushed the raft to her hut, climbed up inside.

Becq fell onto the floor of the hut in a rage of tears. She sobbed, into her blankets, lying on her side, and she drew her knees up to her chest. For minutes she vibrated with anger. When she found that she was too tired to cry any further, she reached inside her bedding and picked up the doll. She held it up and looked at it through stinging eyes. Then, she drew it close to her chest, inhaling deeply.

She lay there for some time hoping the repetitive surf would send her to sleep. Her eyes burned with her sadness. It was over an hour before she began to think rationally: that Manolin was not hers and had never been. He had hardly ever looked her way. Through never really getting to know Manolin, she had formed her own opinions of what he was like, what he wanted, and what he would do for her. She knew she was wrong. She knew that her relationship with Manolin was mainly in her mind. Perhaps that was why she was crying: the realisation that her fantasies were not real.

She believed Yana ought to have known better. Yana knew how she felt. Then, the woman did have her own problems, too. Perhaps she was justified. Becq realised that she was convincing herself that everyone else was right again. Her lack of self confidence, ironically, forced itself to the front of her conscious. She wondered what would be the case if they were all animals. Would everything be such a mess? If they were all hares, running wild on the island, would they have the same worries? Would they have created the same mess? Would hares run around hating each other, being jealous, angry, sad and falling apart? Do hares cry?

She didn't think so. She thought of Arrahd. The god's chubby little face materialised in her imagination. There he was, smiling. It was Arrahd's belief that humans were the most sophisticated of creatures. An animal, if lucky on death, would be reincarnated as a human and have an opportunity to strive for spiritual perfection. She thought it rubbish. She would have given anything to be a simple creature, doing simple things, in a simple group. She thought Arrahd was wrong: being human, or rather one that could think, was a curse.

Then she smiled as she realised that some humans didn't think. They simply went about their lives, not thinking, not appreciating Has-jahn. They woke up, worked, ate and went to bed, unconscious of the damage they did around them, because it didn't matter if they killed too many animals, if they destroyed homes, if they ate too much, if they fucked too much. Who was that hurting? Maybe they weren't animals after all.

Becq sighed. What did any of it matter? Here she was again, with no one to love her. No one to hold when it got cold. And she was getting older, nearly thirty. Who would marry her when she was old? She saw her future ebbing until she could no longer see it.

Yana climbed up into the hut and interrupted her thoughts. The woman sat in the doorway. 'Becq, are you okay?' She pushed back her hair from out of her face.

Becq's head felt heavy, and she strained to look at her. 'I think so.'

'I'm really sorry, Becq. I want to do anything I can to help and make it up to you.'

'Would that make you feel less guilty?'

'No. I want to make you feel better.'

'Look, he wasn't mine and never would be. You can have him if you want.'

'No, that's not what I want. I never wanted him in the first place, Becq. Please, you must understand that. I never wanted him. I don't now, and I won't ever. It was a mistake and the biggest mistake of my life. My relationship with Jefry is ruined and I'll be going home alone.'

Becq reflected on the words, laying the doll beside her. 'Jefry's had a tough time, hasn't he?'

Yana nodded. 'I know.'

'I was never that close to Arth myself. Jefry was, wasn't he?'

'Very. I know he keeps on visiting the site of the pyre. He spends some minutes there, then walks along the beach. He's hurt, and I've hurt him even more. I'm selfish, I know, but it was all one drunken night. I can't even remember it and I regret it so much.'

Becq was silent as she sat up.

'Please forgive me, Becq. You're the only person I can talk to. You're the loveliest person I know. Don't hate me.'

Becq looked down then up at Yana. She sat back, leant on her arms. 'I don't. I needed a reality check.'

'Thanks, Becq. Let's go for a swim together tomorrow, then we can walk whilst the guys prepare to dive.'

'That'd be nice.' Becq nodded, lay down again, in the vague hope that she would get some sleep.

Twenty

'You know what substance they say is most like human blood?' Gabryl announced as the ship cut over the surf. The horizon was grey. Salt and spray filled the air.

'Nope,' Menz said, leaning on the rail.

'Seawater.' Gabryl lifted his chin up as he said it. 'Honest. Seawater and blood are similar, biologically speaking. See—the sea's in all of us, but I reckon my blood is closer to it than others.'

Menz would've been genuinely impressed had it been Gabryl's first interesting fact. 'Shouldn't we've found one by now?'

'Say again?'

'A whaler. We've been in the right area, as you say, for nearly a week.'

'Patience, Menz. How're the girls?'

'Oh fine. They're below.'

'That's good. No real place for a woman when we have to do what we have to.'

'You forget who you're talking about,' Menz said. 'You forget who's in charge.'

'I know, I know. Old habits I guess.'

'Hmm.'

'I guess I don't expect girls to be so angry as them two,' Gabryl said. 'Especially Jella. And Lula—ain't she a delight? I can't believe that someone so sweet as that can shoot as you say she can.'

'Aye, they certainly can handle themselves.'

'Now that's another story entirely. I've been on some ships in my time, and there was always a bit of scurrying under covers. It was to be expected of so many men on their own, but when there's so many men around, and still them women are playing around... Well, it ain't natural.'

'They're in love, Gabryl. That's all there is to it. You've been at sea too long. In Rhoam, there was a lot of it going on. They're entitled to a bit of love in this world, ain't they?'

'Such a waste though,' Gabryl said. 'Anyway, must keep focussed. These things don't steer themselves.'

'True, true. So, when're we going to see a whaler?'

'Should've seen 'em a long time back, in all honesty,' Gabryl said.

'I've known this side of Has-jahn for years, and there's always some around this time of year. Don't see why we need one anyway.'

'It's been explained before.'

'I know, I know. Just like to be sure, that's all. Don't like taking too many risks, especially when the weather's this bad.'

'We got to find one. Ain't no use doing what we're doing without one.'

'Look, how can you really be sure it'll work?'

'Basic ecology, Gabryl. Basic ecology. That and myths, but it'll work. I trust Jella. She's done her reading for years on this. Quidlo is a funny thing. Besides, Jella's done her field research, too. She's seen the thing close-up. She's looked right at it and, to be sure, dropped a bit of whale meat near it. By all accounts she's hardly ever been so scared, and she's a tough nut.'

'Yeah, she mentioned she'd seen it. How long ago was that?'

'Couple years back.'

Gabryl nodded. He stepped back up to the wheel.

Menz patrolled the deck as if it was his own. Yayle was below, feeling sick. Allocen was somewhere within the ship's shadows. Jella and Lula were spending time together. He didn't like the increasing amount of time the couple spent alone. It was not right, he thought. They should be a team, because they could possibly lose their lives. It occurred to him that no one had really spoken in a group for the last couple of weeks. He hoped it was the solitude of being out at sea for so long.

Menz liked his daily chats with Gabryl. Both being men that had served in armed forces they could discuss travels, combats. Both men became proud, then, as time progressed, disillusioned. Despite all that they had given, neither really had a future, or a past that they had built on. They had no family, or wives. There were lovers, as they were only too willing to share, but there were only lovers. There were no children to tell such tales. They were hardened men. They did not like to admit they had avoided the real battles of life: starting a family, providing for children, being by their parents. Ironically, now it was all they could think about.

Menz leaned on the rails staring out to the horizon. The sky was still pale, patches of blue opening out ahead. His eyes settled into a trance, the movements of the boat forcing his eyes to be lazy. It was some seconds before he noticed a ship in profile on the horizon, heading towards the mainland. He stood up straight, turned to face Gabryl.

'Gabryl, look—' He indicated the ship.

'I see it. Well done that man.' Gabryl turned the boat so that it travelled in an arc to intercept the ship. It would be a few hours before they were upon it.

Gabryl looked up at the sails and saw that they had now as much wind in them as before, so he started the ship's engines. The noise of the motors brought Jella and Lula up to the deck. Yayle and Allocen followed, the rumel looking a pale shade of his usual grey, the Qe Falta creature hidden beneath his black cloak.

'Why're the engines on?' Jella asked, her white hair being aired in the gentle winds.

Menz indicated the ship on the horizon.

'Finally,' Jella said. She put her arms around Lula and kissed the side of her jaw. 'Here's the next hurdle.'

With the engines on it took less time then they thought to catch up with the other ship. As they came closer they could see it was indeed a whaling ship. The vessel was twice the size of theirs, with a long, flat deck to the rear, where large mechanisms leered over the side. There were pulleys, cranes and cogs, a system of ropes. Most importantly, there were carcasses of whales. The silhouettes could be seen from a long way off and soon the stench confirmed it.

Jella counted twenty men on board as they stood on the ship's starboard side, staring in her direction. They were some fifty feet away and it was clear that Jella's ship was going to cross in front of the whaler, whose deck was ten feet higher. She heard the other vessel's engines die, in anticipation of a collision, and it turned away slightly. They were upon them surprisingly quick. She went below deck, returned with muskets and pistols. She handed them out, turned to Allocen. 'Off you go.'

Allocen looked at her from the depths of his cloak. Men were looking down at them, shouting in a foreign language. The Qe Falta picked up a grappling hook that was linked to a length of rope, threw it up to the whaler, which was still moving. She watched his cloak air as he made his way up the rope and over the edge. Men on the deck of the whaler crowded around Allocen as he stepped out of site. Commotion followed.

'Shouldn't we ask them first?' Menz asked.

Jella shook her head. 'No risks.'

Then she heard the first screams and the sound of metal cutting air, then wet noises like fish falling on the deck. Pistols fired, metal struck metal.

They stepped back as blood spilled over the sides and they stepped up to find shelter by the ship's wheel. They looked at each other as they heard more screams and shouting. They couldn't see anyone, but still the blood mixed with seawater dripped off of the side as the whaler knocked the side of their own vessel. Men were still firing. More screams. She could see the top of someone's head, so lifted her musket and fired, then watched him buckle forwards. She couldn't see anyone else, but she could certainly hear them. There were agonizing gasps as if they were undergoing surgery without anaesthetic.

Menz shook his head. The others were wide-eyed, shocked at what the Qe Falta could be doing. They could hear his boots running along the deck, followed by another low moan. Then there was only silence.

Allocen's figure peered over the edge of the whaler's deck. He was no longer wearing his cloak, his antennae wafting in the crosswind. Blood soaked his clothing. He raised an arm, put up his thumb. Then he turned.

Jella looked at Menz.

The old rumel merely shook his head. 'We could've at least asked.' Then he stepped towards the rope.

That evening, they all sat around a table in Jella's cabin. She insisted that they ate together, even Allocen. Lula sat next to Jella, and Menz, Yayle and Gabryl opposite. Allocen was standing by the cabin door, his hood drawn over his face. Sometimes, Jella could see the candle reflecting in the creature's eyes.

'So, we've got the whales,' Gabryl said.

'Yep,' Jella said. She sat back, draped an arm over the back of the chair, sipped from her wine glass, then looked out the porthole window opposite.

'Just straight there?' Gabryl said.

'Yep,' Jella said. 'Straight there.'

Gabryl ate tentatively at his fish meal before laying his fork on the plate. 'This thing—it wants a whale?'

'I reckon so.'

'You... *reckon* so?'

Jella said, 'Okay, I *know* so. It'll be like catnip.'

'Then we take it to Escha, right?'

'Right.'

'Sounds a good plan.'

'It is a good plan.' She placed her glass down and regarded Gabryl. She smiled then looked across at Menz then Yayle. Both rumel were staring down at their plates. They had already finished their meal.

'It sounds too easy,' Gabryl said. He wiped some sauce from the edge of his beard with his top lip. 'Anyway, why do it this way, why not other ways?'

'This'll last longer. You see, a bomb will kill. They all die at once. It's good and effective, but people recover. Wounds heal. Buildings are built again.' She indicated Allocen. 'The Qe Falta, like him over there, they had a series of suicide bombers years ago. Took out a few buildings, some people, but nothing much since. Those attacks are soon forgotten by those who're unaffected.'

'Suicide, why? You mean they do it with the intention they pop up to visit Arrahd afterwards?' Gabryl asked.

'No.' She smiled again. 'Hell, no. Not Arrahd. I don't think the Qe Falta believe in a god, no matter what name, particularly that one. They don't believe in creation at all. They go back to the life force, or whatever they believe in. Back to nature, as it were.'

'A strange psychology.' Gabryl nodded to himself; his words seemed to linger in the room.

'Not if you believe in a greater good,' Jella said. 'Not if you want justice for your people. It makes perfect sense. To them.'

'And this Quidlo thing...' Gabryl said.

'Will go on and on. Firstly, it will create a large scale movement of water—a tidal wave. Started so far out at see, that initial impact will be severe, possibly wiping out half that coast. Over a period of time, with Quidlo in the waters, the damage will go on. It'll stop all shipping for a good few years. The damage goes on. That's the great thing.'

Gabryl nodded, raising a fist to his mouth to stifle a belch.

Jella couldn't tell what the man was thinking. She turned to the rumel. 'You're quiet, guys.'

'Yes,' Menz said. 'A bit tired, I think. Repetition of the sea and whatnot.'

Yayle nodded. 'Absolutely.'

'You boys need to learn the ways of the sea,' Gabryl said. He slid his plate forwards. 'I'll make sailors out of you yet.'

'You mean you'll take us below deck and bugger us, pretending we're women?' Yayle said.

Gabryl guffawed loudly. 'Ah, lad. You've got spunk in you, I'll say.'

'I hope that's not a promise?' Yayle said with an eyebrow raised.

'Are you sure you're not having any doubts?' Jella asked. She rested a palm on the table. 'Anyone?'

Menz raised his eyes and held her gaze for a while. 'Don't be silly.'

After the others had gone to sleep, Jella and Lula were standing in loose nightwear on deck feeling the cool night breeze from the trade winds. They were both holding cups of water, leaning, side by side, on the rails. Lula sighed. She looked at the reflection of the stars on the surface of the sea.

'What's wrong?' Jella asked above the noise of the waves hitting the boat.

'Nothing,' Lula said.

'I can tell something's up.'

'Nothing's up, okay.' Lula glanced into her cup, took a swig.

Jella stood closer. 'Look, just tell me. I don't like seeing you like this.'

Lula slid fractionally away. 'Surprised you even noticed.'

'Sorry?' Jella said.

'You heard.'

'I'm not sure I understand.'

'No, no you don't, do you.' Lula smiled vaguely. 'You have no idea what I'm feeling. You haven't cared for ages.'

'That's rubbish. Course I have.'

'Tell me then,' Lula said. 'Tell me what I'm feeling.'

Jella was silent. Her tail was motionless. She looked down into her cup.

'You're too caught up in this,' Lula said. 'You're not even thinking about me. And it's not as though you're busy, is it? I mean, there's not a great deal to do on this thing.'

'I think about you more than you realise.'

'Maybe it's not enough,' Lula said.

'Why're you so insecure? You never used to be like this,' Jella said.

'You say it as if it's a crime. It's not *bad* to be insecure, you know. Everyone is, a little bit.'

'I'm not,' Jella said.

'No,' Lula said. Then, 'No, you're not, are you. You're immune to worry.'

'I'm just rational.'

'People aren't rational. *Human's* aren't,' Lula said. Then, 'Sorry, I didn't mean it like that—'

'Why apologise?' Jella said. 'Nothing offended me.'

'Okay,' Lula said. 'Surely you must be worried about something. Not even the plan?'

'No, it's perfect.'

'Do you worry about whether or not the plan will make you feel as though you achieved what you wanted? Or, will you go on after this looking for the next thing to get involved in?'

'I can't see where you're going with this,' Jella said.

'The more time I spend with you—out here, out away from other distractions—the more I worry about you.'

'There's really no need for you to worry.'

'What d'you really hope to get from all this?' Lula said.

'The destruction of a city.'

'I mean *personally*,' Lula said.

'The destruction of a city.' Jella turned around and leant back on the rail.

Lula sighed and glanced across the dark panorama. It was easy to be distracted by the rhythm of the tide. 'If Lucher was still standing, if you had no need for this, then what d'you reckon you'd be doing?'

'Doing?' Jella looked across at her lover. 'You, ideally.' She smiled, stepped behind Lula, put her arms around the human.

Lula smiled politely. 'I mean what would you be doing as a life, career?'

Jella rested her chin on Lula's shoulder. 'Don't know. I think I'd probably be studying something. Science. It was what my dad wanted.' Then, 'Yes, probably as a researcher or something. Coastal ecology. That's the same thing my dad studied. When I was little he used to talk to me about those sorts of things.'

Lula sighed happily. 'You don't talk about him much. I like it when you talk about your past.'

Jella said, 'I don't really have a past to talk about.'

'I think that's why I don't understand you as much as I'd like to,' Lula said. She ran her cheek along Jella's. 'I don't know what makes you tick.'

'You make me tick,' Jella said. She kissed along Lula's jaw.

'You don't have to *always* fuck me,' Lula said. 'Talk to me. Let me inside your head more.'

'You don't want to be there.'

'What would I see?' Lula said.

'You. Being pleasured.'

'You're sex-obsessed. Why?'

'You say that as if it's a crime…' Jella smiled.

'I think you're using it as an excuse not to talk to me. You'd rather make me horny than open up.'

'Any complaints, genius?' She threw her cup overboard.

'No,' Lula said. 'No and yes. I get worried about you.'

'Well, don't be. I'm fine, really.' Jella ran her tail up between Lula's legs, and the human opened them, leaned forward on the rails, stared out to the horizon.

Lula closed her eyes, accepting the act, believing it to be a strange charity or sorts. She began to think whilst Jella slipped her tail inside. She'd have to fake it again tonight. But at least it would make Jella feel better about herself. She wasn't the only person in the world to do it. It wasn't as though she didn't enjoy it, because she did. To feel those strong, tough-skinned hands on her body was a delight. Sometimes though it needs more than the physical connection. As she felt Jella's tail moving around inside of her, circling with precision, she clutched the rail tightly.

'Are you enjoying this?' Jella asked.

'Oh, yes…' Lula said, and dropped her cup into the sea.

Twenty-One

'So, this is it then,' Forb said, rubbing his hand over the metal of the submersible. It was brown, shaped like a cigar. Its curves seemed to hint at mathematical precision.

'Indeed it is. My own precious secret. A delight. A mystery of technology. I give you, the *Pilar*.' Santiago was standing on the deck with his hands in his pocket. The wind ruffled his vision settled on the doctor, waiting for a reaction.

'It's fantastic,' Forb said. 'Seats six?'

'Yes.'

'A relic you say?'

'Yes. When you're connected as well as I am, you can find some delights on the black market.'

'I thought you were a Collectivist? Didn't think you guys did things on the black market?'

Santiago said, 'It's the economy's fault, not mine.'

'So, where does the gas mixture go?'

'There's room for ten cylinders, which fit around the inside. That can last for twenty-four hours at least. We won't need that much, though. It's a mixture.'

'And you got that from… let me remember, the industrial areas?'

'Absolutely. You remember the mainland well, sir.'

'Yeah, can't forget a heap like that in a hurry.' Forb inspected the six large, glass portholes. He was amazed to see something like this. During the rebellion to science, so much must have been lost. It was awe-inspiring to see such a mechanism had survived, and it suggested only greater things an age ago. Although he had fled the city and his own past, Forb was entranced by the sense of history that the submersible presented. To see something so old, yet far more powerful than current civilisation could create, was humbling. 'How thick is the glass?'

'It isn't glass,' Santiago said. 'We don't know what it is, but it isn't glass.'

'So how deep can we go in it?'

'A few miles, I suspect. But we won't need to go that far. Notice the spotlights on the front.'

'Yes, very effective?'

'Reasonably. Probably a ten foot beam underwater with generators of some description. If I'm honest, it's technology is beyond anything I've known or seen. But the whole thing's perfectly safe. I've used it on a couple of private expeditions before. I've never had any trouble with it.'

'What metal is this made from?'

'Again, we don't know. It looks like brass, but it isn't. It can stand ridiculously strong pressures though. The last age had so much better resources, didn't it. We've things floating around the city that we've no idea what they're used for. What really annoys me is that government have stashed Arrahd-knows how much of it. All growing mould. If only we knew. Of course the public, mostly, have no idea.'

'Yes. It's surprising,' Forb said, and wondered again how Santiago managed to extend his influence so far to acquire such a device. 'What time shall we dive then? When can you get it ready by?'

'Give me an hour,' Santiago said. 'Just need to make sure the rotors are in good condition then lower the thing. I can get it ready for before lunch, then we should still have good light. Not that there is any down the other side of the reef.'

'Great. I'll row back and get the others ready.'

The rest of DeBrelt's crew were sitting on the beach, near where Santiago's ship was anchored, a little way off where the waters were deeper. Everyone struggled to meet each other's vision. Calyban and Soul were watching them all from the shade of a tree. Palms crowded the beach, and the shallow waters were still bright blue despite the shade.

Yana stood up, hunched instantly. She was clutching her stomach and she gasped a little. Everyone turned. 'It's all right. I'm just feeling sick.' Waving a hand, she staggered from side to side.

'Are you okay?' Becq asked.

'Yes, please don't get up. Stay there, okay. Promise you'll stay.'

Becq nodded, her face revealing concern.

Yana groaned as she stumbled, bent double, towards the forest. Her white skirt was long and almost tripped her as she stepped out of sight. Jefry stood up, looked for a moment towards where she went then followed her. Manolin wondered what it was all about.

Yana clutched the side of a palm tree. The rough bark scratched her hand. She held it up, looked at it, couldn't feel a thing. Her other hand was pressed hard below her stomach. The forest was humid. She looked up and saw a trail, followed it, not knowing where it went. It hurt to walk. The forest was a blur of varying shades of greens. She did not notice any of the birds or the insects or the plants, sweat stung her eyes and she gritted her teeth as she stumbled along the trail, into the darkness.

Jefry watched her stepping along the path. White flashed suddenly: her skirt disappearing behind foliage. The rumel wiped his brow, kept a distance so that she would not be worried by his presence. If anyone was worried, it was him. He had never seen her in so much pain. His throat felt dry and he wondered what was wrong with his wife. He brushed back the ferns, and he dipped his head to avoid insects.

Yana had found a cool, deeply-shaded region in the forest. Its remoteness suggested that she thought she could be alone. The forest floor was dry and she slipped on the fine dirt, back against a tree and she gasped as she landed. Tears trickled down her face like sweat. She looked short of breath, as if she had never known such agony. Her skirt was no longer white. Aside from the stains of plants and dirt, there was a thick red streak down the front. Her eyes widened as she struggled to take breaths and looked up to as Jefry stepped around the corner. They held each other's gaze, and it was as if all other sounds in the forest had disappeared.

Jefry stepped down to her. 'Can I help? What's wrong? Tell me.'

She shook her head as she forced out the words, 'I... It hurts. Cramps...'

His heart was racing. He looked in more detail at the red stains. 'Hold on, hold on.' He took her hand.

She bent over, wheezed.

'Is it the baby?'

Her head jerked up and she shook it. Fear was the only emotion in her wide, round eyes.

'It's not for months,' she said. 'It can't be'

'Shall I fetch Santiago? What about the doctor? He might know of some remedy.'

She shook her head again. Her hair, clammy with sweat, spiralled down her shoulders. 'No... I'll be fine, honestly. I—' She gave a cry, hunched over again, then rolled onto her side.

Jefry knelt by her head, feeling completely useless. Yana clawed the forest floor. The rear of her white skirt was coated with blood.

Calmly, he said, 'Yana, I'm going to move your skirt.'

She nodded, rubbing her head in the dirt.

Jefry lifted her skirt up over her legs. The material was sticking to her thighs. His face creased as he saw her legs smeared with blood in places.

'You're bleeding all over, Yana—oh, no.' He moved over, lifted her hair from her face then he kissed her on the forehead. 'You're going to be all right, okay?'

She was crying again, and she nodded, baring her teeth. Jefry felt sick.

A few moments later she screamed.

Manolin looked up as he saw a flock of birds shooting out of the forest and out to sea. He heard the scream, glanced at Becq.

'I'll see what it was,' he said.

Running, he entered the forest. He looked at where there was recently trodden dirt, followed the tracks. A fleck of white material was caught on the side of a tree and he headed down that trail. He could hear crying, but he couldn't see where it was coming from. Following the sound, minutes later he saw two shadows up ahead in the dark, where the canopy was so dense that it blocked sunlight. He jogged, taking wide steps over the low plants, towards the figures.

Jefry was hunched over Yana. The rumel's hands were covered in blood and Yana was sitting against the tree, in the dark, crying in heaving sobs.

Manolin looked again at Jefry's bloodied hands, shocked. 'Jefry, what's going on? What've you done?'

Jefry was facing down, but drew his head up, slowly, to look at Manolin. 'What have *I* done? Me?'

Jefry looked down again, at his hands. He glanced back at Manolin, who was standing with his hands on his hips.

'What have *I* done?' Jefry looked at what was in his hands then threw the contents at Manolin's face. 'Just fuck right off, okay. *Now.* Go on, fuck off!'

Manolin stumbled back, reaching for his face. He walked through the forest, looking back at Jefry. He did not understand what was going on. He looked at his hands. They were red with blood and he noticed something on his neck. He reached to his collarbone, beneath his shirt and drew out what looked and felt like a tiny tentacle from an octopus, like one that he saw in the food markets back in Escha. It was only a couple of inches long, and as he rubbed it though his fingers he could feel the fleshy cartilage. He frowned as he jogged out of the forest and, with his face still showing confusion and disgust, as if a bird had fouled him, he stepped out onto the small beach and to the water. He immediately washed his face and hands in the warm water.

The scene he had witnessed confused him utterly. What was Jefry doing with blood on his hands? Why did he throw blood at Manolin? Was he angry because of his incident with Yana? Manolin didn't like the idea that he'd upset anyone. Obviously his relations with Yana came at a difficult time, and it was inexcusable. But what had just happened was simply bizarre.

Becq approached him. 'What's wrong?'

'Nothing.'

'Are you sure?' she said. 'What was the scream?'

'A bird, that's all.'

'A bird?'

'A bird.'

Becq said, 'Why's your shirt collar red?'

'I caught it on a branch. It's dark. I wasn't looking where I was going.' Across the way, Forb stepped off a raft on to the beach.

Manolin turned to Becq. 'Excuse me for a moment.'

He walked along the sand over to the doctor.

'Ah, Manolin,' Forb said, shading the sun with his hands. 'You looking forward to the dive? What's with the stains?'

'Oh, nothing. Snagged on a branch. When're we off?'

'Couple of hours. Everything all right?'

'Yes, sure,' Manolin said. 'What're we going to do with the siren's body incidentally? Santiago mentioned dissecting her?'

'Hmm. Well possibly,' Forb said. 'I don't want it done on the island. I'd like them to be kept as far away from the ichthyocentaurs as possible, just in case. On board the ship, maybe. I don't think it'll do much good, though. The only way we're going to get on top of things is to get down there and see for ourselves.'

'Fair enough,' Manolin said. 'I'll round Mr Calyban and Soul up then so we can. I think Santiago would probably like to take the body back to the mainland though. For proof.'

The doctor's face darkened. 'Is he going to announce that he got it from here?'

'Would that be a problem?' Manolin said.

The doctor suddenly seemed anxious, desperate even. 'You cannot bring any of the authorities here, Manolin. The navy will come and tear the place up. I'll lose the plants, and the cure.'

'Cure?'

Forb said, 'Cures... sorry. There's so many here. I can't afford them to be lost. You could take some of those plant specimens back to the mainland. Look, I don't want large quantities of people here. When I sent the message out, I knew that there could only ever be a small investigative party sent, if anyone at all. And I was desperate for help. Who'd be stupid enough to send a fleet? I've been meaning to have a word with Santiago. I want him to make clear that no one else should come. You understand?'

'Of course,' Manolin said. 'I'm beginning to regret even our presence here.'

'Why so?'

'We just seem to get things wrong. Between us, that is. I've never known so many problems between us all.'

'You're only human,' Forb said. 'That's what it means to be one—problems, suffering.'

Manolin smiled.

'But you're helping,' Forb said. 'Being here, you're preserving and protecting a whole species. A whole damn species. That's something.'

'Really?' Manolin said. 'How many do we eliminate with our careless actions in a heartbeat? These are only species you can see. Our industries and progress displace and kill… countless more.'

'Don't be downhearted, lad. Every species has a right. By preserving the larger species, you preserve their habitats and their ecosystems. Think how many you can't see that you save. Anyway, this lot are something quite special.'

'Yes, they're certainly unique,' Manolin said. 'I'd love to spend more time learning about them. Time just seems to go quicker and quicker these days. Far too quick.'

'A young man concerned about time?' Forb laughed, as if at some private joke.

'What's so funny about that?'

Forb met Manolin's gaze. 'No, you would understand, of all people, but it's a long story. I'm getting on, and my life's a blur, let me tell you. It seems like yesterday when I landed here and met Myranda for the first time.'

'That's something worth remembering.'

'She's a great woman. She's so simple, too. I mean that in a good way, not a derogatory term—uncomplicated, but I guess that's island life for you. Simplicity is the very essence of things here. She's very intelligent, so I don't mean simple like that. She is intentionally pure in her acts.'

Manolin was silent. He glanced at DeBrelt's ship.

'She likes you,' Forb said. 'She's very fond of you.'

'Haven't been here that long for anyone to like me, surely.'

Forb placed his arm on Manolin's shoulder. 'Look, you can tell me you would love to spend an evening with her.'

Manolin closed his eyes for a second, then opened them, frowning at the doctor. He couldn't work out what he was suggesting. 'Well, she's lovely.'

'Lovely, that's what he says,' Forb said. 'It's all right, I know. It's not difficult to tell. You've been having supper with us, and spending lots of time with us both. I can tell you find her lovely, I'm not stupid.'

Manolin felt uncomfortable, a secret confessed. 'I didn't say you were.'

'She likes you too,' Forb said.

'What?' Manolin said. 'He didn't understand Forb's meaning.'

'She's attracted to you.'

'Look, Forb, I have to say I'm a little uncomfortable with all this.'

'Nonsense. You're both attracted to one another. But, Manolin, tell me: what's happening with you and Yana?'

'What?' Manolin said. 'D'you have magic powers or something? You know an awful lot.'

'I can tell there's a bit of tension. It's the classic story of tragic affection: the fact that you can barely look at one another. I guess that you're all too busy looking around at the island, where as I'm fascinated by all of you. So, what happened?'

Manolin sighed. 'It was one night on the ship. Nothing more, nothing less. I was drunk—we both were. That's all. I'm not attracted to her.'

'Good, good. I believe you. And my wife? You're attracted to her?'

'Yes, all right, she's absolutely charming. Is that what you wanted me to say? I don't feel particularly great for saying it.'

'Don't worry. I'm not mad or anything like that. Truth is, Manolin, if anything happened to me, I'd rather like it if you... looked after her.'

Manolin gave a sideways glance, frowning. 'How do you mean? Kill her?'

'No, no. I mean, take her as yours.'

Manolin shook his head.

'I'm serious,' Forb said. 'Look, it's not an easy thing to do, you know. If I died I would love it if you were to be her husband. I truly like you. I think you and I are the same.'

Manolin felt sweat run down his face. The sun was overhead. Along the beach he could see Myranda walking towards a group of brown children. They ran around her as she met them. It was one of those fantasies, to be here. He had a live on the mainland, a career, the business with his ex wife to sort out. Friends, lifestyle, meetings. But

Forb looked as earnest as any man he had ever seen.

Manolin said, 'I don't know what you're getting at, Forb. I really don't.'

'No, I suppose I'm the only one who can know.'

Keen to move the subject on a little, Manolin said, 'Look, shouldn't we get ready for the dive? We're all keen. I'll get Calyban and Soul, and I'll be back soon, right?'

'Right,' Forb said, and wiped the sweat from his head.

Manolin was last on board *DeBrelt One*. Calyban, Soul and Forb were all standing with Santiago when he stepped on to the deck. The boat was lying against the mangroves and the air was, as it always seemed, clean and humid. The men were gathered around the vessel they were to dive in.

'It doesn't look sturdy enough,' Calyban said.

'Nonsense. This'll get us down and back easily,' Santiago said.

'I'm not sure.'

'Hello, are they complaining?' Manolin said.

'Ah, Manolin,' Santiago said. 'Tell them about the *Pilar*. Tell them how sturdy she is.'

'Yes, she's very good. You used her on a deep dive a few years back, didn't you, Santiago? On that private expedition. Very sound. And we used her in shallow waters last year. The *Pilar* is as sturdy as they come.'

'Moreover, she's made from old technology,' Santiago said. 'Strong, reliable stuff—like they used to make.'

'You mean a relic?' Calyban turned to Santiago. The agent was smirking.

'And you'd know all about that, of course,' Santiago said. 'Look, it's all legit. She's big enough to keep the six of us down for a long time. Which won't be necessary. Anyway, I've fixed the gas up so we're ready to go.' Santiago turned to Manolin. 'Are the others going to come aboard to help lower us?'

Manolin shrugged. 'I asked Becq to wait for them, but there's no sign.'

'What the devil are they playing at?' Santiago said.

Manolin glanced to the deck. 'Look, we need only one to operate the pulley. I'll ask Becq. We can get a villager to inform Yana and Jefry when they see them.'

Santiago nodded.

Manolin walked to the edge of the ship. Becq was on the beach. Myranda was nearby. He called to Becq, waved at her. She was climbing into a raft. It was a little before midday, the sun turning the water to prisms, and he leaned casually on the rails watching her row out to the boat, enjoying the sunshine.

He turned to face the others. 'She's coming.'

'Good. Let's climb aboard then.' Santiago secured the top of *Pilar* to the rope then checked the ropes at both ends. He walked to one side, grabbed the lock-wheel. He turned it over twenty times until he could hear it unlock. He pulled the door open and, with his hand raised, said, 'Enter, gentlemen.'

The *Pilar* was definitely designed for scientific exploration, Manolin thought, and not a luxury cruise. As he sat on the metal seat, with Santiago in the front seat, Forb to his right, and Calyban and Soul behind, he could see the beams of light that came from the several portholes. At the front, there was one, large porthole through which Santiago would navigate. It smelled of rust, although none was present.

The *Pilar* jolted as Becq restarted *DeBrelt One*'s engine. Santiago had brought the boat out so that it was in profile on the ocean side of the reef. After he made the final checks to the submersible, he left Becq in control. One last check, then he went inside.

Becq operated the basic pulley system that lowered the submersible into the rough waters and eventually the ropes went slack. She let the remaining rope drop into the water and looked down to see that the vessel had gone down. She could hear the waves striking the bottom of the ship, feel the cool, sharp breeze, the strong sun on her face. She stood against the rails for some time.

It took them half an hour to allow the gas mixtures to be released fully, then Santiago, sat at the controls, started the motors of the *Pilar*. A bass vibration shuddered across the vessel. Through the large porthole, he could see the clear, sharp tropical waters, and the abundance of marine life that drifted by. Slowly, they descended, hovering past the reef. Santiago steered them downwards. As they descended, light faded, the water became a deeper blue. Fish flashed by the portholes as if the men were watching an aquarium.

Santiago turned *Pilar* so that she was parallel to the reef. 'I think it would be best to follow the reef and see where it ends up.'

'Why?' Calyban said.

Santiago said, 'Because, most of the organics down here depend upon the reef. It would make sense that most food chains will be based around it, including the sirens'.

'It's only a piece of rock, I think we should scout the open waters,'

Soul said. 'Surely we should have some say in the matter of our descent?'

'Fucking idiots,' Santiago said.

'Sorry?' Calyban asked.

'I said you're wrong,' Santiago said.

'Why?' Calyban said.

'The reef is not a piece of rock,' Manolin said. 'It's animal and plant that secrete limestone—'

'A massive symbiosis,' Santiago said.

'I was getting there, y'know.' Manolin turned back to Calyban and Soul. 'Yeah, a symbiosis. The two work together. It'd make sense to go this way as everything in these waters depends upon it. It's the basis of nearly every food web. It's more likely that sirens would be near it. Follow?'

Calyban and Soul looked at each other then looked back. They nodded.

'Good,' Forb said. 'Exciting, isn't it? I've been here for years and never yet seen underwater to any great extent.'

'Really? I'm looking forward to bagging a siren,' Santiago said. 'One of them will fetch a very nice price back home.' His mind raced across all sorts of possibilities—fame, fortune, women.

'San, what about research?' Manolin asked.

'Yes, yes,' Santiago said. 'That too. I can't believe we're finding a myth—an actual myth. We'll be famous.'

'We're not here for fame,' Manolin said.

Santiago said, 'I'm technically your boss, so you ought not to talk like that.'

Manolin said, 'You're so far up your own arse, you know.'

'Beg pardon?'

Manolin sat back on his seat. He wriggled before sitting up again, then turned to the window. 'I said you've forgotten what we operate for. I think this sniff of success has gone to your head.'

'Indeed,' Santiago said, dismissing Manolin's speech as a young man's folly. 'Right, I'm taking us down quicker now. You may experience a change in pressure, but this little vehicle is pressurised. Your head isn't going to explode through your ears.'

They descended for over an hour. Inside, the vessel was dark, and as they fell further, the temperature fell uncomfortably. The sound of water passing around the craft seemed amplified by the metal shell. Santiago reached into a bag that he kept on board, then he handed around thick, woollen jumpers. Manolin pointed out bizarre shapes that spirited past the portholes. None of the scientists knew what the genera were of many of these creatures. Santiago had turned on the spotlight, and as the waters became dark, they had to look out the one large porthole at the front, following the beam. Despite reaching only several feet, the spotlight illuminated a large number of organisms, all of them unknown. Santiago tilted the *Pilar* past the sharp coral ridges, and as the waters became darker he took more caution.

The *Pilar* passed down into even darker water, and Manolin could feel the pressure change in his ears. 'How far now, San?'

'Few hundred feet.'

Manolin nodded, then turned to Calyban and Soul. 'So, come on you two. What're you guys looking for? You're clearly wanting to see something.'

'That's our business, Manolin,' Calyban said.

'Oh, come on,' Manolin said.

'There's no point, Manolin,' Santiago said, calling back over his shoulder. 'They'll hold back any piece of information—they think it's power.'

'We're interested in these sirens, just as you are,' Calyban said. 'But a lot of ships go missing travelling this way. A *lot* of ships.'

'You think the sirens did it?' Manolin said.

Calyban shrugged. 'Who knows?'

The submersible shuddered. 'Sorry,' Santiago said. 'Scraped the reef.'

'Well don't damage it, will you,' Manolin said.

'What, the ship or the reef?' Santiago said.

'Both, if you can help it,' Manolin said. 'Try not to destroy anything natural.'

They descended further, staring at the porthole all the time. The lower their altitude, the less powerful the beam was. Santiago had said that when he had the light replaced when he bought the submersible, they no longer possessed the technology to make the beam effective.

Manolin didn't think the water could get any darker, but it seemed to, and soon the species that he saw were more alien. Impossible shapes and ghost-like matter floated by.

'Are we still following the reef?' Manolin said. He leaned forwards.

'Indeed,' Santiago said.

'Goes rather deep, doesn't it,' Manolin said. 'Can you hover and steer the light towards it?'

'Why?' Santiago said.

'To look at it. I didn't think that reefs came down this far. I thought the plant within the coral needed light. Not much light down here.'

'Good thinking, Manolin,' Forb said, nodding.

'Thanks, doc.'

'It's quite obvious, really,' Santiago said.

'You didn't say it,' Manolin said, feeling slightly smug.

'Fine. Anyway, I'm turning now.' Santiago tilted the submersible so that it was facing the coral rock that still, despite being hundreds of feet below the surface, contained surprising amounts of life. The beam highlighted a bold circle of the substance, and Manolin, Forb and Santiago all leaned forward to look through the large porthole.

'Amazing,' Manolin said. 'Look at the thing. How does it survive?'

'Most irregular,' Santiago said.

'Any of you two experts on the deep? Forb asked.

'Not really,' Manolin said. 'Most of what we do is land based. Shallow waters at the most.'

Forb nodded. 'I've only known shallow waters, too.'

'What are you three confused about?' Calyban said. ' It's just a piece of rock—*sorry*, animal.'

'And plant,' Manolin said. 'And plant. Everything working together.'

'Unlike you lot then,' Soul said.

'What's that supposed to mean?' Santiago said.

'Nothing. Just that you're always too busy fighting amongst yourselves to get on with anything practical.'

'Fuck off,' Santiago said.

'You two shut up,' Manolin said. 'We're trying to concentrate.' He took out a sketchbook from his pocket, began taking notes, describing the structure. The reef seemed alive, even at that depth. Coloured tubes protruded, waving in the currents. A network of eccentric looking animals swam into then away from the spotlight, diving beneath the latticework in the coral. He could see spiked plants, fish that oozed up to the rock and stuck their mouths to the limestone. 'Very odd,' he said.

'What is?' Santiago said.

'I don't understand—shallow waters, where there's plenty of light, you'd expect this abundance. Not down here, not at a few hundred under.'

'Well, it's right there in front of you,' Forb said. 'I've stopped wondering about the natural world. There're weirder things in real life than you can dream up.'

Manolin looked at the reef. He found it difficult to describe in his notes. He couldn't get his head around the shapes and colours and movements. He looked at it for some minutes.

'Are we all done?' Santiago asked.

'Nearly. Another minute.' Manolin gazed at the rock. Suddenly, he thought it moved, a subtle, slow vibration of the rock, up then down. 'Did you see that?'

'What?' Santiago said.

'It moved. The rock—it shuddered.'

'It must've been the current,' Forb said.

'No, I swear it shuddered,' Manolin said. 'A reef shouldn't do that.'

'Tremor?' Santiago said.

'It's possible,' Forb said. 'We've had tremors near the island. Small-scale tidal waves once or twice a year.'

'That'll be it, Manolin,' Santiago said.

Manolin nodded. 'Fine. Okay, let's move on.'

Santiago tilted the *Pilar*. The vessel cut through water parallel to the reef then went down further. They travelled through the blackness for minutes.

Manolin felt as if he was on another planet. 'Make's you realise how little we know about this place, doesn't it? How for down now?'

'Over a thousand feet now,' Santiago said. Then, 'One, one hundred.'

A rush of thin fish shot by the porthole, into the darkness. The group watched, in quiet awe, as other alien shapes drifted in and out of sight. Clouds of plankton were illuminated. Manolin saw a large fin covering one of the side portholes. He could see the scaly texture that covered it. Then he frowned, tapped the porthole.

'What's wrong?' Forb said.

'Damn fish won't move,' Manolin said. 'Ah—there it goes. Funny thing. We seeing much else, Santiago?'

'Nope. It's getting more barren.'

'As I thought,' Manolin said. 'Finally the lack of light is having an effect. Turn her into the reef again.'

'Yes, *master*.' Santiago stopped the *Pilar* then turned it, a clunk of levers indicating his struggle. 'Hang on. The current's strong down here.'

The spotlight fell on to the reef again. Manolin and Forb leaned forwards.

'Well, fuck me,' Santiago said. 'It's still there. You know, I only thought reef formed in warm, shallow tropical waters.'

'Doesn't have to use light though, does it?' Forb said. 'It could feed on the plankton down here or something like that.'

Manolin scribbled further notes.

'Could be anything,' Santiago said. 'Absence of evidence is not evidence of absence. That's what my lecturer used to tell me back in Escha.'

'So, that could mean the fairies feed it,' Manolin said.

'Ah, but did we even think there were sirens before we left home? Nope. And now we have evidence, but that doesn't mean they didn't exist before.'

'Point taken,' Manolin said.

'We have no idea what you're all talking about, but have you seen anything yet?' Calyban said.

'Nothing that'd interest you,' Santiago said.

'We need to see if there're more sirens,' Soul said.

'So do we,' Manolin said.

'Well let's go then, because this is all rather dull and we don't really give a toss about a piece of rock.'

'There—' Manolin said.

'What?' Santiago said.

'The damn reef moved again. It shuddered completely.'

Everyone leaned towards the front porthole, staring at the illuminated area of reef. They could see that the coral was shaking, then stopped. It vibrated. Then again before it went still.

'See, I told you,' Manolin said. 'Is that still a tremor?'

'I've never seen what one can do underwater,' Forb said. 'I guess it could still be. Let's look further down.'

'Indeed. But I don't think we should pay any attention. Let's focus on the sirens.' Santiago steered the submersible down even further.

'How long are we going for?' Calyban said. 'This is getting quite dull and we've found nothing. We should've scouted around the surface, like we wanted.'

'The hell we should,' Santiago said. 'We're taking *Pilar* down further. She's never been this deep and she's holding well. How many men d'you think've ever come this far into the deep? None in our time. We're going further, so enjoy the ride.'

Calyban and Soul slumped on their chairs as the craft descended.

For another ten minutes they headed through the gloom. Few shapes drifted past the portholes. Fewer drifted across the beam. The men began to feel the extreme temperatures. Forb was staring out of the porthole, shivering.

'Come on Santiago, let's go back,' Calyban said.

'Wait,' Forb said.

'What now?' Santiago said.

'Santiago, turn off the spotlight,' Forb said.

'You want it off?'

Forb shuffled in his seat, said, 'Yes.'

'Okay.' Santiago turned the light off and they were surrounded by a total darkness that none of them had ever experienced. Even at night you had starlight, possibly moonlight. Perhaps even the light of a house on the horizon, but this was a sense of utter pitch black.

Forb leaned forwards, staring out of a side porthole. Manolin waited for his eyes to become accustomed to the total black.

'What d'you see?' Santiago asked. He looked back but couldn't see anything. His heart beat quickly.

'A light,' Forb said.

'Can't be,' Santiago said. 'How the hell can it be?'

'Look, to the right,' Forb said.

Santiago hauled leavers to turn the vessel, blindly, to the right. You could hear the others shuffling to look out of the front porthole.

'There,' Forb said. 'To the top right of the window.'

'Some fish?' Manolin said.

'The light isn't moving.' Forb shifted on the hard seat. 'Whatever it is, it's stationary.'

'Don't be silly, man,' Santiago said. 'There wouldn't be any lights down here.' Slowly, Santiago could make out the light. Soon they all could see the light. 'Well, bugger me. He's right.'

'What d'you reckon it is?' Manolin said.

'Haven't a bloody clue. But I'm heading towards it.' Santiago turned on the beam again, directed the *Pilar* away from the reef, towards where he remembered the light to be. Every few moments, Santiago would turn the beam off to trace the source of the light. As the distance decreased, the lights became more discernable against the black water.

Manolin and Forb leaned over Santiago's shoulder. 'See it yet?' Manolin said.

'Only with the light off,' Santiago said.

'What could it possibly be?' Forb said.

'The only thing it could be is bioluminescence,' Santiago said.

'Some sort of fish?' Forb said.

'Probably,' Santiago said. 'Possibly.'

Calyban and Soul crept up to take a closer look. Santiago turned off the beam again, and there, ahead and a little below them, was the glow.

Calyban said to Santiago, 'Where the hell are we?'

'Showing an interest, chaps?' Santiago said. 'Somewhere between the islands, I reckon. We're at a pretty low point—the lowest even. The floor can only rise from here.'

'I think we should keep the beam off, San. I don't want us to scare whatever it is,' Manolin said.

'I reckon there's more than one, Santiago said. 'If you can see, there's more than one source of the light.'

'How far away?' Forb said.

'No idea,' Santiago said. 'All perspective's lost down here. Couple hundred yards, tops.'

'Keep on going then,' Forb said.

As they headed through the black waters towards the light, they could see that the source was not one, but many. The lights were white, blurred. At first you could see a few spots, but as the vessel approached you could see the lights separating, as their perspective altered, and there were in fact hundreds of motionless lights.

'Dam,' Manolin said. 'This is odd.'

'Indeed,' Santiago said. 'Quiet extraordinary. I hope you're taking notes.'

Manolin said, 'Gone through two pencils already.'

'Good stuff.'

The lights were numerous, and their craft was so close that they soon filled the whole of the porthole as if they were looking through a telescope at the night sky.

'This is absolutely unheard of,' Santiago said.

'Kind of bizarre, don't you think?' Forb said.

'Well, it's no animal, that's for sure,' Santiago said. 'Some kind of structure?'

'What the hell can build this?' Manolin said.

Everyone stared, in awe, through the porthole at the hundreds of lights that glistened and as they came closer, the men became more perplexed, more amazed. The lights were arranged in neat rows that led off in various directions, suggesting avenues, paths.

'Kind of looks like Escha from the surrounding hills, don't you think?' Manolin said.

'I say, it does rather,' Santiago said.

'What d'you think made—?'

They all lurched back, their hearts skipping beats. A siren slapped against the porthole. She was looking in, pawing, staring at them. Her eyes were wide and white. Gills opened and closed.

'Hell, there's your answer,' Santiago said.

'Get the thing off, Santiago,' Calyban said.

Santiago said, 'Our little lady friend isn't doing any harm, is she?'

'Doesn't she scare you?' Calyban said. 'Look at her.'

A silence fell as they stared at the creature. She was identical to the one that they had killed up by the beach.

'Get her off,' Calyban said.

'No,' Santiago said. 'How often d'you see one of these things? I'm heading straight for the lights. I'm a betting man, and I'd place a good pile of cash on that being their home.'

Santiago pushed a lever forward and the vessel ploughed the water with more force. He drove straight towards the lights. The siren did not move. Then, a second joined her, was identical. Together, they covered most of the porthole.

Manolin noticed that the other portholes were covered, too. The sirens were all over the *Pilar* and they could hear banging as the sirens began to beat the hollow, metal craft. 'Santiago, I suspect now would be a good time to get them off, if that's possible.'

'I think you're right,' Santiago said. 'Gentlemen, are you wearing shoes?' He turned to take a quick look at their feet.

'I'm not,' Forb said.

'Would you mind standing on Manolin's feet?'

'What?' Forb said.

'Please,' Santiago said. 'Just a precaution. Stand on his toes. Make sure you're not touching the metal floor.'

Manolin and Forb looked at each other. Manolin shrugged. 'We're all friends here.'

Forb stood, awkwardly, on Manolin's toes as they held on to each other's clothing.

'What's the meaning of this Santiago?' Forb said.

'Hold on—' Santiago stood up, bent under the control panel. He pulled out a couple of wires. 'I was never sure what these fellows did when I bought this thing. Discovered this little trick by accident.' He placed the bare wires together, looked toward the porthole. The sirens fled and he thought he could hear a faint scream, followed by silence. He pulled the wires apart and stumbled as he regained the controls again. He sat down with a grunt. 'You can stop hugging each other now.'

Manolin and Forb disentangled. Manolin smiled at Santiago's audacity.

'What did you do, Mr DeBrelt?' Calyban asked.

'I suspect when this thing was built all those centuries ago, that was an actual lever or something. Something must've been connected here.'

'You mean you don't know what it does?' Calyban said.

'Oh yes, one can find that out by trial and error. Trouble is with relics, it's difficult to know what they do and how they work. Believe me, one can find all sorts of crap. Just that no one has a damn clue what to do with them.'

'What did you do just then?' Calyban said.

'When you join the wires together, a shock passes around the outside. Those little creatures didn't like it. They won't touch us now. In fact, we may've scared them off completely.'

With everyone sat in place again, glued to the front porthole, the *Pilar* approached the construct of lights. The water became brighter, the lights still blurred. Silhouettes of sirens passed clearly over the lights. As the craft passed over a ridge on the ocean floor, the structure was revealed to them in its entirety.

'It's a bloody city,' Manolin said.

'A city of sirens?' Santiago shook his head. 'Surely not. It can't be.'

'Well, it's there, in front of your eyes,' Manolin said. 'No need for your absence of evidence stuff. There it is.'

You could see lanes and rows, carved in or out of rock, framed by the light, and sirens were swimming along the paths. Light didn't travel far that deep, so you couldn't be sure of what you saw. The rows extended upwards as well as across, and there were gaps running through. The lights flickered as sirens swam past. In some places, the lights framed more wide shapes, possibly shelter of some kind.

Santiago suggested the structure to be a quarter of a mile tall, and half a mile wide. He couldn't see how far back it went. 'This is absolutely incredible.'

'I would never believe it,' Forb said.

Soon there were several sirens around the *Pilar*, hovering at a distance.

'I wish they'd get out the way,' Santiago said.

'You going to head straight towards the lights?' Forb said.

'Reckon so.'

Calyban and Soul were muttering something.

'Going to share that gossip, chaps?'

'Sorry?' Soul said.

'We'll have no secrets on board,' Santiago said.

'Never you mind,' Calyban said.

They descended upon the structure, the sirens following them, and more came. Santiago steered the craft to the edge of the city of lights. Within a minute, they were there, and could see the first of the lights close up.

'Well, will you take a look at that?' Manolin said.

'Bioluminescence,' Forb said. 'So there's our light source.'

There were thousands of tubes, of some order of life that they couldn't recognise. The tubes moved like flags in the currents, but they were rooted to rock.

'I don't understand,' Forb said. 'They must breed these things, whatever they are.'

'Well, that's simple enough I suppose. What order d'you think they are?' Manolin said.

Forb said, 'Your guess is as good as mine.'

'Amazing,' Manolin said.

'Head down to the ocean floor, Santiago,' Forb said. 'Let's see the structure from the root up.'

When they were at the bottom, the structure towering above them, shimmering, they could see different figures that weren't sirens. They carried large shapes along an illuminated path.

'And what the hell are they?' Manolin said. Then, as they were closer, 'You know, they look a lot like ichthyocentaurs.'

Santiago leaned back with a sigh. 'Ah, of course.' He began to chuckle.

'What?' Manolin said.

'I'll take us closer,' Santiago said. 'I think I see what's been going on all this time.'

At ground level, with sirens spiralling the craft, Santiago turned the spotlight on the faces of the figures. They could see that the shapes they were carrying were structures from wrecked ships: rails, piping, a rudder. The faces of the figures were identical to the ichthyocentaurs on Arya, except there were thicker gills. They stared morosely towards the spotlight, with narrowed eyes. Sirens swam near them, then the creatures looked forwards, continued their labour.

'That's why they're killing 'em,' Santiago said. He could feel his heart beating fast. 'The feisty little sirens are breeding. And of course they are—damn women can't reproduce that well on their own now, can they? No matter how much they'd like to think they could.'

'Are you sure?' Forb said.

'What else can it be—look at them,' Santiago said. 'They're half breeds, I tell you.'

'I can't believe it,' Manolin said. 'They've been taking the ichthyocentaurs for that?'

'Well, only their sperm I guess,' Santiago said.

'What the hell for? And why're they carrying parts of ships?' Manolin said.

'They're carrying parts of ships?' Calyban asked.

'Looks like it.' Santiago said. 'Why d'you ask?'

'Those are probably Eschan ships,' Calyban said. 'Ones that have gone missing.'

'You can't know that for sure,' Manolin said.

'The damn things are sinking Eschan ships,' Calyban said. 'They're responsible for all the disappearances over the years.'

'Now, there's no way you can know that for certain,' Forb said.

'Well it's looking pretty damn much like it,' Soul said, running his hand across his brow.

'Don't jump to any conclusions,' Manolin said.

'Easy now, chaps,' Santiago said. 'I can see we're all getting pretty excited. I'm going to follow and see where they're off to.'

Once again, Santiago switched off the spotlight, steered the craft along the line. He could see that sirens swam up and down the line, as if making sure the half breeds were going the right way. They acted in a manner that suggested a slave labour. Santiago followed from a greater height, looked down to see where the half breeds were taking the scrap. The line went on for a couple of hundred of yards, and the *Pilar,* Santiago noticed, had gained some altitude.

They came to yet another structure. He slowed the *Pilar* then he stood up, stepped around the controls, looked down the front porthole. It was much darker, there being only a few of the luminescent tubes. He could see the outline of what he assumed to be a coral structure, part of the reef. The half breeds were more numerous, and they were attaching the metal that they carried to the reef. He frowned.

'What d'you see, San?' Manolin said.

'They're building something.' Santiago turned on the spotlight. He could see the reef—the stable coral rock—moving, sliding along the ocean floor, and he noted clouds of stirred sediment from where it had moved. The half breeds were attaching the metal wreckage to the rock. He muttered something and his throat felt thick. 'I'd no idea... My... So that's why. Still, I wouldn't think it a problem...'

'What d'you see, San? I can't see at thing,' Manolin tried to look around Santiago's figure, to get a glimpse through the dim waters.

'Nothing.' Santiago stood up then returned to his seat. He turned off the spotlight. Several sirens were hovering around the craft, in the gloom.

'Are you sure—?' Manolin said.

'I didn't see anything,' Santiago said. 'They were building more of the city.' He sat motionless, staring out the porthole. *Of course,* he thought. *That makes perfect sense. But I thought it was much further away from this, hours by boat. Unless it is bigger than I thought...*

'What is it?' Manolin said.

'Nothing. I rather suspect these ladies are getting a little restless with our presence. Shall we head back up? Just a precaution about the air now, that's all.'

'But what about the structures?' Soul said. 'We should go back to the main lights. If they've been taking Eschan ships—'

'All in good time, Mr Soul,' Santiago said. 'All in good time. We've plenty more days yet. I don't want to waste the air all in one day.'

'We heading back up?' Forb said.

'I think that'd be a good idea—it's damn freezing. We've plenty more opportunity. Anyway, we know now what's killing the ichthyocentaurs and why.'

'Well, not really,' Manolin said. 'We don't know *why* they want half breeds, or indeed, the fact that they can have half breeds.'

'They're not too dissimilar,' Santiago said. 'They probably share a history, going back in time. The fact that they are relatively local suggests that. Anyway, this is all up for discussion. We can have a good debate when we're back up.'

'I want to know if they're responsible for sinking the Eschan ships in this area,' Soul said. 'They represent a hazard to the city—'

'We can discuss this later, Soul. Come on, we've plenty of time.' Santiago turned the craft around, the sirens still surrounding it. 'Besides, we've got to shake these ladies off.' Santiago was keen to get back. There had been a lot of information from this, and he wanted it detailed perfectly. He had notes of his own—private documents—that he needed to check, too. Much had been discovered today. Behind him, the conversations continued.

'You're quiet,' Forb said, turning to Manolin.

'Hmm.'

'Everything okay?' Forb leaned in closer.

'Just thinking, that's all,' Manolin said. 'A lot's been happening recently. There's a lot to take in.'

'Quite,' Forb said. 'I can't wait to tell the others. What d'you think they'll make of all this?'

'They probably won't believe us,' Manolin. 'Anyway, I guess they're wrapped up in their own problems.'

'What d'you mean?'

'There was something between Jefry and Yana before we left. Something was wrong with them. I hope they're all right.'

'What was that about Yana?' Santiago asked.

'Nothing,' Manolin said. 'Come on, let's get out of here.'

'Already on to it,' Santiago said. 'We'll have to climb slowly, and it will take a few hours for us to take in the surface air. So we've plenty of time together yet. Anyway, you were saying something about Yana?'

Manolin said, 'Oh, Jefry and Yana were having another fight.'

'Did they tell you what it was about? Do *you* know why they were fighting?'

'No,' Manolin said. 'They're always like it. Guess when you come away, everything's amplified.'

'That's what islands are good for,' Forb said, nodding, smiling.

'Yes, I suppose so,' Santiago said. 'So you don't know then?'

'No. Why, should I?' Manolin said.

'I only wondered that's all. I thought she had a lot on. Her and Jef are on the rocks. Guess he thinks something strange happened on the way over to Arya.'

'Well nothing happened, okay. Have the sirens gone yet?' Manolin looked to Forb. The doctor said nothing.

Santiago sighed. 'There's one or two still swimming around us. They can't do anything. I'll put the spotlight back on in a few minutes.'

'Right,' Manolin said. 'See if you can trace the reef again, I want to take a closer look at it. I thought it was pretty fascinating. And I want to see the tremor again.'

'Doubt you'll see it again,' Santiago said. 'It was a one-off.'

'Well, if we're going up slowly then we might as well get some detail of the rock. If you could bring this thing up at an angle, you could keep the beam up on the coral and I can make some good sketches of the marine life at different altitudes.'

'Fine,' Santiago said. 'That'd be pretty good to discuss back in Escha.'

'If we ever get there,' Soul said. 'How long left do we have on this island now that we've investigated everything?'

'Whoa there. We've only just begun,' Manolin said. 'We'll be here a few weeks yet you know. Why're you so keen to get back?'

'Well, if these sirens are the cause of our Eschan ships do disappear, then it must be reported,' Calyban said. Then, 'We've got to inform the navy. It's been a mystery for decades—'

'The hell you will,' Santiago said. 'No one's reporting anything just yet. All we've done is seen them. There's nothing to suggest they're to blame.

'He's right. And I don't want the navy coming to Arya,' Forb said.

'Why?' Calyban said.

'Why? They'll ruin the place. They'll bring a fleet and destroy the waters. They'll drive their ships through the reef. They'll trash the island. We'll lose tons of important natural resources.'

'Don't worry, Doctor,' Santiago said. 'No one's coming to this island. These little runts will have to get back to the mainland without us first.'

Calyban grunted then smiled.

'Anyway, we can argue up there,' Manolin said. 'I want to concentrate on studying the coral, so if you could all please be quiet.'

Santiago steered the *Pilar* at an angle to the reef so that Manolin could see through the large porthole and study the rock. Manolin made sketches, diagrams, recording the colour and estimated size of each plant or animal he saw. Forb helped him, making quick sketches of plants. Time was passing quickly in this fever of discovery.

They had been travelling up the reef for some time before Manolin noticed the vibration in the rock. He said nothing at first, preferring just to watch. Being in such an alien environment, your imagination tended to entertain itself. It could have been anything. They ascended for an hour, and Manolin noted that the reef shook five times. Eventually, he decided to inform Santiago.

'Well, it could still be tremors,' Santiago said. 'Doc, what do you think?'

'I'm not a geologist,' Forb said. 'I don't know how the land behaves here. To be honest, I never even knew that the reef was one large piece of rock like this. I didn't know they could be distributed in such away. As for tremors, who knows?'

'Are we rising quick enough? Manolin asked.

'A little too quick,' Santiago said. 'We've got plenty of time yet.'

'Good,' Manolin said. 'I want you to start scanning along the reef, then go up and back across. That way we can see a massive section of the coral.'

'Well, we've got the time I suppose,' Santiago said. 'Sure.'

'Oh, come on,' Calyban said, in between sighs. 'How much longer do we have to put up with your crap?'

'Listen you two,' Santiago said. 'We've put up with *your crap* for weeks. We're here on a research expedition, so you'll shut the fuck up and learn something useful. Okay?'

'Fine,' Calyban said. 'Just hurry up. And just remember who you're addressing.'

The submersible travelled to lighter waters, and they could feel the temperature rising. The water became a dark blue. They could see recognisable creatures passing the porthole, into the spotlight.

Manolin continued making his notes. He stood up to get a closer look at some of the species. 'Hold it here for a minute.'

'What's wrong?' Santiago said.

'Nothing. Just fascinated by that line there.' Manolin indicated a thick, white horizontal mark that stretched across the porthole. 'There's no coral on this segment. Just lichens.'

'That's rather a long line,' Santiago said.

'There's no coral polyp here,' Forb said. I wonder why that is.'

'Do you want me to pull back?' Santiago said.

'Sure, so long as the light is still effective,' Manolin said.

'Well, I'll go a few feet back, and perhaps we can see what the line is,' Santiago said. 'Then we'll move on.'

'Forb,' Manolin said, 'come and take a look.'

The doctor joined Manolin at the front. 'Bizarre. There're definitely lichens and barnacles, and it looks like rock. How far are we from the surface?'

'Oh, not far at all now,' Santiago said. 'You could probably swim this far down, with the right apparatus. You can see the water's lighter here.'

They all looked at each other as they were talking.

Then they looked back.

'Bloody hell,' Manolin said. He could feel his heart beating high in his chest. 'What the hell is that?' They were staring at a completely black, glossy surface, and the light of the spotlight was reflecting back.

'Is that what I think it is?' Forb said.

'Bring us back, Santiago,' Manolin said.

Santiago sighed, said, 'I'm trying, damn it.' He pulled the *Pilar* back several feet and the glossy surface still filled their vision.

Everyone stared, wide-eyed, speechless. Then, the tops of the black surface were brought down, the barnacle-encrusted surface sliding till they met. After a moment, they parted again

'For fucksake, get us back,' Calyban said.

'Wait a second,' Manolin said.

'Never mind a second,' Calyban said. 'Pull back, Santiago. Please—'

They could hear, and feel through the metal surface of the submersible, a thundering bass sound.

Manolin was staring at a black eye, almost right through it. Deep within, the light found all the details to suggest this was completely animal, completely alive.

'Uh, Santiago…' Calyban said. 'Come on.'

'How big is that thing?' Manolin said. 'It must be ten feet wide.

Hell, Santiago, pull us back. And turn that damn beam off.'

'Right... Okay.' Santiago turned the spotlight off. Even in the better light, they could still see the reef vibrate as they pulled back.

'This has to be reported,' Calyban said. 'What in Arrahd's name was it?'

'Nothing's being reported without our approval,' Santiago said.

'Sod your approval, this is a... a... fucking eye. What does it belong to?' Calyban said.

'Let's all calm down—' Santiago said.

'Calm down?' Soul said. 'What, with that thing?'

'Look, everybody be quiet and let's review this at the surface,' Santiago said.

'Review?' Soul said. 'It's a beast. Whatever it is, it has to be removed.'

'Removed? The hell you will,' Santiago said. The *Pilar* shuddered as he turned the vehicle away, and steered it towards the surface. He wiped his forehead. They fell backwards into their seats as he tilted the craft.

Manolin tired to not be distracted by the arguments. He was utterly amazed at what he had just seen. If that was an eye, exactly how big was the rest of the creature likely to be? And what was the creature likely to be?

'I don't care what you say, that is a danger. Everything down there is,' Calyban said.

'We must calm down and rationalise this,' Santiago said.

'What's to rationalise?' Calyban said. Then, 'It must be destroyed.'

'We don't even know what it is yet,' Manolin said.

'*Nothing* is being *destroyed*,' Forb said.

'We must return to the mainland immediately, Santiago,' Soul said.

'We're not going anywhere.' The *Pilar* shuddered as Santiago turned off the motors and the vessel cruised through light waters again. Sunlight filtered through he sharp waters, filled the portholes. Prisms of blue stretched away.

'Right,' Santiago said, 'we've to stay here for an hour until the pressure is changed and the air is safe. Do I make myself clear? If you don't, you will die. It's as simple as that. So we've an hour, one hour, in which to discuss exactly what we did and did not see.'

'Okay,' Manolin said. 'Whatever that was, it hasn't harmed anyone. No one has been affected since their stay on the island. We've been down there and back, and we're perfectly safe.'

'This has to be reported,' Soul said.

'You can't report anything,' Forb said. 'I don't want any navy coming to the island. There's too much to lose. You can't destroy something in nature that you don't understand.'

'What's to understand?' Calyban said. 'There's something enormous down there, and those sirens are sinking Eschan ships. It affects our government.'

'How can you possibly know any of this for certain?' Manolin said.

'Either way it has to be investigated,' Calyban said.

'We can do that,' Manolin said.

'No, I mean by the *government*,' Calyban said.

Santiago stood up. He had a pistol in his hand. 'Fuck the government. When has a government done anything to help nature or science?'

Calyban and Soul both looked at the pistol, then at Santiago. Manolin watched his old mentor move with purpose, precisions, in away that told him he wasn't unfamiliar with these situations.

'Might I remind you that it's our responsibility to report our findings to our government,' Soul said. 'Should anything happen to us then the navy will be here.'

'And how're they going to know if anything happens? Eh?' Santiago said.

'Santiago, put the pistol down,' Manolin said.

'You can shut up too.'

'Santiago?' Manolin said, frowning. 'What the hell are you saying? Don't be stupid, and think about what you're doing. No one is going to be shot. Put that thing away.'

'We'll discuss this on the island,' Forb said. 'We'll take a break, have some food and relax. When we're all calm, then we can discuss the matter clearly and logically.'

'Those boys,' Santiago said, indicating the agents with his pistol, 'don't do logic.'

'Santiago, you're not helping. Come on, let's sit down and be civilised. Okay?' Manolin said.

'Right,' Santiago said.

'Good,' Manolin said.

'Fine,' Santiago said.

Twenty-Two

The afternoon sun had burned away people's energy leaving them lethargic, tired. It was dusk, and a cool breeze came from the north. Life emerged once again. In the forest the birds were boisterous. You could smell the fragrance from the trees further up the island. DeBrelt's crew, Calyban, Soul, the villagers and several ichthyocentaurs had gathered around a large fire built alongside the lagoon. For a while, everyone talked amongst themselves. Some of the villagers were sitting cross-legged at the front of a circle.

One of the ichthyocentaur women was carrying a baby, and Manolin and Forb were paying the young creature attention. Manolin beckoned the others forward. Becq came, and Santiago, but Yana and Jefry did not move. They were sitting next to the fire, staring at the infant from a distance. Jefry tried to move Yana, but she was reluctant. He held her arm. Her eyes were round and red. She mouthed some words Manolin couldn't hear. All Jefry could do was squeeze her hand whenever she gripped it. Yana was still cold, silent, but she would talk only with Jefry. Manolin supposed that their relationship was deeper than either had realised.

Forb was signing to the mother, who, with her hands full, couldn't reply properly. Manolin offered to hold the baby. She handed her child to him carefully. Manolin was surprised at how heavy it was. The creature's grey skin was tough. Manolin smiled when he saw the stub of what would become the tail. He made faces at the baby, and it imitated him after a few different facial contortions. The mother grinned and Forb laughed. After the conversation, Manolin reluctantly handed the baby back. The little creature was smiling.

'What a little gem,' he said to Forb.

'I think you're accepted by this lot,' Forb said. 'She let you hold her baby. That's pretty good going.'

Manolin signed, *Thank you. Good luck*, to the female. She nodded. It was nice to feel accepted, especially by something so exotic. In the streets of Escha, people would seldom accept you. They would walk on by, struggled to make eye contact. Occasionally someone would speak, blurting out some kind of offensive madness, or try to sell you something, pawing at your clothes. Groups tended to keep to themselves, never wanted to integrate.

Becq sat down by Jefry and Yana. Manolin sat on her other side. The opposite side of the circle, Myranda was sitting with Lewys. There was a sense of excitement as people chattered because they had been summoned. It was as if they had never been gathered for anything like this before.

Santiago and Forb moved to the centre of the crowd, by the fire. They looked out to the orange and pink horizon, and the darkness of the sea against it. Everyone stood or sat on the sand, in a circle around them. Silence descended, and the fire could be heard crackling. Manolin felt the tension, even though he knew what they would be talking about.

'Right,' Forb said. 'We're going to give some feedback on our trip down the reef.' He signed to the several ichthyocentaurs as he spoke.

'Absolutely,' Santiago said. 'Now, as you may or may not know, we travelled some way down in my submersible and we think we're at the bottom of our mystery.'

Forb continued translating for the ichthyocentaurs.

'This afternoon, for several hours, we followed the reef down. We didn't expect the reef to be so deep. Now, we've basic technology, but we got to the bottom. Somewhere down there,' he indicated the ocean, 'is a city. We saw a construct, possible made out of the coral, or indeed caves, but we couldn't be certain.'

People in the crowd were muttering. Santiago palmed the air. 'Now, let me continue. It was illuminated by some sort of bioluminescent life form. Quite common in deep waters, but I never expected to see them in such quantities.'

Everyone was silent. He tuned to Forb. 'They any idea what I'm talking about?'

The doctor said, 'Stay away from the technical details.'

Santiago nodded, placed his hands on his hips. 'Basically, there is a community of sirens. And the reason they are killing these chaps, I believe,' he indicated the ichthyocentaur group standing between the villagers, 'is to breed. They are taking their sperm. This is quite likely as, when you think about it, they're all female, by the looks of it and couldn't reproduce on their own. Or at least, one would not assume it.'

The crowd muttered.

'What doest thou mean?' a villager said.

'What I mean is that your ichthyocentaur men are being *raped*, for want of a more accurate word. They are being raped so that the sirens can reproduce. Our mystery, therefore, is solved.'

'Tell 'em the rest,' Calyban said.

Santiago looked at him. Forb was no longer signing, but turned to stand by Santiago.

The two agents stood up, stepped over the semi-naked bodies on the sand, to the centre. 'There's more, isn't there?'

'No. These simple people don't need to know anything else,' Santiago said.

'Why don't you tell 'em? Eh?' Calyban said.

'Now would be a good time to take this elsewhere, gentlemen.' Santiago nodded slowly, eyes wide.

'Don't you want them to know,' Calyban said, 'that there's something under the island?'

'No.'

Forb looked across to Santiago. 'We could tell them, you know.'

'No. Now gentlemen, if you want to take this further—'

'What doest he mean?' a villager said.

Santiago turned to the villagers, who were looking at him, their eyes wide and bright against their dark skins. 'There was... Well, we saw something else.'

'What?' someone said.

'Well, to be fair,' Manolin said, pushing himself up from the sand, 'we don't really know what it was.' He wanted to see order maintained here, felt it a duty to prevent an argument, especially since it would be caused by the foreigners. More than anything he wanted to be polite, to fit in.

'Indeed,' Santiago said. 'We saw a black, glossy surface that could've been anything.'

'It was an eye,' Soul said.

'Not necessarily,' Santiago said.

'It was a damn eye. An enormous eye,' Calyban said.

The villagers were talking loudly. Santiago walked up to Calyban and Soul. 'I think we should have this out, face to face.'

'Be careful,' Forb said. 'I don't want trouble. Remember what they said about the navy, Santiago.'

'I wouldn't worry about what they say too much, doc,' Santiago said.

'Oh, why not? ' Calyban said. 'What're *you* going to do about it, eh?'

Santiago stepped forwards, grabbed the collars of Calyban's shirt, and Soul tried to hold Santiago's wrists. Forb squeezed between all three. seconds later Manolin was trying to pull the group apart, as all the men shouted obscenities at each other. Behind the fight, the villagers were shouting, too, and Becq, Jefry and Yana were all standing now, helpless ,before Manolin and Forb managed to pull the fight apart.

Santiago's chest was heaving, his clothing pulled askew.

Calyban reached up to his nose, revealed felt blood. It had dripped on his shirt, too. He looked across at Santiago's silhouette, the setting sun behind him, the villagers still talking, and you could see the cool breeze ruffling his hair. 'That was a mistake, Mr DeBrelt. It was a very regrettable mistake. When the navy get here, you'll be deported from this island and never allowed to work again. Mark my words. I'll see you spend some time behind bars.'

Santiago said, 'The hell I will.'

'Hey—all of you,' Forb said. 'I don't want any naval ships here, okay. I don't want anyone here. Sort out your differences like decent men.'

'That would imply, doc,' Santiago said, 'that these two men *are* decent men.'

'You're not helping, San,' Manolin said.

'Be quiet.'

'For fuck sake,' Manolin said. 'Here we are trying to help you and look at you—'

'I don't need your help,' Santiago said. Then, 'I don't need anybody's help.' He pushed his way past Manolin and back out towards the village.

Manolin looked at the Forb, who shrugged. Calyban and Soul walked away moments later. A group of villagers drifted away. Some remained and talked.

Myranda came to Forb, who was sitting alongside Manolin by the fire. They had eaten two hares on spits. It was dark, but the wind had calmed, the evening became pleasant. Manolin felt as though the nature of the island had soothed the angst he felt earlier.

'Hello, you,' Forb said. 'You okay?'

She nodded. 'I don't like all the arguments. We hardly argued before.'

'I'm sorry for that,' Manolin said. 'We've brought our ways with us, and our problems. For that, I apologise.' He felt a guilt that they had brought all their problems to this paradise.

'Not your fault,' Forb said. 'It's what happens on islands. Small spaces, isolation. Things come to a head.'

'I don't understand any of this. We're such a rabble.' He looked up at Myranda. 'I *am* sorry for it all.'

'Don't be,' she said, and smiled. She stood up, kissed Forb on the top of his head.

Manolin's gaze followed her as she walked down the beach. He turned to see that Forb was watching him.

The doctor said, 'Love and care makes it all better, doesn't it?'

Manolin sighed. 'I wouldn't know about that.'

'Fair enough. So, what d'you think of our sirens?'

'Amazing, wasn't it,' Manolin said. 'To see another race in a whole world different to ours, and to see that they had formed a functioning society with parallels to our own... well, I can't quite sum up the importance of that to science. Here we are thinking humans and rumel are the only creatures capable of such organisation. It's humbling.'

'What d'you reckon about the half breeds?' Forb said.

'Interesting stuff,' Manolin said. 'Just couldn't work out the necessity for killing the ichthyocentaurs. Also, why the need to breed them? The half breeds were labouring. I know it was almost total darkness, and we couldn't quite see, but they were almost like slaves. It just wasn't right.'

'Hmm.' Forb picked some meat out of his teeth. 'And the eye?'

'Might not've been one.'

'But what do *you* think?'

'I think it was an eye,' Manolin said. 'But I wouldn't like to say what it was connected to.'

Forb said, 'I've a theory about the sirens, y'know. Those half breeds were building something, or rather bolting something to the ocean floor. Think about all that metal.'

Manolin nodded. He placed his hands behind him on the sand, stretched his legs out. He turned to face the doctor, said, 'You think they're bolting the thing with the eye, don't you?'

Forb smiled. 'What else could it be?'

Manolin nodded again, both eyebrows raised. 'It's possible. Okay, now let's assume it *was* an eye, and it *was* connected to something. That's pretty damn big, isn't it?'

'The reef grew on top of it. The coral imprisoned it, using the thing as an artificial reef itself.'

'It's all logical, I guess. Coral could do that. But it's a bit fantastical, don't you think?'

'One thing I've learned from this island, and all my life studies, Manolin, is that the natural world is more bizarre than anything our minds can produce.'

Manolin stared out to sea. He listened to the dying fire, to the sounds of the surf. Night birds were still loud in the forest, using their shift to make all manner of disturbance.

'Manolin.'

'Yeah?'

'The navy won't come, will it?'

Manolin could see the concern in the doctor's expression. It must pain the man to think that another government would come to corrupt and destroy his paradise. 'I honestly don't know. One of those two would have to get back to the mainland first. You're worried about that, aren't you?'

'Of course. It's my home. It's home to a lot of us, and it's unspoiled. You know what armies are like. I don't want to lose all the cures we have here. I don't want to lose all my work.'

'I'll make sure you won't,' Manolin said.

'I hope not.'

Each man reflected for a moment in companionable silence.

'I don't want to lose Myranda, either,' Forb said.

'How d'you mean?' Manolin looked at Forb, whose face was pale.

'I don't want anyone to claim her. I don't want that.' He ran his hand over his bald head.

'You don't mean *me*, do you?' Manolin said.

'No.' He smiled. 'Not directly.'

'You're mysterious at times.'

'Mysterious, I like that. I'd prefer mystical. The mystical is that which cannot be explained.'

Manolin inhaled the fresh scented air. 'Like all of us then.'

Forb smiled. 'Yes, like all of us. I guess every man and woman is mystical. I like your attitude to science. You're definitely not part of the old thinking.'

Manolin shrugged. 'It's a way of life for me. For all this crew.'

'Good, good.'

They were silent again. The island did that to people—it made their conversations not as important somehow. Manolin looked at the sky and saw the intensity of the stars. He looked along the beach, and a figure was walking along it, away from the village. Then into the forest.

'Manolin, you hurt Yana, didn't you?'

'I'm sorry—?'

Forb held up his hand. 'Look it's okay, I'm not going to lecture. Have you treated any other women like that?'

'What? No. Look, what happened with me and Yana was a brief moment. I lost my mind, we both did. I would never do anything intentionally. I know how much it hurts. I don't think I can be disrespectful to a partner ever. I'd been going through a very difficult time.'

'Your ex?'

Manolin nodded.

Forb said, 'Sometimes that can make you vengeful though. The human mind is more complex. It can make you want to hurt every lover you come across now.'

Manolin sighed. 'I don't want that. I wouldn't like that. I'd end up like Santiago. Anyway, as stupid and predictable as it sounds, it was Yana that went after me. I was tipsy, to say the least—not that I'm saying I don't like her; she's very pretty—but I was emotional, and in no sound state of mind. She seduced me. Believe it if you will.'

'Yana? And I can see Becq wants you, too.'

'Okay, maybe I was a little spiteful for the whole Yana thing. But nothing bad came from that, did it? Nothing bad happened. Jefry and her have always been at each other's throats. And Becq? Well, I guess I didn't realise she liked me. Anyway, she's not my sort of girl.'

'Not your type?'

'No, just not strong enough. Becq would probably always give in to me too easily; always ask what I wanted to do for a day out. My ex was always in control of things, and I liked it. I guess one reason I stuck by her all that time is that I liked the buzz I got when we argued and made up.'

Forb laughed. 'You want that? You want that spice every day and night for the rest of your life? That'll drive you crazy. It'll make you an angry man.'

Manolin dragged his knees up to his chest, folded his arms around them.

Forb said, 'You can't want that, truly.'

'No offence, Forb, but what're you getting at?' Manolin looked over at Forb. The doctor's face began to show pain.

'It's not easy—this,' Forb said.

'What?'

'All the stuff I've been on about... Myranda likes you. Look this isn't easy.'

'What isn't?' Manolin said.

'Do you have any idea how difficult it is for me to find a partner for Myranda when I'm dead?'

'Dead? Hey, come on now.'

'Yes, fucking dead. Dead. Dead. I've no idea how long I have left—two months, two years. It's not hard to work out what's wrong with me, is it?' He slapped his head. 'Didn't cut it this way.'

'All right, I'm sorry. You... may last a while.' Manolin was uncertain as to what was really wrong with the doctor, and couldn't work out the correct way in which to approach the matter.

'Manolin, I can see that you're both attracted to each other. I want all you guys to stay here for months yet. I want you all to stay, because my plants are wearing off quick.'

'Plants?'

'Yes, the stuff the ichthyocentaur give me to walk straight and keep me on my feet. My medication.'

'Oh,' Manolin said, suddenly realising what was going on. He realised that Forb *needed* the ichthyocentaurs, *needed* their medicinal skills. 'Oh I see now. Look, Forb, I'm not sure how long we're staying. We can only hang around until we have to go back. It's up to Santiago, and if Calyban and Soul persist then we could go soon.'

'I understand. I can't ask you all to stay.'

'I'm flattered, Forb, really. I'm not sure I'm a good man for the job, though.' He began to laugh in a self-deprecating way.

Forb said, 'You remind me of me, when I was a bit younger. The same attitudes and whatnot. You've got a good mind, and you're respectful of nature. You'd enjoy things here.'

'I'm sure I would, really. But, Forb, why do you have to find someone for Myranda? Is there a need?'

Forb glanced at the moon. 'Well, put it this way: if you knew you were dying, wouldn't you want to make sure that the things you loved were looked after?'

Manolin nodded. 'Of course.'

'Well, it's like that. I've been used to this condition for years, and I'm putting off the inevitable. And I can see you're attracted to each other, which when you're in my position, doesn't so much bother you, but it's... a relief. But one that's a real painful thing to come to terms with. Hell, I can't explain it. I guess in the knowledge of death you become less attached to things, at a superficial level at least.'

'I reckon I follow, if I can't completely understand. I'd be seething if I knew someone liked my wife—not that I do, you see—but if someone was like that to mine.' His mind fell back to Escha. He remembered the arguments and her temper. He remembered the nights where she would talk to a guy the other side of a bar, and she'd stand in shadows so that he couldn't see her face. He would never get his own back—he didn't have the confidence. He remembered the waiting for her to return and the emotions that it forced him to feel.

'Manolin.'

'Sorry, I was miles away.'

'I said it's all right.'

'What is?'

'That I can see chemistry between you and Myranda.'

'You know, I'm not sure I could give up a life at home. There's so much there—my research for one. I'd love to publish a lot of my findings. I've got to face my ex-wife at some point, too.'

'I understand,' Forb said, the disappointment clear in his voice.

Manolin thought about the doctor's words. Was this an invitation to leave everything he knew behind, to start all over again in paradise? 'Hey, I'd better be getting some sleep. I'm pretty shattered after all that. We'll talk more, if you'd like?'

'Sure, why not.'

Santiago waded through the dark forest, stepping over ferns, pushing vines aside. He was heading for the hut in which Calyban and Soul were staying. His shirt ripped as he caught it on a branch, but he tugged it then turned to walk straight on, following a trail he that he could just about see in this light. The tops of the palms swayed in the wind, and when he glanced to his left, he could see the moon through the foliage, low in the sky.

He advanced on the hut.

In the dark he stood for a moment, simply staring at it. He knew they were in there. His heart was beating fast and he did not know what to say to them, but he didn't want them to drag his crew back. The agents had power back in the city, but not on this island. His chest felt cold as the wind came through the forest, and he shuddered. He put his hand in his pocket. The pistol was still there.

Santiago stepped towards the hut. When he was by the door he placed his ear against it. He could hear them speaking, but also crackling. He stood against the door for ten minutes. Then, the agents began to talk clearer, louder. Certain words were clear over the noise of static:

'...*Sixteen degrees south... Vessels... Emergency... Repeat... Underwater... Immediate use of weapons...*'

Santiago took a step back and, with the ball of his foot, he kicked the door open. He stepped in to be confronted by Mr Soul, and he could see that Calyban was hunched over a device, which emitted the fizzing static sound. In his hands was an antenna, as well as something that was held close to his mouth. It was dark inside, and their faces were lit only by the moonlight that came through an opening.

Mr Soul said, 'What're you doing here, DeBrelt. Out—'

'What's that?' Santiago pointed at the device, then reached into his pocket.

'Nothing. Get out immediately,' Calyban said.

The device emitted a voice amidst the static: *'Message not quite clear... Please, repeat message...'*

Santiago said, 'What the fuck? Who's on the other end? Who?'

'Santiago, get out now. This does not concern you. I'll be forced to manually eject you—' Calyban said.

'The hell you will.'

Calyban hunched over the device. He was winding a handle on the side whilst speaking in a low tone. 'Please send all Eschan naval—'

Santiago held out the pistol and fired at the device. He hit the box directly and a spark flew off followed by a trail of smoke.

Soul turned back whilst Calyban shouted at Santiago, 'You fucking bastard. Right—'

Santiago fired again, and the device split, small metal pieces shattering on the floor of the hut. 'Communicate with navy will you? Not while I'm here. I knew you had a relic.'

'Too late, Santiago. They're on their way,' Soul said.

'No they're not,' Santiago said. 'They didn't get the message.'

'Yes they did.'

Santiago raised the pistol and pointed it at Calyban's face. He couldn't take the risk. Something had to be done. Fear gripped him. Soul shuffled to the door and Santiago aimed the pistol at his head, then alternated between the two it as the agents edged around the hut.

'Put it down, Santiago,' Calyban said. 'Come on, let's not get like this.'

'Too late. You've already done too much. Tell me, did that message get through?'

Calyban shrugged.

'Damn you, man.'

'You ought not to kill us, Santiago,' Soul said.

'Shut up,' Santiago said. 'Shut up or I'll fire again.'

'He doesn't have the guts and he's not that stupid anyway,' Calyban said to Soul across the hut.

Santiago turned to Soul who was near the doorway.

'Go on,' Calyban said. 'See what that'll do. In a few weeks, every naval vessel on the open seas will centre on Arya. They all know we're here.'

'No. The message didn't get through. I can tell you're bluffing.' Santiago smiled in an attempt that it would force them into making some verbal error that he could use, that he could learn from.

'Try me,' Calyban said. 'Sooner or later they're going to come and find that city and that beast. They're going to destroy it, as soon as they find them. Those sirens are dangerous, Santiago. And that beast is a threat to the seas. Those creatures beneath are guilty of wrecking ships. *Our* Eschan ships.'

Santiago lowered the pistol. He ran his free hand through his hair and sighed. 'All right, sit down then. Let's talk this through sensibly, if we must.' He indicated the floor with the pistol. 'Go on.'

The two agents sat at each end of the hut, glancing hesitantly across at each other. Between them, Santiago was still standing. He paced up and down the hut, could hear his footsteps clearly. Calyban nodded Soul, who shuffled nearer the door, and Santiago noted this movement.

'Right then,' Santiago said. His chest was rising and falling sharply, as if he had raced across the beach. 'I want you to tell me exactly what that device was, and exactly what the message was that you sent. Also, if you've sent any more, hitherto.'

'It's a communication device,' Soul said. 'There's dozens of them. What we said was highly confidential.'

Santiago spun, kicked Soul's shins. 'You bastards. Just tell me, all right? Tell me.'

Soul grasped his legs without making a noise. His eyes narrowed as he glared at Santiago. 'What does it matter? We're warning everyone of a hazard. Why is that so damn bad?'

'Because it's not a damn hazard.' Santiago became calmer, held the pistol at his side. He sighed.

'How can you be so sure?' Calyban said. 'It has to be removed or destroyed, one or the other.'

Santiago thought about a new line of tactic. Obviously hard-man talk was doing now good. Perhaps if he could educate them. 'Why do you think that? Why must you think it that simplistic way? They're natural things. Come on, chaps. We need to be a lot more logical, eh?'

Calyban said, 'Escha is the nearest city to this place. It remains at threat, and therefore—'

'Just leave it here until we return at least, eh? It's not a threat.'

'How can you be so damn sure?' Soul said.

'I am, okay.' Santiago shook his head, smiled. 'Now, please, just tell me, did the message get through?'

Calyban shrugged. Santiago turned to Soul, who gave the same reply, then shook his head. Santiago was staring at him. Then he raised the pistol back and fired at Calyban's face. With a crack the agent's head smacked back against the wall, his mouth open wide, his face ruined, then his body slumped to the floor. Soul stumbled out the door. Santiago lurched after him into the doorway, looked out. He could see him running across the forest and up the slope.

Santiago turned back to Calyban's body. He walked over, looked down. The shot had entered at the corner where the eye and nose met.

Santiago hauled the body up by its arms, began to drag it out of the hut. He stepped outside, and the body dropped onto the forest floor. Through the palms he could see villagers, black against the moonlit beach, advancing towards the edge of the forest.

He dragged the body deeper into the forest, could hear the commotion echoing under the canopy. When he came to an area that was covered with undergrowth, Santiago dropped the body. He pulled at some ferns until he had more foliage with which to cover the body. He took a last look at the mutilated face before laying a fern on top. Then he looked up, across the forest towards the darkness. He had no idea where Soul would be. He heard the voices of the villagers again, and ran.

For an hour or more he stumbled along the forest. He chased every path until he became breathless. Soul was nowhere, long gone. Santiago's ripped shirt was stained green, and he was thirsty. He retraced his steps, and reassured himself that the body was still buried in the dark.

Back at the hut he could see a group of villagers standing outside. The moonlight was reflecting off bald head of the doctor. Santiago reached inside his pocket and drew out a small silver box. He opened it, dabbed his finger in the white powder, brought it to his left nostril and inhaled. He widened his eyes and he swallowed. His nose felt as if he had a cold. He closed the silver box then placed it in his pocket.

Santiago waited until he could feel a strange sensation in his gums as the cocaine kicked in. He needed the confidence boost. It was difficult to maintain such an energetic personality. People expected him to be a certain way, and right now he had to be true to himself. He caught his breath then jogged down to the doctor. 'Forb. Forb, we've trouble.'

Forb said, 'Santiago. I know we've a problem.'

'The agents?' Santiago said.

Forb nodded. 'Well, I think so.' He indicated the hut. Two village men were standing in the doorway. Another was crouched by the steps, looking closely.

'Found blood in there, and a smashed up bit of machinery. Heard a couple of shots earlier too.'

'Yes I know, that was me,' Santiago said.

'You?'

'Look, they've called the navy. They were using a communication device, or something. I shot it to stop them calling the ships, but I'm not sure if I did.'

'The navy?' Forb reached out and held Santiago's elbow. 'Did they get through? Where are they now?'

'I don't know, I simply don't know. They both ran off into the forest and I tried to stop them, but I couldn't find them. Neither of them. They ran along near the edge of the beach to the north of the island. That much I did see. I tried to stop them Forb, I really did.' Santiago could see the whites of the doctor's wide eyes.

'I don't want the navy here,' Forb said. 'They can't come.'

'I know,' Santiago said. 'I know, but we have to stop them both first. What if one of them leaves the island? He could take a small boat and drift on the currents back to the mainland?'

'It's possible, but he'd drift for miles. He wouldn't know how to get back anyway.'

Santiago said, 'I wouldn't be so sure.'

'Look, we've really got to find them tonight.'

They searched for the better part of the evening. Santiago had steered Forb away from where he had covered Calyban's body, suggesting they looked in further places. Forb called off the search eventually. After the initial panic had subsided, he and Santiago stood by the lagoon. Santiago reassured him that the navy would not come if they found the agents.

'They cannot be allowed to leave,' Forb said.

'Well, we can have a better look when the sun's up,' Santiago said. 'We'd be better off having a sleep now.'

'You're right. I'm not sure I'll be able to sleep though.' Forb looked up as a cloud covered the moon, and the island became darker. The wind had become stronger in the last hour. 'It's not going to be the best of days tomorrow. It's not going to storm, but it'll make the search a little easier. It'll be less intense. Cooler. After my surf and breakfast, I'll organise the villagers and we'll arrange a thorough search.'

Santiago nodded. They both went their separate ways.

Santiago pushed a raft onto the lagoon, jumped on it then rowed to his stilted hut. He was tired. His body ached. He secured the raft to his hut and climbed up. His eyes had grown accustomed to the dark. Being careful not to wake Manolin, he pushed himself up and perched by the door. He looked out and could see the stars bordering with the sea, where there was clear sky. Directly above him, the clouds were gathering.

His vision settled on the reef, and was staring for some time.

Forb stood next to his surfboard, staring offshore. Wearing only a pair of short breeches, he looked across the purple and grey horizon. The day was overcast, the sea rough. Three gulls arced out over his head, out to sea. White tips of the waves broke past the reef. The sea had lost a lot of colour. As he waited for the sun to rise behind the clouds, he examined the wave patterns. Behind him he could hear the movement of the palms, which were as loud as the tide.

After a few minutes he picked up his surfboard, placed it under his arm. He walked towards the sea, then into it. He waded out until the water was waist high, could feel the high energy of the day's surf. He placed the board flat on the water then pushed his body up on it. He felt lethargic, his triceps weak.

Laying flat on the board, he paddled out for several minutes until he was past the reef where the water possessed more energy, vaguely wondering if any sirens would come. The wind cut across him, spraying salt in his eyes. Further off shore, the waves were high. He steered the tip of the board towards the biggest waves. He swam out, ducking and diving under the oncoming waves. The water sent a shudder through his body. He glanced back to the island. It seemed quite small from where he was. He paddled west, through the rough waters.

Turning around back to the island, he could see a small boat. A figure was pushing it off the beach. Forb frowned because knew the villagers wouldn't be up for another hour at least. He was always the first up.

His eyes widened.

The agents, he thought. *That must be them trying to get away.*

His heart raced as he ducked through another large wave then shook his head to remove the water. He tried to focus on the boat and remain on his board. The figure was wearing a blue shirt. Another wave struck him before Forb realised it was either Calyban or Soul—perhaps the other was hiding in the boat. They were escaping. They would bring naval ships to the island.

Forb steered the board towards the boat, which was heading to come out around the reef, then he caught a large wave and pushed his body up, distributing his weight to stand up and steer towards the agents and he could feel the wind whipping his body and the cold thrill of riding the wave. The island became large and dark again in the background as he sped nearer the boat. He shifted his weight, lifting the front of the board to his left then he could see the clear shape of the figure inside, and the fedora, so, with his arms wide for balance, he aimed to where the small boat was steering. Within seconds he was on it, the wave coming low and fast and Forb, now seeing that there was definitely one agent, waited until the last second before he lifted the front of the board and crashed through the centre of the boat with a loud crack.

Forb heard a garbled scream and could see strips of wood falling in the water before he fell under. Daylight become a blur. Seawater filled his mouth. Something was moving under the surface, so he grabbed it. It kicked hard. Forb held his breath, clutched what he realised was a flailing limb until it stopped kicking. After a while, it became still.

Forb released his grip then swam up to the surface. He gasped as he came to the surface, and spat out water. His chest ached. He felt agony as he reached out for what was left of his surfboard, but was now a splintered segment of wood.

The tide pushed him back and forth, up and down and he struggled to hold on in the strong surf. Breathing heavily, he drifted nearer the reef, hunched over the wood.

Another wave came and pushed him off, then he fell back and his head struck a raised platform of coral. Blood spat on his face. His eyes closed as he drifted onto his back, catching and spinning in the currents and channels caused by the reef, and felt a strange sensation that he was pushed back, towards the island.

Darkness took him.

Arth Speaking

I thought I was dead too. The particularly interesting thing is: I'm not—I was never even born. I can't explain it that well, but it's only when you're here that you realise what's going on—what's been going on for all this time. It's like a one big secret is revealed; a massive twist in a play or book you've been reading all your life and to be honest it's very exciting, I have to say, from a personal angle, I'm of a mind to suspect that these big picture things are never especially big once you get here. All that stuff about Arrahd and other gods is a complete pile of arse and I'll hear no more about it. Anyway, this is all just confusing, and irrelevant, and it requires a bit of a leap of faith! I never found out who it was that killed me. Apparently, it's not for me to know. Not that I really care now.

But, here I am—hurrah!—and let's leave it at that.

Here is a strange place. I have been told to wait in this *limbo*. I can see what awaits me: there are stone walls, green hills and gorse bushes. It looks colder, and there are shaded paths that lead to a rocky shore. I can see the waves foaming around the rocks; the water looks muddier than any I've seen, and there are gulls circling. There are small cottages and people wearing strange clothes. They are to be my family. The place is rather like Has-jahn, but there is something slightly odd about it. There are no rumel, so I've been told that I'll become a human. Not quite sure how I feel about that. Apparently I'll forget almost all of what I know anyway, but it won't be a bad thing. Again, I can't say how I really feel because there's little point in worrying. Everything does seem to be reassuringly calm though. And I like the sensation.

So I want to talk more about Manolin while I still can. Now, there is a young man who particularly fascinates me at the moment. Here am I with a handful of regrets and wishes (I have been informed that these will wear off after a while) and I can see him in a very enviable position. The lad's had his fair share of troubles, I'll not take that away from him. That wife of his was a tad on the mad side, but there's some of that in more people than you'd think. (In fact, one thing I have discovered is that everyone has their issues, even if they'll tell you otherwise.) So, Manny is at a particularly interesting stage. He's growing up faster than he thinks.

I remember when I met him for the very first time and I thought now here is a bright young fellow. And he's polite and kind. (Easy to see why that wife clung on to him. He was her rock to which she grasped when she needed stability.) I think Manolin is the type of lad us elders can relate to; one which, if I'm honest—and there's not point me having secrets anymore!—one which we all wish we were more like.

I'm not surprised old Yana slept with him. I think deep down we could all see her problems, it's just that it was never our right to actually say anything. (And I know Jef can be a wee bit neglectful at times—who isn't!) I'm not saying that she's bad, or Manny is either, and I certainly am not justifying any actions—even if they are not of a wholesome nature, but the thing I have to keep reminding myself (and it's very easy to see these days) is that shit will happen to people. Groups split up. There is something about the lad which scares Santiago, too. I'll say no more, as it's not my position to say anything—never a gossip—but it's easy to see why one would not only like Manny, but how one could be jealous. Relationships fade. People drift or clash. It seems to be the only one thing certain about life: things will always fall apart, and everything does, inevitably, end in relationships breaking up. (Death comes along at the end, just to make sure.)

You can either be bleak about it, or get up of your arse and just accept that that is what life is about—crack on with living!

Manolin is aware of this, and that is why I'm jealous. He always used to go on about science and how he was part of a new, modern thinking. It requires a little explanation, and here it is in its simplest form.

There are two ways of looking at the world. One is to break everything down and study its component parts. Break life down into the small things, study it and find answers. That's very much Santiago's way of thinking. Manolin is a fan of the new paradigm. Basically, it's all well and good breaking things down, but you can't really get a look at the world unless you look at things from a system level, from the highest perspective. One can see the emergent properties something has, which is greater than the sum of its individual parts. Breaking things up doesn't tell you much about the whole. Santiago would spend his time studying a particular species, whilst Manolin would spend his time looking how that species fits in to the wider community. That's all very basic, of course; and I think they've worked well as a team so far. It was Manolin that convinced Santiago to have complete biological, geological, geographical surveys, because one cannot understand a system by its parts.

Manolin's science is good. It's different and exciting. It seems to encompass life. That lad will really go places. His way of thinking does not just apply to study, but his whole life. He's always looking at the bigger picture, whereas Santiago, Mr Rational, is always breaking things down for logic, logic, logic. Just look at him taking Yana's urine sample, I mean really. That was quite appalling, but only a true classical thinker such as Santiago DeBrelt could've had such a clear mind whilst doing that. Santiago's problem has always been that he's not thinking of the bigger picture.

I worry about Manny at times. He thinks too much. There's no point, believe me—and I really do know. He's always sitting on the beach looking out to sea (he does do it far too much). Thinking gets you nowhere. If you think, you're dead.

Get out there, go and do things, don't wait, seize every damn opportunity, that's what I say. I want to shake him and make him do this!

Do not fall on one's knees and look upwards for any answers. There are none to be given. By all means have some faith, if it helps, but everything that is needed is down there. And even afterwards, it's not all that bad.

Twenty-Three

Manolin and Myranda sat next to the doctor's bed. He had lain there, unconscious, for nineteen days now. By the window, an ichthyocentaur was holding a cup of water that had been mixed with a herb so that it was tinted red. The creature held the cup over Forb's mouth, its hand as steady as coral, then dripped the mixture inside. Manolin had long ago realised that whatever the ichthyocentaur were doing, it was keeping Forb alive.

Sunlight, came through the shutters, casting beams over Forb's resting body.

Manolin thought that he would've spent much of his time reassuring Myranda about the doctor's health, the last couple of weeks, but she seemed almost unaffected by her husband's accident. She was calm, rational. Even Lewys, who was often out playing with Yana and Jefry, seemed fine. The only possible reason, Manolin suspected, was that they must have been aware of the doctor's disease, that they were prepared for his death.

As the ichthyocentaur left the hut, it held the door open for Santiago, who bounded into the hut. 'Ah, how's the patient?' The old man rubbed his face free of sweat with a handkerchief.

'Still the same,' Manolin said.

Santiago nodded, looking at the doctor. 'He'll be up soon. Good breeding, that one. He's made of tough stuff.'

Manolin turned to Santiago and said, 'How's the profiling going?'

'Oh, fine, fine,' Santiago said. 'It's not an easy job, with the sheer diversity of it all, but we're getting a good idea. I suspect most of the species are endemic to this place.'

'Wouldn't surprise me,' Manolin said.

'You know, we'll get so much information to sell back at home. So many sketches, maps, diagrams—so many samples to show off. The ship's getting quite full of arthropod samples. I really think we can make a lot of money from the maps alone.'

They stepped out of the hut, into fresh air, then walked along the beach. Strong winds took away any humidity. It was a day in which work could be done.

Santiago turned to Manolin. 'You going to help us at all?'

'What d'you mean?' Manolin said.

'You've been with Forb for most of the last few days. Bit of help wouldn't go amiss.'

'Someone's got to keep an eye on him,' Manolin said.

'Why you? There're plenty of others.'

'Just think I ought to, that's all. When he wakes up he's going to want to know what's been going on. I'll give him the gossip when he's ready.'

'He'll need to know about Calyban and Soul,' Santiago said.

'I think he'll find out. He'll be more concerned about whether the navy will come.'

'Him and me both.'

'Why're you so bothered?' Manolin said.

'Look, no one's going to think that Soul shot Calyban and tried to escape. They'll think I killed him—perish the thought. If that's the case, then what are the chances of us getting back to Escha and publishing our findings?'

'I guess so,' Manolin said, scrutinising Santiago's words for any hint of a clue as to why he had been acting so suspiciously recently. It was a daily ritual that Santiago would enquire about the doctor's health, return to the agent's hut to examine the remains of their relic device, then stare longingly out to sea, regarding the horizon for any hint of a naval vessel.

'I've half an inkling, and deep down it hurts, that we're not going to be able to show any of our findings publicly. I suspect it'll all be done behind closed doors, and only to those in the know.'

'That's really bad,' Manolin said.

'You're telling me,' Santiago said. 'I was rather hoping to finally make myself a celebrity figure…'

'How're the others?' Manolin said. 'I haven't really spoken to them for a while.'

'No. No you haven't,' Santiago said. Then, 'They're okay, I guess. Soldicring on.'

'Becq?'

'Yes, she's a trooper. Got some cracking sketches. A good eye for detail, that one. Keeps asking after you. Spends a lot of time on her doll.'

'Doll?' Manolin said.

'Yes. You know what girls are like,' Santiago said, waving his hand dismissively.

Manolin shook his head at Santiago's belittling attitudes towards women. 'Yana and Jefry? I see them running around with Lewys and some of the other children from time to time.'

'Yes. They're... they're coping well.'

Manolin looked at Santiago's eyes, trying to read them.

'If coping is the word,' Santiago said. 'They'd a lot on their plate. Still have. Complex thing, life.'

'What d'you mean?' Manolin said. 'I know they had a big argument a while back. I wanted to help, but it seemed a bit too much of an issue.'

Santiago looked Manolin up and down. 'I don't suppose its worth while going into it. A lot has happened to that couple and they've somehow gotten over it. They're getting along fine now, so let's leave them be. I don't think that *you* would be of any help, lad.'

'Why d'you always have to patronise me?'

'I'm not,' Santiago said.

'Yes. You are,' Manolin said. 'It's not like I don't know people, or I don't understand them. I've changed since I've been here. I can handle things. Make decisions. Help people when they need it. You've a nasty habit of belittling me.'

'I don't. But remember, I've spent much of my life teaching you things, and helping you out. You remember who got you where you are, okay?'

'I wish you wouldn't keep coming back with that. It's all you say when I talk you into a corner.'

'It's true though,' Santiago said. 'You'd do well to remember that.'

Manolin sighed. Sometimes, he thought, people don't let go of certain notions. It was pointless talking to Santiago anymore. He turned to the sea, had to shade his eyes because of the glare. 'I'll go back to the ichthyocentaurs and study there. I made a start, and I have conversed with the ones that have come to visit the doctor. I've come to know one or two of the individuals pretty well. I'd like to get to know them more. I've picked up quite a lot of their sign language and I think I'm pretty welcome there.'

'All right,' Santiago said. 'I must say though, I never like my crew fraternising with the natives.'

'It's study,' Manolin said.

'Indeed.'

Manolin was silent for a moment, listening to the thriving coast, then said, 'San, do you actually think that the device Calyban and Soul were using actually worked.'

Santiago placed both hands on his hips, shook his head. 'I've no idea. Really. We'll know in due course. I'll see you later. Just keep me in the frame with what you're doing. I take it you've been making notes.'

'Yes, don't worry, we'll have plenty of information you can sell back on the mainland.'

Manolin sat down on the sand, watched Santiago walk off. Then he watched the sea, was hypnotised by the surf. There were fishing boats coming in from out of the sun. He stood up, walked up the beach until he was in the shade, then sat down under a palm. It was cooler and he closed his eyes. The forest behind him was loud with the throng of insects, birds, mammals—an equal to the noise of any city, although more pleasant to his ears. He could feel the sweat on his legs so rolled his breeches up. Then, once the wind had cool him, he fell asleep against the tree.

He woke up an hour later, when Myranda ran up to him.

'Manolin, he's awake,' she said.

'Yes, just about,' Manolin said. 'I fell asleep for a bit. Is it past lunch?'

'No, Manolin—Forb is awake.'

'Forb?' Manolin jolted up, then stood up, brushed the sand off. 'Come on, show me.'

He followed Myranda along the beach, into the hut. Forb turned his head towards them as they entered. The doctor's eyes were narrowed and he closed them occasionally, turning his head so that he was facing up.

Manolin could see the scar on the back of his head. 'Forb, it's us. Manolin and Myranda. Can you hear us?'

Forb opened his eyes, sighed, nodded.

'Good. Good. Do you know what happened?'

Forb opened his mouth and a breath came out. Then, he whispered, 'Hit the reef.'

'Yes, yes you did. You ran into a boat and hurt yourself. Forb can you hear me clearly?'

Forb nodded, closing his eyes.

'Good. I'll fetch one of the ichthyocentaurs.' Manolin turned to Myranda. 'Will you be all right looking after him for the moment?'

'Yes, of course.'

Manolin smiled. 'I think it'd be nicer for him to wake up and look at you rather than me.'

With kind eyes she turned to Forb.

Manolin returned with two ichthyocentaurs who were both carrying bundles of plants. They set to work on the doctor, fixed him herbal infusions, solid plant matter. Their methods were incredibly efficient. Within hours he was alert enough to converse. Lewys came in to visit, which brought a smile to Forb's face, and for the evening, Manolin left the family to be alone. He asked the villagers, who were keen to visit the doctor, to respect that thought for the evening.

Manolin, too, wanted to be alone. He spent the evening following the ichthyocentaur up to their village. He wanted to know them and understand their methods. He wanted to know how they knew so much about the medicinal values of plants. What he had seen was incredible. How something could be so effective, so quickly, was astonishing.

For hours he ate and talked amongst them in basic sign language. They asked him if the killings would stop. He said he didn't know. He told them he would try and protect them as best as he could. He thought of the half breeds working under the sea.

Manolin played with the young, listened to the elders, walked with the women. He observed their strange anatomy. Tonight, he wanted to forget about Santiago and the others. It had become a mystery why he was on the island, why he was even studying in the first place. The ichthyocentaurs brought it all back for him: the fact that he wanted to work with nature. That's why he spent the night there.

Although unlike humans and rumel, they seemed to have social codes, and a vague, basic economy. He was hypnotised by the strange clicking sounds that they used to talk to each other with. Manolin smiled when he saw the ichthyocentaurs holding birds on their shoulders, was surprised that they didn't fly away. Between the animals there was a respect that he couldn't understand. He frowned when he saw a female taking two males somewhere into the forest, then remembered his conversation with Forb about the liberalness of the creatures. Why did he feel the need to really come here? Was it because of their connection with the natural world? Or was it because of the fact he wanted more distance from DeBrelt's crew. They had become symbols of civilisation, of its problems.

Manolin needed the time to meditate a little. He thought about what Yana and Jefry were doing that day in the forest, wondered what Jefry had done for them to be back together. Did the rumel really knew about him having slept with Yana? That would have explained his anger weeks ago.

It was only when Manolin stopped doing things that he really thought about his own life much. He wanted someone to love him. Or, at the very least, to show some care for him. He felt lonely at times on the island, being far away from the comforts of home, not that there were many—but he was getting used to it. He was getting to an age where he felt he needed to make his career, to settle down. He didn't want to repeat the bad choices he had already made. He wanted to be sensible, and chose a girl who would not hurt him. Vaguely, his mind drifted to Becq.

She wasn't all that bad, he thought. She wouldn't argue much. It would certainly be the rational choice, but he prided himself on not being rational. She would be the settling type. She would not fuck other men in his house.

And that was something to bear in mind.

The next morning, before sunrise, Manolin was ready to walk back down to see Forb. As he was leaving, one of the ichthyocentaurs stopped him, handed him a small leaf package. He opened it to see a crushed blue plant. *He'll need this*, the ichthyocentaur signed.

Manolin nodded, headed down to the beach.

As he entered the hut, Santiago trotted up the steps behind. 'Ah, I hear the patient has recovered.'

'Yes, I'm popping to see how he is.'

'Where were you last night then?'

'Up at the ichthyocentaurs' village,' Manolin said.

'Any reason?' Santiago said.

'Just wanted to get to know them. You know, really understand them, not from a purely scientific view.'

'Fair enough,' Santiago said.

They walked inside.

Forb was sat up on the bed. 'Ah, Manolin, Santiago.'

'Hey, Forb,' Manolin said.

'Doc,' Santiago said.

'I seem to have been away for a bit,' Forb said, laughing. 'I apologise for not being a better host.'

Manolin thought he sounded weak despite his light-heartedness. 'I'll forgive you. Just don't let it happen again.' Then, 'How're you feeling?'

'So, so. Been better, obviously. So, tell me what happened then?'

'You crashed into Soul's boat as he was trying to leave the island,' Manolin said.

'Did I get him?'

'We reckon so,' Santiago said. 'Calyban and Soul had some sort of fight in the night. Soul shot Calyban and tried to flee.'

'Really?' Forb frowned. 'That's odd. Why would he shoot him?'

'Who knows?' Santiago said. 'Disagreement probably. Anyway,

they were trying to send a message, if you remember?'

'Hmm. I think so,' Forb said. 'Can't really remember all of it.'

'Well, you stopped any definite message getting out, by running into Soul,' Santiago said.

Forb blinked. 'Well that's something.'

'Here—' Manolin handed over the plant package. 'I spent last night with the ichthyocentaurs. As I left one gave me this.'

'Oh.' Forb took the package, unwrapped it. His face darkened.

'Not what you expected?' Manolin said. 'Forb?'

'Um, yes... Yes. Thank you.'

Manolin looked over to Santiago. 'If you fancy some rest, then we can leave you to it.'

'Thanks. Oh, Manolin. Can I have a quick word?'

'Sure.' He turned to Santiago. 'I'll be out in a second.'

Santiago nodded, and left the room.

'Manolin, was I given any of this whilst I was unconscious?'

'Um, let me have a look.' Manolin leaned in closer. 'No, definitely not anything that colour. I think they tried, but you couldn't swallow.'

Forb sat back, closed his eyes, sighed.

'Why?' Manolin asked. 'Is everything all right?'

'Remember a while ago I told you about a plant that the ichthyocentaurs had found for me?' His eyes were still closed. A greater level of pain was displayed on his face during the discussion of this subject.

'The one you needed?'

'Yes, well this is it.'

'Oh,' Manolin said.

'And I haven't been taking it,' Forb said.

'Oh. That's...'

'Not good,' Forb said. 'Not good at all.' He opened his eyes, turned to Manolin. Then he reached over and picked up Manolin's hand.

Manolin felt uncomfortable with the gesture. He looked down at the hands and to his left, before he could look Forb in the eye. The doctor was smiling.

Manolin thought it a strange smile, like that of an old man who had just realised he'd been doing the wrong thing all his life, or had been tricked by an old enemy. It was the least happy smile that Manolin had ever seen.

'I'll leave you to think for a while,' Manolin said.

Forb nodded. 'Oh, one last thing. Have any more ichthyocentaurs been killed since I've been here?'

'No. None at all. Perhaps our trip down there scared them off, what with the electric shocks.'

'Perhaps.'

Manolin pulled his hand free, carefully, then left the hut. He had a strange feeling in his chest. As he passed, Myranda and Lewys walked in.

Manolin smiled as he could hear the doctor greeting his son loudly, maintaining a positive air. It took him some moments to contemplate the significance of what Forb was really getting at. Was he dying quickly because of not taking the remedies? It saddened Manolin to think this way. Bonds had formed between the two of them.

He stepped towards the beach to think about the doctor. As he was staring out to the pale horizon, squinting, Becq tapped him on his shoulder.

'Hey,' he said. 'How's things?'

'Good, good,' she said. 'Look, I found some really sweet fruits on the south of the island. Want to come and see?'

'Sure, why not.'

The two walked along the beach around the island. There were a couple of cirrus clouds, thin and pale. It was getting warmer.

'You lonely here?' she asked.

'Lonely?' he said. 'A little. It's quiet here. Forces you to look at yourself. That can make you uncomfortable, I guess. Not so much a loneliness in that respect.'

She nodded. 'Not many people do that.'

'Nope, especially back at home. You don't get the chance to.'

'Or, people don't want to,' she said.

'Possibly,' Manolin said.

'Look, I know it's probably out of line asking you, Manolin, but I know you had a few personal problems when you left Escha.'

Manolin was silent.

'You had a fight with your wife, didn't you? How do you feel now?'

Manolin sighed, stepping the other side of Becq so that he was in the shade from the forest. 'How do I feel? I think the distance helps. There're no reminders—you know, places you visit, bars you go out to. Nothing to remind me of her. I think I'm less angry, too. Again, the distance.'

'Will you see her when you get back?'

'I've never really thought about it. I don't know. Possibly. I don't want to anyway.'

'She hurt you, didn't she?'

Manolin smiled. 'Yeah, something like that.' Then, 'It was good to make that mistake at a young age. At least I won't do it again in a hurry. Or, knowing me, I will.'

Becq was playing with strands of her blonde hair. 'We should all go for some drinks when we get back. Celebrate returning with a clean slate. I think a lot of us feel changed the last few months. I reckon we all feel put right somehow.'

'Really? How've you changed?'

'Well, I feel more confident here. I feel more sensual. Yana's the same. It just makes you more sure of yourself, you know? Anyway, things move too fast in Escha. People don't stop and talk. There's no choice here—you've got to talk. It's pretty rude otherwise.'

'True. Your dad's changed a bit. I'm not sure if he's become more tense or something.'

'I know what you mean. He's ignored me most of my life. Guess you never really see that side of him. I think he would've preferred a son. But, he seems tenser these days. He snaps more.'

'Maybe he doesn't like us youngsters.'

Becq laughed. 'I think you've changed, too.'

'How so?'

'You seem calmer. More assertive.'

'Not having a psycho wife does that to you.'

'I guess so,' Becq said. 'But really, you seem more aware and tolerant—not that you weren't before. I feel I can talk with you more.'

'Well, that's a good thing, I suppose.'

Becq was silent for a moment. 'Manny, what was that thing you all saw? Ever since my dad was down there, he's been different.'

After she said the question, Manolin realised that she had been working up the nerve to pry. The secret of what lay underwater burned away. 'I wish I knew, Becq. I wish I knew.'

'No one's said anything about it since then,' she said. 'I asked him and he continued as if I'd never asked the question.' She stopped at looked across the fringe of the forest. 'We're here. Ah, here's the tree.'

She reached up and picked a large mango. 'Here you go.'

Manolin looked at it. 'Splendid, I was wondering where the natives were getting it from.' Then, smiling, 'I see you're enticing me with your sweet fruit.'

Twenty-Four

Jella and Lula lay naked on the bed below deck, staring at the wooden ceiling, listening to the sound of the waves striking the boat. They were sweating as they had just fucked. They were now talking about the future. Lula turned her head and her eyes settled on Jella's breasts. The rumel woman was conscious of this fact, and she raised her chest a little for Lula to place her hand upon her.

They lay together for some time.

'I'm a little worried,' Lula said.

'I know you are.'

'I love you,' Lula said.

After a moment's silence, Jella said, 'I know.'

'What's wrong?'

'Sorry, Lula. I'm worried, too. I try not to think about it.'

'You should,' Lula said. 'You should open up more, and not be so closed to me.'

Jella sighed, glanced down at the top of Lula's head. She kissed it smelled her fragrant hair. 'You keep saying this. It's just the way I am. I'll try and be different.'

'But we might not have much time left,' Lula said.

'Of course we will.'

'How can you be so sure?'

Lula moved her leg so that it was on top of Jella's. It felt so smooth—that simple difference of skin quality never lost its appeal to the rumel. For someone so rough as her, it was a wonderful escape.

'Because I've studied for years and I have a plan. That's why. I'm confident. We should cheer up because everything will be fine.'

'What will we do when it's all over?' Lula said.

Jella reflected on the question for a few seconds. The last years of their lives had been spent studying, planning, preparing for their mission. It was all their lives consisted of. This line of contemplation would always reach a wall, and it was as if she was not able to get past it. 'Then we'll form another plan.'

'Why? Why can't go somewhere north of Rhoam? I want to settle, and look after you.'

'I'm not that old,' Jella said, laughing.

'I know, but you know what I mean. This is all I've known. I want to do something different. And after this trip, you will have got your justice, wouldn't you?'

'There's a long way to go yet. Getting to Quidlo is only half the job. We've got to trail back to Escha. Then we'll have to go over land again. In fact, we're probably a third of the way there. We can talk about the future later, yes?'

Lula sighed. 'It just feels like the end. It's such a long way to go.'

'Well, the difficult bit's coming up. After that it's easy. Just sailing. Come on, be positive.'

'I know,' Lula said. 'I'm hungry though. We can't keep living off fish.'

'Then we'll stop at an island and get some more fruit.' Jella turned Lula over on her back, kissed her. She drew her tail up the inside of Lula's legs, up to the top. The girl was still wet from before.

'You can't get away with it that easily, you know,' Lula said. Jella kissed her soft neck.

Jella sat up on top of Lula. 'I can try.' She slipped her tail inside. Lula grunted, closed her eyes, drew her knees up, all the time groaning slowly. As Jella leaned forwards to kissed Lula's chest, the girl opened her eyes to stare at the ceiling. Although the rumel could see this, the fact that her human lover might not be fully interested in sex, she continued, would try harder until she gave satisfaction.

Jella stepped up on the deck. Menz, Yayle and Gabryl were all standing on one side of the boat, taking turns at staring through a telescope into the direction from which they had come. She walked over. Above her, the sail was tight with the wind. On one side of the deck were the carcasses of whales. She did not know what species they were, but the stench was horrendous.

'Hey, guys. How're we doing?' she said.

Menz and Gabryl turned. Yayle continued to look out to sea. Menz's tail, which was motionless. Gabryl ran his hand through his beard.

'What's wrong?' she said.

'It appears,' Gabryl said, 'that there are one or two ships following us.'

'One or two?' Jella said. 'What?'

'Well, a few, actually,' Gabryl said.

'Let me—' She stepped past them and took the telescope from Yayle, who stumbled back, cursing. She raised the telescope, thrust it at the horizon. She could see only the sea and the sky. 'Where are they?'

'To the right.' Gabryl tilted the end of the telescope for her.

She could see, in a tight formation and hazy because of the distance, seven shapes, small and neat, facing them.

'Those're the one's we can see,' Menz said. 'Ain't gonna be surprised if there's more.'

'Fucking hell,' Jella said. She glanced at Gabryl. Her eyes were wide, but she made sure she spoke with confidence. 'They're miles and miles away. If we start the engines then we'll get there no problem. Make sure we get there, Gabryl.'

This was no longer as simple as she had hoped. She walked down along the deck then below, almost as if she didn't want to face the fact that her crew was being followed. The risk had just doubled.

Twenty-Five

Manolin woke with a gasp, breathing heavily. He wiped sweat from his forehead. He sat up. The sky was pink, so the sun had not yet risen. Again you could hear the monotony of the tide, soothing, reassuring. It was just what he needed after a dream like that. He took several more deep breaths before lying down again.

'What's wrong with you?' Santiago said.

Manolin tilted his head to see the old man framed by the block of misty light in the doorway, his hat tipped to one side, leaning with his usual casual arrogance.

'Bad dream.' Manolin thought that Santiago sounded surprisingly alert given the time, as if he'd not slept.

'What was it about?' Santiago said.

'Nothing.'

'Come on, talking will rationalise it. Then it's unlikely you'll dream it again.'

'I'm surprised you'd take an interest,' Manolin said. 'Anyway, dreams aren't rational.'

'Don't be so nonsensical. Come on, out with it man.'

'My ex-wife,' Manolin said.

'What about her?'

'I dreamt I was having the conversation with her again. After I caught her. Except it was scarily calm.'

'What were you talking about?'

Manolin sighed, struggled to decipher the images he'd just put to one side. He said, 'She was giving calm reasons why she had to do it. She said that he was more of a man than me.'

'Women tell you that crap to hurt you,' Santiago said. 'They all do it. They know it's the only thing that'll get to you. They think it will make you act in a way *they* want.'

'She's probably right though,' Manolin said.

'Nonsense, man. The amount of chaps that I've seen hurt by a woman—well, there're a lot of them, let's put it that way. And just as many women hurt by men. It's the way of things. It has been for an age. Will be again.'

'Doesn't help much,' Manolin said. 'Still hurts.'

'Was just a dream, Manny. Just a dream.'

'But it wasn't though, was it. She did do those things. You know when you have a dream and it seems so real, then you wake and you spend minutes panicking to make sure it's not real? Well, it's real. She did cheat. I'm hardly a man—'

'Nonsense,' Santiago said. 'And what do you mean by "a man"? You mean you want to go out and fuck as many women as possible? You mean you want to be so distant and never cry in front of a woman? You mean you want to drink yourself into an early grave to prove yourself? Those are the easy things to do. Those are the things that happen when you aren't a man. A real man stands by a family, no matter what. He supports them through every circumstance. That's a man. He can be sensitive, because that's what women are. Sensitive creatures. They need you to be open. And just because you're not like every other man who has to drink to have a good time. Those are all things to avoid being a man. Trust me, lad, you're more than a man than you think. Don't let a dream knock you back.'

Manolin sighed. It was too early for all this talk. The old man sounded bitter, as if years of scorn and hurt were the seeds for such a well-rehearsed speech. Gulls cried out somewhere in the distance, then some unknown creature from the forest called, its voice echoing along the bay. 'So why am I alone?'

'Because you're on an island in the middle of nowhere. And because, lad, that's just the way the wind blows. Nothing more, nothing less. And, ultimately, you're the only one to change it. Back home there're dozens of ideal ladies—and I mean ladies—that are waiting for someone like you. Hell, there's even Becq. She's a great heart, Manny.'

'Sure.' Manolin lay down again, listened to the tide. So many thoughts about the mainland and its opportunities filled his mind. He felt no need to face them, not here. Whether it was because he was hiding, or because of some more noble reason, he didn't know. It was just something he wasn't prepared to examine. Not just yet.

Manolin rowed the raft to the beach. Santiago stepped out cautiously, Manolin following. They were heading to the village for breakfast. It was windy and there were thin clouds. Manolin passed Forb's hut.

'I'm just popping in,' he said.

Santiago continued up the beach.

Manolin looked inside, but there was no one there. *Strange*, he thought. He stepped out as Myranda was walking up the steps. 'Morning. Is the doctor up and about?'

'Yes,' she said, smiling. 'He was walking early this morning and now he's going for a stroll.'

'Is that wise?'

'Oh, I know what he's like. It's not as though anything I say will stop him. I sent Lewys to watch him from a distance.'

'Well, that's all right then.' Manolin paused whilst he held the door open for Myranda. She smiled as she walked by. He noticed that her hair had been tied up in some tribal fashion that he didn't understand, hunks of carved bamboo sticking out. 'I like your hair. It really suits you.'

'Thank you. It's nice that you notice. I have to keep trying here. It's hard competing with all those larger women. Only Forb ever looks at me.'

Manolin followed her inside. 'Well, that's rubbish for a start.'

Lewys could see the bald head of his father from some way away, so he was certain he wouldn't be spotted. His mother had told him that his father was full of pride, so he didn't want to hurt his feelings by being seen. The forest was cool, quiet. He crept through the ferns, off of the path where the opportunity came. His father's movements were slow and considered, his steps hesitant on paths that should have been well known to him. It made him easy to follow.

Lewys liked the forest. It was dark and he could get up to things he couldn't do near the village. There was always something to explore, were always creatures to investigate. The forest was where he could play. He had heard of the cities of the mainland only in stories his father had told him, but he found it hard to believe anything else other than this lush greenery, the intense crowding of nature. It overtook your senses. To be in somewhere so barren, with massive stone buildings was bewildering, alien. It wasn't right, either. Lewys had always been taught how bad they were by his father—that people were unfriendly, that communities were not close. Diversity of life crumbled. Lewys wasn't sure if he could ever be apart from this island. It had become his life, it was the precise limits to his experience. And he was quite happy with that.

It was strange enough with the foreigners here, with their funny clothing and petty arguments. They only seemed to bring trouble with them. Everything was fine before they came along. His father wasn't injured, there were no people being killed by strange devices. They were a weird bunch. Apart from Manolin. Lewys liked him. He was almost like his father. They talked about the same subjects and got on well. The best thing about Manolin was that he treated Lewys like a person. All the other foreigners, and sometimes people from the village, talked down to him. Manolin wasn't like that.

Most of it the forest Lewys knew well, which is why he could tell his father was heading towards the ichthyocentaurs' village. He didn't know why. He followed through shaded paths, past creepers and palms, along the fig region, up the slope. He could see the perspiration on his father's head. Lewys hoped that he wasn't struggling—it wasn't even particularly hot. Every movement his father made suggested pain, which upset Lewys. He wanted to run up and help his father up the slope. But he remembered his mother's instructions, and wouldn't do that.

His father rested his hand on a tree, place his forehead against the back of his hand, and Lewys wanted to shout out. In the growing humidity of the forest, Lewys waited. Forb stood up straight, then continued upwards, through the changing foliage. Lewys saw all the birds he knew up in the canopy, but he did not pay too much attention to them.

The sun came out sending spots of light though the canopy, illuminating his father, who was now limping up the slope. He stumbled on a tree root, but did not fall down. This was a relief to Lewys.

His father changed direction. Lewys leapt behind a fern. He watched his father head away from the village then up to the path to the summit of the volcano. Lewys looked at his father under furrowed brows.

Lewys lost track of his father as he waited until it was safe to enter the bright grass path. Still, he remained close to the forest as if he were stalking a hog. He found the experience exciting in some way he did not understand.

There was a strong breeze as Lewys climbed the slope and saw his father's white shirt waving in the wind. He looked around, noticed that the horizon was pale where there were clouds and you could see the sea now, above the forest, from his position near the volcano summit. It was violent, breaking against the reef with a lot of energy. He turned to see his father dip over the summit.

Lewys ran up.

As he reached the summit he saw his father. Lewys crouched. His father was on his hands and knees, his shirt rippling like sails on a ship. He tried to stand up, span around as if he was trying to examine the panorama. Then he fell.

Lewys saw his father turn on his back and lie flat.

He ran over to him, his legs struggling in the strong wind.

When he reached him, Lewys stopped. His father's eyes were open, staring up. He moved his head so that his father could see him. Lewys shook him, saying nothing, and was met with an expressionless gaze.

It was almost thoughtful, as though his father was realising some great fact. Lewys looked down, noticed that he wasn't breathing. He placed his head sideways on his father's chest. Nothing could be heard.

Lewys remained there for some time, uncertain of what to do. He moved his arms around his father's body until it became stiff. He felt the wind blowing his tears around his eyes and his stomach felt sick. He didn't want to look up. He wanted to stay there, without moving. Somehow he knew—he didn't want it to be true, but he knew. He wanted to stay still, like his father, and not hurt his pride. Not now. He could hear a gull cry overhead. Then Lewys's was fixed on the sea, and the rhythmic movements and sounds. When he was too exhausted from crying, he lay sideways regarding the bright horizon.

A line of ichthyocentaurs walked towards the village. They were carrying a stretcher. As they came to the village, Manolin saw that the body on it was Forb's. Lewys was walking at the rear. A group of semi-naked villagers ran to the ichthyocentaurs, in front of Manolin. They crowded around to see the body. Gasps could be heard. Manolin stood up, pushed through the dozens of villagers. Santiago followed. They came to the centre. Forb lying on the stretcher, colour drained from his face.

Manolin signed to the four ichthyocentaur that lowered the stretcher to the sand. *What happened?*

Lewys brought us to Doctor. Doctor dead, one of them signed.

'Fuck,' Manolin said. He waded through the crowd to Lewys. Manolin crouched next to him. 'Lewys, are you all right?'

Lewys nodded, strands of hair falling across his eyes.

'What happened?' Manolin said.

'Mother asked me to follow him. He was all right, then all of a sudden he fell. When I ran to him he was lying there, still.'

Manolin noticed that Lewys was looking right through him, almost detached from the scene entirely. 'Are you sure you're okay?'

'I'll be all right.'

Just as he spoke, the crowd of muttering villagers parted, and Myranda walked through to her husband's body. Manolin looked up then turned to her. He ushered Lewys towards where his mother knelt by Forb. Manolin glanced across at Santiago, who nodded reassuringly.

'Myranda...' Manolin said. He didn't really know what to say.

Her eyes were filled with tears, although her face was calm. She embraced Lewys. Manolin placed a hand on her shoulder. 'Is there anything I can do? Anything at all?'

She shook her head. He stepped away, motioned with his hands for everyone else to do the same. 'I think we should leave them to it for a moment,' he whispered to several natives.

They separated then stood in small groups further off. Santiago walked with Manolin, away from where they were standing. Becq, Yana and Jefry approached.

'What happened?' Yana asked.

'The doctor's no longer with us,' Santiago said.

'How?' Yana said.

'I think it was his medication,' Manolin said.

'Medication?' she said.

'Yeah,' Manolin said. 'He had cancer, and was using some herb that the ichthyocentaurs had prepared for him. He wasn't able to take any when unconscious. I suspect it was that that got him.'

'Cancer? How could you possibly know that?' Santiago asked.

'He told me,' Manolin said.

'Did he, indeed,' Santiago said.

'Yeah,' Manolin said. Poor Lewys though. The little fellow saw it all.'

'Oh no, is he okay?' Becq asked. Manolin could see the genuine concern and upset on her face.

'I think so. I think he's well aware of what's going on. Kids deal with it differently then us lot do. Almost seems detached, I guess. I don't know. I was the same when I was younger. I'll see if I can help him in any way later.'

'Well, where does that leave us?' Jefry said.

'How d'you mean?' Manolin said.

'What I mean, *Manolin*, is what's our role on the island now? Santiago, what do you think?'

'I think you've go a point,' Santiago said. 'Forb asked us here. He's the only one we've talked to really. I don't ever like fraternising with the natives.'

'Speak for yourself. I've talked in depth with a lot of the others,' Manolin said.

'Indeed. Well, anyway, I'll have a think. We've got most of our data anyway.' Santiago spoke dismissively almost, as if he wanted to get away and this provided a sudden excuse.

'What do you mean "data"?' Manolin said. 'We came to investigate the deaths of the ichthyocentaur and stop them. You've hardly even noticed them.'

'Don't be ridiculous. There's not a lot we can do. Anyway, we came to research the island. Take some samples. We've got an ichthyocentaur body on board the ship. We can go back, publish what we've got.'

'No, no you can't.' Manolin stepped towards Santiago. 'If you go back without the agents, you can't publish anything. Their deaths stop you doing that. You can't even go back to Gio. Whatever happens, they'll think you killed them.'

Santiago looked down and up, then placed a hand on his hip. 'Nonsense. I'll have a think. We'll have the old boy's funeral, and then we can decide. We can stop at a couple of the other islands on the way back and take some notes. This chain extends north—'

'Well fuck you then.' Manolin pushed past Santiago, walked towards the village. He turned back, shouted, 'Fuck you, Santiago DeBrelt,' then marched away.

Santiago turned to the others. 'Fucking runt,' he said, watching Manolin stomp off across the sands. 'That's the thanks I get for showing him all he knows. Don't know what his problem is.' He sighed. 'Anyway. We'll leave in the next couple of days then. We need food and water for the journey. We can get that here.'

'What about Manolin? What about what he said?' Becq asked.

'What about him?' Jefry said, with a chuckle. 'Leave him here.'

'We can't do that.' Becq turned to her father, her eyes wide hopeful. 'Please.'

'I'll have a word.' He nodded to Jefry and Yana. They turned and walked, hand in hand, along the beach. He faced his daughter. 'You really do like him, don't you?'

She nodded, rolling her lips inwards.

'I'll have a word with him.' He placed his arm around his daughter and escorted her back to the huddle of villagers.

As they walked away, they could see Myranda and Lewys, framed by palm trees, sitting next to Forb's body on the sand. She sat Lewys on her lap and they were both holding Forb's hand.

The funeral pyre was lit as the sun became as low and red. The day's low cloud had cleared to leave a purple sky. Manolin watched as Myranda stepped away from the fire. She was holding a torch whilst staring at the body of Forb in the centre of the pyre. She had been like that for some time, and all the natives had gone back to the village. Behind her was the sea. The wind ruffled her hair, but she was not affected by it. She threw the torch to the base of the fire and stepped back.

Manolin walked over to her, placed his hand on her arm. She looked at him, her brown skin seeming darker at dusk, and her eyes were wide and full of emotions that he would have once thought were a world away from his.

'Are you okay?' he said.

'Yes. Thank you. I'll be okay.'

They were interrupted by the laughter of the natives, as, back in the village, one of the men was telling a story about Forb. The celebrations were beginning. Manolin still thought it strange that they celebrated lives, rather than mourned deaths, but he had to admit he didn't feel as glum as he would have thought otherwise.

'We ought to join them,' she said.

'Are you upset?'

Myranda frowned, then her face lightened. 'I'd prepared for this day, but it still hurts. We had been expecting it for years. He never knew when the medicine would wear off. We took each day as if it could be one of our last. I know you can die at anytime, but we were more aware of it—the two of us. With that, either we were less attached, or... I don't know.'

Manolin nodded. 'If I can help in any way—'

'You're kind. I'll be fine. Just rather lonely, immediately after spending much time with him.'

'Well, if you want to talk about anything, and the same goes for Lewys. If he wants to chat or play or whatever, then I'll be more than happy.'

Myranda studied Manolin's face.

'What?' Manolin said.

'You and him were similar in some ways.'

'He thought that too.'

She nodded, her eyes narrowing in what Manolin thought was a pleasant way.

'He liked you,' she said.

'He was a good man. It's such a loss.'

'Don't think of it in that way. He's in a better place.'

Manolin frowned, thinking that she said this nonchalantly. 'Myranda, tell me, there doesn't seem to be any... religion, here. I've seen many places, and, always, there is some kind of belief. In something. In anything.'

'You forget that we descended from those scientists that fled the rebellion all that time ago. No beliefs came with them.'

'So, why do they dance, and entertain at a funeral?'

'Because it feels right. It's an emotional expression in its own way—perhaps it came from the culture of our ancestors. But why not?'

'Good answer.' Manolin laughed dryly, then turned to the pyre. He could hear the stories from the village, the sound of the fire burning, and, there as it always was, the sea.

He and Myranda walked back to the village. Beach fires were lit, and by them, the silhouettes of ichthyocentaurs. It was the first time so many of them had come to the beach for months. He signed greetings to them. His language with them had improved to the level that he could now converse with them.

He listened to the stories of Forb's life, watched Lewys show his memories of his father. Manolin felt a lump in his throat as the child walked back to the crowd. For some time he enjoyed the food and the dancing, sharing in the memories of the dead man.

After an hour, he saw Santiago approaching. Manolin turned to him.

'Good evening, Manolin. Enjoying the festivities?'

'Yes. It's all quite touching,' Manolin said.

'Good, good. Look, we've all had a chat, and I've decided we'll head back tomorrow.'

'Tomorrow?' Manolin said. The word had impact with him.

'Yes, tomorrow. We'll get some meat and fruit, then head off in the morning. There're more islands to see on the way back. I think we've all had enough.'

'Enough? What about the ichthyocentaurs? What about Myranda? Her husband's just died.'

'Damn you, man. We're not to interfere in what goes on in these people's lives. Their existence goes on. We've got a home to go to.'

'You might.'

Santiago put his arm around Manolin, steered him away from the village to the darkness over the lagoon. 'You've got to let it all go, Manny. She's pretty, and you've struck a good relationship with many of them. But you're a good scientist. You're not to get too involved.'

Manolin was silent, his throat thick with emotion.

'Becq is worried about you. She's fond of you. She'll look after you on the way back. And think of the new islands to explore. Then the epic return home. There's a lot to look forward to. Think of our reputations when we return, eh?'

Manolin sighed, sat on the sand.

Santiago stood over him, his hands on his hips. 'I know it's hard. Believe me, when I was younger I got tangled up with tribal girls. I've been there. I've done that and—'

'You've done everything, haven't you? You've done so much and you want to vomit it all out on the rest of us. Well, I can't be arsed listening to it. My experience is a little less shallow than your shenanigans, so let's just leave it. Okay? I'll pack my stuff and be ready for tomorrow. It's best we get this all over with quickly.'

'That's the spirit. Everyone else is packed and ready. We can be off first thing then. We can say our goodbyes and be off.'

'Great.'

'Oh, come on, it's not that bad. At least you've seen a bit of the world.'

'Santiago, shut up. I'll be back to bed later.'

Manolin watched Santiago walk back, then row the raft across the lagoon and to his hut.

Darkness fell as suddenly as it always did out here. The stars were again numerous. Manolin remembered the first night he looked at them from the island. He felt hollow inside. He had to leave paradise.

As you glanced along the beach you could see small fires and the main pyre. Jasmine drifted on the gentle breeze, and as the moon became high and bold, you could see the shadows of palm trees on the sand.

Going home was something he had not thought about. The island had imposed limits on his thoughts—on Arya he didn't have to think much about Escha. He brought his knees to his chest, stared out to sea. Watched each wave rolling in. The temperature fell. He lay down flat on the sand and rested his chin on his hands, and he looked at the edge of the forest.

Two figures loitered on the edge. One was definitely a villager, dark, lean, tall. Male. It took him several moments to notice that the second figure was Becq. He looked on, interested. He could see the figures walk by the edge of the forest. The man was telling Becq something. He was a good foot taller, muscular from years of working fishing nets, chopping wood. Wearing only a loin cloth, he was leaning across to Becq to talk to her. Manolin heard her laugh. He thought it strange seeing her with another man. He couldn't ever recall seeing it back on the mainland. He knew of her overtures towards him—he'd have to have been blind and deaf not to. It did not stop the uneasy feeling, especially when the villager leaned over and tried to kiss her. Manolin couldn't quite see it properly—the leaves of the trees waving in front of them in the breeze.

It seemed a little out of character, but then again, she had become more assertive and confident since being here. He looked on as the villager placed a hand on her shoulder, then Becq pulled away. They kissed again.

Manolin grunted a laugh, shook his head. He pushed himself up off the sand, turned, walked away, not really sure of what he felt any more. He walked to the shore further down and slumped on the sand.

He wasn't certain how long he had been there when Myranda approached, walking cat-like across the sand. When she was nearer you could see the moon actually reflecting off of her skin like a cliché.

'Hello,' she said. She sat next to him on the sand. 'What's making you look so sad?'

'Santiago says we have to leave.' He noticed the moonlit shadows pooling by her collar bone.

'Oh,' she said. Then, 'I hoped you would stay longer.'

'So did I.' He looked at her. Her eyes were bright, round, full of sadness.

She placed her hand on his leg, leaned over. 'I really wanted you all to stay.'

Manolin looked at her hand. 'There's nothing I can do. Santiago's made up his mind.'

She knelt up so that her mouth was within an inch of his ear, and whispered, 'I want you to have me.'

Manolin shivered. He did not know if it was the wind, the tone of her voice or what she had said. 'Beg pardon?'

She pushed his knees down and placed one hand under his chin and one on the back of his head. 'I want you to have me before you go.'

'Myranda,' he said. 'Your husband has just died! This is ridiculous.'

'You are a prude.' She frowned then kissed him on the top of his cheek.

Manolin felt the softness of her lips, and her breath along his cheek. She smelled of coconut. He shook himself clear. It seemed ridiculously sudden, and very strange to say the least. 'Myranda, you don't understand. I'm a bit shocked that you can act like this tonight.'

She looked genuinely upset. 'I... don't understand. Why are you angry with me?'

Manolin reflected for a moment, aware of the importance of the situation. 'You *actually* don't think anything *is* wrong, do you?'

She shrugged. 'I don't understand. I'd been saving myself for you.'

'Saving yourself—' Then, quieter, 'Saving yourself for me? You were married to Forb, woman.'

'I could've been with anyone at anytime. That's the way things are here. I only stay with people I feel a special bond with though, and because I'm not attractive then not many people like me. You do, I can tell this.'

'Myranda, where I come from men would pay a million shillings for a kiss from someone like you.'

She laughed. 'I have no idea what a shilling is.'

'It's a lot of wealth.'

'You're silly.'

'No, really,' he said. 'They would. But, you're saying that you can sleep with anyone here?'

'Haven't you noticed?'

'I hadn't really thought about the people at that level. The ichthyocentaurs, yes, because I studied them.' He paused, thinking. 'Guess I never looked at the people that much. You just expect people's relationships, especially the sexual part, to be normal, whatever that means, wherever you are.' Then, 'So, do you not feel any sadness for Forb?'

'Manolin, I know he told you to have me. I know because I asked him to. And he wanted it too. I'm sad, of course I am. But he wanted you to be with me, especially if he went.'

'What? What kind of lives to you all live here? A husband would be willing to permit wife with another man? I couldn't share. I'm not like that. Where I'm from, a man stays with a woman.' The irony of his wife's infidelities didn't escape him.

'Then don't share. I wanted it with Forb here. He always said it was like owning a beautiful pond, which is like a lagoon but inland. He said that it would be tranquil, and beautiful, and he could swim in it any day he wanted. Some people, who had a nice pond, would not want anyone else to swim in it, but others would enjoy seeing others swim in it and it would make everyone happy. Manolin, I don't understand your ways, but I just wanted you to have me.'

Manolin laughed. 'Oh, I'd love to, believe me. But tonight?'

'Why not? I think you're assuming too much about us.'

'Hello? Your husband's funeral?'

'Life goes on: that's all we know. Anyway, what night could be better? I want to feel good, *especially* tonight, and we won't spend another night together after this. I need you more than I ever could. Tonight, I have never felt sadder and I want comfort from you.'

Manolin knelt next to her. 'I can comfort you, but not how you'd wish.' He couldn't get his head around her attitudes to sexuality. There was a perverse logic involved, but emotions were spinning around his head.

She turned to face him. They both stared at one another as if each were a puzzle. He looked down at the island rag that barely covered her. He felt a swelling in his throat. His mouth was dry. He reached for a strand of her hair, which had spiralled down over her breasts. He pushed her hair out of the way and stared at them like an adolescent. He felt very young, and primal.

'I would love to, Myranda. But, tonight of all nights? I'd feel more than guilty. I'm not sure you really follow. If anything was to happen, and I'm certainly not saying it ought to, then I'd want it to be... well, a little less inconvenient.'

'He wanted it. I want it. I want it so much.' She began to unbutton his shirt eagerly, as if she was unwrapping a present. It was clumsy yet endearing. His arms fell to his side as she slid his shirt off. They were still kneeling, facing each other. He ran his hands down her arm. They stood up then she pulled his breeches down and his first thought was to looked around, paranoid that someone would watch. His hands twitched as if wanting to stop her, but not totally giving in to temptation.

He could feel the cool evening air on his loins. 'Look, let's step nearer the forest.'

They walked, hand in hand, Manolin carrying his clothes under his arm, up the shore then she stopped him. She kissed his neck and could feel her breasts, firm and large against his chest. He held his hands out behind her, uncertain, full of hesitation. He spread his fingers out and touched the muscles of her back, pushed her rags down to the ground, feeling every curve, then dabbed her smooth skin with the back of his hand. He grabbed her waist and he felt something deep within his chest as he realised how firm and small it was and he wanted her, there and then, more than anything, but he was thinking, also, that he shouldn't. He was shaking, stared off into the distance as she kissed his neck.

He thought of Forb, of his ex-wife, of Becq and of Myranda, who was presently running her tongue along his collar-bone. He could hear the sea, loud and raw, when they fell naked on to the sand and he could feel the strange sensation of the tiny grains as they rolled onto their sides. She ran her hands along his hips then brought his hands on to hers, and his fingers dragged along her legs. She paused, looked at him and kissed him on the lips, then nibbled his bottom one. He noted how white and round her eyes were against her skin. He groaned and smiled, feeling that same stirring in his chest, then he felt her cool hand on his groin.

She pushed him so that he was lying flat and, as he closed his eyes, she began to play with his cock like he hoped she might. Her hand was cool, and she kissed down his stomach until she placed his cock in her mouth, began to suck gently.

He stared up at the night sky, worried. She kept playing but he was not becoming turned on. He was conscious of this as the seconds passed. The more he thought about it the less he felt aroused. When she drew back he could feel the wind chilling her saliva on his flaccid penis.

He sat up, saw that she was staring at him. She became suddenly distant, as if he were a stranger. She let go, but he brought her closer.

'Just hold me,' he said. 'I'd really like that.'

She said, 'Do you not like me after all then?' Her words were full of vulnerability.

'Yes, yes, of course I do.' He put his arms around her. 'You have no idea how much I've wanted this. It's just…'

'Forb.' Her shoulders sagged.

'Well, yes.'

'I don't understand you.'

'Where I come from, it's simply not a good thing to do so soon, that's all. Especially if you really like someone. I liked the both of you.'

'But I wanted you to have me,' she said. 'I wanted this. I won't see you again. It's really important.'

'I know. I know. But just holding you all night would make me happy, more than you can understand. I don't know 'bout you.'

She smiled, but Manolin couldn't tell if she felt insulted. 'Yes, I'd like that too.'

'I like you far too much, and I liked Forb, too. It's just my way of respecting him.'

They lay back down on the sand, in the darkness by the forest, and they could hear the villagers in the distance. She curled up next to him, nuzzling by his neck, and he held her close. It was another warm night and he could smell the fragrance from the forest and hear the trees moving in the wind.

As she slept he lay there looking at the stars, replaying his life in his mind. He was thinking of scenes in Escha. He remembered the bustling streets, the smells. Tens of thousands of people and hardly any of them smiled. He thought of the bars, the churches, the brothels, the drug houses—*all ways for people to run away from actually living*, he thought. He reached for his clothes and dragged his shirt over him and Myranda. His left hand was flat on the sand, and he clawed at it, feeling how soft and fine the grains were. He breathed in this clean, fresh air. In the distance he could hear laughter and in the forest behind, a bird squawked. Then, as a firefly zipped in circles above his head, and, as Myranda stirred beneath his jaw, he smiled.

Morning, and Manolin threw his bags on the beach in front of the lagoon. He looked back at the huts that had been his home. The sun was hidden behind a low ridge of nimbus clouds. He thought that they should burn away soon enough, and that the day would turn out all right.

Up ahead on the beach, Santiago, Becq, Jefry and Yana were standing next to two rafts. A group of villagers had gathered around. He could see their ship's sail in the distance, poking up over several palms. *So they were going*, he thought.

To his right, a group of ichthyocentaurs walked down to him with their thick tails, their slightly waddled walk. He smiled because he saw that they looked towards Santiago first, but walked over to him. Seven of the creatures gathered around him and they signed greetings, which he returned.

It's a shame, you are going, Manolin, one said.

Don't feel like that, he said.

But you were such a good thing for us.

How? Manolin signed.

You took an interest in us. We felt comfortable with you around. And you have made an effort to stop the deaths. They have stopped for now. We wish you could stay.

No goodbyes, please. Not necessary. He picked up his bags, placed them on his shoulder, walked towards the village. As he passed the hut that Forb had been sharing with Myranda, he threw his bags on the sand in front.

Myranda opened the door at the sound, then stepped out, her eyes wide.

'Are you going now?' she said.

She was standing, one foot behind the other, her hands held in front of her fingering her ragged skirt, the sadness and confusion in her eyes. He looked up and down her body and brushed his hair back.

He said, 'No. If it's okay with you, I'll stay.'

She looked at him through strands of her hair that blew across her face. 'What?'

'If it's okay with you. I'll just let the others know I shall not be requiring a lift back.'

He doubted if he would forget the smile she gave at that moment. She did not move, did not make the moment too dramatic for him. It was nothing like in the ridiculous plays his ex-wife forced him along to see back in Escha. Her smile was genuine, saying enough. It confirmed that he did not want the competition and drama of the city. He did not want to push his career as far as others wanted. Did not want to spend his shillings with others in bars, drinking away his free time. Did not want to walk on streets brushing shoulders with strangers who glared at him as he knocked them.

He knew men did things like this—they gave up their lives for some girl. He wasn't the first, wouldn't be the last. He didn't care if it all went wrong, so long as he had more nights like the previous one, because he felt sensuality more than he had ever known, and it was like he had felt closer to some spiritual plain.

It wasn't just Myranda, either. It was the island as a whole, the entire system.

And she wasn't just some girl. When he looked at her he saw a million potentials.

He walked along the beach towards Santiago and the rest of the crew. His shirt rippled in the pleasant breeze. He was breathing heavily, nervous at the coming moment. He could feel his heart beating and began to alter his stride, becoming more confident and purposeful. He clenched his fists. The others were hunched over the rafts, loading their belongings.

Santiago turned. 'So, you're here at last.' Brushing his moustache down with is finger and thumb, he looked Manolin up and down. 'Where're your bags, man?'

'Oh, by Myranda's hut.'

'Well then, lad' Santiago said. 'Go get 'em.'

Manolin curled his mouth into a pout, shrugged his shoulders. 'Nope. No need.'

'Manny,' Becq said. 'What d'you mean?'

'Yes, Manolin,' Santiago said. 'What *do* you mean?'

'I won't be going back.'

Yana and Jefry stood up from being hunched over the raft.

Santiago rolled up his shirt sleeves. 'What? The hell you won't. Go get your things.'

Manolin said, 'I'm not sure you actually understand, old man. I'm staying here.'

Becq stepped closer to Manolin. 'But, why would you want to? What's here? There's nothing here.'

Manolin nodded. 'Well, not entirely nothing.'

'What d'you mean?' she said.

'What he means,' Santiago said, 'is that he's being fooled by yet another woman.' He turned to Manolin. 'Don't be a fool, lad. Don't be a fool again.'

'Look, I'm staying. I won't have my life dictated to by an ageing gigolo. I want to be free of all your bickering, your in-fighting, your competition, your work. And it's not because of a woman, it's because I want to discover what it really means to exist. It can't be done in that city.'

They looked at each other without flinching or exchanging a word. Manolin felt their relationship severing, the years together gone on the next and last boat out. All that remained now was their stares.

'Manny,' Becq said. 'Don't be like this.'

'Look, Becq,' Manolin said, 'I'm sorry. But your father has spent most of his life controlling me. Yes, I'm grateful. But sometimes an old man gets jealous from failing his own life.' He glanced up at Santiago then looked Becq right in the eye. 'I know you felt something for me—'

'She's always made bad decisions,' Santiago said.

'For once in your life don't speak. Don't be the man you've always been, the type most men are, and just think about your daughter's emotions.' Manolin looked at Becq and said, 'You've felt something for me, haven't you?'

She gave a vague smile, strong, not wanting to show any defeat. A few months ago she would be upset now, but the island had changed her.

'I think you're smashing,' he said. 'I really do, but your head is screwed on properly. You should find yourself a decent man.' He was amazed at how confidently he spoke. He had never been like that before. 'I'm not going to patronise you like some—' he glanced at Santiago 'but I think you know as well as I do that you've changed since you've been here. You're more than capable of getting some of what you want.'

Becq smiled vaguely.

'Oh, please,' Santiago said. 'Spare me your false heroics. The girl's better off without a wet bastard like you anyway.' He ushered his daughter away from Manolin, and placed her between Yana and Jefry. Yana put her arms around Becq. Santiago turned back, speaking aloud, 'Besides, by all accounts, his sexual technique isn't enough to keep a woman.' He looked directly at Manolin. 'What was it then? Just didn't satisfy your wife?'

Manolin felt like he'd become enlightened over night. None of these words mattered. None of it effected him the slightest. 'Do you realise how pathetic you sound?'

'About as pathetic as you fucking a girl? You're not even a man, you're still a boy, aren't you?'

Yana and Jefry pulled Becq away then walked her past the raft and along the beach.

'You never did get Yana, did you? Is that why you're jealous?'

'Why would I be jealous? Your wife slept with other men—doesn't that say something? Men, not *boys*.'

Manolin looked away.

'Ah, touching a nerve.'

'Why would I care anyway? Look what I've got for the rest of my life—' Manolin indicated back towards Myranda's hut, the forest, the sea. 'Don't think you can get anything as wonderful as Myranda at your age, can you? At least not without paying.'

'Think you're so clever, staying here, don't you?' Santiago said.

'Not at all. I just want to get away from everything, permanently. Anyway, I care for nature. There's no point me studying it through books. I need to stay. Here, I have a role, I have something that I can call mine. Forb's work wasn't complete.' Then, 'And there's something about you, Santiago DeBrelt, that I don't entirely trust.'

Santiago looked out to the horizon, towards the reef. 'No, I don't suppose you can trust anyone if you're such a weak boy.'

'Why am I weak?' Manolin said.

'For bailing out of life.'

'You think that's easy? The easy thing is to go back. Go back to the fucking city, chasing a career till I die. Go back to an empty life and carry on as if nothing has happened. That's what everyone else does—just carry on, doing whatever they think they have to, until they get like you. Old and desperate. No, the hard thing to do is to break my mind away from that way of thinking and adopt whatever I'll find here.'

'And just what is that going to be?'

Manolin shrugged. 'That's the part I'm looking forward to. Whatever Arya has to offer me. It's about how you live life. Here I can actually grow up. I can work with good, honest folk. I can feel the sun on my skin. I can feel the warm waters every time I swim. I can eat wholesome food. I can breathe clean air. This place is more hands on, you know.'

'Aren't you just escaping things at home, really? Escaping real life?' Santiago said.

'Nah, escaping's what some people do when they spend all their time reading bad books, watching bad plays. Or, when they work so hard they find that they've forgotten to live. The thing is, I'm still with real stuff. You can't break everything into components. Like what you do when you work and rationalise everything; rationalise yourself into an early grave. You can only break things down so small 'til you realise you're not seeing the real world anymore. You treat everything as if it were a problem, a puzzle.'

Santiago grunted a laugh. 'And what would you know? You're only young; you've not old enough to know how to go about life.'

'The world can't be solved, San. That's not the point. You're not meant to solve everything.' Manolin could see something fade in the old man. A light went out, somewhere deep within.

'Nonsense,' Santiago said. He was looking past Manolin now, at nothing in particular. *Perhaps*, Manolin thought, *there's no longer anything for him to look at.*

'Anyway, this isn't escaping. It's how I always saw science going. Less rational, more holistic. Hands on. Everything is connected in some way—you told me that once, although I'm not sure you believed it. And I'm studying things here for me, not anyone else, not for the sake of academia. What's the point of that, really?'

Santiago shrugged, shook his head. 'So, what are you going to do about your house back in Escha? And all your belongings?'

'You take 'em. Buy another wife.'

Slowly, Santiago gave a tight nod, placing his hands on his hips. 'Might just do that.'

Manolin smiled. The tensions had faded. There was nothing but talk on philosophy, and that could have gone on for days. Nothing remained to be said.

'So, this is it then?' Santiago said.

'Yep.' Manolin stretched out his hand. 'This is it.'

Santiago looked down at the offered hand and back up at Manolin's face, and his expression suggested he was surprised to see such a sure person behind Manolin's eyes.

The two men shook hands.

'I didn't mean any of that malarkey,' Santiago said.

'I know,' Manolin said.

'Since when did you get so wise?'

'Since last night.'

'I bet you did,' Santiago said. 'Never heard you returning. She is charming, I'll give you that. Enjoy her.'

'Nothing happened, and *we* will enjoy each other, thank you very much. You could be a tad less misogynistic.'

'When have you known me not to be?' Santiago said.

Manolin sighed. 'You'll never change, will you?'

'Don't plan on it, lad. Bit late for that. Look, the others are coming back now. I'd best get my stuff away.'

Manolin said, 'Right. Look, San, just what is going on?'

'Eh?'

'The thing... The thing we saw in the reef,' Manolin said. 'You know what it is, don't you?'

'Nonsense,' Santiago said. 'Look, we'd better get our bags on board.'

'But why have there been no more attacks? Do you at least know that?'

'Well, it's probably from the electrocution on *Pilar*. That was probably enough to sort them out for a few weeks. Possibly months. I don't know exactly. Maybe they're too scared to surface again. Don't forget, we scared them off that night. It only takes a couple of muskets.'

'Right.' Manolin picked up one of Santiago's bags and placed it on the raft. He stood back as Yana, Jefry and Becq returned. Out at sea he could see the horizon clearing, and the clouds were becoming thin. The wind dropped.

'You two friends again?' Yana asked.

Manolin smiled. 'Yeah. So this is it, guys. I'm staying.'

'Rather you than me,' she said.

'Are you sure?' Becq asked.

Manolin nodded.

Yana stepped over and hugged him, giving him a peck on the cheek. 'Look after yourself, won't you.'

He held his hand out to Jefry, who turned away to place his bag on the raft. The rumel sat on the raft, rested his arms on his knees, looked out to the ship. Yana looked at Manolin in a way that told him all he needed to know. She joined Jefry and Santiago followed.

Manolin nodded to Becq. She turned, walked away, joined the others on the raft and a group of villagers gathered there to bid farewell. He hoped she would let him go, that she wouldn't internalise things any more than she already had. Relationships were certainly a complex thing, he considered, especially when they never had a chance to be shown physically.

Manolin noticed a small bag still on the beach. 'Santiago, you forgot this!'

'Keep it, lad,' Santiago said. 'That's yours. Just in case you need it.'

'All right.' Manolin bent over and had a quick look in the bag. There were several pistols inside. He frowned, stood up, but the raft had already pushed off for the ship.

Manolin stared at his connection with the mainland sailing away.

'They've gone then?' Myranda asked, having appeared at his side.

'Yep.' It was a strange sensation now that he had made the decision. Would he regret it? It was something he'd never know.

'Why did you always fall out?' Myranda said. 'You were always such an unstable group. You brought so many problems to this island.'

'That's human and rumel nature, Myranda. We're not like the natural world. I've always thought this.'

'How do you mean?' she said.

'In nature, systems move towards stability as the end point. The end point is something like a complex and stable forest. It's the sort of thing I've spent most of my life studying. Humans and rumel are different. They just love to break every relationship up—in nature and within themselves. They can't help it. Call it the powers of irrational thought.'

'We won't break up, will we?' She took his hand in hers.

He looked down at her, seeing her big eyes that were rounded at the bottom, staring up at him. He looked over her gently perspiring face, and followed the lines of her nose and lips.

He said, 'Hell, no. We can be the exception.'

Santiago, standing with his hands on his hips, looked back as the raft backed away from Arya. He could see Manolin's white shirt standing out in the crowd of almost naked villagers. To his right he took one last look at the lagoon, the huts. Behind the villagers was the forest, and behind that was the volcano. The warm breeze escalated as the raft moved further out. He could feel it in his hair. He could see Myranda standing alongside Manolin. They were holding hands.

Was there any anger inside of him? On the surface, yes, Santiago would admit that. Perhaps he felt that Manolin was brave for taking a route he never would have the guts to. Perhaps being left in paradise was something to be jealous about. Santiago had known Manolin for years, and all that was for nothing. Manolin didn't seem that grateful about just how much Santiago had done for him. Maybe he would be unaware of that forever. It would be a loss to science, to see such a bright mind being left here, without anyone to benefit. Vaguely, Santiago wondered what would become of the young man.

As the raft rounded the corner of a sandbank, crowned with palms, he lost sight of them.

On board *DeBrelt One*, Santiago drew up by rope the last of the bags. He had spent the early morning loading food, fruit and meat, on board. The deck looked like a grocer's market. When he had almost cleared it, he put the sails up then used the motors to push the boat out of the bay. Once it was moving, he shut the motors off, allowed the sails to snap out as wind caught them.

They drifted away from Arya.

The sun was out in its full, brutal glory. In the distance, Santiago could still see Manolin's figure on the beach. The villagers were gone. He supposed they were either weaving baskets, gathering food, preparing fishing nets. Manolin looked small against the frame of the island—the palms, the lagoon. Birds were hovering above the forest, circling routes up the dormant volcano. The water was an intense blue and you could see fish drifting with the currents.

Santiago allowed the wind to cool his face, the bitterness he felt to Manolin slowly being blown away. He closed his eyes, inhaled the last of the island air, and could still sense the jasmine that he had become accustomed to. He felt sad, although he was not sure exactly why. He opened his eyes and placed his hands on the rail.

Ahead of him was the reef.

You could see the tiny islands of seaweed perching upon it. The water changed direction and speed through the different channels that ran through it. He frowned and could think of nothing but the reef for a long while after they had passed it.

Jefry had joined him after a mile's sailing. The rumel stood next to Santiago, staring out at the water. Eventually he said, 'Where to now then, boss?'

'Huh?' Santiago said.

'Next stop. You mentioned other islands to look at?'

'Oh. Right. Samekh. It's about ten or twenty miles from Arya. In the direction we're headed. I didn't realise they were so close until Forb had mentioned it. The chain of islands stretches further out in one direction for over hundreds of miles. I'd visited some before for research.'

'Tough call, the doctor getting it,' Jefry said. 'He was a nice chap. Little weird, but a good heart.'

'Yes. Yes he was, rather,' Santiago said. 'Now Manolin is filling his sandals.'

Jefry grunted.

'We can station on Samekh for a few days,' Santiago said. 'A week, maybe, depending on what's there. I've been to that island, briefly, and there wasn't much if I remember, but we can do a survey.'

'What happens when we get back?' Jefry said. 'I overheard talk about us being wanted as the agents are dead.'

'Nonsense, man,' Santiago said. 'We'll be fine. After all, one of them killed the other. These things happen at sea.'

'Right. So we'll be able to publish your findings?'

'Possibly.' Santiago remembered the body of the ichthyocentaur he had below deck in a barrel. He would love show the scientific community.

'Possibly?' Jefry said. 'Why only possibly?'

'Well, if I'm honest, the mayor might not appreciate his men dying. It might be best to stay undercover for a few months. It'll be a while yet. And besides, Manolin's set up home here. He wouldn't want other scientists and sailors coming, would he?'

'How altruistic of you,' Jefry said. 'So this was all a waste of time? All this travelling and research.'

'Not at all. We did our studies. We know what we've found. The money will come eventually. Anyway, you got your marriage back, didn't you? Wasn't a waste from your perspective.'

Jefry did not respond.

'And besides, we learnt a lot. We might not be able to publish yet, but in a few years... We'll have a good reputation when we get back, in underground circles, of course. But who says we need to go back to Escha? I reckon we can go further north. Business is better up there, they say. We don't need Escha. Hell, who does? Jefry, the options are endless. I know of other towns and cities. I know of a place where it's a cool, mild climate, with plenty of mountains, pine forests, and inns—proper ones—where a shilling can feed you all night, and the barmaids smile when you order the same drink again. But, for now, let's concentrate on the second island. Who knows, we could visit others in the chain.'

Both men looked out to sea, towards two shades of blue. Most of the clouds had been burned away. A few seagulls flew circles overhead. You could hear them cry out over the noise of the boat cutting through water.

Santiago stepped up to the ship's wheel. He checked his charts, steered *DeBrelt One* on course for the island of Samekh. As he looked back, he could how small see Arya was, the volcano and forest hazy in the distance. He leaned over the rail, looking down to the rumel, who was still standing on the deck. Yana joined him. They stood together, his arm around her waist. Santiago wondered why Jefry never hurt Manolin, never so much as punched him. He wondered if Yana ever told him about her baby. He knew she had lost it. She had become attached to the idea. He could see the loss in her eyes and the way she carried herself. There was a slowness, a hint of regret in every movement she made. Everything she looked at, she seemed to look right past it.

Did Manolin ever know he could have been a father? Santiago saw a symbol in Manolin's ignorance of this, an ignorance that also led

Manolin to remain on the island rather than come back to the mainland.

Santiago did not know why he both hated and loved him. He thought that Manolin never appreciated what he had done for him. Was he jealous of a younger, better-looking man? One who had given up on life? Santiago snorted a laugh, brushed down his moustache, and walked below deck. He said, 'I'm sure there must be a bottle of wine lying around somewhere.'

Below deck, Becq was sitting in her cabin. She had opened her bags, thrown her clothes everywhere. On her lap was her doll. Manolin's hair was longer when she had left him on Arya. She would need more wool to lengthen that of the doll's. Also, how would she make the doll's face browner? That's how she remembered him. She brought the doll to her face. Strands of her blonde hair smothered it. She let it go, placed it on the bed. She took out her needle and thread then began to work on it. Every few minutes she stopped to hold the doll to the light from the porthole.

There was a knocking on the door, then it opened. Santiago stood in the doorway, a bottle held by his side.

'Everything all right?' he asked. 'Just thought I'd check and see if it was.'

She watched his gaze flick down to her doll, then around at the clothes, which were all over her cabin floor and bed. When he looked right at her, she nodded. Santiago rolled his lips in a thin smile, nodded back, then closed the door. She could hear his footsteps fading.

She looked at the doll once again, holding it up in front of her. 'Now, that was nice of him, wasn't it? You'd think he was someone's father, wouldn't you?'

She placed the doll back down and continued to work on it.

Twenty-Six

Santiago steered his boat as near to the island as he could. He had a vague memory of where the deeper waters were, could see the dark blue colours clear enough as the sun was still high. After dropping the anchor, he looked off the port side to view Samekh in its entirety. Similar to Arya, it was a quarter the size, and there was no volcano. The same palm species were recognisable. The island was uninhabited—that much he did know. Still, he thought it a nice place to stop on the return voyage. It would give the others, particularly his daughter, a chance to remove their attachment to Arya. He knew these trips affected people psychologically.

Santiago turned from the ship's wheel, picked up a case. He opened it, pulled out several sections of a fishing rod, connected them together. He placed a panama hat on, rolled up his shirt sleeves, then picked out a small pipe and a packet of tobacco from his trouser pocket. After he had lit his pipe, he reached into the case once again and drew out a dried piece of meat. He placed it on the hook and cast his line out into a patch of shallow water. His face was perspiring in the heat. He looked down where his line was, and marvelled at how clean and green the water was. Marine life swam hypnotically around his hook.

He didn't know how long he had been there when Becq stepped up next to him, her flip-flops slipping along the deck.

He said, 'Pick your feet up when you walk.'

'I'm not in the mood,' she said.

'What's wrong with you? I hope you're not going to ruin my peace and quiet by being in a huff.'

'Why're you fishing?'

'Why not?'

'Shouldn't we be surveying the island or something?'

'Not today,' Santiago said. 'There's no point. Let's just settle here for a while. We'll be here for a week or so. It's not a big island. You can take a raft and see what's there if you want.'

She sighed.

'Oh, come on, girl. Be more positive.'

'Why?' she said. 'I wanted to stay longer on Arya.'

'Well, I'm in charge and our work was done.'

'Was it? Did we solve the ichthyocentaur deaths? Everything feels a little incomplete.'

'More or less. We didn't go there just for that. Anyway, the mayor was only interested as it could've been a threat to Escha. Now, you didn't see anything that could threaten anyone, did you?'

'I didn't see what you saw,' she said.

'Meaning?'

'Underwater?'

He turned his head, took out his pipe. 'I wouldn't listen to idle speculation, if I were you.'

She grasped the rail and stared into the water as Santiago replaced his pipe in the corner of his mouth. He could do without being pressed on that matter any more.

'Anyway,' he said, 'we're out to survey and record—that's all. And that's what we're doing here. We're still working. Still charting. Still recording. This world doesn't map itself.'

'All right. I'll go ashore with Yana.'

'Yes, you do that. I'll join you later, maybe. Depends on how good a catch I get.'

She paused. 'Don't you care at all about Manolin?'

Santiago reflected on the question. 'What do you mean by "care"?'

'Forget I mentioned it.' She turned and walked along the deck, her flip-flops skidding on the wood, until she was out of sight.

Santiago shrugged, puffed contently from under the shade of his hat.

That evening, each of them ate alone. Becq sat on the beach, Yana further along to a rocky shore. Jefry and Santiago on the boat. The moon was bright, and soon the two girls met along the shore.

Becq and Yana talked for some time, listening always to the sounds of the surf upon the rocks. It seemed to hold them there forever, repeating. Yana was dark-skinned since she had been on Arya. Becq looked at the woman with envy. The hour made her seem darker, almost like a native.

'What happened, Yana, back on Arya? I can see that you and Jefry are okay now.'

Yana smiled, looked at a crab that was crawling along the rock face. 'Yes. Well, to be honest, I always loved him. I guess I just forgot for a while. That sounds shit, but that's what it feels like. I've remembered my feelings.'

'But you seem intimate, and yet... it doesn't seem... natural. Yes, that's the word. Is it a little forced—your intimacy with him?'

'Well, I've been bad to him. I have, haven't I?' Yana said.
Becq was silent.
'I've been awful,' Yana said. 'And still he stood by me. That said a lot. In fact that's an incredibly powerful thing. And I've been through a lot, too. More than I ever thought.'
'You don't have to talk about it if you don't want to.'
She was staring at the rock that the crab had just crawled past. 'It's all right. You know what happened. I lost... a part of me. All I remember is seeing that ichthyocentaur child *right after*. Why did those animals succeed where I failed? It just seemed to rub it in. Not that I'm denying the creatures the right, but you think that everything goes so easy for us normal people. But he still stood right by me, even when it happened.

'It shocks you, you know, when something like that happens,' Yana continued. 'Puts your mind somewhere weird, or brings it back from somewhere else, whatever. Anyway, the point is, I can't just expect Jefry to have me back and me be the same. I have to *try* and show him more affection. It has to be slow at first, after all that's gone on, but I really am sorry for what I've done. My feelings are a little forced, but that's because I'm scared. I do have to remember how to be *in love* with him. I know that being loved is the safest possible feeling.'

'That seems a little weird—your whole situation.'

'I suppose so,' Yana said. 'But everyone's happy. He's got me back, which is what he insisted, and I've someone to look after me, and I know the value of that now. Anyway, most successful marriages have a few lies holding it together; in my case, everything is out in the open. I can at least start again.'

'Hmm.'

'I'm not asking you to understand, Becq, but just be open-minded. No one else is affected, are they?'

'I suppose not,' Becq said.

'Well, there you go. Anyway, how're you feeling about Manolin?'

Becq's face darkened. 'I don't want to go there.'

'It'll be good for you. At some point in time, you'll get over him, and you'll find someone better. He so wasn't right for you.'

'How can you tell?' Becq said.

'He's always off doing different things. He's young, and he gets distracted by the world. He likes remote places, far away from people. And besides, he's not a tender lover; that's what you need.'

'He's good-looking, he doesn't have to be any good.'

Yana smiled. 'You're learning, girl. The good-looking ones never try hard enough. No, get yourself a man who will *let* you make a fuss of him. That's the sort of girl you are, and that's the kind of guy he wasn't. He loves nature and books more than women. But I don't blame him, after what his ex did to him. He was scarred, and whenever anyone is scarred it takes something extremely potent to change the way he'll think. And you know what the weird thing about Manolin is? He went about his life without really knowing what everyone else knew. Guess that goes the same for all of us. You make your decisions on what you know yourself, oblivious to what goes on behind your back. It's easy to think he was naïve, but we're saying that from the outside. To him, he's wondering around in his own little world, trying to be nice.'

'I wonder if we'll ever hear from him again. It's weird not knowing what happens.'

'Well, that's life, Becq. How many people do you meet and then drift away from. Some people leave your life and you'll never know what happens. In fact, in real life, you seldom get to know someone's full story. It's frustrating when you think about it. That's an important thing to realise. He may turn up, but I think his story has ended for us.'

Becq sighed, felt sad. 'I did like him a lot.'

'But you weren't totally committed. I noticed you near one of the villagers last night.'

Becq gave a coy smile. 'I just wanted to see what he was like. His breath stank though, and he had horrible teeth. I'm entitled to try though, aren't I?'

'Yes, absolutely. You've no commitments, and it's the first time I've seen you confident enough on the subject. Guess the island's changed you more than you think. But he was not quite an island beauty for you then?' Yana was holding back a laugh.

Becq wanted to steer away from the subject. 'Do you think Manolin will be okay?'

'Who knows? I guess so. He'll be a lot happier there than back home. Besides, he's surrounded by beauty.'

'It's horrible that she's so beautiful. I'm so jealous.'

'I meant the island. Don't let it get to you. Men will look, but deep down, they don't want a pretty one to settle down with. Trust me. They're too much hassle, too much effort. High maintenance. Men really want a nice homely girl, someone that will provide support and love. You'd be surprised by what a decent man will want.'

'The problem is,' Santiago announced to Jefry, as he tipped back a glass of the rumel's hidden stash of gin, 'we men want a pretty girl. One with a body to make him cry. What's more, they want her to stay that way.' He slumped back on a chair in his cabin, and his panama fell to the floor. Santiago looked down, frowned at the item, considered reaching it, then sat back up. He looked over at the candle on the table at his side and placed his glass down.

'It's true,' he continued. 'Be they whatever size they prefer—some men like 'em chubby, others like 'em as bendable as willow—they have to be pretty. Unless you're really getting your kicks out of the art of fucking, and want to sleep with the ugliest ones around, and I know a few who will. Some decent chaps, too. People's sexual tastes often amuse me. I know many a politician that likes being buggered by a six foot skinhead. You certainly won't read about that in any of the papers. But that's straying from the issue. Anyway, point being, is that I reckon Manolin is staying there only because of her—Miss Island Beauty.'

'Aye,' Jefry said. 'She was nice. I'll give the little runt that.'

'Oh, no, no. Never say "perfect", Jef. Never. The perfect woman does not exist. The perfect partner does not. You remember that.'

'Or something less misogynistic. Well, she's pretty damn perfect to me. Nice arse. Very polite. So damn caring, too. She'll weather well, I'll bet.'

'Careful, man. The perfect woman only exists in art.'

'Nonsense, Santiago. What crap are you peddling—?'

'You see,' Santiago said, 'the decent painter or composer, will always present to you, in their work, a perfect woman. The... joke... that they all share is that the woman will only, *can only*,' he waved a finger in the air, 'exist in their work.'

'Not sure I follow.' The rumel lay down on Santiago's bed, placed his glass of gin on the floor.'

'You see, they are creating someone that they want to taunt the viewer with. One where you can't see the faults. Specifically unavailable to the likes of anyone. In fact, they may do it to point it out to us that they do not at all exist in the real world. Point being, is that *one* should not even be looking for such a thing. Of course, it makes for a painful life back in said real world. Mark my words. Manolin thought his last wife was, as you say, perfect. Look what happened there.'

'Couldn't happen to a nicer guy,' Jefry said.

Santiago focussed on the rumel. 'Why did you never slap the boy? I was expecting you'd at least do that.'

'I wanted to, no doubt about it. I wanted to kill him, beat him into a pulp. But I'm not like that. I might not be too bright, but these things I like to give a good think to.'

'And…'

'What was the real problem, in your mind, Santiago?'

'The old lecherous serpent of lust rising in the lad?'

'No, no. That weren't it. If you trace it, Yana gave in to him. I had to think why my wife would want to do that. She's never done it before—'

'Don't trust 'em, that's what I say. She may have.'

'Just why do you hate women so much, DeBrelt?'

'I don't *hate* them.'

'Sounds like you do,' Jefry said. 'When was the last time you were with one, you know, *with* one?'

Santiago was silent for a few moments. 'A while, admittedly. Doesn't help being out here.'

'True. But when?'

Santiago sighed. 'I slept with a prostitute once last year. Wasn't even worth the money, miserable sow.'

Jefry said, 'Why're you paying for it?'

'Well, it isn't easy at my age.'

'Damn it, man. They aren't a commodity. You don't select one, like you would a piece of fruit. I think that's why you never settle.'

'Man's not meant to. Philosophically—'

'Bollocks. A man is meant to settle and build a family. Only a man stands by his family. A man doesn't cruise from girl to girl. Not a real one. Don't use your philosophy to cover up what's no more than a weakness of character.'

'If I was less drunk,' Santiago said, 'I'd say that was fighting talk.'

'Shut up and don't be stupid,' Jefry said. 'Stop trying to prove yourself to be a man. Just be one. I reckon you need to see women as companions, not something to stick your dick in when you feel like it.'

'Anyway,' Santiago said. 'If you were a man, you would've at least slapped Yana. I would've slapped my woman if she'd done to me what she'd done to you. Sleep with another.'

Jefry shook his head. 'You're outdated, DeBrelt.'

Santiago said, 'What? You think that they ought not to be beaten for doing that?'

'Damn it,' Jefry said. 'The only time you should hit a woman, Santiago, is if it's necessary only in foreplay, and she's asking you to do it for kicks. That's the *only* time you should not be a gentleman. And you don't need to hit anyone.'

Santiago sighed, stood up. 'Well I can see my thoughts are not sharp enough for tonight. Ignore most of what I've said. Complete bollocks.'

'I know.'

'Right—to bed.' Santiago turned and grasped the doorknob for several seconds. Eventually he opened it and walked away, sliding against the walls of the corridor every now and then.

A minute later he returned to the room, the door still open. 'Jef, this is my cabin.'

'Wondered when you'd notice.' Jefry stood up and walked past Santiago, patting him on the shoulder.

Santiago slumped on his bed and could feel it still warm from the rumel. It was an odd sensation. He was not used to warm beds, and it took him a while to fall asleep.

DeBrelt's crew conducted the same surveys as on Arya. There were geological and biological profiles. Becq continued sketching. For several days, they did their work, collecting specimens, building a bank of information. The weather was the same every day—intense sun, little wind. They swam, ate, taking a great effort to relax in the cool evenings.

On the eighth night on the island, Santiago had rowed ashore from his ship. He wanted an evening stroll. He could see the white sands and the shadows from the bright moon. There was not as much noise on Samekh as Arya. There were fewer birds and arthropods in the forest. The sea, too, seemed gentler. There were no conversations between natives here, not that he ever had many on Arya.

He looked out to the blackness as he walked. He glanced at the moonlit silhouette of his ship, anchored a hundred yards in deeper water, and felt a strange sense of calm, almost a belonging.

Maybe the lad was right, he thought. *Maybe staying on these islands is the right thing to do. Maybe I shouldn't care about anyone else, and shack up with a tribal girl or two.*

He continued along the beach.

It was not as long as he thought it would be by the time he saw the ship again. Then, he frowned. It was his ship. It looked the same, at least. It was positioned differently, in another location. But it was *his* ship.

Ahead, as shadows on the beach, he could see figures. They were bringing something off of a raft. He looked back to the ship again, his heart pounding. It *was* his ship—one of his others. He was breathing quickly, dashed to his right, behind a rock. He watched the figures moving in the dark for a long time. They were a hundred yards away from him. He counted four of them in all. They appeared to be working with urgency. Above the noise of the surf, he could hear them talking, but not clear enough to understand them. He thought he heard a female voice shouting.

Could it be? After all this time? What fortune to cross paths again. I had vague thoughts about them coming to Arya, but... well... they've finally done it.

He walked out from behind the rock, tucked his shirt in, rolled down his sleeves.

He could see them pausing as he approached. They turned, stood in a line. Two of them brought up muskets.

'Hey!' one of them shouted. 'Don't move.'

Santiago stopped. Two ran forward, one with a musket. The other, he could tell, was a rumel. When they were nearer he could see that they were female. He smiled as they approached him. 'Santiago DeBrelt at your disposal, ladies.' He held out his hand. 'Again.'

'What're you doing here?' the rumel said, her face registering equal disbelief as Santiago felt earlier.

'Now, Jella, is that any way to greet an old friend?'

'Sorry. Just a bit shocked. It's a pretty slim chance I thought I'd see you again.' She turned back, shouting, 'It's all right, it's Santiago DeBrelt. Our contact from the west coast.' Her voice echoed along the bay.

She turned to face him. 'So, what the fuck are you doing here then?'

'Well, we've been here a week, doing the usual. Been exploring Arya as I didn't get a chance to last time. Truth be told, we were going to remain indefinitely until I had thought long enough of what to do. And you? I see you got the boat then. My messages were received fine? I must admit I had my reservations since I was going to be away from land for so long.'

'Yes,' Jella said. 'It was where you said it would be. All was fine.'

'Those Qe Falta chaps are really quite efficient,' Santiago said. 'I wish everyone was that organised.'

'Yeah, anyway, we didn't think we'd be here this quick,' Lula said.

Santiago said, 'Really? I thought you were ahead of your rough schedule. Why's that?'

Jella took Santiago's arm. She turned him to face the sea. He could see the horizon as it was where the stars were cut off.

'Let your eyes settle for a minute. You might need this.' She drew out a telescope from her pocket, handed it to Santiago.

He held it up to his eye and searched for the horizon again. 'What am I looking for?'

Jella guided the telescope a few degrees to the right. 'See that line of lights—the one's that are more yellow than the stars...'

Santiago brought the telescope down, still looking out to sea. He ran his hand through his hair. 'Navy. Are they Eschan or have they had help from Rhoam?'

'I'm not sure. I had thoughts we were being tracked whilst crossing the desert. The thing is, the two lads got locked up and we had to break them free. They were arrested on charges of terrorism. So they've been following us for ages now, I think. I'm not sure if they've had help from Escha or now. I don't know. How well are the militaries linked?'

Santiago shrugged. 'Rhoam had kept fairly neutral, but if they suspect you then there's no reason they won't hunt you down with help.'

'We've kept ahead of them,' Jella said. 'But they've maintained this route. I don't know how they could know it was us, or what we planned.'

Santiago nodded thoughtfully. 'I suspect they're Eschan ships going to Arya but probably began tracking you. Eschan navy tend to raid any boat that's not registered with the city, then they plunder. Hell, more pirates than a navy.'

'How do you know?' Jella asked.

'We had a couple of agents with us,' Santiago said. 'Eschan.'

'You were working with Eschan agents?' Lula asked.

Santiago noted the look of anger in her eyes. He could see her fingers twitching on the musket in her hand. Back in the distance, the figures were working on the beach He couldn't see what they were doing. 'They're dead. I killed them. I killed *both* of them. They sent a message using a relic.'

'Bastards. Why did they communicate with the navy?' Jella said.

'They always were. They were investigating the loss of Eschan ships in these waters. Anyway, the point is, we have to get going. Particularly me.'

'Fair enough.'

'Yes, I take it everything is prepared?' Santiago said. 'You got the whale carcasses?'

'Yes, everything's fine. Two carcasses. We can lead a trail back to west coast waters. Explosives are back there—' Jella indicated the others. 'Diving equipment and everything. I'm just a bit anxious about getting to Escha.'

'Don't worry,' Santiago said. 'Once Quidlo's up I'd leave it a bit. I think you'll find it will get rid of that lot.' He nodded towards the boats on the horizon.

'You sure?' Lula asked.

'Madam, you can be sure that it'll leave nothing in the water. The force that it'll make when it gets up will rock the surface. Possibly even send large waves to the mainland. I'd stay here if I were you. Wait. There'll be some survivors and they'll head straight here. Pick them off. Wouldn't leave any alive, just to make sure. Then get the hell out of here. How long till detonation?'

'By dawn I reckon.'

'Good. I'll get going now. I'll leave message with the Qe Falta when I'm back on land. I hope it all goes well.'

'It *will* go well,' Jella said.

'That's the spirit,' Santiago said. 'Right, I'm off. Good luck.' Santiago turned to run along the beach. He did not look back.

It wasn't long until he was out of breath. He walked to the raft then pushed it out and rowed to *DeBrelt One*. Within five minutes he had started the boat's engines and pulled the anchor up. Becq, Jefry and Yana gathered by the ship's wheel as Santiago turned the boat in an arc away to the north of the island, parallel to the horizon.

'What's wrong?' Yana asked. 'Why are we leaving now?'

'I want to go now, that's all,' Santiago said. 'I think there'll be some tricky conditions in the next day or so, and I think we can escape it if we move tonight.'

'How d'you know?' Becq asked.

'Cloud patterns. Weather changes. That sort of thing. A man knows these things.'

Santiago looked as his daughter, who tilted her head up to regard the blanket of stars that stretched across the horizon. 'Right…'

'Indeed. Anyway, we're done here. I think we'll have a little holiday on the south of the mainland. To celebrate. Just a few days. And then drinks. What do you say, Jef?'

'Aye, could do worse,' Jefry said. 'Could do worse.'

'Splendid. Then I'll buy you all some fine food,' Santiago said. 'Onwards.'

The boat gathered speed as it left Samekh. The others went below deck. Santiago glanced to the horizon. He thought he could almost see the ships. His heart was beating hard. His throat felt thick. He switched on another motor. The boat cut through the water and the smells of the plants from the island left him.

That's it now, he thought. *That's it. It'll be done. We can rebuild the place after I get back. Start again. I can put all this science behind me. It'll be a fresh start. Everything makes more sense now. Bring back the Collectivists. We'll organise it all, from the root up. I hope they do it. It's just a fucking marvellous plan. But I'd better make sure we're well and truly out the way. We'll be safe by the time it comes up. I hope so. I've got my doubts though. Maybe it won't work. Actually, thinking about it, it seems tough still. Will two carcasses be enough to keep it interested that long? Do they have enough fuel to get back if they've used it getting here quickly? Well, at least it will be out. That's something. Anyway, it might work. I've helped where I could. It's not a perfect plan. I didn't design it, after all. She did the research. She was convinced she knew what it would do. Not my idea of a tight plan, but I thought I'd help. The Qe Falta thought so, too. They've been here longer than we have, and they said she was right. I don't know. It's not the sort of thing you can prove by experiment. But absence of evidence is not evidence of absence, as my old lecturer always said. I would've done something better. I would've used one of the other islands. She knows that one of them has a fault line. Put the explosives in the fault, let the island subside, and create a tidal wave. Simple. Another plan, perhaps. Another day, if it all goes wrong again. At least, in all this, I would've helped free something. That's got to be good, hasn't it? But now, now I'll have to start things all over again. A positive note to end on, perhaps.*

By the time Jella and Lula were back with Menz and Yayle, they were already wearing their diving equipment.

'Are you ready then?' Jella said.

'Pretty much,' Menz said. He turned to Yayle. 'You set, lad?'

The young rumel nodded, his eyes wide. 'All set.'

'Good. Well, all the explosives and charges are here,' Jella said, indicating the bundle on the small boat. 'I think we should crack on.'

'So, Yayle and I go now. While we lay the explosives, the rest of you will...?'

'We'll prepare for that lot, out there.' She pointed to the dark horizon. 'We haven't got long. Gabryl and Allocen will stay on the boat in case anyone tries to attack it. Lula and me will stay here. We've enough ammunition to kill over a hundred men. When Quidlo rises, it's likely to rock everything in the water. It'll take out the navy no problem. Especially if they fire at it. To be honest, they won't really stand much of a chance. But there'll be survivors and they'll head straight here. We'll take them all then go.'

'What if one of us is injured?' Yayle said.

'It depends. If it's serious then we have to leave them. We can't afford to lose anyone else. This is for the cause, not for the individual. You remember that. At least we're going to take out a whole naval fleet.'

'I don't like that "at least" talk,' Menz said.

'Just covering the options. Right, we haven't long. They'll be on us by dawn. We have until then. We set?'

Menz and Yayle nodded. Menz reached down to check his knife. He drew out the blade then sheathed it again. 'Just in case that something happens like last time.'

'Let's do it then,' Jella said.

Menz and Yayle gathered sacks of explosives from the boat and hauled them over their shoulders. Jella watched the two men walk off towards the water's edge. Their diving suits were black, and so it was difficult for her to see them as they waded in. She saw Menz pat Yayle on the back, then they readjusted their diving masks. They seemed to be talking for a while, lifting their masks as they did. Jella thought that they were talking for an unnaturally long time. Then they waded out further.

Within a couple of minutes she could no longer see them.

She turned to Lula who was unloading muskets and pistols from the boat. The rumel watched her looking up and down the barrels of the weapons, then she loaded several of them.

'We've got a while yet,' Jella said.

Lula said, 'I want to be ready.'

'Are you okay?'

'Fine. Yes.'

Jella stepped nearer Lula. Lula looked up but straight past her.

'What's wrong?' Jella said.

'Everything.'

'What d'you mean?'

'Everything,' Lula said. 'This plan. You, me.'

'I don't follow,' Jella said.

'We're going to end up dead, somehow. What are the chances of this thing, whatever it is, actually following us?'

'I'm confident it will work,' Jella said.

'Are you? Are you really?' Lula placed the muskets back on the boat and looked at Jella. 'What if it does? Then what? What happens when we get back? You haven't even talked about it. All you live for is your planning and your anger.'

'If you'd experienced what I've seen—'

'Well I haven't and I'm sorry. I'm *so* sorry I haven't had as terrible a background. This is a wild plan, Jella, and it's all you've lived for. You've been ignoring me the last few weeks.'

'Is that it?' Jella put her arm around Lula. 'Look, we'll have plenty to do and talk when we get back. We can plan our future on the return journey, once we've led Quidlo into Eschan waters, we can go north and settle. Just you and me, like we've always said.'

Lula said, 'Why couldn't we just've kept the money we had and settled somewhere nice?'

'Because I can't, and you know that. You know what this means. To all of his. You know that.'

Lula was silent. She picked up a bundle of weapons. Then, as she turned away, she said, 'There're some good positions behind those rocks. There's good cover from all angles. I suggest that's where we begin any defence.'

Jella stepped up behind her, kissed her neck. She could feel the warmth of the human. 'I love you, you know that. We'll have such a great time.'

'Have you ever felt like this before?' Lula asked. 'About anyone?'

'Never,' Jella said.' You know I can't resist you.'

'I don't want to know that, I want to know you actually feel something for me.'

'Well I do,' Jella said. 'I love you more than you know.'

'Good,' Lula said.

Lula walked towards the rocks. Jella followed soon after, with more weapons including grenades, boxes of ammunition. They set up their positions so that they had a clear shot of the whole beach. The beach was small, and any survivors, Jella thought, would most likely come that way, especially if they saw the boat.

She wondered about Menz and Yayle. They had been gone ten minutes. The plan was simple, placing explosives along the top of the reef and down one side, fracturing it, breaking Quidlo's bonds, which would allow it to push it away with ease. It would take them another fifteen minutes or so to reach this side of the reef, another hour to plant the explosives along a wide enough section to free Quidlo, another half an hour to return. About two hours to wait in all. She would not see the explosions. She was confident that the explosives the Qe Falta gave her would be of the highest quality. After all, they had been doing this sort of thing as long as she could remember.

She and Lula lay on blankets on the rocks, listening to the waves, and, every minute, checking on the positions of the naval fleet and for Menz and Yayle, should something go wrong. Because she was laying face down, Jella could feel her heart pounding the rocks. Through the gaps, she could see the sea and a glow on the horizon where the sun would soon be showing.

The hour passed and there was not yet any sign of Menz and Yayle.

Jella and Lula had spoken little. The horizon was brighter, but the sun hadn't risen. She could see now the outline of the naval fleet. There were twenty grey ships and the sight made her pulse race. She thought she could hear the sound of explosions, but she wasn't sure. The time would be right.

She nudged Lula, who was holding her musket, scanning the beach.

Lula said, 'Was that it, d'you think?'

Jella nodded and pushed herself up so that she could look over the rocks to the sea. Nothing was happening. She thought it may have been the first explosion. She thought she could hear more.

It seemed an eternity until Menz and Yayle climbed ashore. As soon as they reached the beach, she called over the rocks, waved her arms. Then they jogged towards her.

She stepped down on to the beach. 'All done?'

Menz raised his thumb, his chest heaving. She smiled, beckoned them up to their position on the rocks.

'Was it as you remember?' Jella asked.

'Aye. Seemed even bigger. In fact it's ridiculously large. I'm a bit worried that if we wait too long the thing will get away.'

'It's either that or be in the water when it surfaces, which will probably sink us,' Jella said.

'Fair point,' Menz said. 'If you say so.'

Menz and Yayle removed their diving equipment and picked up muskets. They crouched, looking over the rocks towards the sea.

'Should be up by now,' Menz said.

'Give it time,' Jella said.

'We haven't got time,' Menz said.

'Look... Look at the water's surface,' Yayle said. 'The bugger's coming.'

The surface of the water was rising, slowly, then falling, as if a storm was developing. The sun began to rise from her right, and she could see the long, dark shadows that the high waves cast. The sea sounded louder. White tops were visible as the water collapsed on itself.

'It's coming,' Jella said.

They could see clearly a shape, hundreds of feet long, beginning to surface. Behind, were the masts of the naval fleet.

'It's fucking huge,' Yayle said. 'Much bigger than I thought down there.' Then, quietly, 'This is ridiculous.'

The others remained silent on top of the rocks, staring, wide-eyed, at the creature that was rising in the new morning sun, pushing itself up out from the surface of the water. It's skin was dark. Crumbled segments of coral that fell as it burst through the water. A large wave about six feet high spread then banked up on the shallow waters, climbed high and missed them by inches.

Jella turned to watch the waves crashing through the forest and birds darted out from the canopy as she watched the palms bend and break under the pressure, then she looked at her ship, which had moved a little despite the anchor. Her pulse was racing. The plan was working.

Back out at sea, Quidlo was out, it's tentacles, thick and heavy, trailing out of sight. Its cylindrical face pushed into the air, dominating the horizon. Water sprayed and crashed all around it, coral still falling in pieces. Its head tilted up and they could just see its black eye, dozens of feet across, and it seemed to gasp, exhaling air as if it breathed like a person, remembering daylight. Its body must have been over a mile in length.

'What kind of fucking squid is this thing?' Menz said. His mouth hung open. 'I ain't seen that in any book.'

'Beyond our time,' Jella said. 'And for good reason. You never really believed me, even when we went to see it. Even when you actually saw it. None of you really believed me, did you? I was right.'

They watched the creature turn towards the naval fleet that was sailing through and over the rough waves forming a semi-circle. Jella could see the masts rising and falling. 'Fire at it,' she said. 'Come on, provoke it…'

Within seconds, as if she had willed it herself, some of the grey naval boats began firing, as she knew they would. She could see the plumes of smoke, followed by the sound of explosions.

Quidlo turned towards the fleet. Jella watched amazed as the creature drew its tentacles out of the water hundreds of feet in the air, water spraying all around, its shadow strong in the higher sun, then in crashed them down through the boats, tossed the ships over. She thought she had heard thunder as the sound caught up, then she looked on as the next wave banked up the shallow waters of the island, came racing past and slapped into the forest behind forcing the island to vibrate. The waves were only so shallow here, but on the mainland they would have hundreds of miles of water behind them. The destruction would be phenomenal.

Manolin was looking out to sea. He had joined a group of villagers some way up the volcano. The children had been taken further up, towards the ichthyocentaurs' village, by several adults. He had woken Myranda early, dragged her and Lewys out when he had heard explosions.

Myranda had blown a conch to wake the village and, as they saw the reef fracturing and rising, they ran up the slope, understanding what that would do to the water, to the waves. Manolin carried children in his arms. Many of the villagers took his example and carried them on their backs, in time to look down on a wall of water as it smashed through their huts and into the forest, tossing wood into the air before dragging segments of the village under the froth.

Manolin was breathless as he watched what he guessed to squid climb out of the water and dive again, before it swam towards another island further up the chain. As he was laughing with amazement, the shadow of the creature rose again, its conical shape piercing the sky. Then he saw the tentacles follow up behind and slap down, as if it were pushing itself up from the water, creating an even larger tidal wave. *That must be the size of a city...*

He was so shocked that the sight of the naval fleet on the horizon was the last thing on his min. All he could do was watch with the islanders, as the beast brought its tentacles down, flipped boats in the air. He noted the booming of the guns in the distance, which had no effect on the squid, could hear the thunderous sound as the wave arrived onshore, decimating what remained of the village, snapping back trees, displacing everything in sight. Birds shot out of the forest. You could feel the island shudder on impact.

No one said anything, but Manolin was nodding his head. That explained what he saw in the reef on *Pilar*. He wondered if Santiago had anything to do with it, but suspected that his old colleague was long gone. He wondered what the old man would think about a squid that size.

Myranda approached him, he placed an arm around her wanting to be protective.

'Don't worry at all,' he said. 'A village can be rebuilt.'

She nodded, curled up under his chin. She didn't look sad.

They watched the creature out at sea rise and fall several times. Manolin estimated it to be over a mile if it were measured from end to end. He shook his head in amazement, at the fact that something that size could be hidden within the reef. Everything made sense now: the sirens, what he saw underwater. The enigma of what *exactly* the sirens were doing with the half-bred ichthyocentaurs was becoming clear. *They were keeping this creature down there, chained to the ocean floor. They needed the half-breeds to work, to help.*

After the creature had plunged into the deeper waters in the distance, he felt a strange sense of calm. The waters took a while to return to normal. He couldn't see anymore boats out at sea. The sun was low in the sky, but already strong. With the children still out of the way in the ichthyocentaurs' village, several people returned to the beach, but there was no village there.

'Right,' Jella said. 'I can see the first of the survivors coming now.' She pointed to a small boat that approached the shore. When it was closer, she could see there were over a dozen men crammed on board. 'We'd better be quick about this, then we have to find that fucking giant and bait it.'

'Jella, after seeing that thing, do you *really* think it's going to want to eat only a couple of whales?' Menz said.

'Fucking hell,' Jella said. 'Have some fucking confidence. Look, concentrate on those people, okay?'

'How can I?' Menz said. 'I can't have faith in a plan I doubt.'

'Look,' Jella said. 'If you're not going to be any use, get back on the fucking boat. Now.'

'Jella, we need all the help we can get,' Lula said. She hated to see her lover like this, angry, frustrated. She knew that their plans would go wrong if they got angry.

'No, if she wants me to go, I'll go,' Menz said.

'If you're going, I want out too,' Yayle said.

Jella was furious at this attitude, this abandonment now. 'Fucking bastards! Why the hell bail out? What the fuck for?'

'I never saw it's power before—I never knew just how big it was,' Menz said. 'Do you really think we can keep such a thing like that under control? No. But look, the tidal wave will cause quite some damage. That's enough, I think. It would've killed enough. With that thing free in the waters, it'll do more damage around these seas, and who knows, maybe it'll get to Escha. But we can go back, no? Make more plans.'

'Fuck you,' Jella said. 'Get on the boat. Lula and me—we'll finish them off.'

'Right,' Menz said. 'We'll swim. You can use the boat once you've had enough of killing.'

Menz and Yayle crawled along the rocks then down the other side. They placed their diving gear on, crept out towards their boat.

Lula turned to Jella. 'That wasn't particularly wise, was it?' Jella seemed not to react to her question. Perhaps it didn't need an answer. Perhaps Jella knew that what she'd done was wrong.

Jella placed her musket through a gap in the rocks and aimed it at the boat. As it reached the beach, a couple of the men jumped out into the shallow water. Jella fired, a crack shattering the air, and one man fell to his knees, then forwards into the water.

Jella smiled as the men jumped out of the boat ran for cover, kicking their knees high to get out of the shallow water. Lula fired: another fell over the boat. They both fired again and two more fell over the edge of the boat as they tried to get out. Jella could hear them kicking the water to run away. She and Lula climbed down the rocks and threw one of the grenades towards the boat. She watched it explode in a plume of water, leaving no one on the boat in once piece. They knelt by the base of the rocks on the sand, fired at those who were running. There were seven men on the beach, sprinting towards the forest for cover. Jella fired and missed three times before striking another, this time in the head, and he fell backwards onto the sand in a spray of blood.

Lula held Jella back as the rumel stood up. 'No, they have cover now. We must be careful.'

'Come on, we can take them,' Jella said.

A shot sparked off of the rock behind, followed by four more.

'Fuck, get down,' Lula said, and sprawled in the sand. She looked back towards the forest, but couldn't see where the shots came from.

Still looking at the trees, Lula said, 'Jella, let's get to the boat now. We still have a chance to get back and bait that Quidlo at least.'

Jella stared back at her, her eyes wide and full of pain. She was holding her stomach. Lula could see blood pouring from between her grey fingers.

'No. No, no. Jella, are you okay?'

'Yes…' Jella said. 'I'll be fine. I can still shoot. You get back to the boat. I'll hold it here.'

'No, I'm not going,' Lula said. 'I'm the better markswoman. I can get them.'

'There'll be more after this lot. Get to the boat.'

'No, I'm not going,' Lula said.

Another spark flared off of the rock. Lula knelt up, fired, but she did not aim anywhere specifically. While she reloaded, Jella sat up, her back against the rock. She brought out two pistols from within her breeches.

'I can hold them,' Jella said.

'I'm not going,' Lula said.

'Go.'

'No, I love you too much to just leave you here to die.'

'Lula, just fucking go will you.'

'Why?' Lula stood up and fired where she saw a face in the trees.

She heard a scream then reloaded.

'Look,' Jella said, 'I never liked you that much. I only wanted you for sex and because you were an easy target when I found you, and then I found out how good you were at shooting. Don't hang around for me, because it isn't worth it, believe me.'

Lula stared at Jella, who was loading her pistol again. Why was she saying this? Was it true? It was amazing how quickly something could be shattered. Lula felt sick, refusing to believe what was being said.

The rumel looked up. 'You heard me.'

'I don't believe you,' Lula said.

'Your call. Don't die because of a fuck buddy.'

The word stung aggressively, and was something she couldn't acknowledge. They had a relationship, they had shared so much. 'I wasn't a fuck buddy. I was much more and you know it.' Lula's voice was frail.

Jella laughed. 'Get the hell out of here, fuck buddy.' She fired towards the forest, the shot echoing across the bay, then she screamed, 'Come on, I'll take you all!' She began to laugh then stopped, and stared into the distance.

Lula was no longer able to see effectively because of the tears welling in her eyes. She would be no good at firing now. Considering the words Jella had just spoken, she walked away, all the time looking back.

Jella turned back and saw that Lula was climbing up over the rocks.

Her throat felt thick. She looked down at her wound then at her ammunition. She had a plenty of shots left, could finish the job. She reloaded, tried to remember how many there were. She thought there were two left. She reached in her pocket and brought out her last grenade, then looked towards the forest, watched the palms moving.

A face moved within the darkness and she pulled the pin and threw the grenade as hard as she could. It exploded in the forest, sending shards of wood and leaves onto the beach, but she saw the faces running either side so she fired. One of the men fell out onto the beach, then she waited for the other.

She reached for the musket on the sand beside her, loaded then crawled behind one of the lower rocks, pushed herself up over it. She had cover and the survivor would try to come for her.

There were no more boats at sea. She hoped she could kill more people, more survivors. There were pieces of wood, several barrels floating in the shallow water. She held the musket up over the rock, looked along the barrel through the sight. She scanned the forest, heard another shot, which struck the rock beside her. She saw where it came from and, on seeing a small tree moving against the wind, fired. She watched a man fall through the leaves onto the beach.

She sighed, pushed herself to her feet, the wound causing her a stiffness inside. She stumbled towards the forest. If she was shot at then there would be more of them—that insane decision was all she had left to ascertain the situation.

There were no further shots. She checked the other bodies. She placed a pistol in the mouth of any that were still alive, and forced their eyes open as she pulled the trigger. Every one she killed was with her city of Lucher in mind, an obscene offering to her past.

After she had counted all the dead, she fell to her knees then sat down on the beach. Out to sea, her boat was drifting away. She swallowed hard as she remembered Lula. She looked at her wound. She felt numbed to the pain. For some minutes she checked, but there were no more navy survivors.

It was the right thing to do, about Lula, she thought. How else was I to make her go away? She needed that kick. I saved her. Now they can go on and finish the job. They can sail with the whale overboard and drag Quidlo back to Escha. It'll be like catnip to a pussy. It's easy, so simple. Then it can destroy the coast. I did it. I got some revenge. Lucher got one back. And at least I killed some Eschans.

They'll be safe with Allocen on board, protecting them. I've done my job. We've all done our jobs. It was worth it. Hopefully I can heal. I can somehow get back. I'll catch fish or something, there'll be enough to keep me alive. Then I'll get back. It's easy. I'll make a boat from whatever gets washed up here.

She fell flat on the sand clutching her stomach. She tried to lift her head, but her neck was in pain so she laid on the soft sand. Shuddering, she listened to the waves repeating, lapping nearer her feet on each push. It soothed her, despite the pain, which she felt stronger than ever.

The sky was the sharpest shade of blue. Overhead, gulls circled, and she could hear the palms swaying. In the distance, a strange animal croaked, but she couldn't recognise it.

Then, she heard something else that she didn't recognise, except this time she wanted to lift her head. She couldn't describe the sound. She pushed herself up onto her elbows and looked out to sea. Vision was hazy.

As Jella focussed, she did not believe what she saw.

In front of her in the shallow water, were over a dozen heads and shoulders above the surface, with pale skin and long hair. She knew they were females, but not what they were. They were spaced several feet apart and were motionless. The waves rolled past them towards her. She couldn't explain why, but she thought they were beautiful and it was the last thing she saw before she closed her eyes and collapsed to the sand.

The sirens turned one by one to move further out to the deeper water, then dived under the sea in unison. Below the surface were dozens more of their kind, hovering in the half-light. They swam out to sea until the temperature fell quickly. More joined them until over a hundred sirens had gathered. They glided through the water in neat rows, following in each other's jet-stream. The sirens kicked their tails hard to descend. Those at the front called out and listened, steered the group up into warmer currents to travel quickly. As they looked up they could see the light of day filtering through. They had never swum so fast in their lives and they could feel the water pushing hard against their skins.

They sliced through the sea for what seemed like an endless amount of time, their long hair stretched out behind. The females climbed as they felt a change in the water, and that was when they knew it was near. They could feel Quidlo's drag, then quickened their pace, spread over a wider area, kicking past skates and rays.

At the front she could see the tentacle, thick, long, extending into the darkness ahead, where its body was too far away to be seen. She screamed through the water, called for columns of sirens to swim ahead, into the dark, to the other side of Quidlo. Sirens whistled past, their gills pulsating, whilst a dozen more stayed behind the squid. Then those behind prepared to sing through the water.

Several sirens lingered on each side of Quidlo, and maintained the same pace as the beast, following its drag. She could see segments of coral still attached to the thick hide, whilst more females sliced through the water up ahead. She heard the voices of her kind and they, too, called out. Ahead, sirens by the beast's head sang, low-pitched, a frequency they had never sung for an age, and they hit the same chord.

Quidlo slowed down, its tentacles began to shudder, the ends flapping. Sirens had to swim back to avoid being struck. Muscles vibrated under its hide. The squid halted in the water, hovered in the gloom, before it slid down towards the colder water, and the same notes were maintained, an ultra-low chord, halting the beast, until half the sirens changed pitch, climbing scales and octaves by the fathom. Everything in the water began to shudder.

The sirens surrounded Quidlo over hundreds of feet, and dragged it down with their voices, and they could see that its muscles vibrated more, visibly shaking the water, until they struck the highest note they knew of. The creature's eyes closed, then the squid collapsed on itself, folded in, rapidly, emitted a bass groan, then turned and fell down through the water, and the sirens kicked up, away from the drag towards the light, and looked down until the beast had descended into black and the water was calm.

The hundred sirens stopped singing, reformed in a huddle. Their heads were hung low. Some of them held each other for minutes. Tuna swam past them, but they did not look up. One by one they turned, looking down all the time, and dragged themselves through the water and back the way they came. The sea was silent and there was too much salt in the water for their tears to be noticed by anyone but themselves.

Of course, she knew it was only stunned. For how long, she didn't know. It was sad to have to do that—they couldn't kill this ancient beast. A new reef would have to be built. They would have to sink more ships, regain more of the surface metal. It would take forever. She had no idea how far they were from the islands. Perhaps they were nearer the mainland? How would they breed? Questions floated through her mind.

They would have to start all over again.

Manolin looked across the remains of the village. There was not much for him to see. Wood lay strewn across the beach, dead fish and molluscs amongst the debris. Moments earlier a piece of coral had fallen from a palm tree and nearly hit him on the head.

A group of villagers walked along the lagoon, so he ran up to them. They were all men, and were collecting what few personal belongings they could find.

'We can build it again,' Manolin said. Then, to himself, with a smile, 'I was wondering what I was going to do here. Something to get my teeth into.'

They looked at him but said nothing, their eyes displaying some despair. Behind them, the waves spilt on the beach, dumping cargo from the naval vessels. More metal and wood was being washed up, each wave delivering. Then he saw a small boat approaching the island. There were men inside.

Manolin turned to the villagers. 'Chaps, I don't mean to alarm, but those are naval men out there. Could be a spot of trouble...'

One of the villagers, Mhulo, raised his hand.

Manolin frowned, turned to look at the boat. At the edge of his vision, he saw another group of islanders, women this time, walking along the shore, down to where the water met the sand. They were carrying blow pipes. He looked from the boat to the women and back again. The men were approaching the shallower water. One of them stood up, waved his arms to the women. Manolin watched the women raise their pipes, then form two neat rows. He wondered how the women had seen the boat in advance. The front row knelt down. They all fired and, silently, the men fell into the water or the boat. He could see parts of their bodies shaking until they became still. Oddly, the boat began to drift away again as if the tide was removing it for them. Manolin watched it for several minutes until it had passed around the island as quickly as it had arrived.

The women walked back up the beach and into the forest. He scratched his head, shook it, not quite believing they had just done that. The event was eerie, he thought. And the recognition of that word sent a shudder through his body. He turned around again to see that the village men had gone. They were further up the beach now, a few items under their arms.

He was alone. Myranda had gone to see if Lewys was all right. Manolin knew the boy could look after himself. The sun was high and Manolin was sweating. He had to shade his eyes when he looked back towards where the reef had been. There was nothing there now, no darkness on the surface of the water. The waves approached the island faster, louder and with more energy since there was nothing to act as a breakwater.

He walked along the beach, his hands in his pockets, his head held high as he observed his new home. As you looked along the edge of the palm forest and up at the volcano, large and still, overlooking the island, you could see small birds circling the summit. Shading his eyes with his hand as he scanned along the curve of the shore, wondered where he would build his hut.

He would have to start all over again.

Epilogue

Hundreds of people made their way through the rush hour streets of Escha. Rain sparked off the old stone walls, off cobbled streets. People bumped past each other through thin passageways, their heads facing the puddles. A vendor at a newspaper stood idly, his hat drawn across his eyes, his collar turned up. A group of black rumel youths smoked cigarettes as people passed them. You could smell them streets away. All the time, no one looked at each other as if eye contact was a sin. A beggar huddled in a doorway, his legs drawn in so he wouldn't get kicked. A group of workmen were leaving the docks. They carried their equipment, ladders and tools, though the same streets in which people were crammed, howling shouting obscenities over the voice of the newspaper vendor. If you listened carefully you could hear he was calling out yet more headlines about building work from the tidal wave that struck the city a year ago.

An elderly woman was escorting a little girl past a row of commercial buildings. Oil lanterns had been lit, and the girl looked up with big eyes at the beams of light that forced columns of rain to sparkle. At every shop, the girl pressed her face on the window as she passed. Her breathing steamed them up then she drew lines though the mist with her fingers. She moved on to the next, whilst the woman waited patiently.

People knocked them as they passed and the woman let out a sigh. Some would shout at her to get out of the way, but she turned to keep an eye on the girl. They saw an old man who was selling mussels from an alleyway, arranged in order of size. He looked down at the girl, but did not smile. She skipped on, not really caring about his rudeness.

The girl paused at one particular window. A toy shop. A man with a broad moustache stepped out, one of those old top hats on his head. Then he pulled his coat around him, winked at her, strode down the street.

The girl turned back to the row of dolls behind the glass. She pointed at one in particular. 'I like that one. Why's it got funny clothes? It looks like an explorer. I wonder where he's been. He must have had an adventure.'

The doll had black hair, golden skin. It wore a pair of shortened breeches, a loose shirt, with the sleeves rolled up. It looked noticeably different to any of the others.

The woman took a closer look by the girl's eye-line. 'Yes, it probably is. But come on, your mother wants you home before it gets dark. We can look another time.'

The woman walked on, but the girl remained by the window, careful not to steam it up. She stood on tip-toes to get a better look. Then she looked down at her shoes as someone splashed her. All she could see were people's legs moving rapidly. Everyone in a rush. Everyone was rude. She turned to leave the doll, to find her grandmother again.

In her haste she trotted through the streets forgetting the doll as quickly as she had seen it.

The End

About the Author

Mark Charan Newton lives and works in Nottingham, UK.

His spare time is spent investigating green spaces, finger-picking guitars, reading and, of course, writing.

You can contact him at www.myspace.com/cakesandale or visit his website at www.markcnewton.com.

Coming Soon from
www.pendragonpress.net

We Fade to Grey
Edited by Gary McMahon with an introduction from Mark Morris
Five supernatural novelettes from Paul Finch, Stuart Young
Simon Bestwick, Mark West and Gary McMahon

Kingston to Cable
A short Western novel set in an alternate world,
with a touch of Garth Ennis by Gary Greenwood

The Places Between
A short dark fantasy novel with echoes of Hieronymous Bosch by
Terry Grimwood

Silversands
A short SF novel by Gareth L Powell

*Support the independent press, who in turn support
new and exciting authors.*